D0251198

BELLE CHASSE

THE SENTINELS OF NEW ORLEANS

Royal Street
River Road
Elysian Fields
Pirate's Alley
Belle Chasse

Suzanne Johnson

BELLE CHASSE

A TOM DOHERTY ASSOCIATES BOOK
NEW YORK

BELLE CHASSE

Copyright © 2016 by Suzanne Johnson

A Tor Book
Published by Tom Doherty Associates
175 Fifth Avenue
New York, NY 10010

www.tor-forge.com

Tor® is a registered trademark of Macmillan Publishing Group, LLC.

The Library of Congress Cataloging-in-Publication Data is available upon request.

ISBN 978-0-7653-7699-2 (hardcover)
ISBN 978-1-4668-5285-3 (e-book)

Our books may be purchased in bulk for promotional, educational, or business use. Please contact your local bookseller or the Macmillan Corporate and Premium Sales Department at 1-800-221-7945, extension 5442, or by e-mail at MacmillanSpecialMarkets@macmillan.com.

First Edition: November 2016

Printed in the United States of America

0 9 8 7 6 5 4 3 2 1

Belle Chasse

CHAPTER 1

The full moon blinded me when I landed on my back on the muddy ground, but not enough to obliterate my view of a pirate ghost towering over me with a flambeau and a frown.

"Can you stand, *Jolie*?" Ah, not a ghost pirate, but a historically undead one. Melting snow and plaster dust had turned Jean Lafitte's elegant blue jacket into a mass of off-white lumps. "I fear you are wounded."

"I fear you are right." My leg burned as if someone had used a flambeau to set it afire.

"I'll carry the wizard." My merman friend Rene Delachaise sat near me on the swampy ground. He jerked up the bottom of his sweater and popped a bullet out of his stomach with his fingers. He tossed it down the hill toward the sound of ocean waves and studied the small wound left behind. "Damned elves are gonna pay for this."

He looked over at me. "How's your leg, babe?"

I struggled to a sitting position and looked down stupidly at the blood soaking my left leg from mid-thigh downward. Finally, it all came back to me, along with a stabbing pain that felt as if a nail were being driven into my thigh all the way to the bone. Like Rene, I had a gunshot wound. Unlike Rene, I wasn't a shape-shifter and couldn't pop out my bullet like an overripe pimple.

We'd landed in the transport set up on the Beyond's version of Grand Terre Island after fleeing New Orleans, and I'd been shot by one of the Elven Synod while escaping from what amounted to a death sentence from my own Elders. I'd lost my freedom. I'd lost my job. I'd had to leave without Alex, my lover and significant something-or-other, who'd stayed behind to clear my name and try to prevent the preternatural world from going to war. The leaders of at least three powerful species wanted me dead or under their control, which meant I was stuck for the foreseeable future in the Beyond, specifically in Old Barataria, a circa 1815 version of the South Louisiana wetlands.

On the positive side, at least for the first time in two weeks I wasn't up to my ass in snow. New Orleans had been floundering under blizzard conditions; Old Barataria was downright balmy.

Cursing like a teamster, I managed to roll to my hands and knees but couldn't stand. "Where's the staff?"

"I have your magic stick, *Jolie*." Jean held up the ancient staff of the fire elves, whose proper name was Mahout. It looked like a small, insignificant length of wood in his big hand, but everyone here knew it was the most effective weapon on Jean's well-fortified island, at least in the hands of its owner, which would be me.

"Your magic bag is over here." Rene climbed to his feet, seeming no worse for having been shot by an elf who, thankfully, didn't have the good sense to use silver bullets. Rene had almost healed. I'd be well on my way once I could mix a potion with my portable magic kit, which I hoped was still in the bag.

In the meantime, I had no other excuse for staying on my hands and knees like a horse ready for the glue factory. "I can't get up."

Both Jean and Rene moved into action, each grabbing a forearm and pulling me up with enough force that for a few terrifying seconds, I was airborne. Then I landed on my injured leg and it gave way, sending me halfway to the ground again before Rene scooped me up like Rhett Butler ready to charge up the stairs with Scarlett in his arms—well, if Rhett had been a Cajun aquatic shifter.

"Drusilla should be carried only in my arms, *mon ami*," Jean said to Rene. "She is my . . ."

He paused, unsure of what to call me even though we'd established that we were going to officially be friends without benefits. Or at least I had established it and he hadn't verbalized an objection. Now, my empathic skills told me he was feeling possessive. He needed a reality check.

"Get over it, pirate." Rene hefted me more firmly in his arms and headed toward the narrow beach at the bottom of the hill. "I'm younger and stronger. You need to set up guards to watch this transport in case we're followed by any of those elf or wizard SOBs."

Behind me, I heard Jean mutter, *"Qu'est-ce que c'est SOBs?"*

"Son of a bitch!" I yelled, partly to translate for Jean and partly because Rene's arm pressed against my wound too hard. "Put me down, Rene. I can walk."

"Don't be a stupid wizard. Oh, wait. That was redundant, babe. And no, you can't walk."

He was right, so I shut up and let myself be hauled like a sack of andouille down a mile of moonlit beach. The Gulf of Mexico heaved and tossed waves against the shore to our right, lulling me into a near sleep with my head propped against Rene's shoulder. He wasn't that much taller than me, but he was a wiry kind of muscular and shifter strong. Plus, I trusted him with my life so I let myself relax. I hadn't done much of that lately.

The lights of Maison Rouge, Jean's two-story house near the beach on the eastern end of Grand Terre Island, blinded me again as our ascent up the wooden banquette to the building jolted me awake. Rene reached the front verandah, hauled me inside the wide entry hall, and stopped. "You gonna bleed all over Jean's fancy white couch if I put you down."

I craned my neck and looked at the white-upholstered fainting couch with its richly carved mahogany trim. "Just put me on the floor." At least the hardwood could be wiped off. Hiding out in a place and time without electricity or running water was going to be interesting, although I doubted mine would be the first bloodshed this floor had seen.

"*Mais non,* that is not acceptable, Rene. Take her to my chambers." The master of the *maison* strode through the front door. "I have a thing there which will be of assistance."

"Wait." I struggled until Rene finally set me down, although he kept an arm around my waist to hold me upright. "Where are Eugenie and Jake and Adrian?"

"They are upstairs seeing to their accommodations, *Jolie.*" Jean gestured toward the broad staircase that wound its way to the second floor. I knew there were at least three bedrooms up there in the interior of the house; all of the outside rooms were devoted to cannons. Jean's version of a security blanket.

"Are they all okay?" My best friend, Eugenie Dupre, a human only recently introduced to the wonders of preternatural life, was pregnant with the child of my bond-mate Quince Randolf, aka Rand, chief of the elven fire clan and newly self-appointed head of the Elven Synod.

Rand's determination to control Eugenie and his unborn

child, and the wizarding Elders' determination to give Rand what he wanted lest he break the centuries-old truce between our two species, had set the whole ugly scene in motion that resulted in a jail sentence for Jake and myself. Adrian, a wizard and newly turned vampire, was also on the lam.

Since the wizards' jail was located in Greenland and I had assumed a watered-down version of elven hibernation when I got too cold, it amounted to a death sentence for me.

"They are all unharmed, although Mademoiselle Eugenie is fatigued and seems disturbed that we do not have the convenience of modern plumbing. From its frequency, she seems to have confused her need to pass water with that of a racing horse. Perhaps you might explain this, Drusilla, when you are yourself mended."

Yeah, because I was all about explaining a pregnant woman's frequent need to pee like a racehorse to an undead pirate.

Jean led the way into the interior hallway of the first floor, where I knew his personal rooms lay, as well as a furnished guest suite I'd visited once before. We passed the guest room and followed him into the master chamber.

It was a large room, with masculine, heavy furniture that Jean had no doubt plundered off the Spanish ships from whose goods he'd made much of his considerable fortune. A large, four-poster bed with a full canopy draped in rich reds and browns consumed much of the room, complemented by an assortment of heavy chests in matching dark wood.

Jean strode to one of the armoires, opened it, and pulled out a thick blanket—or so I thought. Once he'd spread out the heavy, densely woven cotton, I was no longer sure. I grasped one of the corner posters of the bed, which was almost as big around as my waist, relieving Rene of the job of holding me up. "What is that?"

"When on a frigate, it is a sail." Jean spread it out on the bed with efficient movements. He'd done this before. "Over the span of my many years, I found it has other uses as well, such as in the bloody business we now must tend to in removing the bullet from your leg."

Uh-oh. I knew my bullet wouldn't pop out like Rene's, but I planned to extract it magically. "I just need to make a potion. I can handle this with magic." I held on to the bedpost as if it were the mast of a frigate caught in a whirlpool. "If you'll give me a little privacy, please." I would not remove my pants with an audience.

They looked at me with uncertainty, then looked at each other. Finally, Jean shrugged. "This must be done in the time of one hour, *Jolie*. We do not have your modern medicines here and you must not risk corruption."

I thought I'd probably been corrupted years ago, but assumed it was some old-world term for infection. He was right; I didn't want to risk it.

For the next hour, I tried everything I could devise. A healing potion would trap the bullet inside and end up killing me. A magnetic charm and an attempt to summon the bullet with the elven staff simply caused the piece of molten lead to ping around inside my thigh like a pinball.

After a few other failed efforts, I struggled back into my jeans and limped to the bedroom door, where Jean and Rene stood side by side, watching anxiously.

"Is the bullet removed?" Jean asked.

"Babe, you look like shit," Rene added.

"I can't do it, so you'll have to," I said, wondering why Rene seemed to be turning gray and fuzzy around the edges. "Try not to kill me."

An argument reached me from somewhere on high. I assumed
that God and Saint Peter were above me, debating whether or not
I should be admitted to heaven. Apparently, it was a toss-up.

I struggled to open my eyes when I realized God was speaking with a French accent and trying to unfasten my jeans. When
Saint Peter told God that the wizard would poke his fucking eyes
out with the elven magic stick if he didn't get his hands off her
zipper, I knew I hadn't died and gone to heaven. I was still alive
and in hell. But at least I was still alive.

"Is it over? Is the bullet out?" My voice sounded puny but it
was enough to silence Jean and Rene.

"*Non,*" Jean said. "We are soon to begin. I had hoped you
would not awaken beforehand."

Just my luck; I'd be awake for the fun. "Go for it."

The pirate disappeared for a few seconds, then returned
wielding a lit candle, a dagger, and a bottle of brandy.

Oh, God in heaven. We were going to reenact every bad
bullet-removal scene from every bad historical movie ever filmed.
Next thing you knew, he'd be offering me something to bite
down on.

"You may bite on this to ease your pain." Jean held up a
leather strap, which I was going to use to beat him with as soon
as I could sit up. Which wasn't now. My leg throbbed in rhythm
with my pulse and felt like a mound of boudin noir stuffed into
a denim sausage casing.

"I need anesthesia." I mentally scanned the contents of my
bag again and came up empty. I didn't think holy water would
help since the wound wasn't technically of demonic origin, although I suspected Satan's evil twin might have been an elf.

My racing thoughts were distracted by a tearing noise and I
raised up on my elbows and watched in horror as Rene used the
dagger to spear a hole in my jeans just below the promised land

and then exercised misuse of shifter strength by ripping off the entire left leg of my jeans.

He stopped, biting his lip, and I flopped back on the pillow when Jean walked up to the other side of the bed and also looked down, confused. "What does this mean, *Jolie?* Who is this man named Harry? Why would you wear his name on your pantalets?"

"I'll explain later." Rene ripped off the left leg of the Harry Potter pajama bottoms I'd donned in New Orleans as makeshift long johns. "But you got nothing to be jealous about. Just worry about her sense of fashion."

"Bah. She has none."

I refused to take part in this conversation. Besides, Jean had reclaimed the dagger and was holding it in the fire. Pain was coming and coming hard.

I've never been a squealing, crying, mewling sort of woman, but I screamed like a banshee—a real one—when Rene poured brandy on my exposed wound.

"*Mon Dieu, non.* She must drink it." Jean snatched the bottle away, lifted my head, and engaged in what felt like the alcoholic version of waterboarding. Brandy dribbled down my chin, ran in my nose, seeped down my cheeks, and seared holes in my eardrums. A lot of it, however, went in my mouth and down my throat, peeling off the lining of my esophagus like battery acid. Before long, my leg still burned like a bonfire but I didn't care so much.

When Jean heated the dagger again, however, I did find the presence of mind to grab Rene's arm and jerk him to me. "Where's that damned strap?"

"I have it, sunshine." Jake Warin eased onto the bed next to me and snuggled close. He smelled of fresh salt air and some kind of citrus soap, a far cry from this boudoir of blood and brandy.

I inhaled him and relaxed. Jake would protect me since Rene had proven untrustworthy. "We're just gonna lay here together awhile, okay?"

I managed a smile. I was glad Jake had found happiness with Collette, his new fiancée. Glad we'd managed to end up friends even though I took full blame for him being turned loup-garou, a rogue werewolf with poor pack skills and poorer control. Alex couldn't be here with me, but his cousin made me feel closer to him.

It wasn't until I realized Rene stood at the foot of the bed, holding both my ankles down with all his shifter might, that I realized Jake wasn't here to comfort me. I opened my mouth to scream, and Jake slapped the leather strap between my teeth, wrapped his arms around me like a vise, and whispered, "Hold on, DJ."

CHAPTER 2

A grinning, gap-toothed pirate set a bowl of steaming brown liquid in front of me. I'd barely eaten in the two days since I'd finally awakened from harrowing pirate surgery and been forced to wear an assortment of Rene's camo shorts, the only thing I'd found that fit me and still gave Nurse Lafitte access to my bandages. Once the bullet had been removed, I'd been able to use one of my healing potions to speed up the process. Didn't work as quickly as in the human world, but it beat healing *au naturel.*

The days had passed in a blur, with the undead pirates given life in Barataria through the strength of Jean's own memories acting as scruffy French nursemaids.

Today, though, instead of inducing nausea, the rich, meaty aroma of food made my taste buds sit up and remind me that I needed my strength if I wanted to keep wallowing. Self-pity was exhausting.

The pirate-turned-waiter bowed and gabbled something that sounded vaguely French. Then he backed out of the room, probably to run off and hide the evidence of poison, which could have been sneaked onto the island by enemy operatives and spiked into the gumbo. Not that I was paranoid.

I picked up one of the heavy, ornate silver spoons that had been polished to a sheen and poked in my bowl at a suspicious floating lump the color of redwood bark.

"Eat, *Jolie*," said my French host. "I would be most grievously injured, as would my cook, should you grow faint from lack of nourishment while you are a guest in my home."

God forbid I should offend Jean Lafitte, Interspecies Council representative for the historical undead and the only person undead or alive standing between me and a subzero cell in Greenland. Fugitives from justice should take whatever suspicious mystery meat is provided.

I gave him a reassuring smile and jabbed an elbow at the merman on my right. We sat near the end of a long wooden table in the early nineteenth-century version of a dining room, in this rustic but somehow elegant mansion. "What is this?" I whispered, frowning at the meat.

Rene leaned over and peered into my bowl. "Turtle, babe. What the hell you think it is—dog?" He laughed; Rene had always been good at amusing himself. "Come to think of it, I ain't seen Alex Warin around here."

"Sore subject." I dipped my spoon in the bowl, capturing a chunk of meat and raising it to my nose. At least it smelled more like filé and spices than undead reptile. I'd eaten food in the Beyond before, but somehow dried mystery meat seemed less suspicious than juicy chunks floating in gumbo.

"*Mon Dieu,* it is turtle, Drusilla. Eat. Rene brought it with him from the . . . er . . ." Jean frowned.

"Rouses Supermarket, the one out on Belle Chasse Highway."

Rene grinned. "Don't worry, babe, it ain't undead turtle. It's dead turtle. That turtle ain't *never* comin' back to life."

Great. Everybody was a comedian, and all I wanted to do was either curl up in a corner for a good cry or use my elven staff to char something to bone and ash.

Or someone. Now that my healing potion had done most of its work, I'd started a list: Candidates for Incineration. My spineless worm of a boss, Wizard Elder Willem Zrakovi, currently sat at the top of the list alongside my elf-mate-in-name-only, Quince Randolph, aka Rand. Also on the list: several other elves and every vampire I'd met with the possible exception of the one lounging around upstairs. The jury remained out on Adrian Hoffman.

Rene hadn't seen Alex Warin around here because my canine shapeshifter remained incommunicado in New Orleans, living his normal life while I hid out like a criminal.

There was a bounty on my head, it was four days before Christmas, and I was having turtle gumbo with a merman, an undead pirate king, two loups-garou, and my best friend—a human pregnant with the half-elven child who had unknowingly helped set this whole debacle in motion. Plus a newbie vampire upstairs who didn't like the smell of food anymore.

We'd make a great reality show except I realized, looking at the motley assortment of people sitting around the mahogany dining table, that nobody would believe reality could be quite this warped.

"What's going on in New Orleans?" I asked Rene, forcing myself to eat the gumbo. The warmth and rich scent of the filé-spiked roux made me feel better despite my best efforts to wallow. Maybe I'd turned a corner.

"Weather finally cleared up since the Winter Prince has gone back to Faery for a while." Rene tore off a ragged chunk from a loaf of French bread the size of a baseball bat and slathered it with butter. "All the weather dudes are jacked about the big global warming conference planned for January."

The scientists would be surprised to learn that New Orleans' historic mid-December snowfall had nothing to do with fossil fuel consumption. Jean Lafitte's newest bromantic interest, Christof, the Faery Prince of Winter, had turned New Orleans into a Frigidaire to torment Jean's enemies, the cold-sensitive elves.

"What about the council?" I asked. Rene's arrival marked our first contact with the modern world since the great escape. "Have they issued warrants for my and Jake's arrest?" There was already a standing warrant for Adrian to cover previous sins; it simply needed updating.

"Not yet." Rene slurped his soup, then reached for more bread. The merman had a prodigious appetite that never resulted in an extra ounce of fat. "But it's comin'. You and Jake can't go home anytime soon. Gonna take a while to sort all this shit out."

A couple of weeks before Thanksgiving, Jake had lost his temper during an argument, shifted, and accidentally infected me with the virulent loup-garou virus. Infecting someone—on purpose or accidentally—was a crime that carried the death penalty. Now, I was under investigation for treason after bonding with Rand to avoid turning loup-garou myself . . . and then lying about it all to protect Jake.

Or at least that was the story. The real reason I was being threatened with incarceration is that I'd first disobeyed Zrakovi's direct order to terminate Eugenie's pregnancy, then refused another order to turn her over to Rand.

Zrakovi wasn't secure in his new position as First Elder, and I had embarrassed him in front of the rest of the Interspecies

Council. He wanted to teach me a lesson and save face while also kissing Rand's elven ass.

Eugenie pushed back her bowl. At eight weeks pregnant in human-elven math, which was constructed mostly of guesswork, she'd gotten past most of the morning sickness that had plagued her first few weeks. Stress wasn't helping her appetite, though.

"Maybe I should just let Rand take me to Elfheim." Her eyes brimmed with tears that might be hormonal or situational. Either option applied. "The Elders will probably drop the charges against you and Jake if we give Rand what he wants. The only reason the wizards are after you is to force you to turn me over to him. You know Rand won't hurt me."

Unspoken was *Rand won't hurt me physically but he might scramble my brains with his sneaky elven mind-magic if I'm not docile.* Or another option: *Rand won't hurt me until after the baby is born and then he'll make sure I'm out of the picture.* Rand wanted his son and heir, no matter what happened to Eugenie. She hadn't even known he was an elf until well past the conception, and I placed the blame squarely on my own head. I should've told her before she got so involved with him.

Should was a useless word; it implied failure. The truth hurt.

"You're not going to Elfheim." My voice was combative. "That's not an option." I'd promised to help her through the political minefield this pregnancy had created, and I still had enough optimism, or maybe stupidity, to believe they could work out an amicable agreement over raising the child, given enough time. Rand wasn't evil. He was an arrogant, selfish, ambitious, and frequently delusional jerk who could do evil things, but he'd also shown himself capable of kindness, especially when he could twist it to his advantage.

I turned back to Rene. "What's your dad saying about the big political picture? What does he think is going to happen?"

The elder merman represented the water folk on the Interspecies Council and if he was anything like Rene, Toussaint Delachaise wasn't shy about sharing his opinions.

"Council's gonna meet again the day after Christmas, but everything's seriously screwed up, babe. Jean prob'ly knows more than me." Rene nodded at our host, who'd been listening in uncharacteristic silence. Very uncharacteristic silence.

"*Non*," Jean said, sipping his brandy and setting the glass aside before ladling a spoonful of soup to his mouth. His expression lay just south of a smile.

Uh-oh. I set down my spoon with a clatter. Jean Lafitte never answered a question with a single word when a dozen would do, and he'd been quiet since we arrived. He was up to something.

"What are you not saying, Jean?" Now that I'd finally focused on something besides my own drama, I noticed the barely restrained mirth around his cobalt-blue eyes. His thick black hair had been pulled back and tied with a leather cord, and he wore his usual white tunic and black pants and knee-high black leather boots—sexy pirate gear, in other words. But he'd been quiet as a cloistered nun, which was as ill-suited to his nature as it sounded, and he looked way too happy considering the landfill most of our lives had been dumped into.

"One should not discuss matters of business while one dines." Jean dabbed at his mouth with a delicate sweep of an improbably white napkin. "It weakens the constitution."

His voice, deep, heavily accented, and authoritative, was likely meant to whip me into line with the rest of his flunkies. That tactic had never worked on me, but he hadn't stopped trying.

"My constitution is strong as a dragon, thanks to your doctoring skills. What are you up to? I was afraid you'd be in trouble with the council because of me. Are you?"

"Because of *us*," Jake said. He and his fiancée, a drop-dead-gorgeous loup-garou named Collette, sat across the table from Rene and me, and had remained quiet through most of the meal, exchanging knowing glances and half-hidden smiles. I don't think Alex and I had ever made googly eyes at each other.

"Don't forget me, too, DJ. And that vampire upstairs doing God knows what—Adrian the fanged wizard. Jean's probably in trouble because of all of us." Eugenie, sitting at the foot of the table opposite Jean, played with her napkin. She was not eating enough for two, and her gesture reminded me that I needed to send Rene on another run to New Orleans with a shopping list for healthy fare. Fresh fruits, dairy, and vegetables were scarce in Old Orleans and Barataria, and who knew how long Rene would be able to come and go without someone following him into a transport or charging him with aiding and abetting.

He'd also need to buy a ton of smoked meats, which Eugenie was craving as mother-to-be of the heir to the elves' fire clan. I needed to start another list.

Jean placed his napkin on the table and sat back in his chair with a sigh. "Very well, if you wish to discuss this now, we shall. The council members have expressed a desire that Jean Lafitte no longer attend their future gatherings until they say otherwise." He gave me a broad smile. "I believe one of the things they shall do at their next gathering is remove me from their number, leaving the historical undead with no one to represent them."

My heart did a thudding somersault. Deep in my heart, I'd known it was likely that Jean would be punished by the Interspecies Council if it was discovered that he'd granted asylum to me and this growing band of criminal misfits. By taking us into his home in the Beyond, he'd essentially thumbed his nose at both the council's decisions and its members' authority, and

none of the others among New Orleans' historical undead—
heavy on authors and artists—had any interest in the power politics of the prete world.

Question was, if Jean was losing his seat on the council, why
did he look so amused? It couldn't be good.

"Eugenie and I need to find another place to stay so you can
retain your position." I pushed my chair back and stood. Whatever Jean was up to, I wanted no part of it. Plenty of trouble had
been heaped on my doorstep already, and I was already drowning without adding pirate shenanigans to my gumbo of misery.
"We can go into Old Orleans. There are plenty of places to hide
there. No one needs to know Eugenie and I were ever in Barataria." Zrakovi might not have any proof that I had fled to Old
Barataria, but it didn't take a mental giant to suspect it. No point
in helping him make his case.

One elf—Betony Stoneman, aka Fred Flintstone, the chief
of the earth clan—had seen Eugenie transporting out of New
Orleans with Jean, but he'd been unconscious when I escaped a
few minutes later, and I trusted Alex to have covered our tracks.
Plus, in my humble opinion, ole Fred wasn't the sharpest knife
in the Republic of Elfheim; he might not remember.

As long as I didn't cross the temporal border back into modern New Orleans, the wizards couldn't detect my unique energy signature. They might suspect I was in Barataria, but unless
they invaded Jean's territory, which I doubted they'd do since
most types of magic didn't work reliably here, they didn't know
it for sure.

"Drusilla, sit! *Asseyez-vous!* You shall not depart." Jean raised
his voice to a thunder, then softened it when my startled *eep*
turned into a scowl. I didn't appreciate being commanded as if
I were one of his minions.

"*S'il vous plaît, Jolie.* This action by the council comes as no surprise. Do you not realize that I foresaw this long before you took refuge here? Did I not give you warning that you would be forced to choose sides?"

I plopped back onto the heavy wooden chair, the center slat of its mahogany back carved with an eagle, its talons outstretched as if grabbing for as much power as it could take. The chair's seat had been covered with stiff, heavy gold fabric over what I suspected was horsehair stuffing. Then again, my discomfort might have nothing to do with the chair.

"I haven't chosen sides." I wasn't sure anyone had. Wizards and elves, faeries and vampires, water species and historical undead, weres and shifters. Every species was protecting its own interests, moving in stealth around New Orleans' human population, which had no clue what the barometric pressure of Hurricane Katrina had unleashed in its midst several years ago.

"I'm a wizard," I said. "That's all I know how to be." Until this whole fiasco with Eugenie's pregnancy had arisen and Zrakovi had issued the unforgiveable order for me to terminate said pregnancy with or without her permission, I'd been sure nothing could make me side with any other group. I still wasn't convinced.

Jean took a sip of his brandy and gave me a serious, steady look that made me squirm; he no longer looked amused. The pirate had left me to my own devices over the past two days, playing the polite host but not attempting discussions either personal or political. He'd let me limp around and feel sorry for myself. Now, however, I felt an overdue discussion aiming for my head like a pirate's cannonball.

Rene apparently sensed it, too. "Hey, Jake, why don't you and Collette and Eugenie help me get the rest of the supplies from the warehouse transport. Then, Jean wants us to shut it down so DJ can set up a transport closer to the house, something easier to guard. I brought in enough shit for an army."

Which, now that I thought about it, told me that Jean was stocking up for a long siege, or a houseful of people.

Or a war.

CHAPTER 3

Once we were alone, I raised an eyebrow at my host. "Say what you need to, but as much as I appreciate your taking us all in and digging the bullet out of my leg, the last thing I want is to hurt your position with the council."

Or mine. My priorities were, first, to protect Eugenie, and, second, to get my job back and be able to live in New Orleans without feeling as if the preternatural version of Mongol hordes were bearing down on me. If Jean's agenda didn't jibe with mine, I needed to get far, far away from him and his plots and schemes. Because he always had a scheme.

Jean poured himself a refill of brandy and stood. "Let us go into the study, then, Drusilla. It is time to discuss matters of much importance and difficult truths."

Truths were always difficult these days, so I grabbed my untouched glass of wine before following him. I'd eaten so little in the past week that a few ounces of alcohol would probably knock me unconscious. That might be a good thing.

We settled into what had become our usual resting places,

although the furnishings had changed. Jean's ornate mahogany chair, placed where he could see all of the room's entry points so as not to be surprised or attacked without warning, had been replaced by a massive recliner, cocooned with enough stuffing to fill the Superdome and covered in rich brown leather. Rene must've hit the La-Z-Boy store before a recent visit.

"Is my reclining chair to your liking?" Jean took his seat, fumbled a few moments with the lever on the right-hand side, and laughed when his legs and black pirate boots popped into an outstretched position. "You once had a similar chair before your house was unfortunately set afire. I would be pleased to share this chair with you, *oui*?"

Actually, I'd gotten rid of my old recliner shortly after Katrina and long before my house had burned down, mostly due to bloodstains as a result of a fight with Jean Lafitte. No point in trotting out unpleasant memories.

"*Oui*. Next time you're not sitting in it, I'll try it." I relaxed when he chuckled. Fending off smarmy comments from Jean put me in familiar territory. "Next time, have Rene bring back a sofa to match."

I perched on the uncomfortable settee whose mahogany legs had been carved in the shape of angry phoenixes. What was it with the pirate and ill-tempered birds?

The room was bathed in rich scarlets and browns, same as Jean's bedroom. The ambience was strong and masculine, wafting rich scents of oil and polish and the undercurrent of savory tobacco and spices that always accompanied the master of the house.

Rene's camo shorts and my red sweater, beginning its third day of wear and adorned with several ragged holes courtesy of my escape from New Orleans, felt shabby in these plush surroundings despite my nightly devotion to washing them. My lank hair suffered from being shampooed with some rudimentary form of soap. Both my clothes and I were trying to stay clean using the big iron tub tucked into the corner of the small room I had moved into on the first floor.

Like my pirate, who had returned to his private suite down the hall from mine, I refused to sleep upstairs where I might be trapped by marauding bands of elves, vampires, faeries, or undead ax murderers. Been there, done that. All of it.

"Do you think Rene brought any clothes for Eugenie and me?" Collette was the only other modern woman on the island that I had seen, and she was half a foot taller than me with a waist circumference the size of my grandmother's knitting needle, which is why I was wearing Rene's shorts.

Jean smiled. "I have arranged for supplies of clothing for both you and Mademoiselle Eugenie. I was simply waiting for your spirit to revive."

In other words, until I stopped my navel-gazing. "Consider it revived. Where'd this supply of clothing come from?" Last time Jean had provided me with a wardrobe, I'd flashed way too much cleavage and had been given a bizarre assortment of early nineteenth-century underwear that I kept putting on backward.

"Bah. It is clothing, Drusilla." Jean waved his hand in a universal *let it go* gesture, so I let it go. For now.

Guess that meant it was time for business and hard truths. "Do you think it's too late to save your seat on the Interspecies Council?"

I opened up my empathic senses to his emotional signature. As a wizard, my limited physical magic didn't work in the Beyond, although my geeky Green Congress ritual magic usually did. Red Congress wizards had the showy physical magic, but it was useless in the Beyond. I wasn't sure about Blue Congress, the magic of creation and re-creation, or Yellow Congress, mental magic. They might or might not work here.

My empathy, however, was one of the elven traits I'd won in the genetic lottery thanks to my late parents, and elven magic worked just fine in the Beyond. I wanted to know what Jean was feeling, not just what he said; he had a tendency to embellish. *Lie* was such a harsh word.

Currently, he was impatient but also something else I couldn't identify.

"The proper question, *Jolie,* is not whether I *shall* keep my seat on the council, but whether or not I *wish* to keep my seat on the council," he said, leaning forward and propping his elbows on his knees.

Anticipatory. Predatory. Those were the emotional traits I'd been trying to name. Jean was like the eagles on his dining room chairs, talons outstretched to snag a tasty mouse. Trouble was, I had no idea which mouse he hoped to devour, or whether I was a fellow eagle or part of his intended meal.

When in doubt, do what the pirate orders. "Okay, let me rephrase my question. Jean, do you *want* to keep your seat on the Interspecies Council?"

He'd worked hard—and quite illegally, I'd heard—to obtain that spot representing the historical undead, famous humans granted immortality by the magic of human memory. Why would he want to give up the power for which he'd fought so hard?

"*Non.*" His eyes grew more animated. "What kind of council is it now, after all? It has proven to be a sporting arena for only the wizards and the elves. The vampires' allegiance sways like reeds in the wind, and they currently have no representative because of this. Rene tells me his father considers leaving the council, for he sees no strength of character. The fae are

fighting among themselves, the were-creatures are but mario-
nettes whose strings are pulled by the wizards, and the other
species are too frightened to form alliances." He shrugged.

I had to admit his summary was accurate. The peace of the
whole prete universe seemed to rest on whether or not the
wizards and elves could salvage their centuries-old truce despite Rand's power plays to control Eugenie and the wizards'
inability to give him what he wanted. Otherwise, we could
face a conflict the likes of which the world had never seen, with
New Orleans sitting at ground zero. The unwitting human cit-
izens of my hometown could easily become collateral damage.

"If there is a war, where will your loyalty lie, Jean?" I kept
my tone even but as I sipped my wine, I could mentally track
its burn all the way down my esophagus and into the pit of my
stomach, where it sizzled like liquid hitting a red-hot pan.
I might be sick.

Jean, oblivious to my physical plight, leaned back and
grinned. "As it must always be, my loyalty lies with Jean Lafitte."

As if that were ever in doubt. "Yes, but if the wizards and
elves go to war, who will you support?"

Jean lit one of his small cigars. Although it had taken some
strong-arming on my part, he'd agreed to limit his pipe and cigar
smoking to this room in deference to Eugenie's pregnancy. Rand
would have an elf-stroke if he thought his unborn son were
being exposed to undead secondhand smoke.

"Drusilla, have I shared with you the events surrounding
the war?"

I'd thought we *were* discussing the war. Unless . . . "Which
war?"

"The battle that took place early in the year 1815, between
your Americans and the English tyrants."

Jean wasn't one to stroll down memory lane without a point.

"I know both sides tried to recruit you. What does that have to do with the current situation?"

Jean leaned back and stared at a faded sepia-toned map of the Gulf of Mexico hanging on the wall opposite his chair. "It has much bearing on the matters we now face. Prior to the grand battle, I placed myself in a position to decide who won control of *Nouvelle Orleans* and, thus, *la rivière,* the Mississippi."

I had read a lot about Jean's role in the Battle of New Orleans, figuring the more I knew about this complex man the better, but I failed to see the connection with our current situation unless the British planned to sail into Barataria Bay with elves manning their warships and the wizards planned to make a stand in a muddy field in St. Bernard Parish.

"I'm sorry, but I'm missing the point."

Jean shook his head at me, and I thought he might be trying to refrain from an eye roll. I hated a dead guy who was smarter than me.

"Understanding escapes you, Drusilla. This disappoints me."

I hated to tell him, but understanding didn't escape me; I'd never had it to begin with. "It disappoints me, too, Jean, but you're going to have to tell me what you mean. Stop dancing around it."

"We will dance later if you like, *Jolie.* I cut quite a fine figure in the ballroom, but I do not see . . . ah." I waited for him to finish figuring out my slang. In a few moments, he nodded his head.

"As preparations were being made to fight this battle, I saw the weaknesses in both sides. In order to reach the city by stealth, the British would have to cross Barataria, which they could not do without my help.

"The Americans had too few men, too few arms, and very little powder, all of which I possessed in abundance."

His meaning sank in as I mentally shuffled through my history lessons. Both the British and Americans had approached Jean Lafitte and his merry band of pirates for help. He'd played both sides, finally twisting the situation brilliantly to ensure the American victory while also benefiting himself and his men.

Things had gone south for him a few years later, but at the time, he had held the fate of the new world in his battle-scarred hands not a month after a warrant had been issued for his arrest on charges of piracy, a hanging offense.

Holy crap. He was going to do it again, or at least he wanted to.

"You think both the elves and wizards will come to you for help?"

He smiled and finished off his glass of wine. "Come to *us* for help, Drusilla. *Oui,* it is possible, if the wizards and elves break truce. An alliance with the vampires would not give either side a decisive victory, and the people of Faery might well be evenly divided between the two princes who are vying for the throne. Whoever Christof supports, Florian will oppose. If Christof and his followers support his good friend Lafitte, well . . ." He smiled. "Better for us, *oui?*"

While he paused to refill his glass, my mind spun with the ramifications. I'd joked to myself a couple of weeks ago that Jean was amassing a motley assortment of allies, only now I realized it was no joke. He'd managed to build what could turn into quite a preternatural army. He'd taken in Jake and Collette, both loups-garou who might be able to enlist the help of other rogue wolves. Because of Jean's friendship with Rene, the water species would support him, especially if Rene's father left the council. Jean could still control the historical undead since they didn't give a crap about preternatural affairs. My former wizard colleague and newbie vampire Adrian Hoffman, living upstairs,

was on the run from wizards and vampires and elves; he had nowhere else to go. He had both fangs and magic; he hadn't been
turned long enough for his Blue Congress magic to have failed.

Last but far from least, Christof, the Faery Prince of
Winter, was Jean Lafitte's trump card. He had potentially half
of Faery at his disposal, and God only knew what all faeries
could do.

Thanks to yours truly, Jean now had a Green Congress
wizard in his entourage, one who could do elven magic.

Except this wizard wasn't enlisting.

"No." I set my wineglass on the side table, still mostly full.
I needed a clear head. "I'm not willing to fight against the
wizards." They were my people. I'd lost my job as sentinel and
my Green Congress license had been suspended pending an investigation, but the wizarding world was the only one I knew.
Besides that, elves were devious, arrogant, spoiled, and morally
ambiguous. I would not back them.

"Even now, *Jolie,* do you insist that your intent aligns with
those of the wizards?" Jean moved to sit beside me on the sofa,
his muscular frame warm and solid, as was the arm he slipped
around my shoulders. "They have sentenced you to what will
be a certain death on ridiculous charges, all because you will not
betray your friend Eugenie and her child to appease the elves.
In particular, *your* elf, who is using his power on the council to
control everyone."

Damn it, he was right. If I turned Eugenie over to Rand, who
now headed up the Elven Synod and was *my elf* whether I wanted
him or not, he'd promised to keep the truce with the wizards.
War could be averted, at least if he kept his word. Which is what
Willem Zrakovi and the Elders wanted, at any cost, because
they feared they'd lose.

For me, the cost of leaving Eugenie to whatever fate Rand

decided on was too high, however, even if Zrakovi agreed to let me off the hook on the other charges. I wasn't convinced of that; Zrakovi needed a scapegoat and I made a very good one.

I hadn't always been the best of friends to Eugenie. I had been selfish at times, distant at others. I could own that. On this matter, however, I had clarity. She was out of her element among all these pretes, and I'd do everything I could to keep her safe.

Who must I fight to do that? Not just Rand but my own people.

"I can't support either the elves or the wizards." I was screwed, in other words, and tears built behind my eyeballs. Tears I would not shed in front of Jean, even if I had to gouge out my eyes to avoid it. I didn't want his pity; I wanted his advice. "What the hell am I going to do?"

"You will support yourself, *Jolie,* alongside your friend Jean and our compatriots. We will do what is best for us all."

"But how will we know what that is if—"

A pair of shots rang out from outside, near the front of the house, followed by shouting. A sudden flood of adrenaline doused my fatigue and political confusion.

Jean's posture straightened, and he rose quickly. "That is Dominique, whose men were watching the transport. Something is amiss."

Ya think? I ran for my bag and pulled out the staff.

Jean slipped a triangular-bladed dagger from beneath his tunic, wrenched open the door to the study, and strode out ahead of me. As always where the pirate was concerned, I trailed along, a step behind.

CHAPTER 4

I edged around Jean in time to see his older half-brother and fellow pirate captain Dominique You dragging a stumbling, bleeding man into the front hallway from outside and shoving him to the floor. I breathed a sigh of relief that it wasn't Alex, followed by a chaser of disappointment that it wasn't Alex, topped by a dollop of concern that our friend Ken Hachette had been shot.

Ken, a human NOPD detective who'd recently been clued in about the big bad world surrounding him, had missed all the recent events due to a family emergency that had taken him out of town.

Why would he be coming to Old Barataria alone via Jean Lafitte's private transport unless Alex sent him? My adrenaline jump-started my heart to another race, this one fueled by worry. Something bad had happened; it was the only explanation.

Jean and Dominique exchanged a rapid-fire torrent of French that went way past my abilities to interpret. "He claims to be a friend to *her*," Dominique finally spat out, and I could tell by the way he said *her,* much as one might say *flesh-eating maggot,* that he referred to me. He'd never liked me; he considered me a bad influence on his baby brother the immortal pirate. As if.

"He *is* my friend." I shot Dominique a nasty look and rushed to help Ken to his feet. "How badly are you hurt?"

"Just a flesh wound." Ken studied the singed, bloody sleeve of his black jacket. "Gunpowder tore through my patch."

The New Orleans Police Department shields that emblazoned Ken's upper sleeves identified him as a homicide detective. His shiny crescent-moon-shaped NOPD badge was clipped to his belt, but I had no doubt that, somewhere on his person, he'd tucked another badge identifying him as an investigator for the Division of Domestic Terror. The DDT had been formed a few months ago as a top-secret preternatural crime unit loosely connected to the FBI and headed by Alex. Ken was the only human member among a small cadre of shifters and werewolves.

"What's happened?" Now that I knew he wasn't going to bleed out on Jean's entry hall floor, my mind conjured horrible visions, most involving Alex hurt or worse.

I only knew that when I left Alex a few nights ago to flee for my life, his last words were *I love you.* It didn't solve any of our problems, which still might prove insurmountable, but we'd both said the L word, and that was a big start.

"I need to talk to you alone, DJ." Ken looked around at Dominique and his hand slipped beneath his jacket. He was packing.

Dominique had the same thought, apparently, since he raised his heavy muzzle-loaded pistol and aimed at Ken's head. "I will not take a shot of warning this time, monsieur. I did such only out of respect for my brother. Not *her.*"

Her raised the elven staff and pointed it at the prickly pirate. "Just try it. Did you know that in modern times Dominique is quite a feminine name for a woman?" Petty, but it made him bristle and shift the gun toward my head instead of Ken's.

"Bah, *arrêter*." Jean grasped the end of the staff and forced it lower, stepping between me and Dominique's gun. He was wise enough, however, not to try wresting the staff away from me. "Drusilla's friends are most welcome in the home of Jean Lafitte unless they prove themselves untrustworthy." Jean looked at me. "Is this man to be trusted? He is Jacob's human friend, one of the human constabulary, *n'est-ce pas?*"

"Totally trustworthy." I made the necessary introductions, grasped the wrist of Ken's uninjured arm, and tugged him toward Jean's study. "And I want to talk to him alone. He needs his wound tended to."

While Jean bustled his grumbling, gun-happy brother back to transport-watch duty, I led Ken into the study, and dug a vial of healing potion from the bag I'd stashed beneath Jean's desk. Just in case there was more shooting, I rested Charlie on the table within easy reach. "Take off your jacket and shirt and let me clean up your arm, but only after you assure me Alex is okay."

"Alex is fine. He sent me." Ken struggled out of the nylon NOPD jacket, untied his Saints tie, and unbuttoned his conservative white dress shirt. Once out of the detective gear, I thought he'd look less like the conservative, control-freak Marine he was. Wrong. He just looked like a shirtless conservative, control-freak Marine. He'd been in Jake's unit in Afghanistan when things had gone badly. In the years since, Jake had found comfort in alcohol; Ken, in control and routine.

"Are you sure Alex is okay?" I paused, water dripping from the napkin I'd wet with water from a decanter next to Jean's stash of brandy. "Have the Elders gone after him?"

That was the thing I feared most. At some point, Zrakovi or Rand would realize the easiest way to force me out of hiding,

maybe to bring Eugenie with me, would be to hurt or threaten
Alex. I'd been trying to think of how to set up a private meeting with Zrakovi and plead my case without getting myself
arrested and shipped off to the frozen tundra.

"Seriously, Alex is fine." Ken winced as I eased the wet rag
down his arm, cleaning off the blood. He was right. It was a surface wound. Dom had been trying to scare him, not kill him.

"Alex wanted to let you know what was going on and since
I haven't been involved in all this council business, we thought
it was safer for me to come. I'm *just a human*"—the words held
a touch of pique—"so no one worries about my comings and
goings."

"Yeah, safer for you except for the getting-shot-by-a-pirate
part." I opened the jar of healing sweet olive and cloves ground
into a magicked lotion and spread it over the wounds.

Ken watched, openmouthed, as the jagged tears in his skin
began to make minute motions to reknit themselves; it would
take a while longer in the Beyond but as soon as he went back
to New Orleans, he'd heal quickly. He had a beautiful complexion the color of rich caramel and serious brown eyes with a
touch of green. The man just needed to lighten up. Then again,
we didn't live in lighthearted days.

"It will still take a while to heal, but take the rest of this vial
of potion with you. It'll work faster once you get out of the
Beyond and you'll be healed by tomorrow."

He looked at me, started to say something, then settled for
blinking a couple of times. "Thanks. Nice shorts, by the way."

I laughed at his *Dawn of the Dead* expression. "I keep forgetting
you've only known for a few weeks that magic existed. And the
shorts are Rene's—long story." Ken had taken the news about the
magical world with his usual calm demeanor, although he'd been
shaky around the edges for a day or two.

Ken pulled his bullet-grazed shirt back on, slipped his shoulder holster into place, carefully rolled up his tie and stuffed it into the pocket of his jacket, and followed me to the settee. We sat side by side, but I turned so I could watch his face. Not that I could read his expressions very well; he was a cop, after all. But my empathy told me he was nervous.

Nervous with a dose of ironic humor. "Yeah, thanks again to you and Alex for letting me know the bad guys I chased as a detective were amateurs compared to the ones from your world."

"Our world," I said. The lines were growing thin between humans and pretes as the species jockeyed for power. Some, including the fae and vampires, favored coming out to the humans. The wizards and elves agreed on one thing only, which was that alerting humans to our existence would be disastrous.

Ken seemed reluctant to speak, so I prodded. "Talk to me, Ken. What's going on that Alex had to send word?" I didn't tell Ken he was projecting nervous energy like a clear-channel radio station. He'd just freak out more.

Ken fidgeted on the sofa. "Alex is pretty sure either the Elders or Quince Randolph, or probably both, are having him followed. They think he'll lead them to you or to Eugenie so he wouldn't dare come himself."

I let out an unladylike snort. "I suspect they know exactly where we are without having to follow Alex."

Ken smiled. "Yeah, they figure you're with Lafitte, but so far they haven't been willing to come after you because they don't know who his allies are or how well he's protected. They know they can't kill him, but he can kill them."

Well, they could kill him, but as an immortal powered by the magic of human memory, he'd just come back angry. Make that *more* angry. "They don't have jurisdiction here anyway."

"Alex thinks if either wizards or elves can figure out who's backing Lafitte and can raise enough fighters to take him on without having to use their magic, they'll stage a raid to try to get you and Eugenie. Mostly Eugenie; she's in the middle of all this. Once her situation is resolved, Alex thinks you'll be cleared." Ken paused.

Which was all well and fine, but he hadn't crossed into the Beyond for political chitchat. "Tell me what's going on." I tucked my feet underneath me and waited.

"It's about . . ." Ken paused and glanced around at the closed door. "Where is Eugenie?"

I frowned. Ken and Eugenie had become friends in recent weeks; they'd learned about the world of insane and occasionally homicidal pretes about the same time. "She went to help Rene and the others get stuff out of the transport. Why?"

He sighed. "I don't want her to hear my news before we decide what to do. DJ, her sister is dead."

I stared at him, a niggle of worry sending a wave of chill bumps across my shoulder blades. "Violette? She lives in Shreveport." And had a husband and twin daughters who were six years old. "Eugenie didn't mention anything about her being sick. Was there an accident?"

Deep in my heart, I knew no accident would make Alex send Ken to Barataria.

Ken took a deep breath and shook his head. "Not a chance. She was found on the sofa in their living room, posed with her ankles crossed and her hands over her chest, four puncture wounds to her neck. She'd been completely drained of blood. The newspapers are all talking about a"—he made quote marks with his fingers—" 'vampire killer.' "

The *tick tick tick* of Jean's grandfather clock sounded abnormally loud in the silence that followed. My mind had frozen at the words *drained of blood*.

Ken leaned forward. "Are you okay? You look like you're about to faint. You're kind of green."

"I . . . No, I'm not okay. None of this is okay." I stood up and began to pace, trying to quell the panic that made me want to jump on one of Jean's frigates that was anchored offshore and sail off to parts unknown. "This is sick. Vampires. Why would vampires want to kill Eugenie's sister? She has little kids. She's in *Junior League,* for God's sake. What about her family?"

"Alex said they're fine—he sent someone up to Shreveport as soon as he heard. They were all home when it happened, but the husband found her. At least it wasn't the kids."

The ostrich side of my brain wanted to convince the hard, practical side that it could be a coincidence. Rogue vampires occasionally killed humans, after all. But deep down, I knew better. A rogue could find an easier target than a young mother in her own home in a suburb of Shreveport, Louisiana.

The vampires as a group would have no interest in hurting Eugenie, or even me, for that matter. They would, however, have an interest in aligning themselves with a more powerful group.

"Rand ordered it." I hated saying those words, hated thinking that my stupid elf-mate could be capable of such an act. He was selfish and arrogant and volatile, but going after Eugenie's family seemed too extreme even for him.

Ken hesitated, then spoke slowly. "Alex thinks so, too, but there's no proof."

I stopped pacing long enough to take a healthy kick at the side of Jean's fancy recliner. "There's no other explanation. The vampires wouldn't even know where Eugenie's sister lived, or care. I can't believe Rand would do it." If for no other reason than it could cause Eugenie enough stress to complicate her pregnancy. Who knew what to expect with half-elven pregnancies?

"I don't understand that damned elf." I kicked the heavy side table, leaving a mark but not budging it. I hoped it wasn't a priceless antique pirated from an early nineteenth-century Spanish vessel.

"Alex wanted you to decide whether or not to tell Eugenie."

"Oh, God." I flopped in Jean's recliner, reached over to the side table for my glass, and drained the remains of the wine I'd left earlier. "How can I tell her? She'll want to go to Shreveport for the funeral, and you can just bet Rand and his elf buddies will be waiting to grab her." And me, because I'd have to go with her. No way would I let her go alone. Although I'd been contemplating a trip to try and talk to Zrakovi in a rational way, so maybe I could meet him in Shreveport.

"I want you to consider something else," Ken said, his voice slow and calm. "Promise you'll hear me out."

I set my glass down and sat up straight. Ken's anxiety level had risen, when it should be lower now that he'd shared his news. "What?"

"Alex didn't consider this because he's too damned loyal for his own good, but I have to wonder if it wasn't the wizards behind it."

"Not a chance." My glare could cut glass.

Ken flinched, but kept talking. "Look, I wasn't there a couple of weeks ago when all the shit went down, but according to Alex, Zrakovi wanted you to abort Eugenie's baby, even by force if necessary. Then he was willing to turn Eugenie over to Rand without a thought as to what it would do to her." Ken took a deep breath. "To me, that sounds like a man determined to hold on to his new position as First Elder and desperate to keep the peace, no matter what it costs."

Ken waited for his words to sink in while I tried to mentally bat them aside. My pro-wizard bat was splintering, however.

"DJ, they consider her expendable." Ken's voice softened. "I'm human and I've felt that kind of condescension from half the pretes I've met, even the noncriminal ones and, except for you, that includes the wizards. They don't think we matter."

I closed my eyes, thinking back to what had driven me to such loggerheads with the Elders in the first place. I'd refused to obey Zrakovi's direct order to abort Eugenie's baby. I'd sidestepped Zrakovi by going to Rand for help. I'd fought Zrakovi at every turn.

"You're right." The words burned my insides worse than the wine. "It could be either wizards or elves. It could be both. The outcome is the same. And I don't know what the hell I'm going to tell Eugenie."

"Then you better decide, DJ, because I'm standing right here."

I hadn't heard the door to the entry hall open, but there Eugenie stood, alongside Collette. Behind them, Jake's soft Mississippi drawl wafted in from the hallway, mingling with Jean's deeper rasp.

"What is it you don't want to tell me? What have those crazy prete people done now?" Her face deepened to a dark claret that clashed with her auburn hair.

"How much of that did you hear?" I really might throw up this time.

"Enough to know somebody has done something bad and it involves me," Eugenie said, giving Ken a peck on the cheek on her way past and taking a seat next to him on the settee. Collette quietly left the room and closed the door behind her. "Start talking."

CHAPTER 5

Ken's face assumed the demeanor of a stag head on a hunting lodge wall—wide-eyed and immobile and wondering how the hell he'd gotten into such a position. His terror at seeing Eugenie skittered over my skin like ants. God forbid a man should have to endure an emotional scene with two women.

I threw the dog's best friend a bone. "Ken, would you mind waiting in the entry hall while Eugenie and I talk?" I thought a moment. "Stick close to Jean. I don't want Dominique to shoot you again."

He'd do it just to annoy me.

"Do you mind if I go on back to New Orleans? I doubt anyone will notice I'm gone, but no point in taking chances." Ken stood up and retrieved his damaged jacket from the settee with desperation-fueled speed.

I wanted to talk to him more, to know how Alex was really doing, but I knew he needed to get out of Barataria. The wizards might consider Ken unimportant in the grand scheme of prete politics, but he was a link to Alex and thus to me and thus to Eugenie.

They might be watching more closely than he and Alex thought.

"Sure, tell Alex . . ." I couldn't bring myself to send my love via Ken. It felt too weird and mushy; I'd barely managed to say it to Alex himself. The words had kind of slipped out accidentally, although I'd had no urge to take them back. "Tell Alex to be careful."

"I will. Oh, wait—I'd forgotten. Alex wanted me to give you this." Ken handed me a wrinkled envelope from his coat pocket, spatters of his blood forming a Rorschach splotch over my name, which had been written across the front in Alex's neat, precise cursive. Something heavy jingled inside.

Ken gave Eugenie a quick look, saw her eyes narrowed in suspicion, and made a hasty about-face toward the door. "Hope you guys can come home soon."

That made a bunch of us. I suspected the only one of us enjoying this experiment in preternatural communal living was our undead host.

Eugenie waited until the door closed behind Ken before pouncing. "What news? You might as well tell me. What awful thing has Rand done now?"

I took a deep breath, folded the bulky envelope and wedged it into my pocket, and settled back into the big armchair. Eugenie and I occupied the reverse spots that Jean and I had taken earlier for our unpleasant conversation. I could grow to hate this room.

"DJ, you're scaring me. Just say it."

My friend's short hair lay limp, its usual spikes beaten down—evidence that she'd been away from her Shear Luck salon and her abundance of tonsorial products for three days. I saw her—really saw her—for the first time since we'd fled New Orleans. I'd missed the dark smudges under her eyes, and if anything she looked as if she'd lost weight. Her hazel eyes regarded me with an open trust that made me loathe myself, my fellow wizards, and any prete who'd ever crossed her path. How had I let her get into this mess? How could I deliver this news gently?

I moved to sit next to her on the sofa and took her hand. Only from sheer will could I force my voice to stay level. "It's about your sister, Eugenie. She's gone."

Gone sounded better than *dead,* but its meaning missed the bull's-eye.

"Violette? Gone where? Why would Ken know about Violette going somewhere?"

"No, Eugie. I mean she's . . . she died. Violette died last night."

The long, awkward silence had a soundtrack. The metallic *click* of Jean's grandfather clock had, if possible, grown even louder since the room's last uncomfortable conversation. I might take Charlie and burn the damned thing to ashes after everyone settled in for the night.

"She can't be gone." Eugenie frowned. I could tell the instant it really sank in, from the widened eyes to the rising panic in her aura. "It's four days before Christmas. Amanda and Amelie are only six." She closed her eyes, and a single tear trailed a jagged line down her cheek, dragging molecules of my guilt and anger along with it. "Was it a car wreck? I always told her she talked on that damned cell phone too much. How's Matt?"

Eugenie's brother-in-law probably wasn't coping well at all, based on the part I hadn't yet told her. "Sweetie, it wasn't an accident."

"What? Was she sick?" Her eyes narrowed and slowly, so slowly, her panic gave way to a numb calm that scared me more than her fear had done. "Tell me the whole thing, DJ. Just say it."

I didn't realize I'd been biting my lower lip until I tasted the blood. "According to Ken, Violette appears to have been killed by"—I took a shaky breath—"by vampires." That sounded blunt, but I didn't know how to make it prettier.

She stared at me a few long moments, and I waited for the tears to come or the hysteria to be resurrected, prayed I'd have the words to help her.

Instead, she wrenched her hand from mine and her voice turned flat. "That's not even possible. Is that what Ken came to say? He's wrong because it's just too ridiculous. Violette lives in Shreveport, for God's sake. There are no vampires in Shreveport."

I didn't want to tell her more, that her sister had been drained and posed on her living room sofa, lifeless and empty—or that vampires were everywhere, even Shreveport. "It's true. Alex sent Ken so we'd know. He wanted to make sure you didn't hear it somewhere else and try to go to Shreveport, because it's a trap. Alex and Ken are sure of it, and I agree."

She continued to stare at me, a frown setting a deep crease between her brows. The truth was going to hit her hard when it finally settled in, but I recognized the whole ostrich game. I'd played it enough myself.

Pretend it's someone else you're discussing.

Pretend it isn't real.

Pretend it won't feel like shit and rip your heart out when you finally acknowledge it.

Her voice remained cold and flat. "Where did it happen?"

I fiddled with a fold in the upholstered seat of Jean's sofa, avoiding eye contact. "At her home. Matt and the kids are fine." Well, not fine at all, I was sure, but at least alive and not bitten. The monsters had been in their home while they were sleeping, though. The monsters might have even taken Violette from her bed without waking Matt. Goose bumps spread over my arms at the idea, followed by a flush of anger that turned my face hot enough to leave grill marks.

Damn it. Going after innocent family members for political advantage was unforgivable no matter who was behind it, and I had no doubt that's exactly what had happened.

"Was it a coincidence?" Anger seeped into her flat tone, giving it heat. "Don't even answer that because it's obvious. The wizards were behind it, weren't they? Your Elder Zrakovi made a deal with the vampires to try to force me to come back."

I looked up, surprised that her first suspect was Zrakovi and not Rand. "Alex thinks it might have been the elves."

Although the more I thought about it, the more certain I became of Rand's innocence. Well, he was far from *innocent*, but at least in this case, I didn't think he was guilty. The act had been too artless and direct, too blunt. Rand was subtle and clever in his deviousness.

"It wasn't Rand." Eugenie looked down at her hands, which were the only part of her that showed the anguish building inside. Her fists clenched so tightly that her knuckles had turned a mottled shade of white.

"How can you be sure?" I wanted to keep her talking, to keep Violette's death as abstract as possible. That way, when reality set in, maybe it wouldn't be as crushing. Yeah, right. Because that always worked so well for me.

"Rand wouldn't go after my family, not like that." I had to trust her instincts; she knew Rand better than I. In a *whole* lot of ways. "Even if he does think humans aren't worth the dirt under his shoes, Rand's lost too many people himself and he's still mourning his mother. No, sorry, DJ, but this was your people."

She shot me an accusatory look, and I closed my eyes.

Speaking of ostriches, however, I had to extract my own head out of Jean Lafitte's sandy beachfront.

"Yeah, it's very possible." I opened my mouth again to say I was sorry, but closed it. The words would come out empty. She knew I'd never condone or excuse this, and if Zrakovi was behind it, I had to know. The more quickly I could set up a meeting with him, the better.

Eugenie stood up and strode toward the door. "I'm getting out of here. Matt and the girls need me." I raced after her, then she stopped and turned so abruptly we collided in front of the door. "Do you have a gun I could borrow? Of course not. I'll ask Jean Lafitte. I bet he has a lot of guns."

Holy crap. Eugenie could not make a run for Shreveport carrying one of Jean's big pistols. She'd either kill someone or end up in jail, where she'd be a pregnant sitting duck for a marauding wizard or elf.

Before I could verbalize that, she'd flung open the door and come face-to-collarbone with what appeared to be a brazenly eavesdropping pirate. He didn't feel the need to pretend he hadn't been listening in on a private conversation. Then again, it was his house.

"*Pardon,* Mademoiselle Eugenie, but Drusilla is right. You must not attempt a trip to see to your family's affairs. The safety of neither you nor your child could be assured."

Smartass pirate. He'd played the safe-baby card before I could.

"But I have to . . . to . . ." Now the tears started, and she threw herself into Jean's arms. He patted her on the back awkwardly and looked at me over the top of her head. "Perhaps you should assemble our friends, *Jolie,* so that we might devise a plan."

A plan was good, plus assembling friends didn't take a lot of work; I didn't have that many. Rene, Jake, and Collette came inside from the broad front porch, and Adrian had already emerged from his upstairs room to see what the fuss was about. We all sprawled around chairs and on the rugs in the study while a couple of pirate flunkies stood guard in the entry hall.

"It ain't safe for any of us." Rene summed the situation up pretty well after I'd gone through the options, including the possibility of Eugenie not going to her sister's funeral, which had brought on a fresh flood of tears. "Even if vamps can't be trottin' out for a daytime funeral, babe, the elves and wizards can."

"I could protect Eugenie using Charlie," I said. "Rand wouldn't hurt me." At least I didn't think he'd hurt me. I might still be of some use to him in the future, plus the whole mating bond threw our relationship into some realm I didn't understand. In killing me, I suspected he'd at least weaken himself.

Rand loved himself way too much for self-sacrifice.

"Your elf might not murder you, Drusilla, but your wizards would imprison you in order to sway the balance of power and that would kill you," Jean said. "I forbid you to make this journey."

Who the hell did he think he was? I swear, the more I hung around the pirate, the more he acted like Alex Warin. We were going to discuss his attitude, and soon.

Right now, however, he was unfortunately correct. "Right, and Jake can't go for the same reason. He could be used as leverage. What about Collette? She isn't on anyone's radar."

"Sure, I'll go." The leggy brunette ignored Jake's frown.

"She can't fight wizards," Jake said, sounding a lot like his bossy cousin, Alex, and his boss, Jean. "They'd throw one of their spells at her, take her out, and Eugenie would be unprotected. Collette doesn't know how to handle a gun well enough."

She gave him a frown of her own, but bit her lip. I had a

feeling they'd be discussing Jake's bossy attitude later and sympathized. I'd had quite a few similar conversations with Alex.

We turned our gazes to Adrian. Since joining the crew at Barataria, he looked more like his old arrogant, obnoxious self and less like the haunted, frightened wizard he'd been a month ago. A handsome black man with a shaven head and a penchant for stylish clothes, his current wardrobe of tight trousers and a white shirt with ballooning sleeves and a frilly lapel made me fear what Jean would find for me to wear. Adrian couldn't go without risking arrest, either, however, even if he could walk in daylight—which he couldn't, nor could the red-haired, fanged girlfriend he was trying to extract from Vampyre.

"Adrian's out," I said. "Rene and Jean can't go for the same reason as Collette; there's no way for them to fight the wizards' physical magic."

When the pirate opened his mouth to protest, I added, "I forbid you to make this journey, Jean."

He rewarded me with a flash of outraged blue eyes followed quickly by a growing look of amusement. God help me, we were way too compatible. Too bad Alex didn't understand me half as well.

For a nanosecond, Alex popped into my mind as a possible escort for Eugenie, but he couldn't protect her without blowing his cover of loyalty with the Elders and putting himself in danger. Plus, I wasn't sure he'd do it and it wouldn't be fair for me to put him in the middle any more than he already was.

I looked at Jean. "What about Christof?"

The Faery Prince of Winter and the pirate Lafitte had formed an odd, unlikely friendship, although I hadn't seen him since we'd all fled the disastrous Interspecies Council meeting. I assumed he was lounging around in Faery doing faery prince stuff, whatever that might be.

"Would he be willing to run interference?" At Jean's frown, I interpreted, "Would he agree to escort Eugenie and keep her safe?"

I wasn't sure what type of magic Christof had at his disposal other than manipulating the weather and changing his appearance, but elves couldn't function in extreme cold, and Christof could freeze out any wizards who approached unexpectedly. The human meteorologists would be delighted.

"Perhaps." Jean crossed his arms and studied the wide cypress floor planks, his expression focused and determined. Thinking. Strategizing. In such a moment, I could easily see him organizing and commanding the thousand men he had under his command in his human life.

About two centuries ago, he'd managed to play one nation against another so that he and his allies flourished. In the end, the world changed into a place where there was no room for a man like him, but for a couple of decades his power and wealth had been unrivaled in this part of the world.

The room fell silent as we waited for *Le Capitaine* to weigh his options. I doubted Christof would help us. He and his brother, Florian, the Faery Prince of Summer, were locked in a struggle for power, anticipating the eventual death of their aunt, the childless Queen Sabine. Openly providing assistance to a member of "the opposition" could have negative political ramifications for him. And everyone currently living at Maison Rouge qualified as opposition.

"Bah, I have no answers," Jean declared. Judging by his sour expression, indecision didn't suit him. "Christof is in Faery, and travel there is much too treacherous at this time. Mademoiselle Eugenie, you simply must not journey to Shreveport."

Eugenie's red-eyed, teary gaze met mine, and I remembered the pain of losing Gerry, of losing Tish, of the look of stark pain

on Rene's face when his twin brother, Robert, had been murdered. We'd seen so much death, but at least we'd had the chance
to publicly mourn our losses and say good-bye. Eugenie deserved
to do the same.

"DJ, I can't miss my sister's funeral." Eugenie's tears flowed
freely. "How could I ever explain? I know they're already trying to find me, and it's adding one more worry. Even if I can't
stay long, I need to be at that funeral."

Yes, she did, and I only knew one way to make it happen.

"Give me until tomorrow morning." Ken had left word with
Jake that the funeral mass was going to be held tomorrow after-
noon. By then, I'd either find help or be dead. "I'm going to
Faery to ask Christof for help."

Jean would shout and try to frighten me out of going, but I
had no intention of going alone. He was going with me; he just
didn't know it yet.

"*Non!* This is unacceptable!"

Yep, there went the shout. Ignoring Jean's bellows of protest, I returned to the study and retrieved my backpack and
Charlie. By the time I reemerged into the entry hallway, the
room was empty but for the outraged pirate. Everyone else had
run like rats escaping the rising flood of Jean's fury.

"You shall not do this, Drusilla." Jean's dark-blue eyes
sparked glints of warning. "You will put down your belongings
and stop where you are, *tout de suite.*"

I edged around him and marched toward the front door. It
was almost a full mile to the transport out in the middle of Grand
Terre Island and there was no time to waste. "Put a sock in it."

The thud of his boot heels followed me across the verandah
and down the steps onto the wooden banquette. The sand
crunched behind me as he trailed a few steps behind but didn't
try to stop me or even talk to me. He was too busy muttering

to himself in French, probably trying to figure out what this had to do with socks. I stifled a grin. Jean would go with me to Faery because he hadn't yet realized I'd figured out how to exploit both his masculine desire to be my protector and his obsession with being in charge.

Dominique was on sentry duty at the transport, which had been etched deeply into the soil of a clearing up the hill from the beach. Despite it being late afternoon, the Beyond's constant full moon still shone so brightly in its midnight-blue abyss it hurt my eyes to look at it directly, but it made the outlines of the transport clear even in the areas outside the range of the flambeau Dominique used for illumination.

As soon as we'd arrived, Jean's muttering had been aimed at his brother. Guess he needed to bitch at someone and knew I wouldn't be receptive, or was trying to enlist Dom's help in keeping me out of the transport without my using Charlie to burn off any of their body parts. My aim had improved.

I interrupted their exchange. "Any clues as to the transport name I need to say?"

Two pairs of eyes, one pair dark blue and the other brown, both annoyed, focused on me. "*Tête de cochon femme*," Jean muttered.

"*Oui*," Dominique said. "*Je vous l'avais bien dit.*"

Jean had either said I was pigheaded or outright called me a pig. I don't know what else Dominique added, but he obviously agreed. They could call me whatever they wanted; my stubbornness would force Jean to go with me. He simply needed an extra nudge.

"Fine. I'll just transport to the name 'Faery' and see where I end up." I knelt and held the staff toward the transport edge, knowing full well Jean would step in at the last second, if only to save me from myself. I might be impulsive, but I wasn't stupid enough to go traipsing off to Faery alone. Jean didn't know that, however.

An inch before Charlie touched the transport edge, at which point I'd have to devise a new trick to manipulate him, Jean stepped in next to me, holding Dominique's pistol in one hand and a dagger in the other.

Heh.

"*Vous serez la mort de moi,* Drusilla," Jean hissed at me, then in a firm baritone pronounced, "Winter Palace, Faery."

Yeah, well, I might be the death of me, too. In fact, my death was much more likely than his. Plus, mine would be permanent. We'd find out once we arrived at the Winter Palace.

Only as time and space compressed around us did it occur to me that I might need a coat.

CHAPTER 6

We landed in the middle of an empty room about ten feet across and perfectly round, its walls of solid ice rising around us and out of sight, as if they reached to heaven itself. Tiny rivulets of water cascaded down the smooth sides, making them glisten. Behind the water the walls were thin enough to reveal shadowy bulks beyond but too thick to see what the shadows were.

"The Winter Palace is made of ice?" I tucked Charlie into my messenger bag and walked toward the edge of the room with my arm stretched out to touch the wall, but got only a single step before my feet went skating without me. I pinwheeled twice and did a graceless, spinning one-eighty before landing on my ass. Guess I'd waited too late to begin my figure-skating career.

My bad-tempered escort stood in place with his arms crossed, looking down at me with a disapproving arch of dark eyebrows. "Did you expect that the Prince of Winter would live in a hot and dry desert, Drusilla?"

Well, when he put it that way.

I tried to get up but couldn't gain purchase even with my

sturdy rubber-soled boots, which formed the height of fashion with the camo shorts that reached just below my knees and a red sweater full of holes. I held out a hand to Jean for a boost and he stared at it without moving.

When would the pirate learn that I'd figured out how to play him?

A threat to destroy the palace around us should work. "Hm . . . I wonder what would happen if I used the elven staff in this room?"

I reached toward where Charlie stuck out the top of my messenger bag, prompting Jean to wedge the dagger beneath his belt, take a slow step forward, grab my arm, and hoist me to my feet much more roughly than I thought necessary. I almost pulled us both down.

He let go of me and regained his solid footing. "You are a menace, Drusilla."

And I worked hard at it, *merci beaucoup.*

Speaking of fire, I hadn't felt the need to start my teeth-chattering, prancing-in-place-to-keep-warm routine, which was odd. Thanks to my fall, my legs were chilly and the backside of Rene's shorts had gotten soaked to the hem. I sensed no need to go into hibernation, however.

"Why isn't it colder in here?"

When Jean ignored me, I pulled the staff out of my messenger bag and poked him with it, just to remind him that I had it within my power to melt the whole Winter Palace of Faery. Not that I had any desire to spark yet another interspecies debacle. "You can be pissed off at me later. While we're here, it might be helpful if we appeared to be on the same side."

Or at least on speaking terms.

Jean sighed. "*Très bien,* but this headstrong behavior must be addressed when we return to Barataria, Drusilla."

Yeah, well, he could get in line behind Alex. "Why is it not cold in here when we're surrounded by ice?" It was wet like melting ice, yet never really melted. There were no puddles.

"This is the receiving chamber of Christof's palace. He chooses not to encase his guests in true ice until he determines whether they are friend or foe." Jean tucked the pistol's barrel beneath his belt within easy reach and switched the short, triangular dagger to his right hand, but made no move to leave.

Maybe because there was no door. I slowly pivoted a complete turn to make sure, being careful to move slowly in case I fell again and Jean refused to help me this time. No doors. No windows. Just ice. "How do we get out of here?"

He shrugged. "We shall either be allowed to leave, or we shall not."

If he didn't grow more forthcoming, I was going use Charlie to beat him over the head, which would get my point across without melting anything. "Jean . . ." I tried to put a warning of violence and mayhem in my voice.

This time, when he glanced down at me, amusement had slipped back into his eyes. Yeah, he knew how to push my buttons, too. "We are being watched, *Jolie,* and weighed. These are dangerous times in Faery. If those who study us determine that our intent is to endanger Christof or his allies, we will find our last breaths to be cold ones indeed. If not, we will be allowed farther into the palace, perhaps to see Christof himself if he is in residence."

I pivoted again, trying to find a camera or other type of surveillance device. Nada. "How long will it take for us to be weighed and measured?" Sort of like fish.

He shrugged. "As long as it takes."

Fab. It wasn't exactly cold in our ice prison but neither was it toasty, especially with a wet butt. I tucked Charlie under my arm and stuffed my hands in the pockets of my shorts, trying to warm my fingers. In my right pocket, I found the envelope Ken had given me, forgotten amid the funeral crisis.

Pulling it out, I slid a fingernail beneath the envelope's seal and saw why it had been so heavy: A long chain tumbled into my palm, from which dangled a heavy gold locket in the shape of a paw print. I couldn't help but smile even as a pang of homesickness cut through me. Leave it to Alex to find something that represented him—or his canine form, a monstrous dog-slash-pony I called Gandalf—without being overtly romantic. I slipped it over my head and let it slide beneath my sweater, near my heart.

"A woman should receive protestations of love and gifts that reflect her beauty," Jean said, eyeing my chest where the locket rested out of sight. "Not chains containing the feet of animals."

I opened my mouth to explain my own theory of romantic gifts, which had more to do with intent than appearance, but was silenced by the door that materialized in the wall before us. It, too, had been carved of ice, but rather than being clear, it shone a translucent, glistening ruby red. A perfect match for the gown of the woman who opened it a moment later.

"You are Lafitte, I am told, and a friend of the prince." She curtsied before Jean with the grace of a feline, which coordinated with the wild mane of amber curls that fell to her waist. "My name is Tamara. Christof is my brother."

I saw the family resemblance. Her moss-green eyes tipped up slightly at the corner and she was slender and fair-skinned, with the high cheekbones that the fae seemed to share. She had a good four inches on me in height, putting her at about five-eight.

Her smile faded as she turned to me. "This one, we do not recognize." She gave me the most thorough head-to-toe visual examination I'd had since trotting out some sexy new lingerie for Alex. "What are you?"

"Drusilla is the consort of Jean Lafitte, official council representative of the historical undead and famous privateer," said the man himself, snaking a hand around my waist and pinching my side along the way. I took that to mean he didn't want me hauling my sentinel ID out of my bag, which was fine since I'd been fired anyway. "Unemployed wizard" wouldn't make a very impressive business card.

"Yes, consort," I said, casually sliding Charlie up the inside of my right sleeve. This consort was packing heat in the form of an elven fire staff, a fact that was on a need-to-know basis as far as Tamara was concerned.

She did a slow stroll around me while Jean held me in place. "So this is what human men enjoy in these times? She is wearing short trousers." Tamara stopped behind me. "Damp trousers."

"Drusilla is beautiful, although her taste in clothing is quite deplorable," Jean said, assuming a regretful tone that I'd heard before. "And she has entirely too many male suitors." Ever tactful, he ignored the comment about my cold, wet ass.

"More than one suitor? Her? Really?" Tamara stopped in front of me again, as if the idea were beyond belief.

Okay, this was getting old. "Could you tell Christof . . ." I paused, gaping, as her bones transformed, liquefying and reshaping her into a shorter woman with shoulder-length honey-blond hair wearing a pair of camouflage long shorts and a ragged red sweater full of holes. Only her face hadn't changed. I'd seen Christof look like everything from a California beach boy to Justin Bieber, but he'd never changed in front of me. Faeries gave shapeshifting a disturbing new twist.

"Mon Dieu." Jean pulled me against him more tightly. "You must stop this immediately, Princess Tamara. I must insist. And it is urgent that we speak to Christof. He will be most aggrieved if we are too long delayed."

Just as quickly as she'd morphed into a poor imitation of me, she morphed back into herself—if the tall lioness was her real self. Jean's clutch on my waist lightened, but not much.

"I do not see the attraction to her," she sniffed, then switched back into a brisk tone. "Christof is not at the palace. If your business is urgent, you will have to find him in the capital, in his office at The Arch."

"What transport should we use?" I asked, earning a sharp look from Tamara and another pinch from Jean. Guess consorts shouldn't ask intelligent questions.

"Transport to the Tower Tavern," she said. "It is neutral ground, and you should be able to get word to Christof from there without fear of Florian's spies unless things have deteriorated since my last visit. I don't have to remind you that Faery is never safe for strangers even in less dangerous times than these."

With those cheery words, she exited the red ice door, which disappeared behind her. How did they do that?

"She was a total creepfest." I wrested myself from Jean's grasp. "And you were pinching your *consort* a bit hard, don't you think?"

Jean continued to frown at the icy spot where the door had been. "My apologies, Drusilla, but when she assumed your lovely visage, I felt I must hold the real woman in my grasp lest I fall prey to the false one."

"That freak show did *not* look like me." I propped my hands on my hips. "She had the size and the hair and the clothes right, but her face never changed. Pointy chin, green eyes. I have a better nose than that."

Jean studied me a moment. "To my sight, she appeared just as you are. Perhaps your magic protects you from her glamour."

"Perhaps." It had never protected me from Christof's everchanging faces and hairstyles. Speaking of which. "Have you been to the capital of Faery before?"

"*Non,* although Christof has told me of it." Jean stepped back into the transport that had been etched into the ice floor. "It is a place of wild magic, Drusilla. Are you certain you wish to embark on such a journey?"

It would be so easy to say no, to have the transport toss us back to nice, warm Barataria. But Eugenie's sad, desperate face would be waiting for us, maybe lit with a moment of hope before realizing I'd failed her. Christof was the only way I could think of to safely get her to Violette's funeral and back. If he would help us.

"I'm not certain that I *want* to go," I told Jean, "but I'm certain that I must."

CHAPTER 7

The first thing I saw when we materialized at the Tower Tavern was a black bear with human hands, wearing a Clemson sweatshirt and holding a frosted glass beer stein from a spot behind a long, highly polished wooden bar.

The second was Florian, the Faery Prince of Summer, standing at the end of the bar and shooting a spinning ball of fire from his outstretched fingertip directly toward my head.

"Holy crap! Down!" I turned and pushed Jean, who was standing behind me, hard enough that he toppled over and pulled me to the floor with him. A couple of wooden barstools fell on top of us. It was hard to hear the pirate's French epithets for all the raucous laughter from the tavern patrons.

I raised my head and looked around to see what was burning, but no signs of fire or even smoke marred the rustic tavern. The placed looked straight out of Victorian London.

"As much as I would enjoy lying alongside you, *Jolie,* this is neither the time nor the proper setting," Jean said, shoving me off him and knocking the barstools aside.

The bear had lumbered around the bar and now reached down with his hand-shaped paw, hauling me to my feet. He turned to help Jean, but my escort had pulled out his pistol and held it steady, aiming at the bear's midsection as he stood up unaided.

I wasn't sure how much damage the gun would do, however. Yogi was humongous in both height and girth. I wondered if he hibernated.

"No shooting inside the building. It's neutral ground. You only get to keep the gun if you don't try to use it." The bear had a deep, growly voice that came out like a garbled phone message, and placid green humanoid eyes. I wasn't sure what he was, species-wise. He didn't have the aura of a shifter or were, but read a total blank like the fae and elves. His lower paws, or maybe they were feet, wore heavy boots that clattered on the wooden floor when he returned to his spot behind the bar.

"If this is neutral ground, why did he get to throw a fireball at me?" I pointed at Florian, who had taken a seat at a corner table and was grinning at the chaos he'd created. "Technically, that was shooting a weapon."

The bear gave me a bemused look, which I wouldn't have thought possible given that he was, like, a *bear*. After a few seconds, the silence that had fallen over the place when Jean pulled out his pistol gave way to soft conversation. We were no longer the center of attention. All was right in crazytown.

"It wasn't real fire, Ms. Jaco," Florian said, making his way toward us, flanked by a pair of oversize—and heavily armed—guys in green tunics and black pants. Perhaps the Summer Prince rated a royal guard; there were vaguely Celtic-looking insignias on their sleeves. "The fire was aimed to evaporate just before it reached you. As he told you, Mick doesn't allow the use of real weapons in the tavern and we respect him as leader of the

Hybrids. If you'd like to step outside the neutral zone, however, I'd be happy to send a real firebomb your way."

Guess Mick was the bear, and while I understood the Hybrid concept—faery plus bear equals Mick?—I had no idea how such a thing might happen and didn't want to think about it too deeply.

Besides, Florian obviously hadn't forgotten or forgiven our encounter at last month's Interspecies Council meeting, when I'd been forced to zap him with Charlie to stop him from burning down the historic New Orleans Criminal District Court Building.

I frowned as he drew closer, trying to figure out what was different about him. His jaw was more angular than when I'd seen him in the past, his long nose a bit sharper, his green eyes almond-shaped and tipped up slightly at the outer edges. His blond hair was fine as corn silk. In fact, he looked a lot like one of Christof's personae, only with harsher angles and lighter hair.

When he got within slapping distance, he drew back with flared nostrils, his eyebrows arching toward his hairline. "You reek of canine. I'd heard you consorted with the new representative of the shapeshifters, but do you never bathe?"

My brain struggled to process *consorted* and *reek* and *representative,* not to mention I'd noticed that Florian's reflection in the big mirror behind the bar looked nothing like the faery standing in front of me. It had dark spiked hair and a rounded face.

"I do not reek." Lame comeback, but it was the best I could do. I didn't know what to make of the strange mirror image, I was apparently good consort material today, and I didn't believe for a minute that Alex Warin represented the shapeshifters and were-creatures on the Interspecies Council.

"Yeah, you kind of do reek," Mick the Bear rumbled. "Nothing personal. You really a wizard?"

"She was the sentinel of New Orleans until she took up with elves and her Elders had the good sense to fire her." Florian had been paying a lot more attention at those council meetings than I thought. "And then, of course, we have the illustrious leader of the historical undead, Captain Jean Lafitte the pirate, who is in league with my bastard of a brother."

"Monsieur Florian, it is a pleasure to renew your acquaintance." Jean sounded about as sincere as a politician the day before an election. He hadn't even bothered to protest being called a pirate. "I have often heard of the Faery capital and thought it a fine day to visit. My friend Drusilla insisted on accompanying me."

He didn't mention Christof, so I took his lead and kept my mouth shut. Jean knew a lot more about the rift between the rival princes than I. Plus, Florian had clearly not joined my fan club.

Jean's story didn't work. "You're here to see my brother, and you might as well admit it." Florian ran a hand through his blond hair. In the mirror, he ran a hand through his brown hair. The discrepancy creeped me out. I wondered what Jean saw.

"I assure you that is not true. Drusilla and I simply wished to visit this beautiful city of which we have heard much." Was it my imagination or had Jean taken a step backward, toward the transport? I followed suit.

Florian laughed. "Is that the best story you can come up with? Tales of your intelligence were highly exaggerated, I think, pirate." The faery crossed his arms and squinted at us. "Here's what I think is the true story. You and Ms. Jaco came to see Christof, no doubt transporting to the Winter Palace. You're probably seeking help in getting Ms. Jaco back into the council's good graces—something quite unlikely. Since my people inform me that my brother is still holed up inside The Arch, too cowardly to come outside, I suspect you were greeted by our traitorous sister Tamara at the palace, and that she directed you toward this transport."

Mick nodded as he polished glass mugs and set them on the shelf. His reflection in the mirror was that of a bear. "Not many folks know there's a transport here. It's only for palace emergencies."

Tamara had either set us up or we had the misfortune of arriving when Florian happened to stop by for a brewski. Either way, we were busted.

Jean seemed to agree. "Perhaps we shall see your city another time, then." He caught my eye and jerked his head toward the transport behind us. "We should be returning to New Orleans, *Jolie*."

Clever pirate, not mentioning Barataria. Florian might not know where in the Beyond Jean lived, so no point in advertising it.

"By all means." Florian took a seat on the nearest upright wooden barstool, crossed his arms, and gave us a dazzling smile. "Enjoy your trip. See you again soon."

An uneasy prickling spread across the back of my neck. A sense of impending trouble had nagged at me since the fireball, but now it grew more fierce. Florian was being too agreeable to people he knew were allies of his brother.

"Send us back, Drusilla." Jean's voice was soft, barely audible. "We should not tarry."

I knelt and touched my finger to the edge of the transport, wondering what wizard had set it up for them. Nothing happened, which shouldn't have surprised me. My native physical magic, which was pathetic to begin with, didn't work in Old Orleans, Elfheim, or Old Barataria. It was only logical that it wouldn't work in Faery, either.

Grasping Charlie from my backpack, where I'd stuck the staff when we left Christof's palace, I touched its wooden tip to the transport's edge and softly spoke our destination, using the name of an open transport in Old Orleans rather than in Old Barataria.

At my words, a flicker of flame the size of a dying Bic lighter shot out briefly, then died. The next time I tried, nothing happened.

"Back already?" Florian laughed, and his duo of flunkies chuckled with him. Mick rolled his green eyes and lumbered to the far end of the bar. "Wizards' magic doesn't work in the Kingdom of Faery, Ms. Jaco, nor does elven magic work on this transport. It can only be powered by one of us. Proving the superiority of faery magic, of course."

"Of course," I said, smiling. Arrogant twit. "Then, Prince Florian, would you power the transport for us, please? As you pointed out, I need a bath." And a good, stiff drink. We'd just have to tie Eugenie to a chair or porch rail to keep her from going back to Shreveport. Or I could shut down Jean's transport and refuse to power it up for her.

"Unfortunately, that transport is, as Mick said, reserved for royal emergencies. Which you are not."

I turned to Mick and noticed that the bar had cleared out except for Florian, his guards, and us. Funny; the other patrons must have anticipated trouble. "Can you power the transport to send us out, Mick?" He seemed like a reasonable bear.

He shook his massive snout from side to side. "My tavern is neutral. I don't interfere in matters between the princes."

Not that I blamed him, but his noninterference policy was less than helpful.

"What is it you wish us to do, then, Monsieur Florian?" Jean's voice was low and lethal. The pirate was angry, but I knew he wouldn't take action unless it had a high probability of success. That he hadn't done anything so far told me he didn't know how to navigate this particular political bayou, either.

"Ah, well. There are powered, open transports in front of both The Arch and The Academy, at the foot of the steps, so you're certainly welcome to use those," Florian said. "Of course, you have to get there alive, but perhaps you'll get lucky."

Judging by the way things had gone so far, Lady Luck had taken a vacation.

CHAPTER 8

Florian delivered his lucky speech without ever losing his smile, which made its implied threat more chilling, as was the fact that Jean—normally as testosterone-filled as any alpha male alive or undead—remained silent and watchful.

I had no clue what an arch or an academy were, but if Florian said Christof was "holed up" at an arch, he was there. Faeries couldn't lie. Obfuscate, yes. Lie by omission, certainly. Answer questions with other questions, absolutely. But not outright lie.

Christof was at The Arch, so that's where we needed to go. Somehow.

"Where is this arch?" I asked Florian.

He grinned. "In the capital."

Faery gnat spawn. I grinned back. "To get to The Arch by the closest route, do we turn right or left when we walk out the front door of the Tower Tavern?" If he thought he could obfuscate his way past me, he had the wrong unemployed sentinel.

His grin drooped. "Left."

"Thank you. How many turns must we make between the

front door of Tower Tavern and this arch, counting our left turn at the door?"

He cursed. "One."

It was a straight shot north then. "Let's go, Jean."

I headed toward the door, reaching into my messenger bag for the spare potions and charms I carried, slipping a couple of vials into the right pocket of my shorts. Just in case. They might work in Faery; they might not. Florian said elven magic didn't work on that transport, not that it didn't work in Faery at all, so I grasped Charlie in my right hand. I slung the long strap of my bag over my head and placed a shaky hand on the door handle. What would we find outside?

I felt Jean close behind me. "Step slowly, *Jolie*," he whispered. "Touch nothing. The Arch should be quite large, from what Christof has told me."

I opened the door to a stabbing pain, virtually blinded by something I hadn't encountered in three days—bright sunlight. Since Old Orleans, Vampyre, and Barataria were always dark, I assumed all of the Beyond lay in perpetual nightfall. Wrong. Blinking, I waited a few seconds for my vision to adjust before stepping outside the tavern. Jean stepped out beside me and closed the door behind us.

We stood on one of a pair of wooden sidewalks that rose a couple of inches on either side of a broad paved street in what looked like a fairy-tale village. On either side of us stretched small storefronts I could only describe as "cute" and even "alpine." Heidi and Grandfather might live in one of them, down the block from Peter the goat herder and his blind grandmother. Shutters and window boxes adorned façades of creamy plaster or intricately patterned wood. Flowers bloomed in profusion.

There wasn't a soul in sight, only a small herd of miniature blue deer about the size of terriers, trotting in erratic patterns past us and disappearing toward the south. I opened my mouth to comment, decided I didn't know what to say, and closed it again. Perhaps they also were Hybrids.

Now, the streets were deserted. Shouldn't the capital city of Faery be bustling?

"Where is everybody? What's this arch place and do you know what it looks like?" I looked up and down the street for something that resembled the only arch I'd seen big enough to hide inside, as Christof was supposedly doing: the big Gateway Arch in St. Louis. The only big anything I saw from outside the tavern was a monolithic, modern building with red reflective glass on the sides. It stood tall and narrow, at least ten or twelve stories high, in the middle of the street to our left. The lanes of the street divided to circle around it. I could only assume they met on the other side and continued.

"Let us walk, *Jolie*. I believe The Arch is on the other end of this street, past the Royal Tower." Jean took my hand and we turned to the left, toward the tower. It looked ridiculous and out of place in these quaint surroundings, like a modern New York high-rise had been plopped halfway between Heidi's house and Peter's.

As we walked, Jean explained what he knew of Faery's structure, learned both from Christof in Old Orleans and also from many years earlier. In those days, he'd traveled the ley lines that shifted and pulsed beneath the Beyond, learning the ins and outs of the various kingdoms. "Faery has the most beings living within its borders," he said. "Although Elfheim has more forest and valley."

Probably because the elves were so contentious, even they didn't want to live near each other. I had Rand for a neighbor in New Orleans and it sucked.

"Where are all the people? I haven't seen anyone." We'd reached the long, dark shadow cast by the tower, and the temperature seemed to drop twenty or thirty degrees.

"I do not know, and this is cause for . . . *Mon Dieu*." Jean stopped abruptly and I looked around to see what caused his reaction. Beyond the far side of the glittering Royal Tower, a shop front lay in ruins. Chunks of plaster appeared to have been blown across the street and, indeed, as we walked closer, I saw that a section of the tower itself had been cracked, probably by flying debris. A spiderweb of cracks inched up its north face, adding extra glitter to the reflective glass for two or three stories.

That was in itself disturbing, but even more so was the heavy snow cloud centered over the ruined building. The shop must have specialized in toys, because intricately carved and painted wooden train engines and golden-spotted giraffes and pink-cheeked baby dolls peeked from fire-blackened piles of debris and the heavy flakes of snow that were beginning to blanket them.

A boom of thunder sounded from above us, loud enough for the windows in the nearest shop front to rattle, and sent my heart thumping against my rib cage. Jean slammed me against the wall of the shop a few feet to our left, my cheek scraping a splintery red-painted shutter just as a blinding bolt of lightning shot from the sky and created a burning crater in the pavement where we'd been standing.

"Holy crap. Where did that come from?" A few seconds ago, we'd been in bright sunlight. Now we had snow and a thunderstorm—simultaneously.

"I suspect Christof and Florian are fighting," Jean said. "When I last spoke to Christof, they had not yet come to violence. Something must be further amiss and the people are hiding. If Florian has taken control of a neutral space, this does not appear as if Christof is prevailing."

No kidding.

The people were smart to have gone into hiding. A dollop of rain thumped the top of my head hard enough to sting, the precursor to a downpour that followed within seconds, plastering my hair to my scalp and soaking my clothes. The heat—except where the snow was beginning to grow deep on the ruined toy shop—had grown so oppressive that breathing grew difficult. It felt like New Orleans in August with a tropical storm building offshore.

"What's going on?" I shouted to Jean, who looked as dazed as I felt, his eyes darting rapidly over the landscape, his jaw tight.

"We must run! *Dépêchez!*" Jean kept a firm grasp on my hand and pulled me as hard and fast as we could go toward the north. We skidded to a sudden stop when the rain turned to sleet, the ice pellets sharp and bruising, the temperature plummeting. Footing grew treacherous. I never realized sleet could hurt, but it did. Christof needed to dial it down a notch.

I stopped long enough to pull the potions vials from my pocket and squinted through the rain at them. One was a melting charm that had been coming in handy during New Orleans' inclement winter, so I pulled out the stopper and arced the contents across the sidewalk in front of us. Nothing happened. Damn it, guess my potions didn't work in Faery, either.

"Come, Drusilla," Jean said. "Travel as close to the buildings as you can. We must reach The Arch." Jean led the way, and I followed, the rough walls of the shop fronts—all of which had CLOSED signs hanging in the doors—scraping against my sleeve. In less than a block, I had pulled enough loose threads from the arm of my red sweater that the whole thing looked on the verge of unraveling. My black bra would look great with the camo shorts. Urban guerrilla swamp girl.

I squinted through the gray sleet and kept my feet sliding

forward, thankful I'd been wearing the rubber-soled boots when I fled New Orleans. Jean and I both careened a few times before suddenly reaching the end of the block, which was again bathed in hot sunlight.

I was never, ever coming to Faery again, at least not willingly. These people and their world were insane. I was going to have to apologize to Jean for dragging him here, if we survived.

The melted ice in my hair blended with the sweat that had formed on my face from the sudden humidity, but at least I wasn't in immediate danger of falling on my backside.

"Let us go in haste while we are able," Jean said, breaking into a trot. I ran and he trotted rather than leave me in the dust, thanks to my shorter stride, but my regular morning runs with Alex paid off. By the time we reached the end of the next block and were almost knocked off our feet by a powerful blast of icy-cold air, Jean was breathing harder than I was.

He wrapped an arm around my shoulders and I held on to his waist as we leaned into the frigid wind. "Look—The Arch is just ahead!" Jean shouted, his voice sounding faint as it was carried and dispersed by the airborne currents.

I struggled to look ahead, but couldn't see a damned thing. The wind hitting my face forced me to keep my eyes cast downward, which was the only thing that kept me from following Jean to the ground when a step appeared in front of us. He stumbled and caught himself on the third of what appeared to be a broad set of marble steps leading upward.

The wind died as quickly as it had begun. For the first time in what seemed like the hour it had taken us to cross that treacherous stretch of five or six city blocks, the air around us was neither hot nor cold. The sky overhead was a clear, robin's egg blue.

We both stopped to gawk at what lay ahead of us. At the

top of the marble stairs stood a neoclassical-style building constructed of what looked like tiny slivers of mosaic glass arranged to form shifting scenes of nature. A dense forest, layered with dappled sunlight and shade, remained static for a few seconds before some of the green and brown shimmers of glass shifted position or flipped around until, instead, we viewed an open sea with restless, shifting swells and a stormy sky.

A jaw-rattling explosion—or was it thunder?—broke the trance we'd been lulled into by the building, and I whirled to look behind us. Florian stood atop a boulder-size chunk of plaster from the ruined building next to the Royal Tower, his arms stretched heavenward.

"Run, *Jolie! Courir!*" Jean raced up the steps, not bothering to drag me behind him. "We must get inside!"

I followed but slowed to take another look over my shoulder at Florian, so I saw the fireball leave his hand. I doubted this one was a fake. I whipped Charlie out of my bag and shot a blast of fire toward his fireball; they collided in midair and exploded, harming nothing. I had no time to congratulate myself on my perfect aim, though; another of Florian's fireballs followed. He'd shot two back-to-back.

"Jean, down!" I threw myself up a couple of steps, grabbed a black boot, and tackled the pirate a half second before the marble in front of us exploded, pelting us with a volley of sharp stone slivers.

Jean reached behind him and I grabbed his wrist. He dodged the damaged steps and put on a burst of speed to reach the top, never releasing his hold on me. The world shrank to noise and pain and motion. I wasn't sure how much I ran and how much I was dragged.

Then it all stopped. Maybe I passed out. All I knew was that I returned to an awareness of my surroundings lying flat on my back in a sea of silence, looking up at a star-studded sky of midnight blue—until a familiar pair of almond-shaped green eyes looked down into mine. The face—high-cheeked, full-lipped, with a slightly upturned nose—was unfamiliar. I'd know those eyes anywhere, however. They were a mossier green than those of the evil prince, which meant it was the prince we'd been seeking.

"Christof?"

"Well, at least you're alive, no thanks to my psychopathic brother." He paused. "Although you stink of canine. You didn't bring a dog here, did you?"

He helped me sit up, and I realized I wasn't outside anymore but lying on the floor in the hallway of a large building; the night sky was a ceiling, an illusion of shadow and light. The marble floor, a confection of blue tones with white veins streaking through it, was spattered with blood. Charlie lay on the floor beside me, as did my messenger bag.

"No dog." I really needed a bath, apparently. What I didn't see around me was my pirate. Panic tightened my throat and I fought the urge to strike out. "Where's Jean?"

"Here, *Jolie*." I finally spotted him across the wide hallway from me, next to broad double doors of dark wood. He, too, sat on the floor, leaning against the wall, his face covered in small bloody cuts, one leg bleeding heavily. "How is she, Christof?"

"You're both going to be sore tomorrow but nothing serious. You were lucky. What the hell are you doing here? Don't you know the capital is a war zone?" Christof cursed as another explosion outside sent what sounded like a rain of marble chips against the doors.

"Come farther inside The Arch. Now that you're here, DJ, maybe you can set up a transport we all can use. I think Florian's blown up the one outside. Never mind that he might need to use it himself, the fool."

He pulled me to my feet, and I took a quick assessment of my body parts while the faery prince helped Jean up. Both knees had been scraped, and blood ran freely down my right leg. My left thigh, still sore from the gunshot wound, screamed at me when I took an experimental couple of steps, but it held my weight. Everything ached but nothing was broken.

"Has something happened? Does Florian always greet visitors this way?" I watched as Jean took a few steps. Other than a slight limp, he, too, looked to have escaped serious injury.

"Sabine has taken ill," Christof said, flipping a switch on the wall that raised the cover to a monitor. The screen showed a view out the front of the building, where a monsoon seemed to be falling now. "And as you can see, Florian is trying to kill me so he can claim the throne without challenge." His voice took a sarcastic edge. "It's so much easier than winning the trust of the majority and letting the people choose their leader."

"If everybody knows he's insane, it probably is easier," I said, and when he arched an eyebrow at me, added, "Sorry."

"No need to apologize. Truth is truth." Christof shut down the monitor. "Come to my office and let's see about that transport. You both need to get out of Faery, and I need an escape hatch Florian doesn't know about."

We followed Christof down a back hallway ending in another set of wide double doors. Open doorways along the corridor had revealed a number of offices and what looked like laboratories. I'd seen nothing that looked even vaguely archlike.

He opened the doors into a plush office the size of my burned-down house in Uptown New Orleans. Two walls held banks of monitors showing different scenes, including the view out the front of the building. The monsoon continued to rage.

"Hold on a minute." Christof sat at a polished desk the dimensions of a queen-size bed and began furiously tapping at a computer keyboard.

On the monitors showing the front of the building, the fall of heavy rain began to slant, coming at a ten-degree angle, then twenty, then thirty. When it was almost horizontal, Christof punched another set of keys, and a wind stiff enough to rip the awnings off a couple of buildings on the capital street blew the rain offscreen. Within moments, a thick fall of snow had taken its place.

"Well, that should take care of the son of a bitch for a little while." Christof slammed his keyboard tray back under his desk and propped on his elbows, studying us. "We have a few minutes, so tell me why you risked coming here before we get to the transport."

"Uh, about that." I limped over to a chair on the other side of the desk and fell into it. "My magic—elven or wizard— didn't work on the transport at the tavern. My wizard's potions don't work at all here, but the elven staff does. Do you think it would work in this building?"

Christof threw up a long, slender hand in a dismissive wave. It was pale against his black sweater and slacks. He could've gotten dressed out of Alex's closet. "Mick's is a neutral transport, which means both Arch and Academy power has gone into it. Your wizard's magic won't work in The Arch, but your elven magic will. You can establish a transport here and power it with the staff you carry."

"What are The Arch and The Academy?" I pushed myself to my feet, yanked my portable magic kit from my bag, and began laying down the interlocking circle and triangle of a small transport in an open corner of the office floor.

"It is the magic of Faery, what in human terms might be called nature and science. There is always tension, and in The Asylum are those who've tried to combine the two." Christof handed Jean a small cigar that I recognized; Jean provided them in bulk to Rene, who I suspect sold them on the sly. I gave a delicate cough when they both lit up, which they ignored. Maybe they wouldn't know I reeked of dog if they smoked awhile.

"Those are the Hybrids, like Mick at the tavern?"

"Yes, Mick is one of the fortunate Hybrids. Some are quite . . . odd." Christof shrugged, obviously not thinking a ginormous human-bear qualified as odd. "This building houses The Arch, symbolizing the laws of nature. At the opposite end of Tower Street is The Academy, our center of physical law. What are you using for the transport?"

"Iron filings—they're strongest." I seemed to remember some fae lore about cold iron and paused. "Should I use something else? Salt isn't as strong but it will work."

"Iron is fine here. In The Academy it would be deadly. Florian and I are Queen Sabine's oldest living family members who possess both Arch and Academy magic—required to be the monarch of Faery." Christof paused. "Before you power the transport, tell me why you're here. It must have been important for you to take such a risk."

While I explained about the death of Eugenie's sister, and our suspicion that it was a trap meant to lure her out of the Beyond, Christof approached me, his green eyes scanning my face, my neck, and my body. Then his gaze zoomed back toward my neck and he used one finger to lift the chain and tug the golden paw locket from beneath my sweater. "What is this?"

I tugged it away from him. "A gift." None of his faery business.

"What is in the locket?" He reached for it again, and I took a step backward. I hadn't even opened the locket, but now I did. Inside was a fuzzy tuft of golden fur that looked suspiciously like that of Alex's canine alter ego, Gandalf.

"Hair of the Dog." Christof's sharp nose wrinkled as if he'd smelled week-old fish. I smelled nothing, but wondered if Alex had put the fur in the locket as an anti-faery charm. We'd learned recently that the fae hated dogs because dogs could see through their glamour and know what they really looked like.

Holy crap. The locket was why I had seen through Tamara's attempt to change into me, and why Florian's image in the mirror had changed but what I saw in front of me hadn't. I doubted Alex had known the locket would have such a useful effect, but I loved him for it anyway. I thought it wisest not to share any of it with Christof—or Jean, at least for now.

"My boyfriend gave it to me; he's a canine shifter," I said. "I apologize for the reek."

"No harm." Christof shrugged. "Now, back to dear Eugenie's sister. Who do you think is behind her murder?"

"The elves could be behind it, since Quince Randolph wants to get his hands on her until his child is born," I said. When Jean cleared his throat, I reluctantly added, "Or the wizards, who think producing her and turning her over to Rand will help their alliance with the elves."

I noted after the fact that I'd said *their* alliance, not *our* alliance. Despite my protestations otherwise, I'd stopped thinking of myself as one of the wizards.

"Abominable, in either case. And how is my lovely Eugenie?" Talk about unlikely friendships. Christof had taken an immediate liking to her during their one or two encounters, and I was pretty sure I disapproved.

"She's determined to go to Violette's funeral, but since we're sure it's a trap, we can't figure out who could protect her and make sure she got there and back safely. I wanted to ask you, although, to be fair, Jean warned me that it was risky to come here. I insisted." An apologetic look toward Jean earned me a small smile, but it was free of *I told you so.* "It looks like you have your hands full."

Christof paced the room, his hands steepled in front of his chin. "If I have a transport in and out of The Arch, I should be able to leave long enough to accompany her and then return before Florian causes too much damage. I have allies who can protect my holdings," he said. "But there's one thing I feel the need to ask."

Jean and I looked at each other. "What is it, *mon ami*?"

"How well is Eugenie guarded in Barataria, with both of you gone?" Christof leaned against the edge of his desk. "How do you know this wasn't a ploy to distract you and take her while you were away?"

This time when Jean and I exchanged glances it was with a rising sense of fear; his alarm grew as quickly as mine. It hadn't even occurred to me.

I moved faster to complete the transport, then went to get Charlie and my bag. She had to be okay. She was far from alone.

"The loups-garou are with her," Jean said. "Also our mutual friend Rene. The vampires. My brother. She is guarded."

Eugenie didn't have to be alone to be vulnerable, though, and we all knew it.

We stepped into the transport, and this time when I knelt to touch the tip of the staff to the interlocking circle and triangle and directed it to "Maison Rouge, Old Barataria," Charlie emitted a satisfying burst of energy.

Within seconds, we landed in the transport on Grand Terre, which lay unguarded. The mile-long run toward the house seemed to take forever, but we finally limped up, breathless and afraid.

The front door stood open, and inside we could see the entry hall, its floor littered with bodies.

CHAPTER 9

As soon we reached the verandah, Jean raced ahead to the blood-covered body of his half-brother, kneeling beside Dominique and placing a hand against his chest. Even I didn't need to feel for a pulse to tell he was dead; Jean was going through the motions, and my skin absorbed the tangled ball of anger and anguish wafting off him. A baseball-size chunk had been torn from the side of Dominique's neck.

Undead or alive, a pirate couldn't survive the loss of a carotid artery, at least not in the short term.

Christof ran past me into the hallway and out of sight, following a snarling, enormous red wolf. I took a deep breath, said a quick prayer, and knelt next to the body of another wolf. Then I asked for forgiveness for being thankful that this injured loup-garou was Collette and not Jake, or at least it was a female. She was alive, her breath coming in shallow pants. When I touched her shoulder, she opened wide brown eyes and emitted a high-pitched whine, struggling to get up and snapping at me simultaneously.

I fought the urge to move away or show fear, not easy since

she'd missed chomping off a finger by mere inches. "You're safe, Collette, and Jake is okay."

As was the case with Jake in his wolf form, I wasn't sure how much her wolf understood but assumed there was at least some cognizance of friend versus enemy. I pressed her shoulders back to the floor, and she let me. "You don't need to move or shift back into human form until you've healed more. Stay here." Weres and shifters healed better in their animal forms. "Jake is fine; I'm going to find him."

And also to find Eugenie, I hoped.

The wolf's responding whine sounded like a *yes* to me, plus the sounds of shouting and breaking glass had begun filtering down from upstairs, and the stench of blood, thick in this room, threatened to empty what little food was left in my system.

The noise also was enough to bring Jean back to his feet. The anger wafting from him surpassed even that he'd expressed toward Etienne Boulard, the vampire who'd betrayed him so badly back in early November. I knew better than to remind him that Dominique would revive; he was fueled both by Jean's memories and his own remembered role in New Orleans history. Jean knew that, but it didn't lessen the pain.

Plus, he'd not tolerate such an invasion of his home and his family.

A writhing pile of vampires formed a bloody, fanged tangle at the top of the staircase. I recognized Terri Ford's bright red hair, and closed my eyes at the sight of Adrian Hoffman baring fangs and snapping off part of another vampire's ear. It might haunt my dreams forever.

Jake's wolf had bulldozed into the mix, and now, with the fight coming to a conclusion, he stopped to howl, dark-maroon vampire blood dripping from his jaws. Chill bumps spread up my arms at the feral, celebratory wail.

What was there to celebrate—more bloodshed? And where the hell was Eugenie? A few of the vampires had fled down the stairway when Jean and I had come running up. Had others gone ahead and taken Eugenie?

"Jacob, *donner la chasse!*" Jean shouted, stopping the wolf in mid-howl. Jake's loup-garou looked briefly at his master—I had to call it what it was because, unlike me, Jake had chosen sides without a backward glance. He loped down the stairs and out the open front door in search of the vampires who'd escaped.

Damn it, the big transport I'd set up on the island for Rene to bring in supplies was still open, giving them an easy highway back to whoever hired them. No way they were acting on their own. As soon as the political struggles began, the vampires had been consistently loyal to whoever paid the most or made the most promises.

I pulled Charlie out, slipped my messenger bag over my head, and dumped it on the stairs. "I'm going to shut down that transport before any more of them can escape," I shouted to Jean, although I doubted he heard me. Wielding his dagger, he was engaged, along with Adrian and Terri, in fending off the remaining vampire, a woman I'd never seen. Hired fangs, maybe. But hired by whom? Maybe Terri, Adrian's vampire paramour, could give us the answers—she'd apparently used the attack as a way to get out of Vampyre. I just hoped she was loyal to Adrian and not to her leaders.

At the front door, I froze when Christof came up the front steps carrying Rene Delachaise. My heart stopped, hitched, and then raced. "Is he . . . ?"

I couldn't even say the words. By God, if they had killed Rene, I'd take Charlie and set fire to every vampire I could find even if I had to march through the Realm of Vampyre like General Sherman tearing through a fanged Civil War Georgia.

"He is alive," Christof said, and his voice was so assured that it calmed me. "Don't bother going out. The wolf you call Jake has caught and destroyed the two vampires who tried to escape. He is hurt only slightly."

Destroying a vampire wasn't simply a matter of stopping their heartbeat. "They'll regenerate unless—"

"Their wretched hearts will beat no more, as they are no longer inside their bodies. In fact, the hearts themselves are no longer in one piece." Christof gave me a cold smile that had nothing to do with his weather-making abilities. "It was a better fate than they deserved."

I brushed aside the image of Jake ripping the heart out of a vampire's chest and did a body count. Dominique was dead but would revive in time. Collette was healing. Jake was okay. Terri, Jean, and Adrian had used fang and knife and, finally, pistol to dispatch the two vampires who remained in the house. Rene was unconscious. Which left only one person unaccounted for.

Christof had come to the same conclusion. "Where is Miss Eugenie?"

An angry baritone came from our left. "Exactly the question I want answered. *Now.* Dru, start talking."

Quince Randolph stood in the front doorway, looking at the carnage like a king surveying the bloody ruins of his realm after a brutal battle. He wore white and didn't have a speck of blood on him. That didn't mean he didn't have blood on his hands in another sense.

"*Vous allez mourir, canaille!*" Jean rushed down the stairs, bloody blade still drawn, but collapsed when he was still a few feet from Rand. He fell to his knees, then curled up in a ball on the floor, clutching his head. Now the leader of the Elven Synod as well as clan chief for the fire elves, Rand glowed from a fire within, as always when he was angry. By glowing and chanting softly in his guttural elven language, he fought Jean off without lifting one well-manicured finger.

Fortunately, I had ways to punish him. Thanks to our blood bond, I could screech at him loud enough to make him cry without ever opening my mouth. He hadn't been able to hear me when I was in the Beyond and he was in modern New Orleans, but by God he'd hear me now. I didn't even try to verbalize, but just screamed. I was shrill, piercing, and as loud as I could imagine a scream being.

Relief flooded Jean's face just as pain crossed Rand's, and the elf clapped his hands to his temples. "Dru, you are incredibly rude. You need to be taught manners before you can take your place in Elfheim as the mate of the Synod leader and stepmother to my son and heir."

I snorted. "Give me some of whatever you've been smoking."

He ignored me. "Tell me where Eugenie has taken my son."

A very good question. Where *was* Eugenie?

"You killed her sister, you elven puffer fish. You really think I'm going to tell you anything?" If Rand was asking me where Eugenie was, he obviously didn't know either. Pretending I *did* know would give me leverage, however. It might be false leverage but I'd take what I could get until I figured out what was going on. "Eugenie's two little nieces will have to grow up without their mother, thanks to you."

Rand blinked at me, a slow closing and opening of those brilliant, clear blue-green eyes so similar to the color of my own, only prettier. "What? Violette is dead? How? When?"

In my peripheral vision, I saw Jean slowly climb to his feet and pick up his dagger. I gave him what I hoped was a subtle shake of my head. Jean couldn't fight Rand, at least not with a dagger. Mental magic outweighed a dagger, and Jean had nothing to counter it. Rand needed to be controlled, not destroyed. At least not tonight.

I gave him my best sneer, the one I'd practiced in the mirror as a teenager pretending to be a big powerful wizard scaring pretes with a single vicious look. Boy, had I been delusional.

"Stop playing dumb. The same vampires you sent to do your dirty work tonight killed Violette last night in the house where her husband and daughters were sleeping. That's low, even for you." I turned my back on Rand and walked away, which I knew would infuriate the arrogant bastard. "Tell me another fairy tale, elf."

The rest of the audience was forgotten as Rand stalked me across the entry hall and into Jean's study. I closed the door behind us. It wasn't that I wanted a word alone with the elf who had lured me into what was essentially a marriage in the elven world. Nor, unfortunately, did I think I was smart enough to outwit him. I simply wanted him away from anyone whose thoughts he could read, which would tell him in a flash that Jean, at least, had no clue of Eugenie's whereabouts. I hoped she was upstairs, hiding under a bed. I didn't know how elves' magic worked on merfolk or faeries.

Elves could read the thoughts of most creatures, however, including wizards—unless the wizard happened to share their blood. Quince Randolph couldn't learn a damned thing from me, even if there had been anything to learn.

Rand paced the study, his shoulder-length blond hair flowing in loose waves instead of pulled back in his usual ponytail. Tall, long-limbed, with eyes a clear cerulean blue and cheekbones to die for, he wore his usual Russian snow prince garb: white sweater with a pale teal thread woven into it. White jeans. White boots. "I don't know what you're talking about, Dru. I didn't send the vampires here. Why would I? They'd scare Eugenie, and that could harm my son."

Damn it. That was the argument I kept stumbling over in blaming Rand for Violette's death. He might not give a rat's ass about Eugenie but he would not put his child at risk. The whole reason he was so adamant about getting my friend locked up in Elfheim was not because he wanted control or power or a political bargaining chip—although he'd consider all those things worthy bonus collateral. He wanted to make sure nobody hurt that baby, intentionally or otherwise.

"If you're innocent, how do you explain being here, searching for Eugenie at the same time a vampire attack is taking place? Even you've gotta admit the circumstantial evidence is pretty damning."

Rand collapsed in Jean's throne chair; the pirate would have a cow if he knew Rand was infecting his fine leather upholstery with elf germs. "I've had people monitoring the transports in and out of the area around Barataria since you escaped with Eugenie. I knew when the merman came here with all those supplies that you were here. I also saw the vampires slip into that same transport tonight and just followed them in. It was careless of you and Lafitte to leave it standing wide open."

"Uh-huh. Nice try." Trouble was, I believed him for the same reason I didn't think he was behind Violette's death. Vampire attacks tended to be sloppy, bloody things. Rand could be cruel. He'd somehow murdered his predecessor on the Synod, Mace Banyan, by arranging to have him crushed beneath a twin-engine Cessna while it was on the ground. But he was creative in his cruelty. If he wanted to storm Maison Rouge and take Eugenie by force, he wouldn't use a bunch of vampire hit men as his first strike.

"You don't know where she is, do you?" Rand leaned forward and brushed a stray strand of hair off my cheek. "You look awful. Need me to send you some clothes or anything?"

Gee, sweet-talk me, why don't you, Rand? "No, thanks. I have what I need." Every girl needed wet camo shorts and unraveling sweaters. "And yes, of course I know where Eugenie is. I'm just not telling you. She's safe, and so is the baby."

God, help me to be telling the truth in some lying, roundabout way. "Go home, Rand. Let me talk to her and work out a time for you to see her."

Rand deserved to be a part of his child's life, even before it was born. He just had to learn how to coexist without bullying Eugenie, threatening her, and scaring her. Like it or not, Rand was as close as she was going to get to an elven midwife, at least until it was time for the birth. Thanks to his already developing ability to mentally communicate with the fetus when he touched Eugenie, he knew the baby was a boy. I wanted Rand to touch her and assure all of us the child was healthy and felt content— he couldn't communicate verbally with the baby but he could tell if it was frightened or upset. It wasn't as if we could give Eugenie a stress-free environment, not in these crazy times.

"I'll just stay here until she comes back from wherever you're hiding her." Rand leaned back in the chair, crossed his arms, and assumed the petulant I-am-Elf look that annoyed the hell out of me. "I can outlast all of you."

Freaking elf. "No you can't. Jean Lafitte can outlast you. He's immortal and you aren't. This is his home. One of the vampires that he thinks you brought here—never mind that you didn't, he thinks you did—murdered his brother." I gave him a smile as cold as Christof's. "Go ahead and sit here in his study, relax in his favorite chair, and act imperious. He will kill you."

Which might kill me. I really needed to find out what would happen to me if Rand went to the elven version of the Rainbow Bridge, which would help me decide how hard I needed to work to protect him.

I could tell by Rand's pout that my point had been well made. "Fine. I'll leave. But I expect to hear from you within twenty-four hours with a firm time for me to see Eugenie. Not a second more."

We both got up and walked toward the door to the entry hall where, if history repeated itself, a nosy pirate would be eaves-dropping. "Or what—you'll send in a squad of goblin hit men this time?" Goblins would be cheap; they'd usually work for bourbon.

"I won't have to. I'll just pay a visit to the shifters' new Inter-species Council representative. Didn't take Alex long to blow you off and suck up to Zrakovi for a political appointment, did it? And I hear he has a new girlfriend."

I gritted my teeth and opened the door to find myself again nose-to-Adam's apple with the Eavesdropper-in-Chief. "Alex is working to change things for the better from inside the system. You might try it."

All bluff and no truth. What was Alex thinking? This was the second time I'd heard this business about the Interspecies Council, and since it was doubtful that the Faery Prince of Summer and the head of the Elven Synod were conspiring, my dogboy had some explaining to do. He could send me a locket full of faery repellent but not mention he'd been named to the Interspecies Council? And, excuse me, a girlfriend?

"Drusilla, do not tell me that you have made a bargain with this devil." Jean refused to clear the doorway.

I didn't want Rand glowing and chanting and doing his mental torture on anyone else so I stepped between them. "Rand wasn't behind the vampire attack; I'll explain later. For now, let him get the hell out of here."

Jake had shifted back to his human self, pulled on a pair of jeans, and stood at the bottom of the steps, bloody and bruised. I hated to see what Collette looked like; she'd left the room. "I'll show Mr. Clean to the transport, sunshine." Jake gestured to Rand. "Get your ass out of here, elf. And don't even *look* at me the wrong way or I'll rip your heart out."

Literally, I suspected. Rand seemed to think so as well. He tried to give me a hug until I elbowed him in the gut, so he *oofed* and strode out the door toward Jake, giving wide berth to the glowering pirate.

Twenty-four hours, Dru, he said in my head. *Send word to my house in New Orleans.*

As soon as he and Jake were out of sight, I went into the front parlor to check on Rene and find out what the hell had happened to Eugenie. To my relief, my favorite merman was sitting up. Sort of. More like he was propped in a sitting position, his eyes at half-mast.

"Hey there, babe, you look like sssssshitzuh." He squinted at me, not quite focusing.

"Is he drunk?" Rene could drink like the fish he was in his shifted form. I hadn't thought he could get sloshed.

"Drunk on vampire pheromones," Christof said, his voice dripping with distaste. "Although he's had trouble articulating all that happened, I gather several of them fed from him at once, and made it feel quite good."

Well, he looked happy enough. His head lolled back against the sofa, and his tongue hung out one side of his mouth like a dog's. Glad someone enjoyed their first vampire bite; mine hadn't been nearly so pleasant. The vampire regent had spat out my blood and said it tasted foul. Plus, it hurt.

"Did you find out where Eugenie is?" I dropped my voice to a near-whisper. Rand should be well gone by now, but no need to take chances.

Christof grinned, and I realized that, since I still wore Alex's locket, the almond-shaped eyes and high cheekbones and dark hair were his real features. I wondered how he looked to the others.

"It was a quite brilliant plan," he said. "As soon as he realized what was happening, while the others fought, Rene took Eugenie to the transport and escorted her to the home of . . . what is that musician's name . . . it's someone you know, Rene said. Lives in Old Orleans."

I blanked for a few moments, then blinked. "Louis Armstrong?"

"That's it." Christof snapped his fingers. "Rene took her to stay with Louis Armstrong."

Over the years since Katrina, Louis had done me a few favors and he was by far my favorite member of the historical undead, discounting my pirate. But he lived in Old Orleans, and Eugenie could get in way too much trouble in the Beyond's lawless version of a Wild West border town.

I wanted to sleep in the worst way, but knew I couldn't until I got Eugenie where I could keep an eye on her. "Guess I better go and find her," I said, turning to Jean. "You have something else I can wear?"

CHAPTER 10

I tugged upward on the ruffled neckline of my dress, which inched its empire waist toward my shoulders. Not a good look for anyone.

Jean sat in his recliner, watching me and enjoying an occasional chuckle at my discomfort. Only my relief at seeing him smile kept me from slapping him upside the head. Sixteen hours after his latest death, Dominique was already back, although weak and confined to bed for a week or two. Thus, Jean's mood had improved.

I scowled at him. "Where the hell is Rene?" I'd had little sleep after a busy night. First, I had to find Louis Armstrong and wait for him to finish his set playing at his favorite Old Orleans nightclub, Beyond and Back. Then he talked my ears off as he took me to his small cottage on the far eastern end of Old Orleans' French Quarter to retrieve Eugenie. She'd been temporarily shocked out of her horror over Violette's death by the vampire attack and the dashing escape to find Louis Armstrong.

As soon as she saw me and I told her Christof had agreed to

take her to the funeral, the tears started anew, but it also calmed her down. We returned to Old Barataria with no further drama, and I sat with her until she fell asleep.

I'd planned to go back downstairs and wait for Rene to come down from his vampire-orgasmic high so I could talk to him about Alex and the vampire attack, but finally gave up on him and went to bed. This morning, I'd sent him on a shopping expedition with a serious vampire hangover. Too bad. In a few hours, Christof was due to return from Faery and take Eugenie to the funeral. We both desperately needed clothes and toiletries.

"Rene will return when he returns," said my ever-helpful companion. "As you do not intend to accompany Mademoiselle Eugenie to say farewell to her sister, your need is not urgent."

Actually, it was. Once Eugenie was safely back from the funeral and back under Jean's guard, I planned to sneak across the border into New Orleans and have a chat with my favorite shapeshifter and, rumor had it, newest member of the Interspecies Council. No one besides me knew that part of the day's agenda. It was risky, but I wanted my life back and needed to find out what was going on.

I also wanted Alex's advice on how to get a safe meeting with Zrakovi. I kept thinking if I could get the man alone in a neutral place long enough to have a rational conversation, I could explain that I was not his enemy. Given my ties to Rand, I could help broker a real truce between the wizards and elves if he'd just let me.

I jerked the fitted empire waist back down below my boobs, which flashed way too much extra cleavage for my audience of one.

"Ah, that is most becoming, *Jolie*. A woman should wear things that accent her beauty." He paused. "And wear them properly."

"*Cochon.*" The pirate didn't seem to take offense when I called him a pig, so I often did. Sometimes the snout fit.

My "morning dress," as Jean called it, was a ruffled nightmare of stiff burgundy fabric that made me look pasty and clashed with the cuts and bruises on my face from my race through Faery. Eugenie's rust-colored version of the dress looked good with her coloring, and the empire waist made me imagine I could see a little baby bump even though it was still too early.

Unfortunately, I also appeared to have a baby bump. Since I wasn't pregnant, that pissed me off even more.

"Only women built like ten-year-old boys should wear these dresses, unless they're pregnant." I hitched the skirt up to my knees and curled up on the end of Jean's settee. His gaze tracked the appearance, folding, and disappearance of my bare legs. I'd refused to wear the stockings, and the rubber boots were in the bedroom. "And the underwear the women of your day had to wear. Oh, my God. It's a nightmare."

Jean gave a mock-serious nod. "I saw that the pantalettes I selected for you remained in your room." His gazed roamed toward my lap, and I smoothed the fabric over my legs to make sure he saw nothing but ugly burgundy cotton. If I was going commando this morning, it was none of his business. "Are you wearing no undergarments at all, *Jolie*? *Excusez-moi* for such an indelicate question, but you did bring the topic to my attention."

"You will never know the answer to that question." At least I hoped not.

"That is a pity." Jean's look was way too heated for this time of morning, or at least I thought it was morning. My cell phone had died and I had no way to recharge it. Portable battery packs were on Rene's extensive shopping list, as was a nice, old-fashioned wristwatch. I couldn't be running to consult Jean's grandfather clock whenever I needed to check the time.

I also was in no mood for sexual banter. "Jean, I thought we'd agreed that I was with Alex and that you and I were going to be friends." We'd had that relationship talk a couple of weeks ago, finally getting everything out in the open.

"As I recall, *Jolie,* what we agreed to, as you say, is that maintaining your affair with *Monsieur Chien* was a great deal of work and that I am a patient man who can wait until you tire of him and realize how well-suited we are for each other. I am not, however, a blind man, and patience does not prevent me from enjoying your beauty, *non?*"

Oh, brother. "Whatever."

Taking that as an assent to . . . something, Jean moved to sit beside me on the settee, and I tucked the full folds of the skirt more tightly around the site of the missing pantalettes. What was he doing sneaking around in my room checking on my underwear status, anyway?

He reached over and wrapped his hand around mine. Never mind his age of about 230, give or take a decade; his hand, though scarred, was tanned and firm, with strong fingers that could probably snap the neck of a misbehaving pirate. Or wizard. "You should not be lonely, *Jolie.*"

"I never said I was lonely." So why did I want to cry all of a sudden? I'd become so pathetic it was pathetic.

And yet . . . once again, Jean had seen me with a clarity I could never achieve. Eugenie's troubles grew by the day, and her baby had to come first. Alex was trying to change things from the inside to make both our lives better—not to mention saving mine. I was surrounded by people, but as selfish as it felt to even think, I longed for real companionship. Someone to be with who didn't have an agenda.

I turned to try and express some of this to Jean, who always had an agenda, but instead found his mouth an inch from mine and moving closer. He kissed me, a soft pressure of lips and then a pulling back, but only a fraction. I didn't react; my brain had frozen, my thoughts drilled down to the scent of cinnamon, the pressure of his hand on my waist, a second kiss.

Did I kiss him back? I wasn't even sure. He smoothed my hair away from my face, still leaning close, his eyes an impossible rich shade of cobalt blue.

I should slap him. Bitch at him. Call him a *cochon*. Not just sit here frozen and staring.

"Well, ain't this cozy?"

I jumped like I'd been beaten with a bullwhip, which I should be. Thank God. I'd never been happier to see Rene Delachaise and it had nothing to do with the armload of bags he dumped on the floor in front of me as I moved to the opposite side of the settee from Jean.

"We were waiting for you." I willed the heat from my face, which had probably turned the shade of the awful pink bikini panties Rene pulled from one of the bags and dangled from his finger.

"Yeah, I can see that, babe." Rene shot the panties like a rubber band toward Jean, who caught them in midair, examining them with much interest. Too much interest.

"Those are not mine," I assured him. I wasn't a pink kind of girl.

"Yeah they are." Rene smiled, but he had fatigue lines around his eyes. Guess vampire orgies were exhausting. "I couldn't get within a block of Eugenie's house or your papa's place in Lakeview or the Hotel Monteleone. I had to shop."

He said *shop* as one might say *horse manure*.

I had a moment of panic. "How much did shopping cost?"

I'd given him a huge list, and I was currently unemployed. Even when I'd been employed, my salary had been barely enough to make ends meet.

"Don't worry about it. I got it covered. It's worth it to see that." Rene nodded toward Jean, who'd set the panties aside and was pulling other goodies out of the nearest bag. Pink bras, teddies, and more pastel panties were taken out and examined, held up for display and turned in different directions. God help me.

Rene could afford it, between his successful shrimping business and his off-the-books smuggling with Jean Lafitte, but I paid my own way. I'd find a way to repay him, eventually.

Jean made an appreciative clucking sound at a particularly lacy pair of garters. Who the hell wore garters? Nobody in my circle. "Those are for Eugenie, and she probably wouldn't appreciate you mauling them," I said, punching Jean in the biceps nearest me. No way Rene would buy me pastels and lacy garters. I didn't own one single pastel stitch of clothing for a reason.

"Oh no, all the pink and lace is for you," Rene said. "The colors are sweet, which you aren't, babe. Plus, I was pissed at having to shop for women's underwear three days before Christmas, me and every loser who'd forgotten to buy his wife a present." He pulled a sheer pale-pink whisper of a negligee from a Victoria's Secret bag and held it up for Jean. "Plus, since I couldn't get the holy water you asked for from your house, I had to steal some from the Prompt Lady of Succor so I'll probably go to hell, too. You owe me."

"I should like to see you wear these items, *Jolie*," Jean said, grinning at the evil look I shot his way.

"Enjoy fondling them; it's as close as you're gonna get." His chuckle told me he thought otherwise, but his chuckle lied. "And the name of the church is Our Lady of Prompt Succor. If you don't know the name of the patron saint of New Orleans, you probably won't go to hell for stealing her holy water."

Rene laughed. "Yeah, you right."

"What's going on at the houses—have the wizards posted guards? Did you try to go to Alex's place, too?" These were things I needed to know before tonight's secret mission, assuming all went according to plan with Eugenie and the funeral.

"There's some kind of magical shit around them, like a force field—the whole buildings. Your office, too. I figured if I went through it, an alarm would go off somewhere we didn't want it to. And yeah, Alex's house is warded. Think he knows?"

Good question. "Yeah, I think he'd have to." Those kinds of wards had to be set in person, so a wizard—probably Green Congress, which made it sting even more—would've had to walk the property, planting charms and sealing it with blood and holy water.

That meant I'd have to catch Alex somewhere in public tonight. Maybe at dinnertime; the man never cooked. One of the things I loved about him was that he didn't expect me to cook, either. I refused to believe he had a new girlfriend; Rand was just trying to torture me.

"Thanks for doing all this shopping." I began gathering the bags. "I need to go up and help Eugenie get dressed." I hoped he'd bought something besides underwear.

Turns out he had not only jeans and sweaters in pretty close to the right size for both of us, but also a few maternity tops for Eugenie and a simple black sheath dress and pumps for her to wear to the funeral. Rene was an unexpectedly good shopper.

"I need hose." Eugenie pulled on the dress, which was at least a size too big but that might be for the best. No one would know she was pregnant unless she wanted to tell them, which meant no explanations. She'd grow into it pretty fast if she had the baby closer to the elven term of seven months instead of the human nine.

"Wear the black tights you had on when you got here." I rummaged around the armoire in the room she'd claimed as hers, near the stairway on the second floor. "It's going to be really cold if Christof has to do his Prince of Winter thing."

If our houses were warded with magical alarms, I doubted this funeral would go off without drama. I hadn't told Eugenie about the security at her house; she was barely holding it together anyway. I'd have to tell Christof, though, so he wouldn't let her talk him into popping over to New Orleans. He was supposed to set up a transport from Faery into Shreveport, which meant Eugenie would transport first to the Winter Palace and then to the new spot, with no need to go anywhere near her house. Still, so much could go wrong.

A soft knock on the door preceded Collette, who stuck her head inside. She was moving a bit slowly after her close encounter of the fanged kind, but had almost healed. "Christof's here." She smiled at Eugenie. "You look beautiful. Pregnant women really do glow."

It was true. Once you got past the dark circles under her eyes, which she'd managed to cover up pretty well with the makeup, Eugenie looked beautiful. Her heart-shaped face had filled out a bit, and her auburn hair shone now that she'd finally been able to wash it with real shampoo. Pregnancy agreed with her, even if the baby's father was a devious, petulant elf.

She picked up the small black purse—Rene had thought of everything, which made me suspect he'd had some help from either one of his string of romantic conquests or one of his sisters. My buddy the merman had a reputation as quite the aquatic playboy.

"I guess I'm ready." Eugenie took a deep breath. "What am I going to tell Matt if he asks me to stay and help with the twins?"

I thought about it on the way downstairs. "Tell him you're having a difficult pregnancy and have some tests scheduled." That was the truth, only her brother-in-law could never guess how difficult, and Eugenie's upcoming meeting with Rand, which we'd set up for tomorrow, already had me feeling testy. "Does Matt have family?" I knew Eugenie's parents had died quite a few years ago, and she and Violette were the only siblings.

"Yes, his parents and a couple of sisters, and they're both within an hour's drive." She nodded. "That's a good idea about the pregnancy. They knew I was seeing someone. Too bad it turned out to be Quince Randolph."

That was the God's honest truth.

Christof stood in the entry hall with Rene and Jean, and he cleaned up nice, as my grandmother back in Alabama would say. He'd gone for a very mainstream human look, with his dark hair short and styled. He did an admirable job of filling out a conservative black suit.

"Oh, I like Christof with the blond hair," Eugenie whispered. "He looks so handsome."

The only blond hair in the room was mine, and I started to say so. Instead, intrigued to try out a theory, I tugged the chain containing Alex's locket from around my neck and laid it on a side table. This time when I looked around at Christof, his hair was almost shoulder length and blond. Unfortunately Rand-like, in my opinion. His features also were softer, his nose and chin less sharp, his cheekbones not as pronounced.

I suspected Christof would not be pleased to know I could see through his glamour, thanks to that little tuft of Gandalf's fur. I'd be wearing it constantly from now on, even if any faeries I encountered thought I reeked of dog. I slipped it back around my neck, relieved to again see Christof as he really looked.

The faery and the merman and the pirate had paid us no attention at all, so deeply were they engrossed in conversation. Nor was it a lighthearted chat, judging by their expressions.

The last phrase I overheard before they noticed us and shut up like uncooked clams was *coup d'état*.

I wasn't sure which state they were talking about, but it had been overthrown.

CHAPTER 11

Okay, let's have it." As soon as the others left, I pounced on the pirate. Christof and Eugenie, looking like a proper mourning couple, had strolled off toward the transport, followed shortly by Rene, who'd be trailing them to Shreveport in case of trouble. "Talk to me."

"*Bien sûr,* Drusilla." Jean's mouth widened in a smile that didn't quite put the usual dancing light in his eyes. "On which topic would you enjoy conversing?"

I'd been patient while Christof admired Eugenie's dress and face and hair ad nauseam, and she admired the blond hair he wore today—wait till I told her he was a brunette.

Those two had entirely too much admiration for each other, which as Eugenie's friend I found terrifying, given the political landscape and the encyclopedic knowledge of what I *didn't* know about faeries. I knew two things. First, the fae were scary as hell: Such was the conclusion I'd reached after my first and, I hoped, only trip to Faery. Second, Eugenie did not need to get mixed up with one of them, especially while she carried a half-elven child and the prete world was on the brink of war. Talk about asking for trouble.

Now my patience had disappeared like last week's New Orleans snowstorm. A faery-induced snowstorm, no less.

"Don't give me that charming routine, Jean. What were you and Christof and Rene talking about when we came downstairs? You're still thinking about it, and it upset you. I can tell."

Jean liked to say he understood me, and he spoke the truth. However, I also understood him. I could read his moods without the benefit of my now-replenished mojo bag. Rene could shop for me anytime.

He sighed. "*Mais oui*. Allow me to speak with Jacob first, and then we shall talk." Without waiting for a response, he turned and strode onto the verandah, where Jake and Collette waited. They planned to spend a romantic day as transport guards. Sometime today, I planned to move Barataria's only transport closer to the house, where Jean claimed he'd have more control over it.

It was isolated. I'd walked down the beach and onto the island interior last night to transport to Old Orleans in my search for Eugenie. My other travel option, sailing a flat-bottomed pirogue steered by an undead pirate, failed to appeal.

In the excitement over losing Eugenie, and then getting her home from Louis Armstrong's apartment in the Old Orleans version of Storyville, the 1920s New Orleans jazz and red-light district, I had overlooked an important point about the vampire attack. We didn't actually know what they were after, or who their target was. We assumed it was Eugenie, but what if it wasn't?

If Rand hadn't planned it, and I didn't think he had, then who were the vampires' targets? What was their endgame? Going after Jean, Dominique, or any of the other undead pirates made no sense because, really, what was the point? One could kill them but in a few days or a couple of weeks at most, they'd be good as new and out for revenge. Plus, although I'd never share this opinion with Captain Lafitte, in the grand scheme of pre-ternatural politics, he wasn't that important.

He might become very, very important if things fell apart in the way he anticipated, but not yet.

I couldn't imagine any reason that the vampires, or anyone who might hire them, would be after Jake or Collette. The loups-garou didn't have a power structure; the whole idea of leaders ran counter to their anti-pack nature. They didn't even partici-pate in the were-shifter alliance.

Terri Ford, Adrian's main squeeze, had seen an opportunity to escape Vampyre, where she'd been under the watchful gaze of the Vice-Regent, hoping she'd lure Adrian back to be con-trolled and used as a weapon. I believed her when she said she didn't know who'd hired the vampires; she had everything to lose by lying.

That left two potential targets among Jean's current menag-erie: Adrian and me. Adrian had very little power. His wizard's Blue Congress magic worked a little in the Beyond but not reli-ably. He hadn't been a vampire long enough to know what he was capable of or how strong he might become vampire-wise, but his magic would eventually wane. He was considered tainted merchandise by the wizards but he might be of interest to the elves or vampires in case of war—if they could control him. My gut told me Adrian wasn't the target of tonight's raid, however.

Which left me. In trying to figure out who might want to kill me, the list was long and ugly. I had value because I could do both wizard's and elven magic. I was dangerous because I'd proven unwilling to blindly follow orders. I was a threat to Willem Zrakovi's political ambitions, and vampire Vice-Regent Garrett Melnick didn't exactly belong to my fan club. Rand had made no secret that he wanted me living with him in Elfheim, but I'd already scratched him off tonight's list of suspects—this wasn't his style.

Zrakovi had the biggest target on his forehead. I didn't necessarily think he wanted me dead; I thought he wanted me under his control, and if I died in the process? Oh well. He'd look like a stronger leader if he taught me a lesson, plus he'd have a clearer shot at Eugenie and a better chance of solidifying his alliance with the elves.

The idea that my own people had sent vampires to capture me, with Eugenie as a bonus, was both depressing and infuriating. Didn't Zrakovi know that I *wanted* to support the wizards? That until a month ago I'd actually admired him? That I'd supported his promotion to First Elder?

He sure wasn't making it easy.

I needed to think about something else, at least until I could set up a meeting with him.

I went to my bedroom, picked up a big blue and white plastic Walmart bag from among Rene's purchases, and took it to Jean's study or, as I was tempted to now think of it, The Room That Shall Not Be Named.

Rene had done a good job of either buying or stealing what I needed to replace the scrying gear I'd requested from my late father's half-gutted, Katrina-flooded, and now-unapproachable house in Lakeview. First was a large mixing bowl made of dark glass, followed by a package of pungent patchouli incense cones and enough holy water to fill three bowls. I laughed; Rene must have cleaned out Our Lady of Prompt Succor. Was this their first holy water theft? Did one report the theft of holy water to the sheriff of St. Bernard Parish?

The final thing I'd need for scrying was Charlie, and I pulled the ancient elven staff from my messenger bag and laid it on the table alongside the other materials. The magic would work better with some of the ruby chips I kept in a glass jar in my makeshift workroom at Gerry's, but the constant full moon of the Beyond, which amped up magic, should more than compensate. I had never tried scrying from the Beyond, but since it was elven magic, I thought it would work.

I planned to watch the funeral, and then I planned to track down Alex Warin. I only wished I'd thought of it sooner so I'd know what was going on. The only wizard still alive who understood what I could do with my ability to scry was Adrian Hoffman and, strange though it seemed, he and I were on the same team. We'd never be friends, but we were coexisting, albeit mostly by ignoring each other. Being members of Jean's band of misfits had made us allies.

Team Lafitte was a good name. Or maybe, since the people who lived in the small town named Jean Lafitte, Louisiana, sometimes referred to themselves as Lafitians, that would work. *Hi, my name is DJ, and I'm a Lafitian.*

Yeah, it had a ring to it. Kind of like Martian, only more bizarre.

When Jean returned from checking on the transport, I was ready for him. "What were you saying about a coup d'état? What's happened?"

Jean poured himself a brandy and handed me my own poison of choice, Diet Coke in a plastic bottle. Rene had brought me a case, and I didn't let a little thing like a lack of refrigeration bother me. Room-temperature soda held its fizz longer.

If the conversation went badly, Rene also had brought in a monster-size bottle of Four Roses, Jake's favorite bourbon.

My pirate sprawled on the settee, so I claimed his throne. I understood its attraction; the dark buttery leather surrounded me in pillows of comfort. It must have cost a fortune by early

nineteenth-century standards, and the room now had the pleasant scent of leather along with cinnamon and polished wood. It
was hard to relax, however, until I knew which revolution had
begun.

"Christof arrived with news of a most disturbing nature."
Jean's emotional aura read like a road map—going in every
direction. "Sabine is dead, and Florian has taken control of the
Royal Tower and holds it by force. Christof suspects his brother
of killing their aunt, but has been unable to get into the tower
to find proof."

Good grief. Faery had gone into a meltdown.

"Just because Florian's moved into the tower doesn't make
him king, does it?" Surely possession wasn't nine-tenths of a
monarchy. The idea of Faery being under the control of that
fireball-tossing freakadoodle made my skin crawl. Never mind
that he hated me. Worse, he hated his brother, who somehow
had ended up an ally of the Lafitians.

"What is Christof doing about it? He should have canceled
taking Eugenie to that funeral." It was an awful thing to say,
but Eugenie couldn't help Violette by going to her funeral and
Christof could help a lot of people—including his allies in this
house—if he wrested control of Faery from his brother. The less
time Florian had to get entrenched, the easier it would be to oust
him from the tower.

"Christof is quite fond of Eugenie and insisted that he keep
his promise to help her, although both Rene and I urged him
to do otherwise." Jean shrugged. "However, it might be a safer
place for him at present. Florian has his own followers and they
are torturing and murdering Christof's allies, including their
sister Tamara. When Christof left Barataria last evening to see to
his affairs at the Winter Palace, he found his home in ruins and
his sister dead."

Holy crap. She'd been Florian's sister, too, although she'd clearly chosen sides. All the more reason Christof didn't need to be sitting in a Catholic church in Shreveport, Louisiana. "What is he going to do?"

Jean shook his head. "There will be civil war in Faery, I fear, and the concern is that the whole of the nonhuman world will be drawn into it because of another action that Florian has taken. Christof must gather his troops and take control, of course, but this other matter is one we must answer first."

What was this *we* business? *We* had no part to play in the politics of Faery. I hated to ask. "What else has Florian done and how does it involve us?"

"Christof sensed elven magic near the ruins of his palace."

A chill ran across my shoulder blades and I choked on my hot soda. Between hacking coughs, I managed a strangled question. "He thinks the elves are already backing Florian?"

Jean stared at me a moment before answering, and I didn't like the cold look that had settled on his face. It was an expression I could only imagine had preceded some act of extreme violence back in his human life.

"I do not know if the elves are aligned with Florian or if he has managed to hire at least one elf to help him," Jean said. "It is likely the latter. But of greater concern is the story Florian intends to take to the next Interspecies Council meeting, if the rumors Christof hears are true."

I had a very bad feeling about this. Jean's aura of scattered emotions had coalesced into one: anger. Deep, deep fury. "What story would that be?"

"Florian claims to have an eyewitness who will testify that the destruction of the Winter Palace was caused by Christof himself. They will present it as his means of gaining sympathy to his cause," Jean said slowly.

Heart pounding, I held my breath. I had a dawning horror of what was coming. "What else?"

"His witness will swear an oath that the person assisting Christof with elven magic, which is illegal to use in Faery, was you, *Jolie*."

CHAPTER 12

Holy crap. At the rate charges and accusations were piling up against me, I'd have to sleep the rest of my life—probably a short life—with one eye open, no matter where I lived. Forget about going home; I'd never again see sunlight reflecting off the spire of St. Louis Cathedral.

"Who is the so-called eyewitness?" I asked Jean, pouring my soda into a heavy glass and adding a generous splash of bourbon. After a moment, I added a second splash. Being framed by faeries earned one an extra dose of bourbon.

"This person's name is not one with which I am familiar—Orloff," Jean said. "One of Florian's associates, perhaps. It matters not. By naming you, the Summer Prince accomplishes much."

However I'd like to think otherwise, I wasn't that important, so I didn't see the benefit. I was no longer even gainfully employed. "What does he accomplish, other than probably getting me killed?" Maybe that was enough for him.

Jean set his drink on a side table and leaned forward. "He rids himself of someone Christof considers an ally and ensures your Elders will not grant you pardon. Perhaps he frightens away some who might otherwise support his brother. Also, by formally aligning you with Christof, he weakens his brother's standing with the wizards who wish to arrest you. They are more likely to support Florian in his bid for the monarchy if you are his enemy."

Maybe I needed a third splash of bourbon. Apparently, being associated with me was political suicide. Thank God Jean thrived on political chaos.

"Still, Florian got someone to do elven magic in Faery." I tried to work it out in my head, no easy task. Prete politics these days were too tangled. "We know I didn't do it, so do you think he is working out a deal with the elves?"

In which case, the wizards were about to get a big, ugly surprise. I had to talk to Rand to see what was going on.

The elves and the fae, or at least Florian and his followers, banding together against the wizards? It was the Elders' worst-case scenario. The wishy-washy vamps, of course, would go with the majority. Maybe the Elders had betrayed me, or saw me as a renegade who'd betrayed them, but I didn't want to see my people crushed beneath a preternatural freight train.

"Perhaps they are aligning themselves, although Florian also might simply have hired someone among the elves to do the magic in order to cast blame on you." Jean lit his pipe, in-fusing the room with the deep, rich scent of tobacco. It sent a sudden pang of loss through me. Gerry had smoked a pipe, and many of my deepest childhood memories were infused with that sweet scent. I missed him, and wished he were here to rant and rave about what arrogant gits the Elders were, as he always used to do.

This time, I wouldn't defend the Elders or dismiss Gerry's opinions as I so often had. I hated the way my father had died, in a position of weakness. He had placed his trust in a preternatural world that wasn't trustworthy because of a wizarding world that also wasn't trustworthy. I understood that now.

Everyone kept telling me I was Gerry's daughter, so was I doing the same thing? I studied Jean Lafitte, the undead scoundrel in whom I'd placed my trust, while he, in turn, studied my scrying setup. No, it was different. I trusted Jean because he'd earned it, time and again, being loyal to me if not to the wizards as a group. Sure, he always had an agenda, but didn't everyone? He was just smarter than most.

And unlike Gerry, I wasn't trying to overthrow the whole prete world and bring about radical change. I just wanted to survive. To get my life back. To have a home. To be with Alex again.

I wanted peace.

The likelihood of any of those pipe dreams coming true had just taken another nosedive.

"What are these items, *Jolie*? You asked Rene to obtain them for you?" Jean held a cone of patchouli incense to his nose, wrinkled it as if he'd gotten a whiff of two-month-old rotten tilapia, and then sneezed. "*Mon Dieu*, what is this foul substance?"

I shoved Florian's frame job to the back of my mind for now. If I could track down Alex later, he might be able to tell me more—but only if we could safely get Eugenie back from Violette's funeral. That had to come first. Then Alex. Then setting up something with Zrakovi. Rand, I'd see when he came to visit Eugenie.

"This foul substance"—I picked up four cones of patchouli from the oversize plastic bag filled with them—"is incense. It's part of an elven ritual I'm going to try so that we can watch what's going on at the funeral."

I looked around the room. Outside one of the big front

windows, tall enough for even Jean to step through onto the front porch, I spotted the full moon, shimmering a soft golden yellow in the indigo night. It was half past two in the afternoon across the border in New Orleans, but here, the full moon floated high in the sky.

"Is there a table outside I could use?" I asked Jean. "If I could do this by moonlight, I think it would work better."

"Perhaps the small table on the verandah might meet your needs. I will place it on the banquette." Jean hefted the big glass mixing bowl and proved how well I knew my pirate by walking through the open window. I picked up Charlie and the incense, following Jean through the window and onto the porch. The gulf breeze was cool and dry with a fresh, salty tang, and it rustled the leaves of the banana trees that grew around the porch, sounding like the feet of ghost children playing in the dense foliage.

Jean moved the round, waist-high table to the wooden planks that stretched from the bottom of the steps out to the beach, an old-fashioned banquette or sidewalk. In the modern world, this area was underwater thanks to erosion and rising seas, its view of the Gulf dotted with oil rigs.

Yet in Old Barataria, frozen in the early nineteenth century by Jean's own memories, the barrier island of Grand Terre rose from the sea big and solid, with a ridge of live oaks marching across the center and a strip of sandy beach stretching across the Gulf side. North of the long horizontal island lay deep, sheltered Barataria Bay. North of that on the mainland, in the modern world, lay the small town of Jean Lafitte, Louisiana, where the modern Lafitians lived.

"Mind if I join you?" A male voice with the accent of an educated Englishman sounded from the dark edge of the porch, and my heart stuttered for a moment. I'd been thinking of Gerry, who'd never lost his English accent even after thirty years in

New Orleans. After that first jolt and a flash of sorrow, I recognized the dulcet tones of Adrian Hoffman.

I pitied Adrian despite all the awful things he'd said and done to me in the past. No matter that his weakness and indecision had almost gotten both Alex and me killed.

He'd be horrified by my pity, but all he'd done wrong, other than being an arrogant jerk like his father, was to fall in love with Terri Ford, vampire assistant of Regent Etienne Boulard. He'd paid for it dearly. No job. A horrific betrayal by his own father, who he then saw murdered a few feet away from him. Abandonment by the fellow wizards for whom he'd worked his whole career.

Sounded a little like me minus the red-haired vampire lover. If I wanted to host another pity party, misery would have company.

I waved him over. "Join us. I'm going to watch what's happening at the funeral, or at least try."

He picked up the heavy bowl, which Jean had abandoned on the porch when he moved the table, and brought it down the steps. "How often must I tell you that scrying is an illegal activity and that . . ."

I raised an eyebrow and he stopped himself, then we both laughed. "Add it to my litany of crimes," I said. "It's getting to be a pretty long list."

"You've done nothing wrong." The vehemence in his voice surprised me. Adrian rarely had a kind word for me and, to be fair, it went both ways.

"We've both been betrayed," I reminded him, and looked away from the raw, bleak misery that settled on his face. Gerry might have died from his own bad decisions, but he hadn't deliberately sold me out like Adrian's father had done to his only child.

"Oui," Jean said, his voice so soft that the sound of the waves

almost overwhelmed it. "There has been much betrayal for all of us."

There was nothing else to add; we all were feeling a bit maudlin. I set about measuring the holy water and pouring part of it into the bowl. At each of the four points around the bowl, I set a cone of incense along with an item I'd cadged from Eugenie's room: a pair of earrings and a bracelet she'd been wearing the night we fled New Orleans, one of a stack of romance novels Rene had brought her on his first haul, and a nail file I'd found on the dresser.

Despite the flicker of flambeaux along the sides of the banquette, the moon provided the brightest illumination here, and its soft glow reflected on the holy water.

I glanced at my new wristwatch, which I'd set to Central Standard Time. The mass had been scheduled in a small church just outside Shreveport, followed by a family-only graveside service. If anyone were going to make a move against Eugenie, the most likely spot would be the cemetery—out in the open. Plenty of tombs to hide behind. Plenty of spots to set up a transport.

I used a match from my portable magic kit, fed a shot of energy from Charlie into the blend of herbs and holy water, closed my eyes, and focused my thoughts on Eugenie.

"*Mon Dieu.*" Jean's exclamation, which came a few seconds later, was tinged with alarm. Good, that meant it had worked.

"There they are. You're quite good at this." Adrian had seen my scrying abilities before; as I recalled, he had been as alarmed as Jean the first time.

"I'm not *this* good." The image on the surface of the water was as clear as a high-definition TV screen—and there was sound, which I'd never gotten doing this at home. "It must be the combination of moonlight, being in the Beyond, and fueling the ritual with the staff."

Eugenie sat on a wooden pew with her head down, looking at her hands. She was twisting a gold ring with some type of emerald-cut gemstone around her left ring finger, almost obsessively. I changed the angle of the elven staff to get closer. I'd never seen that ring before; it must have been Violette's. If Christof's feelings had progressed to giving her jewelry, I didn't want to know about it.

The clarity of the moon-illuminated image showed us every dark shadow under my friend's eyes, the tear-swollen skin purplish and puffy. I couldn't imagine what she was going through. I'd been an only child, and Eugenie was the closest I had to a sister. I'd always envied her relationship with Violette a little; they didn't have much in common in terms of interests or lifestyle, but their family love remained deep.

My only family bonds were with that insufferable elf Rand, an uncle, Lennox, whom I'd met once, a cousin, Audrey, on whom I'd never laid eyes, and my grandmother in Alabama, who still clung to the hope I'd give up wizardry and come home to marry a human and spawn babies.

"You possess skill of which I was quite unaware, *Jolie*." I looked up to find Jean looking not at the image of Eugenie, but at me. He wore the thoughtful, assessing expression that usually meant he was considering how a situation or person might be used to his advantage.

That blasted pirate would try to talk me into scrying every hour I was awake, spying on his enemies, who apparently were also now my enemies. The worst part of that realization was that I wish I'd thought of it four days ago.

"Yeah, I'm just full of surprises." Jean could scheme and plot all he wanted. For now, I had to focus on my friend. Make that friends, plural, I guess. Christof was an ally, whether I wanted him or not. I didn't know what he could do or who he was inside his variety of faux exteriors, so he hadn't reached friend status. He sat on Eugenie's left, elegant in his black suit, his demeanor appropriately somber. For me, he had dark hair, and I itched to ask Jean if Christof looked blond to him. I wasn't sure I wanted the pirate to know about that skill yet, however, because I didn't yet want Jean's new BFF to know.

"Who is the gentleman sitting to the right of Mademoiselle Eugenie?" Jean had finally stopped plotting and leaned over the bowl to see better. I recognized Matt from photos I'd seen at Eugenie's house. "It's Violette's husband." I didn't see the twins, or anyone who might be Matt's parents. They must have been keeping the girls away from the funeral, which was good. If a preternatural catastrophe sent the whole funeral service into the twilight zone, children could make convenient pawns. This family had suffered too much already.

Christof leaned toward Eugenie and said something I couldn't hear, then put his arm around her shoulders and settled her closer to him. I didn't like that move one bit. "Jean, you need to have a talk with Christof. As much as I appreciate him taking Eugenie to the funeral, especially given his political problems at home, he doesn't need to form any kind of relationship with her. She doesn't have the political skills to handle it, and with Rand on the warpath . . ." I shrugged.

No need to tell the pirate anything more; he was already nodding. "In this matter, I must agree, Drusilla. I will speak to Christof when they return."

I was relieved that he agreed, but shouldn't be surprised. For an intelligent man with the heart of a dreamer, Jean Lafitte also could be extremely practical, especially where politics or money were concerned.

He watched them a moment longer. "In normal times, I would not begrudge my friend an attachment to such a lovely woman as Mademoiselle Eugenie, but her child's paternity raises difficulties."

"You can say that again," I muttered.

He looked at me, puzzlement narrowing his eyes. "Very well. In normal times, I would not begrudge—"

I held up my hand. "It's okay. I heard you." Sometimes, conversation with Jean could be a lot like a "Who's on First" riddle.

The funeral mass began, with much sitting and standing and praying. I didn't understand most of it, having been brought up with my magic-eschewing grandparents in a casserole-toting Methodist household until moving in with Gerry at age seven. His interaction with organized religion consisted of driving past churches on the way to buy groceries.

In twenty minutes, it was over, and I held my breath as the family left through a different exit than the public. "Look for anything that appears to be out of place," I told Jean and Adrian. "Watch the perimeters."

As the family walked to the small gated cemetery beside the church and I manipulated Charlie, the view in the scrying bowl moved with them.

"Wait, look there near that tree—and that one, too." Adrian held a finger above the water on the right side of the bowl, then the left. "I know those men; they're both Blue Congress wizards from New Orleans."

The Blues had been Adrian's congress, specializing in re-creation and illusion. I'd seen him do amazing things from animating the ruins of the Katrina-flooded Six Flags amusement park to moving a live oak tree the size of a building close enough for us to escape off the roof of the city's museum. They could also alter memories in humans. The only time Blue Congress wizards were on standby was when trouble was expected that they might need to clean up.

"Damn it. What are they up to?"

We watched as the priest spoke to each family member. When he got to Eugenie, I fed an extra bit of energy from Charlie into the water, hoping to amp up the volume. It worked.

"Thank you," Eugenie was saying to the priest. "I'm sorry it was so hard for the family to reach me. I'd gone . . ." She ran out of steam and looked at Christof.

"We had gone away for a few days," said Mr. Smooth Faery, who seemed to be playing up his accent. It sounded vaguely Eastern European. "I am Eugenie's intended, Christof Prince. Between planning our wedding and with Eugenie carrying our child, we needed to relax and thus were difficult to reach."

"Mon Dieu," Jean muttered just before I said, "Holy crap."

The priest, to his credit, only blinked at the news of an impending shotgun wedding and a pregnant bride, not realizing it was a clever ruse to explain his presence. At least I prayed it was a ruse. And thankfully, he didn't know *Prince* was a title rather than a surname.

"You are *not* that child's father, you faery bastard. He is elf. You'll never get near him."

"Oh God." I'd know Quince Randolph's imperious voice anywhere.

Freaking elf.

CHAPTER 13

I don't know what bush Quince Randolph had been hiding behind, but he clearly didn't want the Winter Prince of Faery claiming fatherhood to the heir of the elven fire clan.

Just in case things weren't spiraling into Wonderland territory already, Rand began glowing as he made a grab for Eugenie's hand. Instead, his fingers ran into the midsection of Christof, who'd stepped in front of her and began his own soft chanting. He raised his fingers toward the sky, which couldn't be a good thing.

"Oh no no no no," I groaned. What a train wreck. I didn't want to know whether Rand's fire would melt Christof's ice, or if the elf would spontaneously hibernate there in the graveyard, which would serve him right.

Adrian moved closer. "Where's the merman? Wasn't he supposed to get Eugenie out if this happened?"

Jean, Adrian, and I bumped shoulders as we crowded around the scrying bowl, scanning the image on the water's surface and searching for a glimpse of Rene. He wasn't there. I knew, because

I could see the face of everyone gathered for the graveside service. They'd formed a circle around Rand and Christof, with Eugenie behind the faery and the hapless priest trying to talk down creatures that, if he realized they existed, would have him on his knees before the altar, praying for divine intervention. Even the grieving widower stood frozen in place, wide-eyed.

Since divine intervention probably wasn't forthcoming, they might have to settle for wizard intervention. "What are your Blue Congress wizards doing to stop this?" I leaned farther in, trying to find them.

"Standing around with their thumbs up their arses, apparently." Adrian pointed toward a tree on the far side of the cemetery, under which the two wizards appeared to be smoking cigarettes, oblivious to anything else going on.

"*Pardon,* Monsieur Hoffman, but why would these wizards place their thumbs up their—"

"He doesn't mean it literally," I assured Jean, although they might as well be plugged up, for all the crap they were letting amass. "Damn it, I'm going over there. Something's happened to Rene, and Eugenie's going to get stuck right in the middle of a preternatural showdown."

Maybe Christof had somehow become my ally, but I didn't trust him any more than I trusted my elf.

I jerked Charlie from the scrying bowl, blanking out the scene, and wheeled around to return to the house.

Jean grabbed my sweater from behind, stopping me midstep. "This is not acceptable, *Jolie.* Haste will prove your undoing. In order to go to this place you must travel through Faery. Do you not imagine Florian will be watching the Winter Palace, if the transport still exists?"

"Thank you for caring about me." I turned and threw my arms around Jean's neck, giving him a tight hug. The shock of it threw him off his game so much that I was able to push away from him and stalk toward the door before he figured out my ploy.

"The transport is still there," I said over my shoulder. "Otherwise, Christof and Eugenie wouldn't have been able to make it to Shreveport. I'm going."

He caught up with me. "Then I shall accompany you."

"Then you're both fools. It's a trap." Adrian caught up with both of us, and I stopped. Daylight was wasting, at least in Shreveport.

I tamped down the anger that threatened to boil over. "Adrian, you're probably right, but I have to try to get Eugenie out of there. I'll move fast, and my elven magic will work in Faery if there's trouble."

I turned to the pirate, whose own anger approached my own. Speaking of other people's unwanted feelings, I needed to grab my mojo bag on the way out.

I appealed to his practical nature. "Jean, you need to be here if Rene somehow does make it back with Eugenie or if Rand shows up, with or without Christof. The people here need you."

I appealed to his pride. "You're the only one who can protect Maison Rouge if Florian sends his people here looking for his brother."

I appealed to his ego. "And you're the only one I trust to protect Eugenie if they come back."

His aura reeked of indecision. "This is not a safe move for you, *Jolie*. Your enemies are watching the borders, and, pardon me for saying thus, but you have many enemies."

More and more by the hour. "I will be careful." Somehow.

I stopped by my room and grabbed the mojo bag, the small packet of herbs and magic-infused gemstones that tamped down my empathic abilities. Sliding it onto a long leather cord, I slipped it over my neck and tucked it inside my sweater. It nestled against Alex's anti-faery locket. Into my pocket went two or three pre-made potions from my bag, the only ones I had left. They wouldn't work in Faery, but they would be fine in Shreveport.

Tucking Charlie into a thigh holster Alex had made for me back when the Axeman of New Orleans was chasing me, I raced out the front door and down the beach a few yards to where I'd powered up a new transport after destroying the old one in the center of the island.

Jake and Collette reclined on the sand on either side of the transport. She still looked pale, but had no trouble jumping to her feet before I got halfway down the length of the banquette.

"Where d'you think you're going, sunshine?" Jake moved even faster than Collette, blocking my path to the transport.

"I'm going to get Eugenie out of Shreveport. Rand and Christof are having a preternatural pissing match in the grave-yard of Our Lady of Perpetual Help." I shoved past him and stepped into the transport. As I knelt to touch the elven staff and take off for the Winter Palace of Faery, I looked up to see Jean standing in the doorway, loading the semiautomatic Rene had brought him and that Jean had always refused to use. I wasn't sure if he was going to use it on me or insist on going with me.

"Jean, I really need you to stay here."

He walked to the transport and held the gun out to me, butt first. "*Oui,* but I insist you take this. It is quite simple to use. Perhaps your bullet will find its target better than your fire."

I thought it more likely I'd shoot my own ass off before ac-tually hitting an intended target, but I took the gun, made sure the safety was on as Alex had taught me, and stuck it in the back waistband of my jeans so that I could literally shoot myself in the ass should the opportunity arise.

Jean placed a hand on my neck and pulled me gently toward

him, giving me a kiss that was both bittersweet and filled with promise. "Courage, *Jolie*. I shall wait for you."

"I'm counting on it." I smiled at him as I fired up the transport, and as I squeezed through space and time on my way to God only knew what, I heard him ask Jake, "Why is she counting?"

I'd sure miss that pirate if I died today.

I stayed in a crouch during the transport, which intensified the feeling of being squeezed through a toothpaste tube but made me a smaller target should anyone decide to kill anything arriving at the Winter Palace.

Or what was left of it. The round floor of ice where Jean and I had transported earlier remained, although large cracks crossed it in jagged, twisted lines. The part of the round wall where the doorway had appeared was no more than piles of shattered ice that looked slick, as if it had melted and refrozen. The magical warmth of the area held, however, so at least I didn't have to worry about hibernating.

Beyond the demolished wall, impaled on a thick stalagmite that rose from the floor, was Tamara's head; her body lay a few feet away. Acid rose in the back of my throat, and I was glad I had skipped lunch. Her long amber hair fell in crimson-covered, bedraggled waves. More blood ran down the melting stalagmite, staining it a jolting, festive color of magenta.

Lying near her headless body was one with its head still intact. The man's face wasn't visible but I'd know that grungy LSU sweatshirt anywhere. Rene.

Heart pounding, I stayed in a crouch and forced myself to look in all directions before crawling my way toward a guy who, against all odds, had become one of my best friends. Somebody was going to pay for this. Somebody named Florian.

I let out a breath when I got close enough to see that he was still alive. An outcropping of ice that had probably formed part of another wall sat a few feet to his left, so I crawled to him as quickly as I could on the slippery surface and dragged him to the small hidden space behind it.

This part of the palace ruins were a lot colder than the transport room, and my breath billowed out in front of my face like a cloud. I couldn't stay here long. Rene's face was white and pale but his breathing was steady, so I pulled out the potions vials from my pocket and studied them. I kept a random supply in my portable kit and had no idea what I'd had left. I hoped if I combined them with a shot of elven magic, they'd work.

A freezing potion would be a fine joke—for Rand. I stuck that one back in my pocket. A confusion charm wouldn't work; things were confusing enough already. The aroma charm had the most potential. It was great to use in controlling gremlin outbreaks, not that there had been many. They were so fond of alcohol that an aromatic that smelled like rum could lure them off a cliff like lemmings.

The only thing Rene liked more than sex—well, as much as sex; well, almost as much as sex—was food. Thanks to our power-share a few months ago, I knew he was a sucker for andouille, a smoked sausage of which I was pretty fond myself. So it was simple enough to tip the edge of the staff into the small jar, infuse some nice elven magic, and imagine a heaping plate of andouille just out of the smoker. Within seconds, the ruins of the Winter Palace smelled like Jacob's Smokehouse in LaPlace, Louisiana, the andouille world capital.

Despite the knowledge that poor Tamara's head was piked a few feet away on the other side of the ice pile, my stomach rumbled.

"Rene, wake up." My voice sounded so loud in the quiet, icy surroundings I might as well have used a bullhorn. I held the vial close to his nose. "Hungry? Rene, I have sausage."

"Go away, babe," he mumbled. A few seconds later, his eyes flew open, a beautiful dark liquid brown that almost looked black. "I smell andouille."

He sat up and looked around. "And where's the iceberg with the dead chick's head on it?"

Thank God, he'd survived with both his bluntness and lack of tact. "On the other side of this pile of ice. It's Christof's sister. What happened to you?"

"His sister? Oh man." Rene rubbed his eyes. "I got no clue what happened. I followed Christof and Eugenie here, about five minutes behind them. Soon as I landed in that round ice room, somebody shot me." He pulled out the bottom of his sweatshirt and stuck his finger through a jagged hole. There was blood around it, although it was hard to see since the sweatshirt was a dark brown.

"Why hasn't it healed?" I edged the bottom of his sweatshirt up farther and saw where the bullet had gone in, near his rib cage. There was an open, oozing spot in the shape of a bullet hole. "Did your body pop out the bullet?"

"Yeah, but something ain't right, babe. I've got a nasty head-ache and the room's spinning."

"We need to get out of here." I helped him to his feet. Rene was solid and muscular, but with me in boots, he wasn't that much taller. I pulled his left arm around my shoulders, and we walked slowly back toward the transport under the open, sight-less eyes of Tamara.

"I feel like we should do something for her," I said, pausing as Rene stopped to catch his breath. He'd gone from icy pale to kind of green, and I wondered if the bullet was tainted in some way. Shifters like Rene, as opposed to were-animals, were not poisoned by silver, so a silver bullet wouldn't do this. But God only knew what faeries had in their arsenals.

"Ain't nothing we can do to help her now. Let's get out of here."

I settled him into the transport. "I'm sending you back to Jean's house in Old Barataria. Then I'm going to Shreveport to get Eugenie, assuming this transport's still set up for it."

"No, DJ, that's too dangerous. I'll go with you." Rene tried to stand up, but couldn't. He sat back down with an *oof,* then rolled onto his side. "Shit, what did those faery freaks do to me?"

"I don't know, but if you don't improve soon, better go and talk to your people's doctor." I assumed mermen had doctors. Before he could argue, I touched Charlie to the edge of the transport and sent him to Maison Rouge.

Once Rene was gone, I checked around me again to be sure there weren't faeries skulking around, and then went back to where Rene had been shot. After shoving some ice chips and chunks around with the toe of my boot, I finally saw the bullet, a misshapen lump of metal that had a bronze cast to it. Not a normal spent bullet, or at least not one like I'd seen before. Being with Alex meant I'd seen my share of bullets.

I stuffed this one in my pocket. I'd show it to Alex later, assuming I got back from Shreveport in one piece. And assuming I'd found Eugenie and gotten her back safely. And assuming I could even find Alex.

Those were a hell of a lot of assumptions.

CHAPTER 14

I had no clue where the faery transport into Shreveport had been drawn, but I landed in a clearing, the transport symbols etched in some kind of white powder into a thickly matted bed of pine straw. Around me, spindly but closely spaced trees formed a dense barrier, and I stayed in a kneeling position until I got a clear view around me and saw no one.

"Hey!" A loud click drew my attention to the right, where a burly guy with a shotgun stepped from behind the tree line. Not as tall as Alex, but at least six feet and built like a big shaven-headed linebacker. His buzzy energy was more like Jake's than Alex's or Rene's, so he was a were-something. Hired security, then. Probably werewolf; they were the most common.

I let out a girly squeal. "Oh my God, you scared me!" *Girly* fit the winter-white jeans and pastel pink sweater I wore with my glitter-covered white boots. All of which, at some point, Rene was going to get an earful about.

Then I crumpled into a heap on the ground and lay still. I'd never pretended to faint before, but how hard could it be? I'd had the forethought to stick my hand in my pocket as I fell, so I got the top off one of the two remaining potions vials. Now that I was back in the modern world, they'd work just fine.

"Hey, get up. Uh, lady?" Wolfie's heavy boots came into view but weren't yet close enough. He stopped, probably trying to decide what to do. I willed myself to look as small and helpless as possible, which sadly wasn't hard. "Damn. You're the sentinel, aren't you? Nobody thought you'd really be stupid enough to show up. Wait'll they see what I caught. I can't believe you fainted. Ain't so tough now, are you, sweetcheeks?"

What an oaf. I'd sweeten his cheeks.

He moved closer, squatted in front of me, and pulled his cell phone from his pocket. I didn't want him announcing his catch to anyone nearby, so while his gaze was on his phone, I slid the vial from my pocket and flung the contents in his face.

Ah, the freezing charm. One of my favorite old standbys. Wolfie turned into a big old werewolf statue, brown eyes wide and surprised, mouth hanging open, phone still clutched in his fingers. I plucked the phone from his hand to make sure he hadn't made a call, then decided to keep it. It might come in handy since mine was dead and I wasn't supposed to be here anyway.

"Don't worry, sweetcheeks." I considered trying to move him somewhere to camouflage him, but decided it would take too long. If I could find Eugenie and get back to the transport, we'd just roll him out of the way. "You'll thaw out in about four hours." Maybe five. It had been a full vial.

He couldn't move his vocal cords, so his only response was a barely audible snort of air through his open mouth.

"What was that? You're sorry for scaring poor little old me? No problem. Gotta run now, honeybun. Bye."

I left him snorting fiercely (but quietly) and headed in the direction from which he'd appeared since that seemed the most likely spot for the church. Sure enough, once I reached the far side of the tree line, I had a clear view of the cemetery, where Christof and Rand still stood, still shouting at each other. I glanced at my watch. It seemed like hours since I'd left Maison Rouge, but less than fifteen minutes had passed. Damn, I was efficient.

Good thing; the situation was deteriorating fast. The priest was still trying to make peace between Rand and Christof, but the sky above them had turned gray and roiling. Rand chanted in his gutteral elven language and glowed; Christof wiggled his fingers toward the sky and muttered in his more lyrical tongue.

I remembered why I'd been so attracted to Jake Warin when we first met, before he'd been turned loup-garou and he'd been the nice human cousin of the insufferable Alex Warin. Jake had been so damn normal. Unlike the faery prince and the elven clan chief facing off about twenty yards in front of me.

Was that snow or rain? Or both? White flakes fell from the sky, melting into raindrops hot enough to sizzle when they hit the ground. Both the elf and faery were working hard, their faces tense and hard, eyes locked on each other.

The weather war continued. Snow drifted down for a few seconds, then turned to blistering hard rain, then just as suddenly back to snow. After a minute of this, the poor bereaved widower, the other mourners who'd followed them outside, and the priest made a hasty retreat to the church. Eugenie remained rooted to her spot behind Christof. Good. That would make my work easier.

I looked around the area to find the two Blue Congress wizards, who'd finished their cigarettes and were sitting on a couple of grave markers, playing cards. Idiots.

Seeing no other werewolves, I skirted the edge of the clearing until I could make a run for the side of the church. From this vantage point, I was facing Eugenie and Christof, and Rand's back was to me. Perfect.

I waved to get Christof's attention. His only reaction at spotting me was a quick couple of blinks, followed by a slow smile directed at Rand.

Dru?

Holy crap. Rand was picking up mental static from me. We didn't dare have a mental chat; my response would come in too clearly and he'd know I was here. I began slamming up every mental weapon in my arsenal. He'd get no more vibes from me, at least not until I could get Eugenie out of Shreveport.

She hadn't spotted me yet, which was a good thing. Her acting skills were worse than mine. She wouldn't even be able to feign a fainting spell for a less-than-genius werewolf.

Christof raised his voice. "Let us leave, Randolph, or I'll put you in the ground."

Kind of melodramatic, but effective. Rand glowed brighter than ever, and the grass near Christof's feet burst into low flames. Damn. I'd always wondered what would happen if Rand glowed and chanted long enough. Fire elf. Duh.

I expected Christof to start a snowstorm above Rand's head. What I didn't expect was for the prince to lower his head and charge Rand like a raging bull, head-butting him in the midsection. They hit the ground, and I saw my chance at the same time Eugenie spotted me.

I motioned her toward the woods where the transport lay. To hell with the Blue Congress wizards. We were going to make a run for it while Christof kept Rand too busy to notice.

She set off for the woods, and I met her halfway. "My family thinks I'm crazy!" she wailed, loud enough to draw the attention of the tall, skinny Blue Congress wizard with the rooster haircut.

"Hey, stop!"

Holy crap. I whipped out the elven staff, paused long enough to aim Charlie just to the right of the wizards. They already had their hands up and were doing some of their nifty Blue Congress magic when I released my fire and blew up the tombstone next to them, sending a rain of marble and playing cards onto their heads. Around us, evidence of their magic appeared as tombstones began moving to block our escape route.

I grabbed Eugenie's arm and pulled her around a marble stag the size of a small SUV that had lowered its head and pawed the ground as if to charge. Blue Congress magic was so damned cool—create and re-create.

"Stop, DJ!" Eugenie grabbed my arm as I tried to race past her. "A sinkhole!"

I looked stupidly at the ground in front of us, which had opened a gulf big enough to drive a Greyhound bus into. "Go around and run fast," I shouted, sending another shot of the staff toward the Blue Congress wizards and blowing up a ginormous marble eagle perched atop a nearby tomb.

We didn't stop to see if the stag was chasing us, but ran for all we were worth. At the edge of the tree line, I hazarded a look back at Christof and Rand. The faery stood watching us; the elf had crumpled on the ground. Not dead, though, because in my head, far behind my protective barriers, I heard him yelling my name.

Christof grinned and motioned for us to move along. He didn't have to motion twice, because the wizards were chasing us, still chanting and doing their finger dance. The stag was getting way too close.

I raised the staff and blew a hole in the earth in front of the advancing stag, forcing him to change direction. Luck was on our side for a change—the stag began charging toward the wizards instead, who had to stop pursuing us in order to protect themselves from being trampled beneath marble hooves.

"Let's run to the transport before those idiot wizards can get out from under the stag." I grabbed Eugenie's hand and we ran to the clearing. "Help me roll this frozen werewolf out of the way."

To her credit, she didn't ask a single question. We tipped the werewolf onto his side and rolled him outside the interlocking circle and triangle, leaving him at an awkward angle with his feet in the air. Oh well.

I touched the staff to the edge of the transport and said, "Winter Palace, Faery" just before the Blue Congress wizards reached the edge of the clearing. I waved at them as the transport sucked the air out of my lungs. They were too late.

Of course, they could follow us to Faery, but I didn't think their magic would work there. Adrian's didn't seem to work anywhere in the Beyond.

As soon as we materialized on the round floor of ice in the Winter Palace, Eugenie screamed. I figured she was getting her first look at the grisly remains of Tamara until a blinding light knocked me off my feet and a big crack appeared in the ice between us.

"Where is my brother?"

I whirled around to see Florian sitting on a block of ice behind us bundled in a heavy coat, a blanket spread beneath him, no doubt to protect his royal assets from getting cold and wet.

"He's in Shreveport, Louisiana, at Our Lady of Perpetual Help church, having a fistfight with an elf," I said, pretty confident that of all the things he might expect me to say, that wasn't it. "I'm sure he'll be along at any minute." Especially since the elf appeared to be incapacitated at the moment.

"Then we'll all just wait for him, yes?" Florian squinted at me. "You still reek of dog. I thought you might have taken care of that little problem. Maybe it's permanent."

"Could be." Eugenie and I still held hands, and I pulled her back into the center of the transport. So far, Florian hadn't attempted to force us out of it. Bending down and touching Charlie to the symbols would be too obvious, but not if I fainted again. "When I scream, drop to the floor," I whispered to Eugenie.

"No talking, witch." Florian grinned. I'm sure he knew the worst thing one could call a wizard was *witch*; they were wannabe mages and nothing more.

"I was just asking Eugenie where your sister was. Tamara. Nice woman. I met her when I was here with Jean Lafitte."

"Your paramour, right." Florian laughed. "I came so close to getting you with that last lightning bolt. Oh—look! Tamara's here. She's right behind you."

I caught Eugenie's gaze and nodded slightly, then turned toward the gruesome sight. The head had tilted at a precarious angle as the stalagmite upon which it had been impaled melted. Soon, it would fall off and roll away.

A deep, burning anger set my gut on fire. Florian had done this to his own sister, with no visible remorse. He should be set upon by a whole pack of dogs, perhaps rottweilers, and I'd like to be the one who sent them his way.

Screaming at the awful sight of Tamara didn't take a huge stretch of imagination, so I screeched a good one and crumpled to the ground near the edge of the transport, Charlie in my hand. Eugenie hit the ice before I did, so I immediately whispered "Maison Rouge" and sent a jolt of energy from the staff to the transport.

Florian screamed in rage, thunder boomed overhead, and lightning again cracked too close for safety, but he was too late.

The transport had already begun, and we landed with a splash in a foot of warm salty water and the sight of two loups-garou with guns drawn.

Thank God. The adrenaline drained from my muscles and I crawled out of the surf and flopped on the sand like a rag doll. Faux-fainting used up a lot of energy.

"You guys okay? We didn't realize the transport would go underwater at high tide."

Collette helped Eugenie up, and I opened my eyes to look at an upside-down Jake, leaning over to look at me. "Did you faint, sunshine?"

"Twice." I moaned and managed to sit up, not turning down the hand he held down to help me to my feet. I could sleep for a month.

"Eugenie, are you okay?" I thought, on the whole, she looked better than me.

"Yeah, I'm just done. You can tell Rand . . ." She stared at the ground, then shrugged. "You can tell him whatever you want to. I don't care."

"Eugenie, why don't we let him come here and see you tomorrow like we'd planned. We'll make sure you're not alone with him, and it might settle him down." Rand had a right to see her, and to make sure his child was safe. Besides, I needed to find out if the elves were forming an alliance with Florian or if some faery had sold his or her services in order to set me up.

Eugenie sighed, too tired to argue. "Fine. Tomorrow afternoon, though, not evening. I'm having dinner with Chris."

Chris?

Oh. Holy. Mother. of. Prompt. Succor. "Chris? As in short for Christof ?"

She smiled, a coy look that told me nothing good was afoot. "Of course. Such a nice man."

My friend turned and walked into the house. I couldn't speak. Christof was not a nice man. He was a very powerful prince of Faery currently locked in a power struggle with his homicidal, sociopathic brother. He was Trouble. He was Dangerous. He was Unpredictable. He was not a Nice Man.

"Well, ain't that sweet." Jake shook his head. "In the meantime, we got another problem."

"Fabulous." I glared at him. "What now? Did Rene make it back okay?"

"That's the problem. Come on." Jake kissed Collette and left her beaming at him before resuming her seat on the beach near the transport. *Jake* was a nice man. Unfortunately, he had some anger-management issues and was spoken for.

"Rene's really sick, and we don't know what's wrong." Jake and I walked into the house and up the stairway. He knocked on a door down an upstairs hallway, and led me into a dimly lit room. Rene had his shirt off, and a sheen of sweat coated his upper body, which was covered with skillfully done tattoos—a painful, exacting process for a shifter. His face was as pale as a fish belly. All traces of the gunshot wound had disappeared, but he was either unconscious or sleeping deeply. Why hadn't he shifted?

"*Jolie,* now I will rest more easily, knowing you to be safe." Jean pulled me into a tight hug, and I hugged him back. It felt good to know someone was genuinely glad to see me, to be greeted not with lectures or censure, but affection and relief. His hand rubbed my back in a comforting way . . . then slid a bit too far south.

I pushed him away and glared up at his smirk. Thank God. Jean Lafitte and I had almost shared A Moment. At least one of us had the good sense to ruin it.

I wondered what kind of reception I'd get from Alex.

"Tell me about Rene," I said. "His gunshot wound is

healed"—I pointed at the spot where it had been—"but he was already getting dizzy and sick when he transported."

I filled them in on the situation at the Winter Palace, dug the spent bullet out of my pocket, and handed it to Jean. "That's what he was shot with. It's a weird color."

Jean turned it around in his palm, but shook his head. "This is unknown to me. Jacob?"

Jake held it under the light to get a better look, then sniffed it. "Has a funny smell and the color's off—you're right about that. I don't have a clue. There's one person who could tell you, though."

I nodded, took a deep breath, and headed back into the hallway. "I've got to find Alex."

CHAPTER 15

I couldn't exactly pop over the New Orleans border into the arms of a wizard enforcer or a shifter security guard. This trip needed some advance prep work.

After checking on Eugenie, who defiantly refused to talk about either "Chris" or Rand but claimed to have a raging case of morning sickness (or in this case, late afternoon sickness), I returned to my room. I'd transformed one corner into a makeshift work area for potions and charms.

My supplies were limited and I had no electricity, so I was thankful I'd stuck one of Gerry's black grimoires into my messenger bag the night I fled New Orleans. Laughing, I'd thrown it in as a joke because I knew I'd get screwed that night at the Interspecies Council meeting. I hadn't anticipated how badly I'd be screwed, though. Even my well-honed paranoia hadn't prepared me for the notion that I could end up running for my life before my own Elders could lock me up in Greenland.

Did Zrakovi realize that sending me to the wizard hospital-slash-prison in Ittoqqortoormiit was a passive-aggressive death sentence? The first time I "accidentally" got locked outside, my cold-sensitive elven genes would kick in, and I wouldn't survive an hour.

Zrakovi had proven willfully ignorant of either my elven abilities or the price I paid for them, however. I was willing to give him the benefit of the doubt and believe he wanted to lock me away, not kill me. Maybe Alex had explained that by now, assuming Zrakovi would listen.

At any rate, I had made it into my pirate hideaway with the illegal book of spells. Gerry had several grimoires that I'd found in his flooded-out house after Hurricane Katrina, warded with so much black magic that even my house burning down around them didn't leave a smudge.

I doubted that he'd done more than collect the books. Until his final days, my father had tried to be the loud, squeaky wheel working inside a system in which he didn't believe. All it had done was earn him the reputation as a rogue wizard and a job in the insignificant outpost of New Orleans. Only now that outpost wasn't insignificant at all, and if he'd never been sent here, I'd never have been born. I guess in some ways he'd had the last laugh; he just didn't survive to enjoy it.

And the real St. Simon family rogue, the one operating outside the system, was turning out to be me.

I smiled and fingered the shabby, worn cover of the little black book, about the size of one of those spindly paperback romances I used to find in my grandmother's nightstand drawer when I was plundering. How Gerry would have thrived in the chaos of today's prete world. He'd be right in there with Jean Lafitte, plotting and scheming.

Instead, there was me. I didn't want to plot and scheme. I didn't want to be a key player in a band of misfits led by an undead pirate who excelled at plotting and scheming. Yet here I was.

This bout of nostalgia bordered on self-pity, and it was getting me nowhere. I wanted to see Alex almost as much as I didn't want to see him. I wanted to feel his arms around me, to hear how he missed me, to smell the warmth of him, to savor the sweet clean taste of his skin, to remind myself what it felt to really be alive in the present.

But.

I didn't want to hear how I'd risked too much to cross the border, or how impulsive I was, or how much my unintentional alliance with Christof was going to cost me, or how I should just let Rand take Eugenie to Elfheim against her will, which might make a lot of this trouble go away.

Which of those scenarios was more likely to happen? Total crapshoot.

Opening the book, I flipped through the pages, looking for something that would help me slip into New Orleans with a minimum of risk, that didn't take long to make, and that only called for a few simple ingredients. Which left exactly one viable potion.

The mixture was brilliantly uncomplicated, as long as elven magic would power it. If it succeeded, I'd have a window of time—the book was a little vague on how big a window—when my aura would be masked. If the wizards were on alert for my unique magical energy signature to enter one of the New Orleans transports, it should fool them.

The mixture of common herbs and extracts dissolved into the cup of the holy water with a noxious stench, and my stomach flip-flopped at the thought of drinking it. Maybe it tasted better than it smelled, or maybe the infusion of magic would improve its palatability.

No such luck. After zapping the mixture with a bit of energy from Charlie, I drank it and then hung my head over the side of the big metal "bathing tub" in the corner of my bedroom for what seemed like an hour, swallowing continuously until I thought I could move without heaving. The only thing that kept it down was the knowledge that if I threw it up, I'd have to drink more.

After changing into some clean jeans—blue, this time—I brushed my teeth in the hopes of eliminating the taste of skunk-tainted road tar, and stopped by Jean's study for a shot of bourbon to take care of what the toothpaste had missed. He lounged in his tufted throne of an armchair, smoking his pipe and reading.

"Catching up on your Eudora Welty?" I poured a finger of Four Roses into a glass, pondered the bottle of soda, and decided I should drink it straight. It might help me forget the baby-pink sweater I'd decided to keep on.

"*Non,* I fear Madame Welty's stories are not to my liking." He held up a copy of *Moby Dick* that was almost as dog-eared as Gerry's black grimoire. "Rene suggested this book, although I find it quite disturbing. Monsieur Ahab was quite full of himself."

Uh-huh. Jean should identify with Monsieur Ahab, and Rene had been a busy thief on his last trip to the city. The book had a New Orleans Public Library stamp on it.

"How's Rene doing?" I needed to get a move on. If the elves were using special ammunition, Alex needed to know about it and tell me what we could do to help Rene recover. I might not be sure whether Christof was a reliable ally, but I had no doubts whatsoever about my merman. I wouldn't lose him.

"Rene is much the same. Do you believe Monsieur Warin will know how to assist him?"

Now that Jean needed something from Alex, he was *Monsieur Warin* and not *Monsieur Chien.* "I hope so. I'm leaving in a few minutes, as soon as I use the scrying bowl again and find out where he is."

Jean followed me to where my scrying gear remained set up

on the upper banquette of Maison Rouge. In a few moments, I'd cleared away the items that allowed me to scry Eugenie and replaced them with the locket Alex had given me, the note and envelope he'd sent with the locket, and a photo of him I kept tucked in the zippered compartment of my messenger bag. So sue me; I'm sentimental, plus in the photo he wore a rare smile that showed off that almost-but-not-quite-a-dimple crease to the left of his mouth. Sexy, that one.

Pouring out the first batch of holy water, I took more of the supply Rene had stolen and refilled the bowl. I had enough left over for one more scrying session. Maybe I could rob St. Louis Cathedral while I skulked around New Orleans tonight.

I took a few deep breaths to clear my mind and focused on my significant something-or-other. *Boyfriend* seemed too adolescent; *lover* too shallow; *friend* too coy. Part of the time we were all of the above. Other times, we only accomplished one of the three. The *lover* part was rarely a problem. I thought Alex was sex on a stick and while I didn't quite know what he thought of me, he'd never kicked me out of bed.

My head full of lust and longing, I stuck Charlie into the water and waited for an image to appear. I hoped it would tell me where Alex was.

Jean's arm brushed my shoulder as he moved in for a look. "Monsieur Warin looks quite happy, does he not, *Jolie*?" He barely kept the chuckle out of his own voice.

"Doesn't he, though." Alex was somewhere public—a restaurant, from the looks of it—and he was smiling. No, not smiling. The dog was laughing. How dare he have dinner at a restaurant, with real electricity and a modern kitchen, and laugh? I'd endured lightning strikes, crazed faeries, boot-wearing bears, arrogant elves (redundant), and a drink of skunk-tainted road tar mixed with holy water. How dare Alex enjoy himself?

"Might you be able to discern his whereabouts?"

Jean seemed way too fascinated with scrying and I had a feeling that sooner rather than later, he'd concoct some way to exploit it.

"Let me move the perspective around a bit." I wanted to know who was so damn funny, since he was laughing again. I changed Charlie's position in the water and the view shifted. "Wait, I recognize that swamp mural with Christmas lights running through it—he's at Jacques-Imo's."

Not only was he laughing, he was doing it at my favorite restaurant.

I shifted Charlie again, anxious to see who was making him laugh. So help me, if it was Elder Willem Zrakovi, Alex was going to be one sorry dog.

Not Zrakovi. Not by a long shot.

"What a lovely young woman Monsieur Warin dines with, *Jolie*." Jean's pleasure at the sight of Alex with another woman seeped out of his aura and battled with my own displeasure. My annoyance won.

"She's scrawny and pale." And young, tall, brunette, and pretty.

"I am certain Monsieur Warin is only feigning amusement to make her feel worthy or to use her in some manner," Jean said, slipping an arm around my shoulder.

The pirate was skating on thin skin. "Of course he is."

"After all, a man grows lonely when he must work at his relationship with a woman and then she is absent."

I regretted ever teaching him the word *relationship* and admitting that Alex and I had to work at ours. If we still had one.

"I'm out of here." I pulled Charlie out of the scrying bowl, ending Jean's peep show, and headed up the banquette toward the front door. "I'll use the small transport at Audubon Park;

it's closer to where he is than the one in the French Quarter."
He'd be at the restaurant awhile; it looked like they were still
on appetizers, thanks to my in-depth knowledge of the Jacques-
Imo's menu.

Jean caught up with me when I stopped to grab my bag and
tuck Charlie back into the thigh holster, just in case I needed to
shoot a stray Elder. Or Alex.

I pulled my hair into a ponytail, picked up Rene's LSU baseball cap, and wedged as much hair as I could into it, pulling the
bill low over my forehead. It wouldn't win me any awards at a
Mardi Gras costume ball and its purple and gold colors clashed
horribly with my outfit from baby-pastel hell, but it would have
to do.

"Do you still have the pistol?" Jean asked as we climbed the
stairs.

I tripped on the step, too embarrassed to admit that I'd run
all over Faery and Shreveport with a gun in my pants and had
totally forgotten about it. Some badass I was. I'd found it when
I changed clothes and tucked it in my waistband. "Got it."

It's just as well I'd forgotten about it. Shooting a werewolf
security guard, or Rand, or Christof, or even Christof's batshit-
crazy brother would only have reinforced my status as a fugitive
from justice.

"Use it only if you must in order to return safely to Barataria,
Drusilla." Jean followed me back through the entry hall, out the
front door, and down the banquette toward the transport. "The
fewer wizards you encounter, the more easily things will go for
you."

"You think?" We reached the transport, and Jean motioned
for Collette to leave us alone. Oh, goody. We were going to have
another Moment.

"Be safe." He leaned down and brushed a kiss across my

cheek, knocking Rene's cap askew. "I would accompany you but I do not wish to raise the ire of *Monsieur Chien* by my presence."

He knew it always made me laugh when he called Alex *Mr. Dog,* and it worked. "You aren't going to try and stop me from going?"

"Ah, *Jolie.*" Jean smiled. "There are many who underestimate your abilities, but not Jean Lafitte. Much woe to the man who ever truly forces you to abandon your caution."

"Thank you. Being underestimated gets old." Speaking of Alex, it was time for me to leave. I had a sick merman to diagnose and a laughing six-foot three-inch hound who had some explaining to do.

CHAPTER 16

I spotted the werewolf guard as soon as I landed in the Audubon Park transport, which had been carved into the soil beneath a mammoth live oak tree. During Jean's human days and even a century before then, men had fought duels here to settle their disputes. Too bad Zrakovi, Rand, and Christof couldn't just count off twenty paces and fire. It would save us all a lot of angst and create orgasmic excitement among the world's meteorologists.

Six months ago, I'd been convinced the wizards were the proper ones to head the Interspecies Council and control the borders. Now, not so much, although I wasn't sure the alternatives were any better.

The guard was short, bearded, and burly; he also held one of the old-fashioned trackers that could identify when any type of nonhuman was in the vicinity. If I were lucky, he had the tracker calibrated to buzz only when it sensed my unique magical signature.

If I were lucky, the black potion would work, and my aura would be camouflaged.

Of course if I were all that lucky, I wouldn't need to sneak into my own hometown to discuss illegal weapons and strange women with my own significant shifter.

The guard had his attention focused on his phone when I arrived, so I stepped quickly outside the transport. By the time he looked up, frowned, and studied his tracker, I was walking away from him, toward St. Charles Avenue and the streetcar named *Desire-to-Get-DJ-the-Hell-Away-from-Here*. It took every bit of nerve I could muster to walk at a leisurely pace with my back to him. I figured running while looking over my shoulder might arouse suspicions.

My right fingers twitched near Charlie, ready to go on the defensive if he approached from behind. I'd left my mojo bag at home, all the better to detect prete energy with my own built-in tracker. His werewolf buzz had already begun to fade, however, so I knew he wasn't following me. Thank God all the security people I'd encountered in the last twenty-four hours had been idiots.

I crossed St. Charles, waited a few moments at the streetcar stop, and then realized I didn't have the dollar-fifty for the fare. Pathetic. By the time I made it a block toward the big bend in the Mississippi River, my muscles had relaxed their death grip on my vital organs. Walking would be therapeutic. Another block and I cut through the Uptown neighborhoods toward Oak Street and Jacques-Imo's, feeling free for the first time in a couple of weeks and enjoying even the waning daylight. I hadn't realized how tense and claustrophobic I'd felt stuck in the dark of Old Barataria, thankful though I was to have a refuge.

With the Winter Prince of Faery's focus off New Orleans, the nightmarish winter we'd suffered through most of December had eased into typical NOLA Christmas weather. The cold, heavy wind blew Rene's hat off twice, and I had to chase it down the sidewalks, which were broken and uneven from the spreading roots of the live oaks.

Twenty minutes later, I reached the restaurant with a fine sheen of chilly sweat covering most of my body. Anyone who thought hot weather was a necessary ingredient for sweaty conditions had never spent a winter in New Orleans.

In front of the door to Jacques-Imo's sat the signature wreck of a pickup truck with the logo on both doors and a long green alligator stretching along the sides. In the bed of the pickup, a couple sat at a table for two, shivering in the cold wind while slurping down oysters.

I wasn't sure what the building had been in its previous lives, but like the rest of the structures on this stretch of Oak Street, it was a two-story Victorian-era New Orleans cottage. The front was narrow, but I knew from previous visits that it stretched back a deep city block, making the restaurant much larger than it looked from the sidewalk.

It might be a Tuesday night at only six p.m., but bodies packed the long tunnel of the bar. Along the left side, a scuffed wooden pew sagged under the weight of chattering patrons crammed shoulder to shoulder, waiting for their tables. Along the right side, bartenders hustled, slinging drinks and banter despite the deafening cacophony of voices.

This was not a place for quiet conversation unless, of course, one could communicate telepathically. I could have a nice dinner and conversation here with Rand without the outside noise interfering. Well, except that it was Rand.

To talk to Alex, I'd have to get him outside.

A line of people stood in the middle of the room, waiting to be added to the list by the hostess, who stood guardian over the door in the back that led to the rest of the restaurant.

I finally made it to the head of the line, hoping I didn't look as penniless as I felt and wondering if Alex would offer to feed me. "I'm joining some friends," I shouted to the red-haired young woman at the desk. With her short hair and big green eyes, she looked so much like a happy, normal Eugenie that it sent a wave of sadness through me—and a renewed determination that my friend was coming out the other side of this current hot mess not only with her baby, but with her spirit intact.

The hostess leaned toward me. "What's the name?"

Good question. I had no idea who Alex was with. "Warin?"

She scanned her sheet and nodded. "They're in the swamp room, all the way back."

I gave her an OK sign and climbed the stairs into the kitchen, where cooks shouted and sweated and concocted some of the best dishes in a town full of great dishes. They joked and waved at the patrons, all of whom had to pass through the kitchen to reach the dining rooms. My stomach rumbled at the savory aromas of crab and steak and gator sausage, but hunger had to wait.

The dining rooms were almost as crowded as the bar, the wait staff performing acrobatic pirouettes between closely placed tables and diners while balancing heavy trays aloft.

Combine my lack of mojo bag with the noise, the crowds, and the kaleidoscope of color on the walls—covered in courtyard and swamp murals, brightly colored lights, and jumbles of primitive artwork—and my senses hummed with an almost physical burn.

I couldn't stay in here long. Most of the vibes I pulled off the diners were happy and alcohol-enhanced, but my head had already begun to pound.

I walked all the way through the restaurant and out the back door into the courtyard—a generous term for a patch of grass and square of concrete barely big enough for two small tables, currently empty because the temperature was dropping a little too much for al fresco dining. The couple in the pickup truck had chosen novelty over comfort.

Where had Alex gone?

I turned back to study the dining room from the outer doorway, and spotted him in the corner, at an angle I'd missed from the other direction. He sat facing me, ever the trained killer, with his back to the wall so no one could sneak up on him. My heart sped up at the sight of him. A delayed reaction to my long walk, no doubt. I was much too sensible to have my heart jackrabbit at the mere sight of the most gorgeous man to ever come out of Picayune, Mississippi.

His dinner companion—I refused to call her a date—sat with her back to me, but she was a waver. Her long arms flew in dramatic arcs. I hated people who couldn't talk without gestures; it was like advertising a diminished vocabulary. Then again, I shouldn't judge. Of all the misjudged people in the world, I above all shouldn't judge. I vowed to do better.

Before I could duck back into the courtyard, Alex spotted me. He'd been smiling at his companion, and then the smile melted off his face as if it had been wax on a burning candle. Those dark chocolate-brown eyes that I dreamed of at night widened, then narrowed, then were drawn askew by one raised eyebrow. A two-day stubble and dark hair with just enough curl to make it look tousled, plus his usual man-in-black wardrobe, completed the picture of the perfectly beautiful enforcer. Who could be ill-tempered and snarky, or surprisingly sweet. Which Alexander Warin would I talk to tonight?

He leaned forward and said something to his friend but it couldn't have been much because he was out that back door and hustling me toward the corner of the courtyard faster than a speeding vampire.

"DJ, what the . . ." Emotions rolled off him in confused

waves, and I gave him a crooked smile. There was more love and happiness in his tangle of feeling than anger and worry and fear. I didn't care who was making him laugh over dinner; I was the one he loved.

"I just had to *mmph*—"

My words were cut short by his mouth landing on mine with enough force to push me against the rough wood siding of the building, our dark corner not visible from the dining room. We might have been apart only four days, but it had felt like four years, with no promise of when things might get better. If they ever did.

I missed him. I wanted him. I was tired and scared and totally at sea, and I poured all that into the heat and promise of a long, drawn-out kiss.

Then we just held each other. My fingers traced the contours of his back, firm and warm beneath his black sweater, trying to memorize every muscle and curve. He smelled like his favorite shower gel, masculine but sweet. He felt like home.

"You shouldn't have come; it's so dangerous." His words were soft, and had no anger behind them. "Is there an emergency?"

I pulled away and looked up at him, jolted back to reality. I dug in my pocket and pulled out the spent bullet that had shot Rene. "This look familiar?"

He sat at one of the empty tables and I took the chair next to his, watching as he held the lump of metal up to the dim light, sniffed it, then touched his tongue to it. He spat on the ground next to his chair. "It's coated in something . . ." He tasted again, and spat it out again. "Bitter orange, I think. Nasty stuff when it's this concentrated, especially for shifters. It can be fatal. Where'd you get it?"

"Rene was shot with it, in Faery."

Alex set the bullet on the table, and I could tell he was measuring his words by the way he stared at the table instead of at me. "Why was Rene in Faery? Were you with him? Do you—"

"Alex, before we get into that, tell me what we can do for Rene." There would always be time for him to ruin whatever time we had left by scolding me like a mother hen.

"My guess is he hasn't been able to shift?"

I shook my head. "He made it back to Barataria but has been unconscious since then."

Alex frowned and thrummed his fingers on the tabletop. "It's because he's aquatic, I bet. He can only shift in the water. So get him in the water, let him shift, and he should be able to shake it off. He has to shift; otherwise, it'll eventually kill him."

Holy crap. Deep in my soul, I'd prayed Rene's problem would be minor, that I could spend the night with Alex, reconnect with him not just physically but emotionally. But I couldn't. Rene had to come first. "I have to get back to him, then. I hope it isn't too late."

"Wait." Alex took my hands in his and leaned toward me, so close I could feel the heat from his shifter warmth radiating against my skin. "I want you to meet someone."

"The woman you're having dinner with?" I kept my voice pleasant and neutral. I was above jealousy. Mostly.

"Yes, you won't believe it. She's going to help us . . . What was that?"

Alex dropped my hands, stood, and turned toward the door. I hadn't heard anything earlier, but now the sound of loud voices came from the dining room. He looked back at me. "You sense anything?"

I edged around him and stayed against the wall, moving closer to the door. A shiver ran across my shoulder blades. "Red Congress magic, and shifters. Weres, I think."

"Shit. You've gotta get out of here. If I slow them down, can you make a transport out here?"

I looked around quickly. "A small one, yes."

"Do it." He stood between me and the door while I pulled a vial of sea salt from my messenger bag and drew a hasty interlocking circle and triangle.

I'd just taken Charlie out of the thigh holster when a crash sounded from inside and thick smoke billowed out the door. Something in the dining room had exploded, judging by the sounds and smoke. Frantic screams blended with the crash of breaking glass, chairs falling on hard flooring, and trampling feet.

I jumped into the transport but paused when a tall brunette tripped on her way out the door, coughing furiously. "I slowed them down, but it won't last long," she said between hacks, her accent British and upper-crust. "DJ must leave now."

"Who are you?" She was Alex's dinner companion, and she was close enough now for me to tell she was a wizard from her familiar energy buzz. But what wizard?

"DJ, zap me with the staff—just enough to knock me out," Alex said. "That way, they won't suspect me of helping you escape. It's okay to burn me a little."

"Okay. I guess." Made sense. I was already a fleeing criminal and Alex was my mole on the inside. I held out the staff, touching it to Alex's shoulder, but hesitated. I couldn't zap him, mole or not, and I didn't trust myself not to really hurt him. "I can't—"

"Oh, bloody hell. We don't have time for this. The flipping werewolves are on the march!" The brunette jerked Charlie out of my outstretched hand and, in one smooth motion, beaned Alex over the head with it. Hard. His face registered shock for about two seconds before he crumpled.

"What have you done? He could have a concussion." I snatched Charlie out of her hand, but was prevented from going to Alex when the woman shoved me back into the transport. "Get out of here, DJ. Now."

She was right. The scuffling sounds were near the door of the restaurant. I leaned over and touched Charlie to the transport, praying Alex had nothing but a minor lump on the head as well as a good cover story. "Who are you?" I asked, before mumbling, "Maison Rouge, Barataria."

Her voice came through faintly as I transported out. "I'm your cousin Audrey. Lovely to meet you!"

CHAPTER 17

An hour later, I supervised while Jake carried the still-unconscious Rene across Grand Terre Island like a five-foot-nine-inch sleeping Cajun toddler. The eternal full moon peeked through a scattered cloud cover, providing enough illumination for loup-garou vision but not for wizard vision. I had a flashlight, a useful little item Rene had purchased on his last shopping trip. I didn't even mind its casing of pink camo.

I pondered the mystery of my cousin Audrey, five years younger and probably fifteen annoying pounds lighter than me, although I'm sure my extra curves were all muscle. I guess I'd expected her to look more like me, not to be an Amazon with short, waifish dark hair, a porcelain complexion, and my father's blue-gray eyes. Well, technically, *her* father's blue-gray eyes.

Eye color was one of the few things Gerry and his brother Lennox St. Simon had shared. Gerry was a dreamer while Lennox was a straight arrow. Gerry had fought the system and lost. Lennox had recently become an Elder and already had his sights on the First Elder's seat.

I hadn't yet formed an opinion of my uncle, and although I liked the idea of a cousin, Audrey was another big question mark. Rumor had it she'd twice flunked the exam to be licensed to the Red Congress and Lennox had all but washed his hands of her, which begged the question: Why was she in New Orleans, where Lennox was now living and acting as the temporary sentinel?

When we first met a couple of weeks ago, my uncle had revealed that his only child was undisciplined and he thought I might set a good example for her. I'd probably destroyed that crazy notion.

The other burning questions: Whose side was she on, and why was she having dinner with Alex? I hadn't had time to ask him about setting up a meeting with Zrakovi, or about his supposed seat on the Interspecies Council. I'd only added to the questions. Sneaking in to see him again would be virtually impossible, however, even if the Elders believed I'd knocked him out with Charlie upside the head.

"How's Rene doing?" I asked Jake. Although the merman hadn't awakened and he'd grown feverish, his breathing remained strong and I was pretty sure he'd recover once we got him in the water. Or at least Alex seemed sure, and if anyone knew weapons and ammunition and shapeshifters, it was Alex Warin.

"About the same, but I still don't see why I couldn't just drop him in the ocean instead of hauling his scaly ass all over this damned island." Jake had been grumbling since I'd nagged him into carrying Rene instead of having some of Jean's undead pirate flunkies drag him on a makeshift travois. "He's a fish, DJ. He ain't gonna be that picky about his water source."

"Yes, but he's my fish, and I want him in a contained area of freshwater." I knew a few of Rene's secrets from having lived in his head when we'd done the ill-advised power-share that had helped us find a killer. Unfortunately, it hadn't been in time to save Rene's twin brother from becoming a victim. Big, open bodies of water freaked him out, which is the main reason he lived on the river in Plaquemines Parish rather than at his family's compound up in St. Bernard. Those wetlands stretched directly into the Gulf of Mexico.

Rene didn't share that quirk with anyone, and I didn't plan to either. We'd never even spoken of it to each other. Everyone had some embarrassing habit or trait or fear, and friends kept their friends' secrets.

As a result, I didn't want Rene shifting and trying to heal in the Beyond's version of the Gulf of Mexico, where he'd be stressed out and have trouble getting his bearings. I'd hounded Jake into hauling him to a small freshwater lake that Jean told me about. We finally found it near the centermost, highest point of the island. It stretched before us, a wide expanse of black glass with silvery moonlight glinting off its still surface.

A loud splash sounded from somewhere in the darkness. "You think there's anything in the water that will hurt him?"

Jake gave a rude, huffing snort. "I'm a loup-garou, DJ. We don't exactly go in for water sports."

He stepped to the edge of the lake and tossed the unconscious merman out over the water like a man-shaped beach ball. Rene landed with a splash, headfirst, about six feet offshore.

"What are you doing?" I tried to keep my voice calm, but I imagined Rene sinking to the bottom like a boulder. I'd thought we could settle him gently into the water at the edge of the lake and ease him into shifting. "He's going to drown before he can change."

I stepped up to the water's edge and stopped. What the hell was I thinking? I couldn't swim.

"Go in after him," I told Jake. *"Tout de suite."*

Hey, it worked for the pirate.

"Good Lord, woman, he's a water shifter. He grows gills. He isn't going to drown." Jake planted his feet and crossed his arms over his chest. I was still glaring at him when he jerked his head toward the water. "Look."

I turned and saw a moonlit version of Flipper nose his way out of the water. Rene's aquatic self could adapt to a saltwater dolphin or a river dolphin, depending on circumstance. Since river dolphins weren't known to inhabit Louisiana, he rarely let anyone see him fully shifted and did most of his swimming in the federally protected waters near the mouth of the Mississippi. But I'd seen him in his shifted form, and this was definitely Rene, letting us know he was okay.

He did a halfhearted splash over the surface—probably the best he could do after being poisoned—and disappeared.

Jake slung an arm around my shoulder and hugged me. "Feel better?"

"Definitely." So much better. I wasn't sure I could stand to lose Rene. The list of people I trusted completely was a short one and he was at the very top. I was ashamed to admit it, even to myself, but Rene was ahead of Alex. Worse, Jean Lafitte was slightly ahead of Alex in the trust department, too, but that was another of my own little secrets. Alex's blind faith in the Elders had hurt his position on my trust-o-meter, although his star was rising now that he'd helped me escape the Elders twice. Jake was pretty high on my trust list, too, as was Eugenie. Who knew? I might even begin to trust Adrian Hoffman one of these days. Or not.

Maybe I really was a Lafitian, although my inner jury remained undecided about Christof.

Jake and I started the walk back to the pirate mansion in companionable silence. Another admission: I was glad things hadn't worked for Jake and me romantically. We worked much better as friends.

"What did you think about your cousin? What was her name?"

"Audrey St. Simon. I'm not sure yet."

"Does she look like you?"

"Polar opposites. Take Audrey Hepburn in *Breakfast at Tiffany's,* give her a British accent and a miniskirt, and stretch her out so she's a foot taller."

Jake laughed. "Doesn't sound like you, sunshine."

Understatement. "You didn't know Gerry, but I can see him in her. Her eyes, and something about the shape of her face." That alone was enough to make me predisposed to like her. If she turned out to be another wizard toady, I would be disappointed.

"Why is she in New Orleans? Watch out for that hole." Jake grabbed my arm and pulled me off our path a moment before I'd have stepped in a deep sand pit and, with the way things had gone lately, would have broken my leg and had to be put down like a lame, unemployed mule. Which, sadly, didn't sound like such a bad fate.

"I don't know why she's here, except she saved Alex and me both tonight." We finally reached the flat stretch of narrow beach that gave us a straight shot to Maison Rouge. "I'm anxious to talk to her." Although how I'd manage that, I wasn't sure.

If she ever came here, I'd have to issue Cousin Audrey a few warnings about sexy pirates with wandering hands, said pirate's brother with a bad attitude, elven and vampire invasions, love-struck faeries, interspecies birth control, and other matters of survival.

Collette met us about forty yards from the house, and I became yesterday's news as Jake focused on his fiancée. Which was as it should be. I wished them a good night and walked up the banquette toward the lights. My scrying materials still sat at the foot of the steps, so I emptied the big bowl and placed it on the porch, gathered my locket and photo, and left the table for someone with preternatural strength to move it back to its spot beside the front door. There were several candidates, and I wasn't one of them.

I heard voices from the entry hall before I reached the door. From the top step, I had a clear view into the hallway. I wouldn't have to wait long for my chat with my cousin; she stood a few feet away, talking to Jean Lafitte.

I bit my lip to avoid laughing at his expression, which lay somewhere between perplexed, annoyed, and fascinated. Not fascinated like *I want to rip off your corset and ravish you,* but fascinated like *Whatever condition she has, I hope it isn't contagious.*

Audrey was a talker and, as I'd observed earlier, a waver. Her hand gestures were embellishing what sounded like an account of the events at Jacques-Imo's. Jean's gaze followed the wide arcs of her long arms as she demonstrated an explosion.

I wanted in on that conversation. "Wait. Start over; tell me what happened. Everything." I shrugged at Jean as he turned a raised brow in my direction.

"Is this really your *cousine, Jolie?* She is most . . . effusive."

I'd known the pirate long enough to recognize a veiled insult when I heard it, but let it pass. "Let's go in the study. I want to hear about Jacques-Imo's, and why Audrey is here. I hope nothing was too badly damaged."

In the past two weeks, I'd witnessed the destruction of the Orleans Parish Criminal District Court Building at Tulane and Broad, the history building at Tulane University, and part of the New Orleans Museum of Art. Those hadn't been my fault; well, not entirely. Tonight's damage might not have come at my hand, but it would be laid on my doorstep as most things seemed to be these days.

Audrey had changed from her short going-to-dinner-with-Alex dress, one of those little clingy things only very young women with very long legs could wear, into a winter-white sweater and jeans with black boots, as if she needed heels. Rand would love it; Jean Lafitte would consider it worthy of a farm-hand, which is what he thought of my own wardrobe.

I still wore my jeans and the baby-pink angora sweater that felt like heaven—if heaven held only cast-off baby clothing. Jean had complimented me on the femininity of the color, which made me hate it all the more.

Pouring a healthy shot of Four Roses to counterbalance the sweetness of the sweater, I settled into my favorite corner of Jean's settee and patted the cushion for Audrey to sit next to me.

"He's one sexy dead guy," she whispered as Jean barked orders at Jake and Collette, who'd dallied too long before returning to their transport post.

I tried to muster up some jealousy over Audrey's appraisal of the pirate, but it just wasn't there. For one thing, Jean wasn't mine to be jealous over, not that that would stop me. Mostly, though, she wasn't his type; he would only tolerate her for my sake if I considered her trustworthy. I knew this in some deep, instinctive way that I didn't want to examine too deep.

"That he is, very sexy for a dead guy," I said. "Accent on the word *dead*."

She shrugged. "He's immortal, right? That renders *dead* meaningless."

Jean returned to his chair, set his brandy on the side table, and fixed his gaze on me, his eyes dark cobalt blue and deep enough to drown in. "Mademoiselle Audrey speaks words of truth, *oui*? What does death mean when it loses its ability to end life?"

"You shouldn't eavesdrop; it's rude." He had a point, but it didn't change the fact that I'd made my choice, and that choice was Alex. Jean had hinted that he'd wait for me, but he might not feel so ardent when I had four chins and frizzy white hair while he remained a virile thirty-five. Wizards aged slowly, but we weren't immortal.

Although the way my life had gone since Hurricane Katrina came blowing through town, I might not live long enough to worry about the chins or the hair.

"Why are you in town, Audrey? Does your father know? I thought you were on bad terms. How did you meet Alex?" I fired off questions as if she were a fleeing Spanish galleon and I was one of Jean Lafitte's artillerymen.

"I should like to hear these answers as well, Mademoiselle Audrey." Jean settled in his recliner but he left the footrest down and never fully leaned back into the cushions. The pirate remained on high alert, which was wise. Audrey St. Simon might be my cousin by blood, but I didn't know her. She didn't get an automatic pass. In fact, it made her sudden appearance more suspicious.

I handed her the glass of whiskey to loosen her tongue. She took a sip and made a choking noise. "That's awful."

"Give it back, then. You want a soda?"

"Diet soda, no ice, please."

I fetched it, not reading much into her DJ-like preference for room-temperature soda since only Americans seemed to have the fetish for icy drinks. "I'm sorry to sound suspicious." I handed the bottle to her. "I appreciate your quick thinking at the restaurant. Do you know if Alex is okay?" I turned to Jean. "Audrey beat Alex over the head with my elven staff and knocked him unconscious."

Jean grinned. "*Très bien*. This tale shall bring me great enjoyment."

I thought it would.

"Okay, so where to start . . . Oh!" Audrey sipped her drink, then set it down on the side table, the better to wave her hands around. "First, to answer your question, Alex is a bloody trooper, he is. Pretended to be out when the werewolf security guys charged into the alley . . ." She paused. "Should one call that an alley or a courtyard?"

"Courtyard." I twirled my finger in the *keep-talking* movement.

"When they managed to rouse him, he pretended to be so confused he didn't remember what happened to him—or even if you'd been there."

I hoped he was acting and not concussing. I also hoped he didn't overact to the point of rousing Zrakovi's suspicion. So far, Zrakovi trusted Alex and therefore might be more inclined to talk to me if we could work out an opportunity. "So what did you do in the restaurant before you came into the courtyard?"

She shrugged. "My dad always says I have no control over my emotions." She deepened her voice. *"You shall never become a worthy Red Congress wizard as long as you react rather than think, Audrey. You bring me nothing but shame."*

I smiled. "I don't know your father well, but yeah, that sounded like him."

"I've heard that my whole bloody life. I say, why bother to get your name on a card admitting you to a club—or Congress, in this case—full of stiff old fools who never have an original thought among them?"

Uh-huh. She'd failed the Red Congress test, all right, and sounded a whole lot like her Uncle Gerry, even though she'd never met him. "You realize your dad is one of the stiff old fools?"

"The stiffest . . . well, no." She gave me a sharp look that aroused my suspicion antennae. "The First Elder, Zrakovi. He's much worse, from what I've overheard my dad say." She blushed. "Eavesdropping's the only way to learn anything from my dad. He considers Zrakovi a weak old bastard, I think, and some of the other wizards are starting to think so as well."

Interesting. Until he'd ordered me to kill Eugenie's baby, I'd liked Willem Zrakovi. My opinion of him had been rapidly declining. He handled power badly, and threats to his power worse. "How did you meet Alex?"

"I had to deliver some papers to him after he was named to represent the shifters on the big prete council," she said. Damn it. I'd heard about that from everyone except Alex. "My father is paying me to run errands and do household tidying for him so that I have enough money to rent my own flat in the French Quarter. What a lovely place New Orleans is. Have you been to The Cat's Meow?"

Once, and once too many. "Bourbon Street karaoke clubs aren't exactly my style. So you met Alex when you delivered papers?"

"Right. We had a bit of a chat and realized we had a lot in common."

Oh, really now? A great many people loved The Cat's Meow, but I couldn't see Alex being one of them. "Such as?"

"Well, we both think you've gotten a bloody awful treatment from Zrakovi, first off. Alex still trusts the guy, you know, but doesn't like what he's done to you. That's sort of why I'm here. It was Alex's idea for me to be your carrier pigeon."

CHAPTER 18

I stared at Audrey, imagining a world in which I might write an encoded letter to Alex, roll it into a tube, strap it to one of Audrey's long legs, and send her flying off in a transport. I did not want to live in that world.

Besides, Rene could deliver messages. The Elders might monitor his movements and suspect what he was up to, but he was smart enough to avoid getting caught.

Jean remained quiet, but gave me a somber look that told me he wasn't keen on the idea either.

"Audrey, that doesn't seem practical." I spoke slowly, choosing my words with care. I'd need verification from Alex before I'd ever believe this scheme, and even then, he might have been sucked in by her long legs and windmill arms. "With everything in New Orleans so dangerous right now, your dad will want to keep tabs on when you come and go. He'll wonder why you're seeing so much of Alex. If you make too many trips into the Beyond, he'll wonder where you're going."

She laughed. "Bloody hell, DJ. Contrary to anything my

father told you, I'm not that stupid. Alex and I are pretending to date, so my dad doesn't think anything of it at all. In fact, he's quite glad Alex is 'moving on' "—she made little air quotes with her fingers—"by getting past his infatuation with you. He thinks it's helping Alex to fall in line with the wizards on the council. Plus, Dad thinks Alex will be a good influence on me."

Yeah, well, Dad thought I'd be a good influence on her, too, and look how that turned out. I wasn't jealous over the dating ruse. Our courtyard kiss had been enough to reassure me that Alex wasn't "past his infatuation" at all, but that didn't mean I bought the rest of her story. She might be running home and telling daddy dearest everything Alex said to her. I didn't know how I was going to do it, but I had to talk to him again.

Not to mention put Audrey to the test.

I forced a smile. "That's just awesome. You guys thought of everything." I gave Jean a warning look and got an arched eyebrow in return. "Could you take a message back to Alex for me tonight, then? I didn't get a chance to tell him, what with all the chaos, but it's really important."

Audrey looked as if Santa had arrived early in Old Barataria, bearing a load of size zero designer dresses and screw-me heels in a pirogue pulled by eight tiny alligators. "Of course! I mean, that's the whole idea, right? You can write him a note or tell me what to say—however you'd prefer." She grinned. "He told me you'd be too suspicious to trust me if he didn't present the idea to you himself. Won't he be gobsmacked that you trusted me right off?"

"Totally gobsmacked." I pondered what my message to Alex should be. "Okay, then. Tell Alex that he needs to call Robert Delachaise right away and let him know that Robert's brother has recovered. And here's the most important part: Alex needs to tell Robert that we want him to offer his clan's allegiance to the elves."

Jean's mouth widened in a slow smile. He, like Alex, knew very well that Rene's twin brother, Robert, was dead. If word got back to Toussaint Delachaise that his deceased son was brokering deals with the elves, we'd know Cousin Audrey was either a double agent or, at best, had a very big mouth with no filter between it and her brain. Alex would realize she was being tested and if he was smart he wouldn't give it away. Alex Warin was many things, but he was not stupid.

I made Audrey repeat the message back to me twice, and sent her on her way.

"You are most devious, *Jolie*." Jean laughed and refilled his brandy glass. "It is a plan worthy of Jean Lafitte himself."

I'd take that as a compliment, coming from the king of deviousness. "We'll see if it works." Having an alternate way to get messages to and from Alex without risking arrest would be great, if the messenger were trustworthy. Rene was probably going to end up moving to Barataria if the water species left the Interspecies Council, and it might be harder for him to come and go.

Audrey's appearance had been awfully convenient, though. One day she was incommunicado with her father and the next she was in town and on his payroll. Not to mention suddenly dating Alex and offering to be a gopher. Something smelled fishy in Old Barataria and it wasn't a merman.

A screech from outside sent both Jean and me running through the open window onto the verandah. We stopped at the same time. Jean laughed and I tried hard not to, but failed.

Audrey stood on the beach. Between her and the transport, looking up at her, was a shorter and very naked merman. Rene's full range of tattoos, including a particularly fascinating diving bottle-nosed dolphin, were on full display. He stood with his legs apart in a pirate stance, hands on his hips, giving her the infamous Delachaise scowl. Her arms were waving and her mouth was motoring, although I couldn't understand what she was saying because of the surf and my own choked-back guffaws.

Jean nudged me with his elbow. "Perhaps you should intervene, Drusilla, lest your cousin reveal the nature of the message she carries."

Holy crap. I jumped off the front of the verandah and trotted down to the beach, waving the staff in the air and talking fast. "Bob, this is my cousin Audrey. Audrey, this is Bob; he has an aversion to clothing. Sorry, Bob, but Audrey has to run. Get in the transport, and I'll power it up. I really need that message to get to Alex."

Audrey looked at me. "But he . . ." She shook her head as if trying to rattle the pieces of her brain back in place. I guess the sudden appearance of a heavily tattooed naked guy would be startling.

"Right then. Off to St. Louis Cathedral." Audrey stepped into the watery transport, and I knelt and touched Charlie against the edge. If she had rented a place in the Quarter, the cathedral transport would probably be closest for now. If by some miracle she turned out to be a legitimate option as a go-between for Alex and me, maybe I could help her set up a transport in her apartment.

"What's this Bob shit?"

I'd forgotten the naked merman on the beach, so I filled Rene in on everything as we returned to the house, starting with when I found him at the Winter Palace. The last thing he remembered was being shot. He was walking a bit slower than usual, but other than that and some missing short-term memory, he seemed to have fully recovered.

"So you puttin' this cousin to the test using my dead brother?" Rene's voice was grumpier than usual.

"Sorry, it was the first thing I thought of that Alex would know but my uncle Lennox wouldn't." It hadn't been that long since Robert Delachaise had died. The fact that he'd brought much of the trouble on himself didn't help Rene cope one bit. I knew this because I still mourned my father, and it was his own actions that had led to his death as well. That knowledge hadn't helped me either.

I'd avoided talking with Rene about Robert's death. Guys tended to get fidgety with emotional subjects anyway, and Rene was worse than most. He'd mentioned it only once or twice, and I had figured if he wanted to talk about it, he would. Since I'd opened the door, however, I might as well walk through it. "How are you doing?"

"How am I doing with the poison bullet or with losing my brother?" Rene didn't make eye contact and since he had the highest pain tolerance of anyone I'd met—that dolphin tattoo couldn't have been anything less than excruciating—I knew it was Robert's death that weighed on him.

"I'm talking about Robert. The holidays make things worse; that's when I miss Gerry and Tish the most. Thanksgiving was really hard." I gave Rene an awkward side-hug once we got back in the entry hall. Jean had retreated to his study. "Sorry I brought it up, but if you ever want to talk, I'm here, you know?"

"Yeah, babe, I know. Lemme get dressed and we'll deck the halls or something."

Yeah, because tomorrow was Christmas Eve, and even if Santa didn't make an appearance at Maison Rouge, we'd have at least one elf in the house.

While Jake and Collette took a trip into Old Orleans for a few supplies, Jean and Rene started a game of poker at the game table in the study. Eugenie stretched out on the recliner, toes aloft, while I painted her toenails a startling shade of blue. She'd already done my toes, which, combined with my pink clothing, made me look like someone had coughed up a nursery.

"Let's get a game plan ready for when Rand gets here tomorrow at four—stop moving your feet!" I cleaned a wide swipe of nail polish off the top of her foot, the result of a twitch when I mentioned Rand's name.

"I don't know what to do about him." Eugenie banged a fist against her forehead. "I wish he'd just go away. I can't believe I thought I loved that freak."

Probably because he was a drop-dead-gorgeous freak who could be charming when he wanted to. Getting close to Eugenie had gotten him close to me, his intended target for political purposes. I'd often wondered if he had manipulated Eugenie's emotions to make her think she loved him, but hadn't had the courage to ask. If he admitted it, I'd hate that bond even more, although I couldn't regret doing it. Otherwise, I'd be running on four paws across the island with Jake and Collette, except with wizard and elf mixed into loup-garou DNA. As bad as things were, that would've been worse.

I finished the final coat on Eugenie's left toenails before setting the bottle out of throwing range and venturing my opinion. She wasn't going to like it. "The way I see it, Eugenie, you're going to have to set up regular visits with Rand. You're going to have to treat this whole visitation thing as if the baby were already here and you were sharing custody."

She lowered the footrest of the recliner with a thump and looked straight ahead. Her expression was so odd that I dropped my empathic shielding to do a bit of emotional eavesdropping. The anger I expected. The confusion I expected. The guilt surprised me.

I nudged her blue toenails with mine. "What's going on, Eugie?"

She lowered her voice, probably thinking Jean and Rene wouldn't hear. I hated to tell her but, like most shifters, Rene would hear her anywhere in this house if he wanted to, no matter how softly she whispered. "Christof offered to kill Rand," she said. "I told him I'd think about it, but I don't know if I can go through with it. Could I? Would it be wrong after all he's done?"

I glanced around at the guys and met Rene's fierce gaze. He gave an almost imperceptible shake of the head. There was no need; I'd never go along with this idea, and I was mad as hell at Christof for offering.

"It would be very wrong." On so many levels. "Rand is this baby's father, Eugie, like it or not. Your little boy will have some elven skills—maybe just a few, or maybe a whole lot. He's going to need Rand to teach him how to use them."

Her face settled into the mulish look she got when she was preparing for a fight. Her lips thinned, eyes narrowed, nostrils flared. "But he—"

I wasn't letting this go any further. It wasn't even worthy of a discussion. "Eugenie, no. Absolutely, unequivocally no. I don't care what Rand's done in the past. Let all that crap go. You need him and your baby needs him. It's that simple. Plus, killing him would be downright wrong. You know that."

I could've gone on and on. About politics and ramifications and power struggles. But I didn't get into any of that because, in the end, the only thing that mattered was this: I believed in moral absolutes that surpassed whatever political or religious labels we tried to put on them. Call them commandments or universal truths or federal laws or whatever you want. There was absolute right and absolute wrong. Murder was wrong.

Rand had been wrong to murder his Synod leader Mace Banyan, which I knew he'd done no matter how many airplane accidents he concocted. I hated Mace, but that didn't make it right. No matter how hurt she was, or scared, or angry, Eugenie could not murder Rand. That blood would be on her hands whether she actually did the killing or not.

I'd been staring at my locket, twisting the dog's paw around and around, thinking about how much time I'd spent blithering about clarity and how I needed some in a life that had become mired in gray. Now I realized I'd always had areas of clarity, lines I wouldn't cross. I'd simply needed to mine more deeply, to reach the bedrock of who I was. It's why being forced to use Charlie against Jean last month had almost killed me.

When I looked back at my friend, to try and explain where I was coming from in what seemed like an inconsistent attitude toward Quince Randolph, I saw it wasn't necessary. Eugenie's face shone with tears, and her aura was coated in shame.

"I know it's wrong, DJ. I feel guilty for even thinking it, no matter what he's done." She swallowed hard and brushed the tears away from her eyes with the heels of her palms. "I just feel so helpless, and so afraid for my baby."

"Scoot over." I joined her in the massive recliner and pulled her into a hug, peeking around to see Rene's faint smile as he returned to his card game with Jean. The pirate, with mere mortal hearing, had been none the wiser about this particular drama. "If there's an upside to this, Eugenie, it's that Rand already loves this baby. He might be the biggest horse's ass to ever father a child, but I really think he could turn out to be a good father. He'd protect this baby with his life."

I believed that, and hoped my non-husband the elf didn't prove me wrong.

A familiar scream sounded from outside, from the front of the house. This time, no one jumped up and ran out the windows. Jean merely took a sip of brandy and leaned back, look-ing across the verandah. "*Jolie,* if I am not mistaken, your *cousine* has returned. Please discuss this screeching habit with her if she is to continue coming here, *s'il vous plaît.* It is quite annoying."

CHAPTER 19

Audrey had a legitimate reason for screaming. She faced an undead and mostly toothless pirate with a big pistol aimed at her head as soon as she materialized into the Barataria transport. Plus, high tide was coming in and she'd landed in warm salt water up to her knees.

By the time I dragged her into the house and settled her into Jean's chair with a glass of wine, she'd stopped hyperventilating. Her hand shook so badly the wine almost sloshed out of the glass before it reached her mouth. After a couple of sips, she calmed down. Honestly, if the girl was going to live in New Orleans—either the preternatural or human version—she needed to remain stoic at the sight of a gun.

"If I was killed in the Beyond by an undead guy, in a place where everything is kind of undead itself, would I really be dead or would it be, like, a bad dream?" She looked bug-eyed but hopeful.

"Sorry, no, unless you were already dead and famous or

remembered by someone famous, you'd be pretty well screwed."
Unfortunate, but true.

She took a few moments to absorb this inequity, and I noticed "Bob" had left the room with Eugenie and Jean had settled into a dark corner armchair, pretending to read while he
eavesdropped. Good. I wanted his opinion after she left.

"Why are you back so quickly?" I glanced at my wristwatch,
wondering not for the first time how Rene had found one with
a pink band. She'd been gone only two hours.

"Well, I delivered your message to Alex." She smiled. "I
thought it sounded like a serious message. You *acted* like it was
serious. But it made him laugh, and he asked me to bring you
this." She held out an envelope exactly like the one Ken had
brought, minus the blood spatter. "He made me wait in the
other room while he wrote it. Was your message a test of some
kind?"

"Sort of." As near as I could tell, she hadn't opened the envelope. I tore off the end and pulled out the single sheet, written on my own Mardi Gras–colored argyle stationery that I'd
left on Alex's desk:

*Good one, DJ. Glad to see you're as paranoid as you need to
be. Audrey is okay. She knows how to keep her mouth shut.
I've tested her a few times myself. Lennox isn't watching her
because he doesn't think she has enough common sense to operate
a transport. He flew her to New Orleans coach class when she got
in trouble at her school in London for setting the dormitory on fire.
I think there's a family resemblance.*

   *She's smart and honest, and doesn't mind letting Lennox
continue to believe she's a hopeless case. She knows virtually
nothing about the magical world except what she's read in books,*

and too much time with her father has turned her against the
bureaucracy, so use her and teach her. We might need her.
    Remember what we did the first night of the blizzard? On
the living room floor? I want to do that again. Now.

                                                —*Alex*

"Oh look, your face is turning the color of your sweater. He said something sweet. Did he say something sweet?" Audrey craned her neck, which was already quite giraffelike, and tried to see.

I cleared my throat, folded the letter, and tucked it in my pocket, the rush of heat from that memory reaching far, far lower than my face. There had been nothing sweet about it. Hot? Yes. Frantic and a little rough? Oh yeah. But not sweet. "Never mind that. He's vouching for you. That's what matters."

I got up to replenish my glass of soda and slipped the letter to Jean. I didn't care if he read the sexy bit. If Audrey was going to be screeching her way in and out of Old Barataria on a regular basis, Jean needed to know everything about her that I did.

Plus, as much as I loved Alex Warin, Jean had a very keen sense of who was and was not trustworthy and followed his own counsel. Alex was wired to respect authority, and he'd refused to question his trust in Zrakovi until it was too late, or at least too late for me. Even now, he thought the situation could be salvaged. I hoped he was right, but I wasn't going to risk the safety of everyone Jean had sheltered here.

"Do you need to go back to New Orleans tonight?" Audrey's trips to the Beyond and back should be limited, and used to best advantage. Besides, if she stayed, I could find out how much she really knew about the magical world. Not being a wizard, Alex couldn't gauge that.

"Sadly, yes. Dad insists we have Christmas Eve breakfast

together before the Interspecies Council meets at noon, and then exchange gifts afterward, although we've never done anything together over the holidays before. I suspect my mum put him up to it, although I'd rather stay and visit with you. Guess I should get back to my flat in case he calls to firm up our plans."

Too bad, because I'd like time to write a note that would keep Alex hot and bothered through the holidays. I'd have to settle for a more tangible gift.

"I have something for you to take to Alex." I dragged my messenger bag from behind the settee and dug around for the rest of the vile-tasting potion I'd concocted to change my aura. I figure it had worked for about an hour. "Tell him this is for emergencies only, if he needs to see me. It might give him an hour, tops, for him to move around undetected. Emergencies only."

This was a bigger test. If she gave it to Alex without telling anyone, great. I doubted Alex would use it, thus my "emergency" warning. So if it got confiscated or they followed him around for a while it shouldn't matter.

We walked back toward the transport. I'd give Audrey credit; she didn't even make a face when getting inside the interlocking circle and triangle that now had her in waist-high water. The outlines of the transport glowed faintly through the waves.

"Anything else you need to tell Alex?" She held the vial above her head as a high wave came in and splashed up to her shoulders. It would be above my head, so I might need to move the transport closer to the house. Drowning in a transport would be a pathetic way to go.

"Yeah, tell him I love him." How brazen was that? "And bring some holy water back with you next time you come to Barataria. As much as you can carry."

I had some scrying to do.

CHAPTER 20

I spent most of Christmas Eve morning staring at the Beyond's version of the Gulf of Mexico, deep in worry and feeling needy.

I needed to learn what Rand knew about Florian framing me, along with Christof, in the destruction of the Winter Palace. Did he know? Had he been in on it? Were the elves and Florian's pack on the verge of an alliance and, if so, did the wizards know about it? If so, Zrakovi would be more desperate than ever.

I also needed to figure out how to convince Rand that an amicable visitation arrangement with Eugenie was a win-win for everyone, especially his baby. She could live here in Barataria and he could have semi-supervised visits.

I needed Alex, too, and wished I'd sent him a Christmas gift via Audrey, even if it was an undead seashell. The gym club membership that I'd bought him, wrapped inside an "As Seen on TV" Perfect Bacon Bowl, was trapped in my wizard-warded house. It seemed too frivolous now that things had gotten more grim, and what I needed from him was two strong arms wrapped around me, holding me together.

Instead, I'd sent that potion, which now seemed dangerous. If Audrey told Lennox, that type of gift coming from me might cast doubt on Alex's loyalty. I badly needed her to be as dependable as Alex thought.

Last, but far from least, I still needed to talk to Willem Zrakovi, to make one final effort to meet him halfway if it wasn't already too late. Hell, I'd meet him three-quarters of the way, just to get my life back. Even if I permanently lost my Green Congress license and my job, I'd be able to rebuild my house, see Alex when I wanted, and live in the city I loved.

For the first time, I realized there was something else I needed, and this was one desire I might be able to get if I could play the blood-relation card.

I sat on the verandah with my bare feet hanging over the edge, watching Jake and Collette as they watched the transport. They always took back-to-back shifts and stayed together the whole time. It was sweet and romantic, but boring. As much as I loved Alex, I wasn't sure I could sit with him for twelve hours straight, watching a transport and talking. We'd be arguing within a half hour, even if we had to make up something to argue about.

That probably wasn't the sign of a healthy relationship, but I'd worry about that later.

A motion caught my eye and I blinked to see what it was in the flickering light of the flambeaux that Jake had planted on either side of the transport. My watch told me that it was only eight a.m. New Orleans time, so Audrey should be busy having breakfast with Lennox.

It wasn't a person that materialized, but a covered bin, one of those big plastic things sold by the gross in discount stores for less than five bucks.

I jumped off the verandah and walked down to the beach, trying not to *eep* when something skittered out of the sand and over my bare foot. Another need: footwear that wasn't shrimp boots. It was too warm here for them. I'd even wear pink running shoes rather than dirty bare feet.

"Stay back, DJ. Collette, you, too." Jake waved us away. "Something's in the box but I can't tell what it is."

He picked up a battery-powered portable floodlight resting in the sand next to one of the flambeaux and approached the bin slowly, crouching as he got closer to try looking through it. Then he leaned toward it and sniffed.

"You expecting a shipment of water, sunshine?" He looked up and frowned at me. "I swear that's what it is—a bunch of jars full of water."

"I bet it's holy water. Let me look." Damn, but Audrey was efficient—and why hadn't it occurred to me that she could send me stuff without coming herself? Although how she lugged that much water to the transport behind St. Louis Cathedral in broad daylight was a mystery; Jake could barely lift the bin himself.

Then again, she might have stolen the water from the cathedral, in which case she didn't have far to drag it. I hoped it was real holy water and that the jars in which it had been placed were blessed as well. Otherwise, it would be tainted and might not work.

As soon as Jake got it to the verandah, I opened the bin and looked at the jars. There was no mistaking this for plain tap water. A strong aura of peace and power surrounded it, which told me that both the jars and contents had been blessed by a priest. It was the most important ingredient in ritual magic and I'd always used it for scrying because it seemed to amp up my abilities. A full-blooded elf probably could use anything.

All together, there were probably five or six gallons in the bin, worth dozens of hours of scrying time.

I removed the jars carefully; the bin could be useful for sending things back and forth if I could get a transport set up in Audrey's apartment—preferably one Daddy couldn't see. A niggling at the back of my brain still told me it was too easy. Since Hurricane Katrina had blown our world to pieces and opened the floodgates to reorganize the prete world, nothing had been simple. Nothing.

Alex trusted Audrey, however, and I trusted Alex. Mostly. Which meant I didn't quite trust Audrey. Not yet. I would use her, but needed to be more careful. This was fine. She could tell Lennox all she wanted about holy water. Unless he was more up to date on elven rituals than the other wizards I'd met, he'd have no clue why I wanted it. I'd make up something to tell her without mentioning my ability to scry.

In the bottom of the bin was a note, written on a French Quarter note card like those sold by the set in every souvenir shop in New Orleans. This one featured pastel sketches of Jackson Square in the full bloom of spring, when a rainbow of azalea blossoms framed the statue of a horse-riding Andrew Jackson himself.

Hullo, DJ—Used a bit of the magic to ramble around the bowels of the cathedral and found their supply of holy water. I hope this is what you need! If you want anything else, send a note via transport at noon. I will be waiting and can get it for you while Dad and the other gits will be at the council meeting. —Audrey

I'd have her pick up some transport-making stuff both for me and for herself. If Audrey were playing double agent, would it hurt anything for Lennox to know if she had a transport in her apartment? I don't see how it could. The Elders were watching the transports and all of our houses anyway; it would just give them one more place to watch. Since Alex had a transport in his house, she could use their relationship as an excuse.

Plus, I could find out how much magic Audrey really knew. A novice at transport making was easy to spot.

Scrounging around on Jean's desk, I was surprised to spot a nice, normal gel pen among his assortment of inkwells and maps and quills. I scratched out a note on the back of Audrey's, asking her to pick up some sea salt from the grocery and to wear a ring she liked next time she came. If she didn't have a ring, she should buy one and bring it with her.

If what Lennox told me was true, and it probably was since he'd told me before he realized I would never be a good influence on his wayward daughter, Audrey had trouble controlling her physical magic. Although my own native magic was weak, Gerry had taught me to control it using a ring as a focal object. Audrey's magic wouldn't work in Barataria—at least I didn't think it would. Mine sure didn't. But I could still give her some basic instructions and she could practice on her own time.

"Writing the great American wizard novel?"

I gritted my teeth out of habit. Adrian Hoffman no longer irritated me, at least not most of the time, but I'd disliked him for so long that whenever he spoke, my first reaction was a knee-jerk negative. I needed to get over that. *Adrian is my ally. Adrian is my ally.* Rinse and repeat a few hundred times.

I turned to find him lounging in the doorway to the study. "Sending a note to my cousin to bring a few things from New Orleans next time she comes. You need anything?"

"You trust her?"

If anyone knew how the Elders worked, it was Adrian. His father had been First Elder, after all, and Adrian himself had worked at Elder Central in Edinburgh for years. I needed to consult him on matters more often. Like whether they'd enlist one of their young family members to spy for them. Since I'd once employed the undead Louis Armstrong as my spy, I had no room to judge. Although Louis was the worst spy ever.

"I'm not sure, so I'm being careful what I entrust to her. She sent some holy water after I asked for it, for example, but I never said what it was for. It could be to bless Jean's undead fleet of pirate ships for all she knows. I don't intend to tell her I will be using it to scry. I doubt anyone among the Elders would figure that out."

"Agreed," Adrian said. "It's too far outside the realm of their skills, so they tend to forget you can do a lot of elven magic. I wondered if you were going to watch the Interspecies Council meeting today. I don't know what time it will be."

I nodded. "It's at noon, and I'm going to be set up and ready. Florian is trying to frame me for conspiring with Christof and stirring things up between the fae and the elves, so I want to hear what he's going to say."

Adrian leaned against the doorjamb. "Do you know where they're meeting? Surely they're running out of public buildings to destroy."

One would think. "No idea, but I can scry Alex. Since he's on the council now, representing the weres and shifters, that should put me with him at the meeting."

Adrian raised an eyebrow, reminding me of the smartass he used to be. "Isn't that a conflict of interest? I'm surprised Willem Zrakovi put him in that position. It makes me wonder: How sure are you that Alex Warin is still loyal to you?"

I thought of Alex's expression as he'd looked in the courtyard a couple of nights ago, his face full of longing and sadness bordering on desperation. "I'm certain of it. But I'm also certain he won't backstab Zrakovi. I'm sure our new First Elder knows that, too." Which is why Alex was so miserable and torn.

"Our new First Elder." Adrian looked at the floor, and a pang of guilt shot through me. I hated Geoffrey Hoffman; he'd been the power behind the whole debacle last month that had cost me so much. He'd given permission to have Adrian turned vampire for political gain, without his son's knowledge. But he was still Adrian's father.

"How far will Alex blindly follow Zrakovi?" Adrian's voice grew softer. "What would it take for him to finally turn his back on the Elders? Or will he follow them right into giving up everything to avoid a war, whether or not he personally believes it's the right thing to do?"

My temper rose, but I tamped it back down. It was a reasonable question, as much as I hated hearing it, because I didn't like the answer I had to give. "I don't know. I really don't."

I'd like to believe Alex had his own true north, his own moral absolutes, and that there was some line that, when crossed, it would turn him away if Zrakovi's path strayed too far from his own beliefs. I didn't have a clue what that tipping point might be, however. For me, it had been Zrakovi's attempt to get rid of Eugenie's baby, and his willingness to turn her over to Rand without considering the consequences to her. Even then, I'd tried to work within the system—sort of. All it had gotten me was an unspecified period in Greenland, during which I'd die from elven survival syndrome.

Alex had urged me to run to Barataria, had even helped me escape. But he had been adamant about staying behind.

I'd had no answers then. I had none now.

"Oh well, guess I'll take some of your scrying stuff outside for you then." Adrian turned to leave. "I'm on transport duty for the next few hours anyway, and I wouldn't miss this meeting for anything."

"Wait a sec." I walked with him to the verandah, set the jars of holy water aside, and placed the note in the big plastic bin. "I want to set this in the transport and send it to the cathedral right at noon. Can you still power a transport?"

Adrian's nostrils flared as if he'd smelled a forest of skunk spray. "I most certainly can."

"Hey, no offense." I held my hands up in a gesture of surrender. "I wasn't referring to you losing your powers; I know that won't happen for a while." Hell, he'd managed to run the whole holiday light show at City Park last week. "It's just that my physical magic doesn't work at all here and I didn't know if yours did or not."

"Mine is obviously superior to yours."

Yeah, and he had a bigger pair than me, too. Just when I started to like the guy he'd remind me why I didn't like him. "Obviously. Okay then, would you mind sending this at noon? Do you have a watch?"

He held up his wrist. I bit my lip to keep the smile off my face. His watchband was as pink as mine. Which is why I adored Rene.

Adrian took the bin down to the beach, relieving Jake and Collette on transport duty.

I had another task to complete before Rand arrived, another letter to write. This one, I'd ask Rand to hand-deliver.

It was to my Uncle Lennox.

CHAPTER 21

About fifteen minutes before noon, Jean assigned an undead pirate flunky to transport duty—I think it was the toothless guy who'd served our gumbo a couple of days ago—so that Adrian could join us in watching the Interspecies Council meeting.

The Christmas Eve meeting had been forced on the council by Florian, and Jean had spent most of the morning in Old Orleans with Christof. The Winter Prince of Faery had been so angry that the Beyond's border town was crippled beneath an ice storm.

"Is Christof going to the meeting?" I placed the same items I'd used to scry Alex last time at the four points around the bowl of magic-infused holy water.

We'd moved the scrying bowl to the verandah itself so we could watch more comfortably, and Jean settled into one of the chairs we'd pulled up around it. Our own theater in the round.

"Christof feels he must go in an attempt to protect himself against whatever schemes Florian has devised." Jean lit one of his small cigars. Eugenie was napping or, more likely, trying to steel herself for the meeting with Rand, so he didn't have to worry about the smoke. "I encouraged him to bring some of his allies in case he must escape quickly and needs assistance. Rene is joining them."

Rene and Christof got along quite well, but I hadn't realized they were good enough friends for Rene to openly side with the faery prince in front of the council. "Christof thinks he will need help from Rene?"

"*Non,* Rene will be there should his father Toussaint meet with any resistance if he decides to leave the council."

Good grief. The Interspecies Council had become a joke. The historical undead and vampires were no longer represented. If the water species walked out, that left only the wizards, elves, fae, and shifter reps on the council. The at-large seat, reserved for the smaller species groups and originally filled by one of the goblins, had already been abandoned, the elves had a leadership void with two of their four Synod members under the age of consent, and the fae had embarked on a civil war.

Then again, the wizards, fae, and elves were the three largest groups, and the were/shifters had always been employed by the wizards. The vampires weren't far behind the elves in terms of population, but since their Vice-Regent had a warrant out for his arrest, they hadn't shown any signs of wanting other representation. Hired thugs seemed to be their new role.

I had no idea what to expect from this meeting.

Shortly before noon, I used Charlie to power up the scrying magic, and quickly saw Alex sitting in an armchair that looked familiar. "Where was the meeting being held?" I asked Jean.

"I know not." He leaned forward. "It looks like a home."

I adjusted Charlie's angle and a blast of anger shot through my veins. "Yeah, it's a home, all right. Mine."

They were meeting at Gerry's house—my house now—in Lakeview. The upstairs of the Katrina-flooded home remained a gutted, empty shell, but Alex and Jake had worked to make the first floor livable as a surprise for me after my house in Uptown New Orleans had burned down.

How dare they meet in my home! Sit on my furniture! If they blew up my house, the elven staff and I were going to do some damage.

Cursing under my breath, mentally calling Willem Zrakovi and Lennox St. Simon every evil name I could devise—because one of them was behind this choice of venue, I had no doubt—I shifted the staff again to see who was present.

Alex lounged in the armchair nearest the sofa, on which Zrakovi and Lennox sat like stiff, business-suited bookends with an empty space between them. Toussaint Delachaise, shorter and wirier than Rene, with a floating mane of Einstein-white hair, sat away from the group, on the brick hearth. Should he decide to leave, the French doors Alex had installed to replace Gerry's old sliding glass patio door lay directly to his right.

Shifting the staff farther to the center of the bowl, I spotted Rand sitting on one end of a long bench facing Zrakovi and Lennox. Next to him, short and swarthy, sat his new lapdog, Betony Stoneman, aka Fred Flintstone. I'd never seen that bench, so it must have been scrounged up to compensate for my inadequate seating. Which is what they got for stealing my house.

At the other end of the bench, side by side physically but miles apart in their body language, sat Florian and Christof. I knew the brothers looked very much alike in their natural states, although Christof was a couple of inches taller, his hair darker, and his features a bit softer and more handsome. Today, however, since my tuft of Gandalf's fur was being used for the scrying ritual, I was treated to their glamour.

"Faeries are absurd," Adrian observed in a flagrant under-statement. The Faery Prince of Summer wore a yellow and white seersucker suit and straw boater hat, which would be fine if he'd been a New Orleans attorney in the summer of 1910 who'd been shopping at Haspel. On Christmas Eve of modern times, it looked ridiculous. Plus, his blond hair was now medium brown hair and arranged in a fluffed-up mod cut that made him look like a mushroom wearing a straw boater.

Christof had gone the undertaker route, with a severe black suit, white shirt, and black-and-gray-striped tie, his dark hair short and slicked back, a white carnation in his lapel. The effect was ruined only by the white patent-leather shoes he'd chosen to go with his ensemble, which kind of took it from undertaker into mob boss territory.

Although a barefoot, unemployed wizard wearing a white T-shirt with pink rhinestone hearts on the front had little room to judge.

Zrakovi rapped on my coffee table with his knuckles to call the meeting to order. I was glad I'd had the paranoia to hide the rest of Gerry's black grimoires above a beam in the unfinished second floor. The First Elder would love to figure out a way to charge me with doing illegal magic. Unfortunately, it wouldn't take much figuring.

"I must apologize for such a hastily called meeting in such inadequate surroundings," Zrakovi began.

"Asshat." The First Elder had not only stolen my home, he was apologizing for its inadequacy.

"Hush." Adrian kicked the leg of my chair.

"Before we get to other matters, I'd like to announce that a warrant has been issued for the arrest of Jacob Warin, for failure to report infecting former Sentinel Drusilla Jaco with the loup-garou curse last month and for escaping before he could serve his one-year sentence at the wizarding facility in Ittoqqortoormiit, Greenland. His sentence will be extended to two years once he is apprehended."

Zrakovi could eat dirt for all Jake cared. Not being able to see his family in Picayune, Mississippi, often enough was Jake's only regret at leaving New Orleans behind, and he figured he could slip over to see his relatives occasionally. Picayune wasn't a magical hot spot. He'd never go back to New Orleans and didn't care; he'd already arranged to transfer ownership of his bar, the Green Gator, to his manager, Leyla.

Zrakovi droned on. "Also, a warrant has been issued for the arrest of former Sentinel Jaco for not reporting that same inci-dent. Although this is a wizarding matter, I also would like to assure the council that because Ms. Jaco chose to run away rather than face her charges, the loss of her Green Congress license and, of course, her position as sentinel has been made permanent. Her sentence at Ittoqqortoormiit, too, will be lengthened."

How, exactly, did one lengthen my "unspecified term" of imprisonment? I ground my teeth and mentally told Charlie to prepare to char the first name on his incineration list, then had to remind myself about moral absolutes and murder and all that intellectual crap I'd been spouting earlier.

"If I might, Elder Zrakovi?"

I shifted Charlie around to find the speaker. Florian stood up in his seersucker suit, his hair arranged in oily swoops and his lips snarled. He resembled a young Jerry Lee Lewis; I hoped he didn't pop out his great balls of fire in the middle of my living room. I'd already had one house burn down.

"Prince Florian, Faery's political situation is on our agenda if you don't mind waiting." Zrakovi gave him a fierce look and even without sitting in the room and feeling it, I knew his blood pressure had begun to rise.

"This concerns the former sentinel." Florian adjusted his lapels. "I have eyewitness testimony that proves Ms. Jaco's charges are much more serious than this council knows and have grown beyond a wizard-only concern."

"Oh, holy crap. Here it comes."

Jean reached out a hand and grasped mine. I let him.

Zrakovi sat back, looking pleased. The angle from which we saw him via Charlie enlarged his nose and bugged out his eyes. Maybe I'd make an illegal potion to render him that way permanently. "Please enlighten us, Prince Florian."

I took a deep breath, ready for my name to be dragged through the political sludge. Again. In the corner of my frame of view, Alex sat up straighter, a frown drawing his dark eyebrows together. On the other end of the bench, Rand leaned forward to get a better look at Florian.

The Prince of Summer assumed a slow, somber tone. "Most of you have heard about the tragic passing of my great aunt, the Queen Sabine, which I fear was foul play."

Yeah, because you killed her, you lunatic fringe mop.

"It is a time of great mourning in the monarchy of Faery."

Lying toadstool.

"Unfortunately, my attempts to peacefully reconcile the assumption of the monarchy with my brother have been unsuccessful."

Since when does beheading one's sister constitute a peaceful anything?

"Rather than compromise or leave the decision to our people, Christof has willfully destroyed much of our capital city—even his own palace—and brutally murdered our dear sister, Tamara. And he has done so using elven magic with the assistance of Drusilla Jaco and her self-professed paramour, Captain Jean Lafitte."

Jean propelled himself from his chair. I wrenched my hand free of his before he could drag me to the floor and dislodge Charlie from my hand. *"C'est des conneries!"*

Yeah, what he said. Whatever it meant.

Zrakovi exchanged looks across the empty sofa cushion at Lennox. I'd give anything to be in that room so I could read their auras. Having to interpret body language and expressions was annoying. If I had to guess, Zrakovi was so pleased he was practically doing the tango in his seat. Lennox, however, looked troubled.

Jean continued to pace and mutter to himself in French.

"Can you turn up the volume on that bowl?" Adrian asked, glaring at Jean but not daring to tell his meal ticket to shut up.

I urged Charlie to amp it up a bit, and the volume increased. I loved that staff.

I'd missed the first part of his comments, but Christof had entered the fray. ". . . a blithering idiot."

"He's talking about Florian," I told Adrian, who nodded.

"Florian and his squad of Hybrids took over the Royal Palace while Sabine was still alive—ailing, but alive." As Christof talked, his breath began coming out in mists of condensation. Around the room, everyone except shifters Alex and Toussaint Delachaise drew jackets more tightly around them. "He killed our queen and assumed control of the tower in order to rob the people of a chance to elect the ruler of their choice."

Uh, excuse me. But what about me? I was being set up.

"Prince Christof, please." Zrakovi held his hands up, palms outward, placating. "I understand your plight, and sympathize with the difficult decisions you face. But the fact is that the decision as to which of you will rule Faery is a matter for the fae to decide. It is not a matter for the Interspecies Council."

"Even if a wizard sentinel is attempting to throw support to the prince who is most opposed to the wizards?" Florian's face had turned downright florid. "Christof is no friend to you. And even if that same wizard has used elven magic, thinking to cast a shadow on the relationship between the fae and the elves, and as a by-product, the elves' alliance with the wizards?"

"It is you who is antagonistic toward the wizards, you lying buffoon!" Christof shouted louder, and behind me, Jean urged his friend to hold his temper. Even Toussaint and Alex pulled on their jackets.

"Jean, what is he doing?" I changed Charlie's angle slightly so I could get a better look at Rand. "This is making Christof look like the crazy one."

"*Oui,* this is most distressing, but Christof is a man of passion, much like myself. It is difficult to respond with reason when one's heart is in anguish."

Whatever. Passionate or short-tempered, he still needed to calm down. And at the risk of sounding selfish, but what about me, damn it?

Alex looked like a treed cat and I knew him well enough to read that expression. He wanted to stand up for me but didn't want to jeopardize his position. Torn between love and duty yet again.

I closed my eyes and mentally screeched as loud as I could: *Quince Randolph, do something, you elven jackass!*

I hadn't expected him to hear me; my earlier attempts at telepathy between the Beyond and the modern world hadn't worked. Then again, I hadn't had the elven staff stuck into a bowl of holy water in a scrying ritual at the time.

Because this time, he heard me. He jolted as if he'd been stuck up the backside with an electric cattle prod and clapped his hands to his ears. *Dru?*

Florian is lying. I had nothing to do with the war in Faery. Florian killed his aunt and his sister. Well, I didn't know that, but my gut told me Christof hadn't done it.

Rand stood slowly. "Since the elves and their allies, past and present, have been brought up here, I'd like to speak. As all of you know, former sentinel Jaco is my bond-mate. The only way she would use elven magic in Faery would be on my orders, and I assure you, the elves have no desire to involve themselves in the fight over the fae monarchy, at least not yet."

A long silence followed. There were so many things to respond to, not the least of which was the implication that the elves might join the fae power struggle in the future.

Zrakovi, however, honed in on the most obvious.

"Are you intimating that you are in contact with your"—he coughed indelicately into his hand—"mate, and that she follows your orders? Think carefully, Mr. Randolph, because with all due respect, Drusilla Jaco is much like her late father Gerald, with apologies to my friend Lennox." He and my uncle exchanged grave nods. "Drusilla Jaco does not follow orders from anyone, period."

Damn straight and suddenly proud of it.

"She follows the orders of those she respects, Mr. Zrakovi." Rand paused long enough for me to snicker and Zrakovi's face to turn the color of a pickled beet. "Dru and I have a very mutually respectful relationship."

Right. Hope he remembered that when he came to visit Eugenie later today.

Rand sat back down but continued talking. "The point being, I assure you that Prince Florian's eyewitness was mistaken. If elven magic was used, then I will find out who committed such an atrocity, and will report it to the princes and to the council. Justice will be swift."

Yeah, and we all knew what form Rand's justice took. He

wasn't saddled by such an inconvenience as moral absolutes or, more likely, his absolutes had a different set of morals attached. He'd once offered to kill Zrakovi for me. I'd pretended he was kidding but, really, I knew better.

"I accept this offer, and thank Mr. Randolph for his level head." Christof gave Rand a solemn nod. One would never suspect those two had been in a recent battle of wills outside a Shreveport Catholic church.

"So, let me make sure I understand this, Christof." Florian began a dramatic pacing around the crowded room; one had to admire his dexterity as he twisted and swiveled around chairs, benches, and tables. "Mr. Randolph has no objections that his bond-mate and her friend Mr. Lafitte came to Faery two days ago and solicited your help in preventing you from seeing the mother of your unborn child as she attended her sister's funeral?"

Damn it, Dru, is that true? That was your doing? That faery goes nowhere near my child. Ever! I clapped one hand to one temple since using both hands to stop the jarring noise in my head from his mental shouts would have required me to drop Charlie.

Rand's voice grew deeper and as cold as Christof's temper. "I assure you, my mate and I will be discussing this matter later today."

Florian's mouth widened in a smirk. "Elder Zrakovi, since Mr. Randolph clearly knows the whereabouts of Ms. Jaco, can't you have her arrested today? And perhaps Jean Lafitte, for harboring a fugitive?"

Zrakovi cleared his throat and fidgeted. "As you know, the council has no jurisdiction in Old Orleans or its outposts such as Barataria. I assure you we are watching the borders carefully."

I held my breath. Zrakovi had to know I was in town last night; only my unique energy signature would have tipped off the werewolf guards to show up at Jacques-Imo's. That I had escaped would be yet another embarrassment to him, and I waited to see if anyone brought it up. Lennox could use it to make Z look incompetent. Florian could do the same. Rand would figure out a way to use it to his advantage.

Alex's only nervous tell, when playing poker or living his life, was thrumming his fingers, and his right-hand digits beat a slow cadence on the leather arm of the chair. Otherwise, he sat still as a vampire.

"Well, then, am I to understand that the official stance of the Interspecies Council regarding the monarchy of Faery is that it has no stance?" Florian spoke after what seemed like an hour-long pause but was probably less than five seconds. I began to breathe again, and Alex stopped thrumming. Assuming Zrakovi knew I had breached security last night, he wasn't sharing that information and enforcers were trained not to talk.

It's also possible that the guards, backing up Alex, hadn't told Z about it at all.

If Audrey had told Lennox, he was keeping it to himself.

Zrakovi began shuffling papers in his lap. "That is accurate, Prince Florian. I wish the best to both you and Prince Christof, and hope that you will be able to settle the matter peaceably. I assume that you both will remain on the council, and once the monarchy is decided, the fae are entitled to a third representative. You may let me know when that happens."

He was washing his hands of the fae, and Christof and Florian exchanged looks that promised violence and retribution.

It was going to be ugly.

CHAPTER 22

The rest of the council meeting was quick, decisive, and mostly unsurprising. The biggest surprises to me were that Toussaint Delachaise didn't resign from the council and Alex didn't open his mouth.

The others debated whether or not to appoint new representatives for the no-longer-represented species and decided the answer, for now, was no. The vampire leaders were criminals, the at-large groups didn't seem interested, and the leader of the historical undead was on shaky legal ground himself.

Speaking of whom, they discussed whether or not Jean Lafitte should be arrested when he next came into the city because he was clearly harboring fugitives. The decision on that was yes, which made Jean chuckle. He'd proven over the centuries, both alive and undead, that he went where he wished, when he wished, and rarely got caught.

Florian made one more attempt to convince Zrakovi to storm Barataria and arrest me, but the First Elder refused on the jurisdiction grounds again. Jurisdiction be damned; he'd come and get me if he thought it would work, but his physical magic wouldn't knock down a pine cone here and that meant, with Charlie in hand, I had the superior firepower. Plus backup from a vampire, a couple of loups-garou, a merman, and a legion of undead pirates.

Finally, Rand said he had delivered a proposal to Zrakovi involving the "future viability" of the Interspecies Council, and he hoped to meet as soon as possible after Christmas to discuss it either privately or before the full council, whichever Zrakovi preferred.

What the hell was up with that?

I guess I'd find out soon enough. There was an hour before Rand was due to arrive for his meeting with Eugenie, but I doubted he'd wait, so with Adrian's and Jean's help we got the scrying materials put away within minutes.

"I will accompany you to the transport, Monsieur Hoffman." Jean gestured for Adrian to head toward the water. "We will ensure that the elf does not arrive armed."

Jean had a short memory; Rand didn't need to wield a weapon. "Don't touch him, and don't get close enough for him to touch you," I reminded him. "If he starts that glowing thing, stay the hell away from him."

"We must discuss your language again, *Jolie*." Jean spun on his pirate boot heels and swaggered toward the beach, testosterone on parade.

As Jean himself would say, *Bah*.

I went inside and gave Eugenie a quick rundown on what had happened. "Rand's going to be awful about what happened at the funeral, isn't he?" She'd styled her hair, put on just enough makeup to play up her pretty eyes, and wore a deep turquoise V-neck top that tied in the back. Rand would love it.

"Don't worry." Famous last words. "He's mad at me, not you, because he knows Jean and I went to Christof for help. He's jealous of Christof—he's jealous of anyone who spends time with you right now—so whatever you think of Christof, don't share it with Rand. In fact, don't mention the faery at all. If Rand asks, act indifferent."

"But I like Christof. . . . Oh, okay. I know. Tell Rand what he wants to hear." Eugenie laughed. "Play nice. You catch more elves with honey than vinegar and all that stuff."

"Exactly. Have you given more thought to a regular visitation schedule?"

We left her room and walked down the stairs to the entry hall foyer. "Yes, if he'll let me keep living here—as long as that's okay with Jean—I'm willing to meet with him. Maybe once every week or two? I thought a lot about what you said. You know, about Rand making a good father, and how important it was for him to be part of this baby's life, even before he's born. You're right."

I opened my mouth to answer but was interrupted by a deep voice from below. "I'm glad to hear that, Eugenie."

Neither of us had noticed Rand standing just inside the doorway, blending in with the cream-colored walls with his blond hair and ivory skin and cream sweater. At least he'd worn jeans and black boots to tone down the Russian snow prince look, although he was still the prettiest elf on the planet.

Eugenie blushed, which made her look even prettier, and Rand wasn't immune, no matter how much he looked down on her for being human and, God forbid, a hair stylist.

He came to a stop a couple of feet in front of her and stretched out his hand toward her belly. "May I?"

I bit my lower lip to keep from asking where the real Quince Randolph had gone and could he stay there because this kinder, gentler version was much nicer. Instead, I suggested we go into the study.

I followed them like the suspicious third wheel that I was, and held my breath when Rand pulled Eugenie down into Jean's huge recliner with him. I got no sense that he was manipulating her. He kept his movements gentle and slow as he slid his hand beneath her top and rested it on her belly.

Rand closed his eyes and relaxed his face into the genuine, sweet smile we rarely saw, as opposed to the devious, flirtatious, conniving, or imperious smile we saw way too often. "He's growing stronger, bigger. He's healthy. You're doing great, Eugenie."

She placed her hand on top of his. I couldn't believe she was actually touching him. It might be a day for miracles. "DJ, would you leave us alone for a little while?"

I gave her my best what-the-hell-are-you-thinking look, but she ignored it. Since I couldn't browbeat her, I had a mental beatdown on Rand instead.

Okay, elf. I'm going to leave you alone with her. If I get even a whiff that you're influencing her moods, manipulating her free will, or trying to change her in any way whatsoever, I will . . . I will . . .

Rand grinned. *You will what, Dru? Come on. Talk dirty to me.*

I narrowed my eyes and filled them with promise. *I will screech at you so loud and so hard that your brain will explode, and I will do it all day, every day, for the rest of our godforsaken lives.*

Ow. Harsh. "I promise not to do anything. Just let us spend some time together, Eugenie and the baby and me. Then we have some stuff to talk about ourselves."

Yeah, we did, and I had a letter for him to deliver.

I assumed my regular spot on the front steps of the verandah, watching as the full moon disappeared and the world turned from pitch-black to a gloomy shade of dark gray. I rarely missed being outside during what passed for sunset in Old Barataria. Within an hour, the darkness would return until the "gray sun" returned for an hour at dawn.

If I'd tried hard enough, I could've eavesdropped on Eugenie and Rand, whose soft voices drifted out the open study window. I wanted to respect their privacy, at least as long as they seemed to be playing nicely and no screaming or shouting ensued. I even heard Eugenie laugh a couple of times. Damn, but I hated that her life had become as tense and screwed up as mine. Worse, really, because I did have tools at my disposal; she couldn't fight back.

Jean had gone into Old Orleans to take the temperature of his allies there among the historical undead as well as other species. Adrian had gone inside for the hour of daylight, although I thought even a vampire could walk around under this gray sky without fear. Jake and Collette remained in Old Orleans, where they'd spent the day, and Rene was spending Christmas Eve with his family in St. Bernard Parish. It would be their first Christmas without his brother Robert; I hoped they managed to find some joy.

Deep in thought, I jolted in alarm when Rand plopped down on the steps next to me. Sneaky elf.

"How'd it go?" I crossed my fingers where Rand couldn't see them.

"Good. Do you think Eugenie is safe here, with Lafitte and his band of criminals?"

Excuse me? "I'll have you know that just because that self-serving council has put out warrants, we aren't criminals."

Rand laughed and slipped an arm around my shoulders. I looked at his hand dangling near my left collarbone and considered biting it. "I wasn't talking about you guys—I meant the pirates."

Oh, those criminals. "Yes, I do think she's safe here. You heard Zrakovi. He says he won't try to come into Barataria because of jurisdiction, but it's really because he knows he doesn't stand a chance. Wizards without their physical magic are very limited." Except those with a powerful elven staff, of course.

"But someone was behind that vampire hit squad, and it wasn't me. I swear to it."

I patted his knee, pleased that the old Rand hadn't yet shown up. "I know it wasn't you, and so does Jean. It was most likely the wizards, but we've moved the transport so we can keep a closer eye on it. They won't get in here like that again."

Plus, although I didn't say so, Adrian's girlfriend Terri was slipping in and out of Vampyre periodically. She'd proven proficient at keeping up with the affairs of the fanged without getting caught. They were laying low and waiting to see how the other prete groups paired up before committing to an alliance—and probably waiting for a cash signing bonus.

"Let's take a walk." Rand stood up and held a hand out for me. "We need to talk and I don't want anyone listening in."

I stood up without his assistance but gave him a smile. I could play nice as long as he did. "There's a lake up in the middle of the island I've been wanting to see while it was light—well, as light as it gets here. We can walk up there. But before we go, will you do me a favor?"

He gave me his quirky, charming grin. "Of course. You want to do it here?"

Good grief. I dug an envelope out of my pocket. "This is a letter for my uncle Lennox. Would you mail it to him, or drop it off at his apartment? I really need him to get it tonight."

Rand looked at the letter. I hadn't sealed it because I knew he'd read it anyway and I thought I'd save him the trouble of trying to seal it back. "Why are you writing your uncle?"

"I want to meet with him, here. I don't know where his head's at in all this political mess and I want to see if there's any chance he'll support me."

Rand shrugged, folded the envelope, and stuck the letter in his pocket. "Sure, but I don't know if it'll do any good. He strikes me as a suck-up. He'll probably take it to Zrakovi."

Probably, but I thought it was worth a try.

We set off down the beach, and I brought the subject back to the immediate problem. "If you're asking about Eugenie's safety at Maison Rouge, does that mean you're okay with her living here?"

He picked up a stick and threw it toward the ocean. "I'd rather have her in Elfheim, but for now, I'm okay with it. I'm spending so much time in New Orleans because of the wizards and their political nonsense that I don't get home often anyway. Eugenie has agreed for us to meet every day about four, so I can keep up with my son's progress."

Thank God, although Eugenie's generosity surprised me. I'd have to make sure he hadn't mentally influenced her with elven mind crap. "I'm really glad, Rand. Eugenie needs you, but don't forget how new this whole world is for her. She's afraid, so you need to be gentle with her."

"I know. I'm trying to be understanding. Well, at least until the baby is born, and then you and I need to decide where we're going to raise him."

I halted, digging my blue toenails in the gritty wet sand. "Excuse me?"

He turned and grinned. "Just kidding."

Yeah, right. Then again, maybe it *was* a day for miracles and he'd given up on this notion that we'd ever be a couple in more than name.

"Talk to me about the fae," he said, stopping to examine a

small fan-shaped seashell, then slipping it into his jeans pocket. "How often is Christof here? Has Lafitte formed an alliance with him that goes beyond their friendship? Will Lafitte throw his people's support against Florian?"

I pondered my answer. I didn't trust Christof, but I also didn't trust Rand. Oh, he wouldn't hurt me physically, but he was a political loose cannon and, as he'd shown with Mace Banyan and his falling airplane, Rand wouldn't hesitate to take out someone he saw as an enemy. Was his enemy Christof or Florian?

"I've seen very little of Christof since I've been here." That much was true; Jean had been meeting him in Old Orleans. "He and Jean are friends but, to my knowledge, they haven't made any kind of formal political alliance."

Also true, although if Christof needed him, I had no doubt Jean would place the Lafitians at his disposal. Whether or not I'd step into that mudhole, I didn't know. Today, my answer would be no.

"If you and Eugenie have reached an agreement about the baby and your access to her—at least for now—doesn't that settle what you call the political nonsense with the wizards?" Wasn't appeasing Rand and giving him access to his child what this month's whole dustup had been about?

Not that it would make any difference in my standing with the wizards, from what I'd heard Zrakovi say earlier, but it should ease tensions between the elves and the wizards.

Rand didn't answer for a while, not until we turned north toward the center of the island. I figured we should reach the lake with about twenty minutes of light to spare.

Once we began climbing through the marshy, tall grass, Rand cleared his throat. "Before I talk to you about political things I need a couple of reassurances from you." He stopped, so I stopped. "Not reassurances. Promises. Promises that you'll swear on Alex Warin's life. You break the promise; he pays the price."

A cold chill stole across my shoulders, and I could pretend it was caused by the winds blowing off the Gulf, but that would be a lie.

"I don't know that I can make a promise like that, no matter what it is. I'll swear on my own life, but not on Alex's."

He smiled at me, and this wasn't the sweet smile. It sent the chill bumps racing across my scalp. "Then the deal's off. I'll leave Eugenie alone until one day, when your guard is down—and it will be eventually. Then I will take her. I'll fry her mind so deeply she'll never be worth a damn again. Once my son is born, she will be returned to you. Useless."

We might be in the wide-open span of Grand Terre Island's highest point, but my chest constricted as if I were trying to draw air in a closed coffin. The only thing that kept me breathing was anger.

"By the way, what happens to one of us if the other dies, Rand?" Forget moral absolutes. I had Charlie tucked in his secret holster and I would fry Quince Randolph right here.

He looked genuinely surprised. "Why would you ask that? I would never let anything happen to you. Never, no matter how much we disagreed."

God help me, I hated this elf. "Answer my question."

He huffed and started walking again. We crossed a small ridge, and there was the lake. Its water was crystal clear and laced with bright green spatterdock. How it grew with no light was beyond me, but maybe that's why it was called the Beyond.

"If one of us dies, the other might die as well—would certainly be weakened." Rand's voice had grown soft. "When my father was killed, my mother, Vervain, slowly began to die as well. Even if she hadn't been murdered last month, she wouldn't have lived much longer. Her will was failing."

I had a feeling my will wouldn't fail, nor would Rand's. "But that was because they truly were mates, right? They loved each other?"

Rand quirked an eyebrow at me and laughed softly, then sat at the edge of the lake. "Bonds in Elfheim rarely have anything to do with love, Dru. They're always political. If there's a physical attraction between mates, that's considered something to be highly celebrated." He looked up at me. "That's why our union is so special. We're physically attracted to each other."

I stared at him, aghast. No wonder he couldn't understand why I hadn't, and would never ever ever, respond to his overtures. He'd grown up in a society where a bonding like ours was as good as it got.

"That's awful," I finally choked out, sitting next to him. It made things a lot clearer. He would love to get Alex out of the way, so these promises must be doozies.

"What are the two promises you want me to make—not that I'm going to. But before I gamble with either Alex's life or Eugenie's, I need to know what you're after. And, by the way, no matter which way I go, I will never forgive you for this. Never."

My fingers itched to take Charlie and get it over with, and if it cost me my will to live, so be it. If I were responsible for Eugenie's sanity or Alex's death, I wouldn't want to live anyway.

"The first promise is this." He shifted toward me, and in the fading light I recognized the stubborn, imperious elven prince I truly despised. "That if things become unsafe here, if you see any sign at all that Eugenie and my child might be in danger of being used as political pawns, you will let me know so that I can get her to safety in Elfheim."

Jackass. Like I'd deliberately leave Eugenie in danger. "And the other promise?"

He reached out and grabbed my hand, and no amount of tugging on my part could free it. Fine. He could hold my hand; he couldn't read my mind anymore so if it gave him a thrill, let him go for it.

"You must promise, on Alex's life, that you will not share what I am about to tell you."

"Then why tell me?" Idiot elf.

"Because I want you to be prepared, and to keep yourself safe. You can't do that if you're ignorant of what's really going on."

I should hit him with Charlie just for using the word *ignorant*. "Does this have something to do with the proposal you gave to Zrakovi about the council?"

He sidled a look my way. "You were listening. You tell me."

I shrugged. "So no, I don't know what your proposal is, only that you made one and didn't seem to be giving Zrakovi much choice in responding quickly."

"Well, do you agree to make these promises on my terms?"

My mind raced in aimless loops and circles. "This is a huge request, Rand. Can you give me until you come to visit Eugenie tomorrow to give you an answer?"

It was getting dark, but there was still enough light for me to see his eyes narrow. "So you can talk it over with Lafitte?"

"So I can think about whether I can make these promises in good faith. Maybe so I can come up with a counteroffer." Definitely a counteroffer.

"Fine." He got up and this time, didn't offer me a hand. I wouldn't have taken it anyway.

We descended the rise at a fast clip so we could reach the flat beach before full dark. "I'll give you a freebie to ponder while you're making up your mind." Rand was striding about two feet ahead of me, using his long stride so I'd have to run to catch up.

"What?" I refused to run, so I had to shout to be heard above the waves as the tide grew higher.

He turned and waited for me. "Zrakovi ordered the vampire attack. They were to take both you and Eugenie. Our First Elder, however, overestimated the vampires' motivation and underestimated how many allies Lafitte has living here. The vampires want nothing to do with the loups-garou, and there are at least two here. But Zrakovi wants to punish you for making him look weak and foolish. He doesn't realize how easy that is to do. He was a strong Elder during times of peace, but peacetime leaders don't always make good wartime generals."

How well I knew that. Among the many lessons learned from Hurricane Katrina's assault on New Orleans was that the people who made good leaders in prosperous days often fell apart during a crisis. The unlikeliest heroes had stepped up in those dark days after the levee failures.

Zrakovi had been a good Elder. It had only been since the political waters got murky that he'd grown desperate. Desperate men can do evil things.

"How do you know it was Zrakovi who ordered the raid?" I wouldn't exactly take the word of any of the vampire leaders.

"I have his office bugged." Rand shrugged, as if that were the most normal pronouncement he could make. "You can learn a lot that way."

CHAPTER 23

I'd been pacing around the study for an hour, waiting for Jean to get home, when Jake stuck his head in the door on his way to transport duty and said the pirate would be staying in Old Orleans for the night. I was so focused on Rand that I didn't spend more than a passing moment wondering about where he'd stay, and with whom he might be staying.

Eugenie had gone to bed early, in a blue funk over Violette's death, being alone on Christmas instead of comforting her nieces, and the prospect of seeing Rand every day. Rene had planned a big Christmas Eve with his family. Jake and Collette would be on the beach watching the transport for the next eight hours and making googly eyes at each other in the flambeau light. Adrian was upstairs with Terri, trading blood and fangs and God knows what. I didn't want to know.

I had been left alone with my thoughts, and they weren't good ones. The more I pondered over Rand and his *promises,* the more I wanted to choke the elven life out of him and screw my moral absolutes.

I would promise to keep Eugenie safe, although if I thought Barataria was getting dangerous for her, I'd take her somewhere other than Elfheim. That would be my counteroffer on Eugenie. My first idea was that I would stash her with Louis Armstrong again, but he had known ties to all of us and it might not be possible for him to protect her. Maybe Faery, but it was no safe place these days, either. I'd have to give it some thought.

As for the secret plot business Rand said he'd share for my own protection, he could keep his lousy information. I had plenty of holy water and unlimited time for scrying. I'd find a way to watch Zrakovi and, whatever the scheme was, I'd find it out for myself and tell whoever I chose.

What those promise demands revealed to me was that Rand was preparing to make a big move, one which would throw everyone into danger. He wanted to cover his ass by making sure his bond-mate and the mother of his child were safe. It would be a great pity if I got killed and he lost his will to live just as he was getting all the power he wanted.

Freakin' elf.

"Hey, DJ—special delivery." Collette knocked on the study door and came in holding a letter that sent my heart skittering. Had Lennox answered already? Had he turned me down?

I looked at the envelope, which featured a fleur-de-lis on the flap and was the same size as the earlier note from Audrey.

"How'd it keep from getting wet?" The transport was way underwater by now.

"It came in that same cheap plastic bin with the top on it." Collette laughed. "It's perfect for our transport because it floats."

I opened the letter while she grabbed a couple of sodas and headed back out to Jake.

Happy Christmas, cousin! Please come to 147 Dauphine Street in Old Orleans right away. Your Christmas present is wrapped and waiting in room 104!

xoxox—Audrey

Uh-huh, because I was falling right into that trap. I had a new Eugenie hand-me-down romance novel waiting on my bed and my least-frilly pink negligee was clean. That was my Christmas present.

Halfway to my bedroom, I looked at the note again. It would be stupid to go, no doubt about it. I'd be taking a risk based on nothing but curiosity and boredom, a combination that had killed more than one cat.

Oh, what the hell. If this hellcat died, her elven tomcat would be close behind. It might be worth it.

Inside my head, Alex's voice chastised me the entire time I spent getting dressed in my best pink sweater and jeans, strapping on my pink wristwatch, and pulling on my (thankfully brown leather) boots. You're being impulsive, he said. You're taking too many chances. You invite chaos.

Yeah, well, it was nine o'clock on Christmas Eve and I was going out. Maybe I'd run into Jean and Christof, maybe with their friend the undead Truman Capote. We'd all go to hear Louis Armstrong play. Talk about chaos.

I ran upstairs and poked my head in Eugenie's room, but she was asleep, so I went back down, grabbed my messenger bag, tucked Charlie inside, and headed out the front door toward the beach.

"Where you going, sunshine?" Jake stood up, his stance wide and ready to stop me. "If you think you're going to New Orleans, you need to think again. I heard what happened at the council meeting today. Jean left instructions that *Jolie* wasn't to go anywhere."

Yeah, I bet he did, bossy pirate. "I'm going to Old Orleans to meet my cousin and that's nonnegotiable." Or I could be meeting Zrakovi with a goon squad, which would be truly ironic since I was going to so much trouble to try to arrange a meeting with him.

Jake relaxed a little. Just a little. "I don't know if that's a good idea, DJ. You want me to get Adrian to go with you?"

"No way. If I drag him away from his romantic Christmas Eve tryst, he'll bitch my ears off all the way to Old Orleans and back."

"You could go with DJ while I watch the transport, and make sure it's really her cousin and not a setup," Collette said. "Just don't stay gone too long." Her smile held all kinds of promises, and not the kind Quince Randolph was asking for.

"Good grief, guys. I don't need a chaperone." I did, however, need a rubber wet suit. "I'm going to move this transport above the tide line."

"Nope, don't move it." Jake checked the clip in his pistol and stuck it back in his shoulder holster. "Jean decided he likes it where it is. The water will throw off anyone who comes in not expecting it, so it's safer for us to keep it open. In fact, he's talking about having you move it farther out."

If I moved it much farther, I'd be completely underwater, and this little wizard wasn't going there.

"Come on, a little water won't hurt you," Jake said. "And don't argue—I'm going with you." He rolled up his pants legs, like that was going to help anyone shorter than Andre the Giant. "Let's see the address."

I handed him the note. "Is there a transport near that spot so I don't have to use the big one at St. Louis Cathedral?" If

I ran into anyone I knew, it would happen at the cathedral transport.

"Yeah, there's one on Dauphine that's gotta be closer. Let's do it."

He gave Collette a lingering kiss, so lingering that I was up to my hips in water by the time he sloshed out to join me. "Does that magic stick work in water?"

"This magic stick works everywhere." I loved Charlie, who gave and gave and never asked anything in return except an occasional polish. If only I could find a man as dependable.

I didn't need the staff in this transport since it was open, however, so I simply spoke the transport name Jake gave me: *Dauphine Express*. Cute.

Turns out it was the name of a hotel and bar a few doors from the transport, which lay in the middle of Dauphine Street. Jake looked at the note again. "This is it, the Dauphine Inn Express."

It lay on a quiet block—at least it was quiet for Old Orleans, a mind-boggling mirror version of the modern city, with working artifacts from different eras. A few places had electricity, and they were always crowded with a variety of species. Goblins took up space at most of the bars serving modern alcohol smuggled in by Rene and Jean, from which they earned an enviable income. At least on this block, there weren't hookers of every species offering their services from open doorways and windows.

One would never know it was Christmas Eve, either. Not a bit of mistletoe in sight.

Jake started toward the hotel but stopped when he realized I wasn't following. I'd need to send him back to Barataria, unless . . . "Is this an open transport?"

I knelt and touched a finger to the interlocking circle and triangle etched into the brick of the street. It had an odd vibe to it. It was open, but what the hell had it been powered with?

"It's an old wizard transport that Christof adapted to work with faery magic, so it's a secretly open transport we can use. If you tried to use wizard's magic on it, it wouldn't work," Jake said. "Of course, now that I've told you it's here, I'll have to kill you—unless you promise not to tell."

I'd heard a lot of that today. Since he didn't need me to get him back to his fiancée in Barataria, I'd let Jake be chivalrous and escort me to the mystery room. I couldn't imagine what Audrey had done, and half expected to see Lennox or Zrakovi, backed by a cadre of muscle, when I knocked on the door.

What I didn't expect to see was Alex, wearing nothing but a tight pair of black boxer briefs and a red velvet bow around his neck. I swear I almost swooned. I definitely drooled.

"Oh my God. I'm scarred for life. I'll never be able to unsee that." Jake slapped his hands over his eyes and headed back down the hallway, so he missed Alex's grin. "I'm outta here. Use that transport to get back, DJ."

I didn't manage to thank Jake. I wasn't sure I could even talk. Every moment of awkward, geeky shyness I'd ever experienced came back to visit. At least until Alex gave me that devilish smile I hadn't seen in forever, slightly lopsided and settling a crease to the left of his mouth that wasn't quite a dimple but was sexy as hell. "I missed you."

So I did what any love-struck woman would do when faced with the half-naked man of her dreams wrapped up in a red bow, saying he missed her: I burst into tears. Which pissed me off, and that in turn made me cry more. Leave it to good old romantic DJ. I finally got to hold the man I love, to touch him, to kiss him, and instead I wept like an idiot.

He drew me into the room and held me. "Let it out." His voice cracked. Maybe I wasn't the only emotional wreck in the Dauphine Express. "God, I've missed you."

I finally pulled away and kissed him, long and hard and thoroughly.

"Hold that thought." Alex crossed the room, painted hot pink and filled with black furniture, and propped a straight-backed chair under the doorknob. Then he set an electronic gadget in front of the chair. When he twisted a few knobs and switches, the device chirped twice and its LED light turned green.

It looked like an updated tracker to let us know if a prete were approaching. Although this was Old Orleans, so I didn't know how effective it would be. Anyone passing by the door would be a prete of some kind since few humans knew this world existed.

What the tracker did accomplish was to give me a sobering reminder of how big a chance Alex had taken in coming here, which dried up the rest of my tears.

Before I could chastise him for coming, or he could chastise me for responding to such a vague note, we were in each other's arms again. We lay on the bed, just touching, remembering the feel of each other. With our world on the brink of war, we might never get this chance again, and as much as I wanted to feel him inside me, what I wanted more was closeness. Awareness. Touch.

This.

We held each other, and I rested my head on his shoulder, taking in his scent of citrusy soap and minty aftershave. I also detected a hint of leather, from the leather jacket that lay draped over the back of a chair next to the bed, a pistol in a holster peeking from underneath. The jacket had a blob of something white near the back of one shoulder. Mr. Neat had actually missed a spot; he needed me.

His heart beat a steady cadence against my cheek, so I sped it up by letting my fingers take a leisurely stroll down his chest and southward.

"You're asking for trouble, woman." At the gruff tone of his voice, I raised my head and met his dark, chocolate-brown eyes, rimmed by long lashes that didn't take an ounce away from his masculinity. I wanted to drown in those eyes.

"I like trouble, remember? Almost as much as I like opening presents." I tugged on his red bow, slid it from around his neck, and tossed it aside.

In another time, another situation, that comment about liking trouble could've opened the door to an argument. Not tonight. "You'd be in even more trouble if you got rid of those clothes," he said.

"Promise?" I slowly pulled off the white T-shirt covered with pink rhinestones, exposing my least-offensive pink lacy bra and, a few moments later, the matching bikinis.

Alex propped himself up on his elbows, those sexy lips widened in a wicked smile. "You even have a pink watch. Am I missing a new phase in your life?"

I laughed and jumped on the bed so he could finish the undressing. "Yeah, the phase where Rene had to buy me underwear four days before Christmas and chose a passive-aggressive way of showing me what he thought of the experience."

He slowly lowered the straps of the bra, narrow nothings of fabric attached to lots of dainty lace. "Hm. I don't know how I feel about another man handling your underwear."

Then I wouldn't share with him the fact that these particular panties had been zoomed slingshot-style between Rene and Jean Lafitte. They *had* been washed.

They proved their airworthiness again as Alex stripped them away and tossed them halfway across the room. My ability to talk disappeared, and we lost ourselves in each other with a desperation born of need, longing, and fear.

Later, although I wasn't sure how much later because the

pink watch had gone flying at some point, we simply lay together again. The heat of his body, the steady thrum of his heart
against mine, gave me a sense of peace I hadn't felt in weeks.
We'd wasted so much time arguing before I'd been forced to
leave.

"I guess we have to talk." Alex turned onto his side and
pulled me against him more tightly. "I used your emergency
tonic to cross the border. That was some nasty stuff."

No argument from me. "It's worn off by now."

"I thought if I crossed back in the middle of the night, I
might slip back into New Orleans unnoticed."

At least I could send him back via the secret faery transport,
which would help to shield him. As a shifter, his energy signature wasn't as unique and trackable as my wizard's energy. He
should be okay.

He reached over and lifted the paw-shaped locket. "Did this
work like it was supposed to?"

I propped on my elbow. "It lets me see through faery glamour. Did you know it would do that? It's brilliant."

He smiled. "I hoped it would work. Once I found out the
fae didn't like dogs, I got Audrey to clip off some fur while I
shifted. I figured if you were going to be around Christof very
much, you'd need it."

"You still trust Audrey, then?"

He hesitated a fraction too long. "Within limits. She really
doesn't know a lot about the magical world except from her
lessons. Since she hasn't been able to pass her exams for Red
Congress, her father has kept her isolated from his work."

"Speaking of Lennox, I sent a letter to him this afternoon
when Rand came to visit Eugenie." I'd debated whether to tell
Alex about it, but of all the people I knew, he had the best handle
on Zrakovi's state of mind. Plus, my days of keeping secrets from

Alex were over. I hoped. "I asked him to come to Barataria tomorrow and talk to me."

Alex traced his fingers up and down my arm. "I don't think he'll double-cross you on Lafitte's turf, but what do you hope to gain from it? Audrey says he doesn't like Zrakovi, but he plays the game really well."

I wondered how much Lennox confided in his daughter. I had no idea, thus my own lingering caution. "I want him to set up a meeting between Zrakovi and me, or at least talk to him about the possibility. I'm hoping that, as my uncle, he'll be able to tell me what might calm Zrakovi down and make him understand that I'm more of an asset to the wizards than I am a liability to him."

Alex was quiet for a few moments while he digested that idea. "I don't know, DJ. Zrakovi's determined to make an example of you. He's beyond Rand and the baby issue and political alliances at this point. You outsmarted him and everyone knows it, so he's embarrassed. Then Rand made it worse by using your information to threaten him. He thinks he can solidify his power by taking you down."

My laugh was bitter. "First, I'm not that important in the grand scheme of things. Plus, he's already fired me and stripped my Green Congress license. All that's left to *take me down* is sending me to Ittoqqortoormiit, which he has to realize would kill me because of that elven survival thing."

I thought of a new wrinkle. "Killing me would kill Quince Randolph, too, eventually. It might take a year or two but he'd die. I don't want Zrakovi to know that, though. He'd come after me even harder."

Alex sat up and looked at me in alarm. "You mean if I off that elven jackass it will kill you?"

I nodded and sighed. The mention of the elven jackass

officially ended the romantic part of the evening. "I finally got an answer out of him, and that's what he told me. The elves don't advertise it, of course, or else their enemies would only need to target their bond-mates."

I shrugged. "He might be blowing smoke up my ass but I don't have any choice but to believe him."

I decided not to share the part about elves not factoring love into their marriages. That had been a major revelation to me because it told me Rand really considered our union a marriage. I'd been sure he'd eventually snap out of his delusion and realize what we had was a business arrangement.

To an elf, apparently, they were the same thing.

As long as I was running my mouth, I might as well keep going. "Speaking of the elven jackass, I also got an interesting ultimatum from him today."

I told Alex about the promises Rand wanted from me, all of the details, including the threat on his life. He responded pretty much as I expected, with barely restrained fury.

"That son of a bitch." He got up and pulled on his pants. Yep, talking about Quince Randolph had definitely ended our romantic interlude. "And now I can't even kill him, which royally sucks."

I finished dressing. "I plan to make a counteroffer." I shared my idea about Louis Armstrong, hesitating when I got to the part about planning to scry Zrakovi. I had to trust Alex, however. It wasn't right that I professed to love him and yet put Rene and Jean higher on my trust-o-meter.

"Here's what I think about Rand and his secret-keeping. Did you hear what he said to Zrakovi at the end of the Interspecies Council meeting earlier today?" I thought Alex had been talking to Toussaint Delachaise and probably hadn't heard. Thanks to Charlie's super-amplification, I'd caught it all.

Alex looked surprised. "You were watching?"

"And listening—I can hear pretty well scrying from the Beyond."

He frowned and I waited a moment for him to express his disapproval at my unorthodox technique of spying on his boss. "Good. I'm glad you have a way of keeping up with what's going on without me or Audrey interpreting it. What did Randolph say?"

I told him about the elf's so-called proposal. "My guess is that he's demanding something pretty radical, something Zrakovi's not going to like. And since Rand is all hot to make sure Eugenie's protected and I'm forewarned, he must be expecting an ugly fight."

"Or provoking one." Alex leaned over and pulled my pink watch from beneath the rickety bedside table. The room had been furnished in an eclectic hodgepodge of fine antiques and cheap fiberboard junk, all painted black, which somehow worked with the hot-pink walls. "Do you want me to warn Zrakovi or wait and see how it plays out?"

The fact that he had asked, and not stomped out to tell his boss without any regard for what it might mean, almost brought on the tears again. I'd cry when I got back to Barataria. For now, I needed to think like a shark. Or an elf.

"I'd appreciate it if you wouldn't say anything, especially since we don't know what the proposal is. But be on your guard in case Zrakovi does something crazy. I don't want you caught in the middle."

Alex smiled, but it was a sad one. "I'm already there."

CHAPTER 24

I slept late Christmas morning and woke to find the lamp lit and a pirate sitting on the edge of my bed. Well, his bed, technically. After my startled heart returned to a semi-normal pace, I threw a pillow at Jean. "It's rude to watch people sleep."

What bothered me more than Jean slipping into my room was the fact that I'd slept through it. What if he'd been a vampire or an elf or a fireball-wielding faery? Obviously, sex dulled my edge. "I want a lock for this door, please."

"Ah, *Jolie*. Would you rob a lonely man of the pleasure of watching you dream? Also, I wished to present my Christmas gift to you without observation from watchful eyes."

"Um . . ." I hadn't gotten him a gift. What a loser. "I'm sorry, Jean. I don't deserve a gift; I didn't buy anything for you. For anyone. I've been too busy feeling sorry for myself, I guess." A self-obsessed loser.

"Bah. The giver receives the joy of seeing his gift appreciated. That is enough, and I hope you will appreciate this gift, Drusilla." He handed me a long, slim, velvet-covered box, such as might hold a bracelet. If he'd gotten me expensive jewelry, I'd feel even worse. Plus, I'd have to worry about whether or not he'd given me stolen goods and from what century they'd been stolen.

I opened the box cautiously, and laughter burbled up from my gut—I couldn't stop it. "This is perfect!"

I pulled out a slim silver dagger, its blade glinting in the lamplight, its hilt ornately carved with a crane standing among tall reeds. Jean and his birds.

"I had my silversmith make it especially for you, *Jolie*. The blade is of pure silver, so it will be useful if you need to defend yourself against a werewolf or other creature of the moon, and the hilt is small enough for your hand to wield it without discomfort."

I held it closer to the light; the craftsmanship was exquisite, even detailed, down to the fish hanging from the crane's mouth. "What's the significance of the bird? You seem to like them."

"They represent the ways of the wild, do they not? They fly free, take what they need, protect their mates and their young, and do not kill for sport. Men could learn much from them."

True, although except for my crane, Jean did seem to prefer raptors. Plus, birds got put in cages. "Thank you. I hope I don't need it today."

"It is my hope that it will never be needed, only admired." Jean shifted on the bed and propped himself up on an elbow. "What will occur today that might incite its need?"

I told him about the possible meeting with Lennox at noon. "Of course, he might not even show up."

I paused, not wanting to overstep my guest status; I'd pushed it by arranging a meeting with Lennox before talking to Jean, although I'd sent him a message by way of Jake and he hadn't objected. "If he does show up, it might be better if Christof is not here, or at least not where Lennox can see him."

Jean nodded. "To this I agree. Christof's plight worsens, and I fear for his safety. His allies are scattering to the far reaches of Faery, for those who are caught in the capital are being publicly tortured and killed by Florian's followers. Their bodies have been displayed on pikes along the main thoroughfare."

Florian scared the crap out of me, even more than some of the scary elves I'd met. "Is Christof still in The Arch?"

"*Oui,* but he is making plans to move it to a safer location."

My horrific trip to Faery was still fresh, and I was pretty sure The Arch was one huge, honking building. "How can he move it?"

Jean smiled. "We shall see, shall we not?"

In other words, none of my business. Maybe The Arch was the magic itself and not the building. But how did one move magic?

I looked at my watch and did a double take. "It's almost eleven and I'm not dressed. Thank you for the gift, but I must get ready to meet my uncle, *tout de suite.*"

"Does this mean you wish for me to leave, even after such a special gift?"

I gave him my sweetest smile. "Thank you for the beautiful dagger. Now, leave."

A half hour later, I sat on the front steps, waiting to see if my uncle cared enough to respond to my request, and if he'd come alone as I asked. He owed me nothing, after all. He might be Gerry's younger brother, but they'd been far from close. I hadn't known he existed until a few weeks ago, when he was named to represent the UK and the European Union on the Congress of Elders.

Adrian had been the regularly assigned transport guard, but Jean had decided to take the post himself while Lennox was here, and I knew his brother Dominique, an expert artilleryman in his human life and his undead one as well, was upstairs with a small cannon aimed at the transport.

Jean was willing to let me hold a peace talk at Maison Rouge, but his malleability only went so far. He'd also insisted I move the transport, although I only took it a couple of feet farther into the Gulf. I wasn't learning to swim at my advanced age just to avoid drowning in my own transport. Wizards plus water equaled disaster. I'd almost drowned earlier in the year, and one round of merman CPR was enough, thank you.

Shortly before noon, I sensed a disturbance in the air and stood up a second or two before Lennox St. Simon appeared in the ankle-deep water; we were at low tide. He wasn't dressed like an Elder—in his usual dark business suit, in other words. He wore khakis, a blue sweater, and a lightweight black leather jacket. The sight of him sent a pang of sadness through me. For just a moment, with the light of the flambeaux on his face, I realized he looked more like Gerry than I'd originally thought.

"Rather a clever spot for a transport." He sloshed out of the water and waited at the foot of the banquette for me to reach him. Smart. That told me he was willing to respect this as Jean's home and not overstep.

I stopped in front of him, willing myself not to cry again. I swear, I must have seasonal affective disorder. Because only a physiological response to a lack of sunlight could bring out the tears this easily. It couldn't possibly be my screwed-up life.

"Happy Christmas, DJ." Lennox smiled and before I realized I was moving, I'd wrapped my arms around his neck. He hugged me back, a real hug, then pulled back and smoothed the hair away from my face. Make that my splotchy, almost-in-tears face. "You've gotten into a rather bad spot, haven't you?"

I smiled at his British understatement skills. "Rather. Thank you for coming."

"Of course. You are my niece. You're family."

As simple as that? Not simple at all, but it was a start. "Come on, let's go inside so you can dry off your shoes."

I saw Lennox into the entry hall, then went to thank Jean for standing watch. When I returned, Lennox was barefoot and trying to wring water from the bottom of his trouser cuffs.

"Sorry about that. Having a transport in the water seems like a great idea until one actually has to use it."

He chuckled. "It's brilliant, actually. Transporting is such unpleasant business anyway that landing in water makes for a bit of a shocker."

I poured a soda for myself and Lennox chose to try Jean's brandy. He'd taken a seat on the settee, so I took the power position in the monster-recliner.

"I'll admit I was rather surprised when Quince Randolph delivered your letter. I hate to bear bad news, but I believe he read it."

I laughed. "Of course he did. I didn't bother sealing it to save him the trouble of having to pry it open. I don't mind him knowing that I want to improve my situation with the council." He sure hadn't done anything to help me.

"Not your situation with the council, DJ, but with Willem Zrakovi. If we're going to speak, let us speak frankly. What you say to me will go no further, and I hope you will grant me the same discretion."

How much nicer to ask me for discretion rather than threatening the life of someone I loved to force my silence. I hadn't yet decided to let him know my involvement with Audrey, however. Partly because I still wasn't sure who to trust, and partly to keep her from getting in trouble with her father. I might not completely trust her yet, but I did like her.

"Of course." I paused, pondering where to begin this delicate dance of words. "Rand—Quince Randolph—and my friend Eugenie Dupre have reached an agreement on visitation during her pregnancy, so he's backed off his demands to have her live in Elfheim." I paused to mentally gather my argument. "That means his threat to the alliance of the elves and wizards no longer applies."

Lennox took a sip of the brandy and studied the glass with appreciation in his aura, which up until now had been completely flat and calm. "Very nice brandy. Is it French?"

I laughed. "Yes, and very old." I'd poured it from Jean's private stash. "Anyway, I had hoped that you'd be willing to set up a meeting between Elder Zrakovi and myself, so that I could try to convince him how useful I would be to the wizards—even to him—if I were reinstated, or at least allowed to return to New Orleans without being sent to Ittoqqortoormiit.

"Because of a condition I inherited when Rand and I formed our bond, I can't live long in very cold weather. It's essentially a death sentence."

Lennox frowned and set his glass on the side table that filled the corner between our seats. "Is Zrakovi aware of this?"

I reminded myself to be fair. Lennox might be my uncle, but he was still an Elder and Zrakovi was his political superior.

"I don't have proof that he took it into consideration when he pronounced my sentence. I don't have proof that he realized it was the same as a death sentence for me. But he does know about my condition." I spared him the story of going into hibernation in the middle of Royal Street in broad daylight a couple of weeks ago.

"This is most disturbing." Lennox leaned forward and propped his elbows on his knees. "I wonder if our First Elder is not even more unbalanced than I'd feared."

I'd been wondering the same thing. "The point is, I really

could be an asset to the wizards. I am not their enemy. Not *your* enemy, and not Zrakovi's."

At least I was trying like hell not to be.

Lennox pursed his lips with a very Gerry-like frown. "I quite agree that you are an invaluable asset to the wizards, especially as alliances grow thinner. To my knowledge, you are the only wizard capable of doing both wizards' and elven magic. You are Green Congress, correct?"

"I *was* Green Congress." Now I was unemployed and unlicensed. It didn't mean my magic had been stripped from me, only that I couldn't legally use it outside my own home. If I had a home. "And I *am* a wizard, first and foremost. Sometimes I think Elder Zrakovi forgets that."

Lennon retrieved his brandy glass and traced a finger around the rim, staring at the rich brown liquid. "Willem Zrakovi advanced to First Elder under very trying conditions, but he has proven himself a weak leader under pressure. DJ, you managed to expose his every weakness within a few days of his assuming the First Elder position—his arrogance, lack of imagination, fear of looking weak, inability to negotiate effectively. Bloody hell, you couldn't have undermined the man more brilliantly if you'd been trying."

My uncle didn't know about my empathic abilities, or at least I didn't think so. Outside my circle of friends, Zrakovi was the only one, other than Adrian, who knew the extent of my elven abilities, and he tended to dismiss them as insignificant. I once considered the empathy a hindrance, but I'd been wrong. It was priceless.

Because of that particular skill, I knew that Lennox was proud of what I'd done to Zrakovi, knowledge that both relieved and horrified me. Relieved because he wasn't likely to turn me in or reveal this conversation; horrified because he was so delighted that he might want to use me against Zrakovi to pursue his own ambitions.

"I didn't intend to weaken his position as First Elder." I really wanted Lennox to understand that. "Willem Zrakovi has been my boss for years. As head of the North American wizarding communities, he has always been fair and reasonable." I had honestly liked the man. I had defended him. I'd *wanted* him to become First Elder.

"Sadly, DJ, the stress of trying to lead during such an unsettled and crucial time has made him desperate and rash. He is in over his head, and his decisions have weakened the wizards' power structure. The Elders were once feared and respected by the other ruling groups. Now, they are at best equals, at worst a joke."

Which meant things on the Interspecies Council were worse than I realized. "So do you think it would be a mistake to meet with Zrakovi? Or would he even agree to meet with me?"

Lennox finished off his brandy and set his glass aside. "I can try to arrange it, although I'm doubtful such a meeting would do any good. Things can't get much worse, however, so we'll try it. Let's figure out how and where you can arrange it so that you don't end up dead or incarcerated on an iceberg."

An hour later, I walked with Lennox back toward the transport, plans in place. He'd rolled up his pants cuffs and carried his shoes and socks, prepared this time for a wade in the surf.

As for the proposed meeting, I was as prepared as I could be. Lennox carried a carefully worded letter to Zrakovi, which he said he'd hire a runner to slip under the door of the First Elder's rental condo on St. Charles Avenue. We'd agreed to request a public meeting place in modern New Orleans, a concession Lennox thought I'd have to make—Zrakovi would never meet in the Beyond, where he was unable to use his magic.

We talked about security and exit strategies if things went badly, which Lennox felt was fairly certain.

That didn't fill me with a lot of confidence.

We paused at the end of the banquette. I'd been thinking about how to find out if he knew about Rand's proposal without admitting I knew it existed. I liked my uncle, so far. Did I trust him? Not by a long shot.

"How are relations between the elves and wizards?" I asked, fishing for info. "They should improve now that Rand and Eugenie have reached a truce." Fish fish fish.

Lennox didn't take the bait, or at least he didn't seem to recognize the bait. "Unfortunately, I don't think the child even factors into negotiations at this stage; it was merely a diversion." Lennox put on his leather jacket, which looked odd with his bare feet but would probably feel good when he returned to New Orleans and a thirty-degree drop in temperature. "Relations seem to be deteriorating. It's clear that Randolph and his fellow elven council member, Betony Stoneman, have no respect for the First Elder and, therefore, for the wizards."

I knew Rand didn't respect Zrakovi, and whatever Rand thought, so agreed Fred Flintstone. "So all of the posturing last month, all of the threats that eventually sent Jake Warin and me on the run—all of that drama was for nothing? All that drama and there's still no peace in sight?"

It wasn't for nothing, however. Eugenie and her baby were safe, and that had been my first priority.

Lennox put his hands on my shoulders and waited until I looked up into those blue-gray eyes that were so much like my father's. "Prepare yourself, DJ, because I don't see any clear way to avoid a war between the wizards and elves, which will put you and your allies here right in the middle. The only thing keeping the peace currently is the civil war in Faery. No one knows where their loyalties might fall but I've seen no signs that Zrakovi is trying to curry favor with either Florian or Christof, and I can't circumvent him."

I shook my head, watching as my uncle waded into the transport. "I hate to think all our fates could lie with the whack-adoodles from Faery."

Lennox gave a solemn nod as he began to dematerialize. "My sentiments precisely."

CHAPTER 25

After six days in the dark cocoon of Old Barataria, modern New Orleans seemed abnormally bright, noisy, and crowded. It was not a typical winter day in my hometown, which would have been about fifty degrees, overcast, and damp. Instead, it was about seventy-five degrees and the southerly wind was dry and warm. It whipped my hair into Medusa snakes as I peeked around the northeastern corner of St. Louis Cathedral.

If it hadn't been the day after Christmas, and well out of season, I'd swear it was the kind of dry wind that preceded a tropical storm.

I'd downed a double helping of the illegal potion to mask my energy signature and slipped into town using another secret fae transport, this one landing me in a French Quarter alley off Iberville. With the help of a wizard-for-hire, Jean had told me, Christof had created secret transports all over the Beyond and the human world like a warren of mole tunnels.

The beauty? Wizards' magic would render them unusable. They were open transports but only worked if you knew the words to say and where to find them. If a wizard tried to power one, it would shut down temporarily. Only Christof and a few close allies knew about them, and for better or worse, I'd made it onto the need-to-know list. Jean had even given me a sketched-out map.

I had arrived early and walked the length of the Quarter to see if Zrakovi had set up a trap for me at the wizards' open St. Louis Cathedral transport. I'd gotten word via a note from Lennox that Zrakovi had agreed to meet me but to "be cautious." Which meant my uncle suspected a trap. What a surprise.

This was me, being cautious.

Two tall, beefy guys stood near the transport. A New Orleanian could identify tourists by their very clean white tennis shoes because our fair city, while extremely high on the entertainment scale, ranked pretty low on the cleanliness meter. Both of these guys were more scruffy than well-scrubbed. One had stringy blond hair that looked like he'd been washing his hair using the soap in Old Barataria and a long goatee that looked like the tail of an anemic squirrel. The other had shoulder-length braids and wore a Saints jersey.

Not tourists, but enforcers, waiting to grab me when I transported in for the noon meeting.

I headed back through the Quarter, staying on Bourbon and Royal to keep myself surrounded by the tourists who wandered the streets, shopping and eating, and the locals, who'd only venture into the city's old district in the winter, when the tourists were at a minimum.

The people around me barely registered, though, because my fury had overshadowed everything else. Zrakovi had failed me again. My First Elder was probably sitting at home by his phone, waiting for word that I'd been apprehended so he could gloat. I wasn't sure what pissed me off more—that he'd set a trap before hearing me out, or that he thought I'd be stupid enough to walk into such an obvious setup.

Or that I'd come without backup. I smiled at the sight of Jean's brother Pierre and one of his undead minions strolling a block ahead of me, heading for the rendezvous point at the Napoleon House. Too bad the transport there had been closed; it would've been convenient today.

The plan was for Pierre to get me the hell out of Dodge if Zrakovi showed up with guards in tow. Otherwise, the pirate and his companion would have a drink, stay hidden, and transport back to Old Orleans. Pierre wasn't anywhere near as strongly remembered in the modern world as his baby brother Jean, but he had enough memory magic to levy a day or so at a time in the modern world.

I had objected to the plan because, like Jean's half-brother Dominique You, Pierre Lafitte had little regard for me. I wasn't a hundred percent sure he'd save me, especially since Dom was still gimping around from his latest death.

Thus, my dagger and Charlie. I could handle myself. Alex once said that everyone looked at me and saw a young woman, not a strong wizard, so they always underestimated me. Zrakovi sure did. He could've at least sent enforcers that didn't *look* like enforcers.

It was still a few minutes before noon, so I took a seat inside the first-floor bar of a restaurant near the corner of St. Louis and Chartres, close enough to see the entrance of our proposed meeting spot and decide on my next tactic.

The movement of clouds to the south caught my eye, dark gray-edged billows forming a solid wall. Maybe I could get out of the city before it started raining, because that looked like a frog-splasher. Then again, it wasn't like I wouldn't get wet transporting back to Barataria.

The Napoleon House had always been one of my favorite spots in New Orleans, seeped in elegant decay and early nineteenth-century New Orleans ambience. The bar played classical music, served sweet, bubbly Pimm's Cups with cucumber garnishes, and was open on the side along St. Louis Street to provide patrons with a prime people-watching spot. The central courtyard dining room surrounded diners with banana trees and brick.

Upstairs, in the second-floor room rented out for parties, Jean Lafitte and I had formed our first uneasy alliance in the days following Katrina. If anyone had told me then that the pirate would become one of my closest allies and confidantes, I would have laughed.

I also would never have imagined myself watching the door of the restaurant to see if the wizarding world's highest-ranking member would show up for a meeting or send his hired muscle to arrest me, maybe to kill me if I resisted. Surely Zrakovi wouldn't be that brazen in the middle of a crowded restaurant at midday. At least that was the strategy.

I glanced at my watch. Ten minutes had passed since our meeting time, so Zrakovi should have gotten word that I was a no-show at the transport. I pondered my options and decided I'd wait for him inside the Napoleon House bar since a table had become available on the side that opened on St. Louis—the better to make a quick escape. If Zrakovi didn't show up, I'd have a drink and leave. I should have about forty-five minutes of energy-shielding time left, judging by the amount of foul swill I'd chugged down.

Checking to make sure Charlie was within easy reach in my bag and my new dagger from Jean was tucked into a makeshift sheath on my forearm, I ambled across the street and took a seat facing the door.

I ordered a Pimm's Cup and got it in no time, delivered by a flirtatious waiter. In New Orleans, wait staff were either surly or shameless; no middle ground existed.

"This your first time in town, darlin'?"

I must look awfully clean—had to be the pink sweater. "Nope, I'm a local, but I've been out of town. We expecting a storm?"

His eyes widened. "You have been gone. Honey, we went under a hurricane warning this morning. There's a cat two headed straight for us—rain should be starting anytime."

A hurricane in December? "That's insane."

"Yeah, you right. You want a sandwich?"

I assured him I was waiting for someone but would probably want another drink, and he went off to flirt with a tourist more likely to leave a big tip. I'd just taken my first sip when a short, sour-faced man with an oversize nose and a navy suit filled the doorway. At least for now, no guards were visible behind him.

I waved, and Willem Zrakovi's anger reached me all the way across the crowded bar. He jerked out the scarred wooden chair opposite mine and flounced into it more like an angry teenage drama queen than the king of all wizardkind.

"Don't look so put out just because I didn't fall into the waiting arms of the were-goons you had waiting at the cathedral transport. All I want is to try and have a conversation with you, sir."

I'd already decided that I was not going to be meek. I wouldn't plead and beg, especially since he'd tried to set me up. I would, however, try to be respectful and reasonable. *Try* being the operative word.

He didn't deny setting the trap, but instead ordered a scotch and soda from the waiter, who wisely turned off the flirtatious charm. Zrakovi and I stared at each other until his drink arrived. It was awkward, but small talk seemed inappropriate.

His first question astounded me with its shortsightedness. "How did you get here without a transport?"

No, let's not talk about the looming war, or how I can help you, or how you can help me, or how we can promote peace, love, understanding, and preternatural world accord. Let's talk about transportation.

"I did use a transport, just not the one you expected me to use. I'm sure you understand why I felt the need for extra precaution."

He leaned back and studied me, so I did the same. Dark circles rimmed his lower lashes and his eyes were bloodshot. He looked exhausted, but I had trouble summoning any sympathy.

"What do you want, DJ? I'm frankly surprised you reached out to me considering all the harm you've done."

The only harm I'd done had been to his ego, and maybe indirectly via my escape, to the roof of the New Orleans Museum of Art.

I'd play his game, however. "I'm sorry things went so badly earlier this month, but I reached out because I hoped you'd realize that I am loyal to the wizards. I *am* a wizard. I want to support you."

At least I wanted to if he wouldn't make it so damned hard.

I took a deep breath and continued. "I hoped I could make you realize that, with my ability to do some elven magic, I could be an asset to the wizards should the two groups not be able to reach an accord."

Because whether Zrakovi knew it yet or not, Rand had a scheme in the works and it had nothing to do with Eugenie. He needed me, damn it.

Time for the final push. "I'd hoped enough time had passed that you realized why I made the choices I did, and would be willing to move forward."

With my job and license back, preferably.

He sneered. There was no other word that fit the curled lips and flared nostrils. "And in return for all that forgiveness and understanding, I get what—you? An arrogant renegade who lies, refuses to follow orders, and flaunts her use of illegal magic? I think not."

I swallowed a lump of anger, along with some fizzy liqueur and soda. *Think before you talk, DJ.* "So your solution is to kill me? Because that's what would happen at Ittoqqortoormiit; I'd go into elven survival mode and never come back from it. That's really what you want?"

He blinked and looked away. I'd needed to be sure he realized what that unspecified jail sentence meant for me, and the discomfort and guilt he radiated told me he knew exactly what he was doing. I'd known it deep inside, but it still hurt as if Jean's dagger had been shoved into my gut. Zrakovi wanted me dead.

"If you want to kill me, why be so passive about it? If you want to show your power, why didn't you have me executed right there at the meeting?" I'd gone off-script, but the raging bull was out of its pen. "Why send me off to freeze to death? Why, for God's sake, sneak around and hire a crew of vampire thugs to come and get me in Barataria?"

"I have no idea—"

"Why have you gone to so much trouble to avoid killing me outright? Oh, wait. I know the answer. Because I've done nothing to deserve a death sentence and you damn well know it. You wanted to keep your hands clean."

His face assumed the hue of a ripe creole tomato in June. "How dare you speak to me this way, in such a tone! You're just like—"

"My father, I know. So you've said." I took a deep breath. I'd never intended to go off on him. "I apologize for my tone,

Elder Zrakovi, but I am a *wizard*. Whatever you thought of Gerry St. Simon, he raised me as a wizard and I have always been loyal to my kind. Last month, you asked me to do something that I truly believed was wrong—to use my magic to take a life, not in self-defense, but for political reasons. The life of my best friend's child. I couldn't do it.

"I wish I'd found a way to avoid it without disobeying your orders, but I can't apologize for making the only decision I could live with. I can only promise to try my best to work with you in the future. I can help you."

He looked at me with a blank, steady gaze that seemed to last a week and a half. "This meeting is over. There is nothing else to be said."

God, this had been a mistake. Alex and Lennox had been right. Maybe if I'd come in crawling and simpering it would have . . .

Hands the size of baseball mitts dropped onto my shoulders, and I tried to struggle from beneath them. When fingers slipped beneath the neck of my sweater and dug into my skin, holding me in place, I craned my neck up to see Dreadlocks gloating down at me from behind. One of his front teeth had been capped in gold and had a star shape cut into it. Squirrel Chin stood beside him.

Damn it, I'd lost my temper and stopped watching my back. Where was that damned pirate?

CHAPTER 26

I suggest you stand slowly and walk out with my men," Zrakovi said, tapping a napkin against his lying, two-faced mouth
and putting a twenty on the table to cover the drinks. "If you
make a scene, innocent humans will be injured. I have a Blue
Congress cleanup team in place, however, so if you want to fight
in public and damage a few humans, knock yourself out. It will
only add to your list of crimes."

I stood slowly, gritting my teeth when Squirrel Chin patted
me down while feeling me up and making it look like a romantic moment. He'd been so busy feeling the naughty bits that he
missed both Charlie, sitting in my bag next to my foot, and the
dagger attached to my inner forearm.

Idiot. Alex would never have been so sloppy. If Alex had
patted me down, he'd have found not only the weapons but also
the portable magic kit.

From the corner of my eye, I saw a tourist taking cell phone
shots of us. He'd no doubt email them to all his friends back

home with stories of those crazy New Orleanians and their public displays of affection.

I considered trying the faux fainting trick again, but I was too badly outnumbered for it to work. Like my friend Jean Lafitte, whose help I could use about now, I didn't want to try something unless it had a reasonable chance at succeeding. I also didn't want to pull Charlie out and risk humans getting hurt.

Pierre Lafitte was AWOL. He'd probably seen me with Zrakovi, spotted no enforcers, and gone home.

"Walk out the door onto Chartres and turn straight toward the cathedral." Zrakovi pulled his jacket aside enough for me to see a shoulder holster. I hadn't even known the man could hold a gun, although for all I knew about guns it could be a water pistol.

The walk to the cathedral transport was three very long city blocks. My best escape opportunity would be near Jackson Square. When the muscular goons tried to turn me left toward the cathedral, I'd try to break and run right toward the river, where I could get lost among the wharves and docks long enough to draw and power a transport. Of course in order to run, I'd have to get away from the clinch of Dreadlocks and Squirrel Chin. Charlie could take care of that.

I slipped the messenger bag over my head slowly, and not even Zrakovi noticed the stick of wood protruding from the top by a couple of inches.

Not to be redundant, but . . . idiots.

None of us spoke as we proceeded down Chartres Street, where, to our south, the clouds continued to build. The wind had grown stronger and drier. The hurricane was sucking all the humidity out of the air, all the better to gain intensity. I hoped Zrakovi, a Bostonian, would enjoy his first storm. I hoped a live oak landed on his head.

He'd been walking behind me, but now he stepped along-side me and pointed ahead. "What the hell is that?"

At first I thought he meant the clouds, but then I saw an-other threatening sight. A block down Chartres, moving slowly toward us, pranced a man in a red glitter-covered suit and hat. He shuffled his red shoes in time to the small brass band that followed him, trumpets and trombones and a big bass drum, all played by young men in black pants and white shirts. They cranked out a sloppy rendition of Rebirth Brass Band's "Do Watcha Wanna," a classic New Orleans second-line tune.

It was a good second-line parade, too. New Orleanians often formed their own impromptu parades, dancing down the streets behind other parades (the first line), jazz funerals, or just for the hell of it.

In this case, behind the official parade loomed a massive pro-cession of people clad in red and white satin dresses and suits, and behind them, as near as I could tell, a throng of tagalong people joining in the fun—sort of a third line. About half of the official procession twirled lavishly decorated red and white um-brellas above their heads, and the other half danced in circles, waving white handkerchiefs.

"It's a New Orleans second-line parade," I told Zrakovi, rais-ing my voice so he could hear me over the slightly off-key trill of the trumpets. "It's a tradition."

"It's stupid, is what it is." Zrakovi poked at Squirrel Chin, shouting, "Go around it."

The enforcer tried to cut left to the sidewalk, but the side-walks had already begun filling with people and we were in the middle of the block. There was nowhere to go but through the crowd, straight ahead.

Even with the onslaught of emotions coming from the people approaching us, I could tell Zrakovi's blood pressure was shooting into stroke territory. If only I'd be so lucky and he'd just keel over on the pavement.

My adrenaline level, on the other hand, was shooting sky-high. Never had a second-line parade been better timed.

"Hold on to her!" Zrakovi shouted at Dreadlocks. "Don't let her go!"

This was my chance. Dreadlocks kept a tight grip on my left arm as the brass band weaved around us with deafening blares of their horns. Then came the satin-clad procession itself, jostling and bumping us. I firmed up my grasp on Charlie, whose presence remained unnoticed.

I waited for the right time. Waited. Waited. Waited. Finally, as a tall woman in a poufy red dress waltzed past, twirling her umbrella over her head, I gave Dreadlocks a good zap with the staff, shoved him toward her, ducked, and zoomed through the crowd like a pinball, head-butting anyone who didn't move fast enough. I bounced off an umbrella twirler and was shoved toward a handkerchief waver, then did it again. At the end of the procession there was a lull where three guys in elaborate full-face court jester masks were doing a dance routine on Chartres in between the official marchers and the crowd of tourists and tagalongs. I put Charlie away and prepared to go through them.

All three were about the same height and build, all wearing fitted black long-sleeved T-shirts and black pants. Each mask was slightly different, but it made an eerie sight as they did a slow, hypnotic dance, moving their bodies in rhythm to the brass band but with their heads tilting only slightly to left and right. They weren't very good at it, but it was still creepy.

The guy in the center seemed to be focused on me, dark eyes glittering behind the eyeholes of his mask of ivory, gold, and royal blue, with blue and gold jester bells coming off the headpiece. He was paying way too much attention to me. I zigzagged toward the sidewalk, hoping to get lost in the crowd, but the jester left his dance, grabbed my arm, and hustled me ahead of him so fast that I almost fell.

What the hell? I planted my feet and pulled Charlie back out of the thigh holster, prepared to zap him as soon as I got a clear shot. He cocked his head, and though his voice was muffled behind the mask and all the noise, his words were clear: "Put that damn stick away and run, babe."

Only one person called me *babe*. "Rene?"

"Who the hell you think it is, Santa Claus?"

He didn't have to tell me twice. We raced down Chartres, separating around the large groups of tagalongs. He was headed toward the cathedral but I had a closer spot and screamed, "Cut left on Toulouse!"

We turned, ran another block, and I pulled Rene into a souvenir shop at the corner of Toulouse and Royal. In the back, between rows of T-shirts and shelves of shot glasses, was a small transport that had been set up by Christof. "You want to go with me or help your friends in case Zrakovi figured out you were helping me?"

Rene looked toward the front of the shop, but no way we could be seen from the street. He pulled out his cell and punched the screen a few times. "I'll text and see where they are."

He nodded a couple of times. "They're good. Zrakovi's standing in the middle of Chartres, yelling at those stupid dudes. He never saw us, so let's get outta here, wizard."

Slipping the phone in his pocket, he jammed himself into the transport with me. I hugged him and whispered, "Thank you," and then, "Maison Rouge, Old Barataria." In seconds, we were knee-deep in salty water, in the middle of a downpour.

Only the lights from the house offered any illumination. It was the first rain I'd seen in Barataria, the first time clouds had blocked out the full moon.

"Bloody hell, woman, get out of the water before you get electrocuted." Adrian had no sooner shouted the words than a jagged bolt of lightning struck a nearby banana tree with a deafening crack.

"Holy crap!"

Rene and I took off for the house, feet slipping on the wet banquette. When we finally reached the verandah, I stopped and looked back at the maelstrom. Whatever New Orleans was about to get, Barataria was getting it ten times worse.

"Come inside quickly, *Jolie*. Christof won a battle in the capital of Faery today and Florian is seeking revenge. We have much planning to do." Jean stood in the open doorway, stepping aside to let Rene and me enter.

He closed the door behind us and led us into the study. For the first time in my visits to Barataria, the floor-to-ceiling windows were closed and wooden hurricane shutters had been pulled shut and secured to protect the glass panes from the onslaught of wind and rain. It made me claustrophobic. "How long has this been going on?"

"Started 'bout an hour ago." Jake stood in the study door, pulling on a heavy black rain slicker with a hood. Behind him, Collette was doing the same. "We're gonna relieve Adrian on transport watch. I don't think vampires are cut out for this kind of shit."

He was probably right, judging by the misery on a very wet Adrian Hoffman's face when he sloshed inside a few minutes later. "It's coming a bloody hurricane out there."

"*Oui,* and it is only now beginning. It will be many hours

before the eye crosses the island. I have raised the red flag, which means all on the island must leave to find other shelter."

I half smiled when I looked around at Jean, because he was joking, right?

The pirate had never looked more serious.

CHAPTER 27

An hour later, I stood in the wide foyer with two plastic bags full of mostly pink clothing, my messenger bag with the few magic-making supplies I had in Barataria, and Charlie. I still wore the silver dagger on my forearm.

Around me, with varying containers of personal belongings, bustled Jean, Adrian, Eugenie, Jake, Collette, and Rene. I had drawn off and powered a transport on the floor in the middle of the room—three times. Each time I drew one off, Jean moved furniture and insisted I make it larger.

"What are you planning to transport, a herd of cows?" I grumbled as he and Jake shoved a large seating group toward the corner of the room, making more space.

"Just make it larger, Drusilla. *Tout de suite.* You must leave now."

What was this *you* business?

I had no idea where he thought I'd go. Transporting into the modern city would be a very bad idea, given the disaster I'd just experienced with Zrakovi. Enforcers worked during hurricanes, I felt certain. This particular wizard was persona non grata in Vampyre, and I'd rather ride out a hurricane here than pop over to Elfheim or Faery.

Unless I sailed up the byzantine bayous branching off Barataria Bay onto the mainland, which would include a several-mile trek in what felt like a cat five hurricane bearing down on us, I knew of no safe transport to go to. I assumed if a hurricane was heading for Old Barataria, it also was barreling toward Old Orleans.

"What usually happens when a hurricane hits Old Barataria?" I asked Jean as he barked orders at several of his pirates, all of whom looked scared as hell. Frightened undead pirates didn't make a reassuring picture.

"We do not have hurricanes here, as they are not things I wish to be here." Jean paced the room like an angry lion, distraught that the world built from his own memories was being manipulated by someone else's will. "This *disastre* is Florian's doing, and I do not know what will happen. Dominique has agreed to stay here, as he is still not well enough to travel, and Jake and Collette have agreed to guard our transport as long as they feel safe doing so. We must go to Old Orleans."

"I'm pretty sure it's tearing through Old Orleans. It's even impacting the modern world. New Orleans is bracing for a cat two hurricane, which is unheard of this time of year."

"Why must you talk of *les chats*? This is no time for idle chatter, Drusilla." Jean was getting snippy, and if he wanted this wizard to keep making larger transports without explaining why, he needed to dial it down a notch.

"It's the modern way of explaining the size and power of a hurricane," I explained, turning my head from side to side to watch him pace. I felt like a spectator at Wimbledon. "Category one or two storms—cats one and two—are relatively small and with lower wind speeds than, say, a category five, which is the largest on record."

Jean stared at me as if I'd lost my mind with my talk of cats. It didn't matter. All that mattered was Old Barataria was about to be socked, for the first time, by a very bad hurricane of fae origin. If Florian knew his storms, and I assume he did as the Prince of Summer, he'd move the hurricane's eye just to the west of Grand Terre, which would put the worst of the wind and storm surge right on top of us.

"Drusilla, you and Rene must transport immediately." Jean paused as a very drenched Jake and Collette battled their way through the front door and, with some effort, closed it behind them. The wind had risen, and it screamed around the corners of the house with a low, eerie wail that sounded like the ago-nized cry of a woman. It sent chills up my spine. I couldn't get out of here soon enough. Elfheim was even sounding like a viable option.

"Where you want us?" Rene grabbed my messenger bag and handed it to me, along with Charlie. "DJ, the rest of that stuff's gonna have to come later."

"Use the fae transport nearest Place d'Armes." Jean turned to me. "Once there, *Jolie,* Rene will take you to my home in the city so that you may set up a transport that links to this one. Then the rest of us shall join you."

I nodded, my mind numb and my body on autopilot, not even questioning that he had a home in Old Orleans, which was news to me.

All I could think was *hurricane.* After Katrina, I didn't think I'd ever hear the word again without replaying the horrific scenes that remained long after the storm, poor construction, and chronic neglect had caused the levees around the city to collapse.

"C'mon, DJ." Rene pulled me into the transport, and I knelt

to power it. My hands shook so badly it took three tries to touch Charlie to the circle.

"What's the destination name?"

"Pontalba," Rene said, and I sent us there, closing my eyes at the pressure of leaving, then opening them to the sensation of hot, heavy rain beating against my face. Oh yeah, Old Orleans definitely was having a hurricane.

We landed in pitch-blackness, and I couldn't see enough to even get my bearings. No one but us, apparently, was stupid enough to be out strolling in a hurricane.

"Where are we?" I shouted to Rene, grabbing his arm to avoid being blown away and losing him.

"Transport's in the middle of Jackson Square, about where the statue of Andrew Jackson would be in the modern city." Rene held his mouth to my ear so I could hear him. "Jean's place is in the Upper Pontalba, but I can't tell which way we're facing."

I fumbled in my messenger bag for the pink flashlight and finally found it. Now I understood why Rene didn't want me bringing the rest of my stuff. This was a nightmare.

"Let's walk until we figure out where we are," I yelled, tucking my left arm firmly in the crook of his right and training the flashlight beam on the ground—or what I assumed was ground beneath the layers of mud and water.

I wasn't letting him take a step without me. We'd try to walk straight and would either run into the cathedral or fall in the Mississippi River, where Rene's chances of survival were a hell of a lot better than mine.

I lost sense of time as we sloshed in what I hoped was a straight line. Every few yards, one of us would trip over something. Twice, we both tripped at once and ended up on the ground in a couple of inches of standing water. I shone the flashlight in Rene's face, and couldn't stop the giggles. He was more drowned rat than dolphin. Shifting the light onto my own face so he could appreciate the moment, I heard him laughing, too.

We struggled to our feet and kept going until, seemingly out of nowhere, a stone wall loomed in front of us and we both ran into it. We'd hit the cathedral—literally—and automatically turned to the right. Now the heavy, slanting rain, driven by strong gusts of wind, slapped our faces. Every inch was hard won.

We finally reached the edge of the stretch of apartments on the side of Jackson Square where, in modern times, one would find the row of apartments called the Lower Pontalba, America's oldest apartment buildings. I held on to the back of Rene's jacket and let him lead me about halfway down the row, where he stopped, pulled a key from his jacket, and, after fumbling a moment, opened a door.

We fell more than walked inside, and Rene had to fight to get the door closed behind us. I shone the flashlight around the room, looking for lanterns or even a light switch. "Does he have electricity here?"

"Our pirate don't do electricity, babe. Wait." He reached for the flashlight and took it to a far corner, where he struck a match and lit a lantern. Obviously, he'd been here before, since he walked straight to another lantern in the opposite corner.

An elegant parlor came to life around me, and I had no trouble recognizing Jean's taste. The walls held framed maps of the Gulf of Mexico and ships, and heavy, dark mahogany furnishings filled the room. The walls were a simple cream-colored plaster, and the elegant fireplace had been painted the same color.

While Rene lit other lanterns and went to secure all the shutters downstairs and upstairs, I began lugging furniture out of the way to clear space for a transport approximately the size of the one I'd ended up with at Maison Rouge. While I marked it off, trying to keep from dripping water on my drawing chalk and breaking my own circle and triangle, I studied my surroundings.

I'd never been inside any of the Pontalba apartments, which framed the east and west sides of Jackson Square. The waiting list to buy one was about fifteen years, last I heard. They weren't so different from the mid-century houses around town, with high ceilings, elaborate millwork, and shiny wide-plank floors.

Once the transport was drawn and powered, I yelled to Rene, who was banging around somewhere upstairs. "I'm going back to Maison Rouge."

He yelled something back that I couldn't understand because everything was drowned out by the howling, crying wind. Using Charlie to add extra oomph to the transport, I closed my eyes and in a few seconds stood again in Maison Rouge.

One of the hurricane shutters over the tall window next to the front door had blown off. The window had shattered, and the horizontal rain blew straight into the entry hall, which was more of a parlor than a hall.

Jean stood on the bottom step, surveying the destruction of his magical kingdom with a set jaw and fire in his eyes. He sprang into action as soon as he saw me. "We must get everyone from the back," he shouted. "Is the storm also in Old Orleans?"

I nodded. I couldn't outshout the sound of the storm, near-deafening with the open window.

Following Jean into the back hallway, I helped Eugenie, Adrian, and Terri collect their stuff and hustled them to the transport. Adrian looked annoyed, but both Terri and Eugenie were pale and wide-eyed. I shoved the last three bags of clothing and a bulging purse into the transport, while Jean added four or five very heavy trunks, which I assumed to be weapons and ammunition.

We hauled out stuff for Jake and Collette as well. "Why are you staying?" I shouted; the acoustics were better in the back bedroom in which they'd been sheltering.

"In case that damned elf tries to come in here at four. Don't want him to drown and cause a war to start," Jake said. "It's only another hour and we can make it that long. If he don't show up, we'll leave. If he does show up, we'll leave and bring him with us."

Great. Riding out a hurricane with Quince Randolph was high on my bucket list. Or not.

I hugged them both, hoping Rand had the good sense to stay away. It was too chaotic to focus here, but as soon as I got back to Jean's apartment, I'd try communicating with him telepathically. If I was able to warn him off, I could come back for Jake and Collette.

I joined Eugenie in the transport and motioned for Jean to join us. "I have one more thing, *Jolie*. Take Mademoiselle Eugenie and I will follow shortly."

Shrugging, I whispered "Pontalba" and off we went—trunks, bags, pregnant woman, and all.

While I'd been gone, Rene had lit a fire, had the lanterns all lit, and had changed into dry clothes. I stepped out of the transport and got halfway across the room before realizing Eugenie hadn't followed me. She sat on the floor in the transport, surrounded by piles of stuff, looking kind of green. Her arms were wrapped around her middle.

I ran back to her and knelt. "Are you okay? Are you in pain?"

She nodded and smiled. "Just started cramping a little. It's been a stressful day."

No kidding. "Can you stand up? We need to get you to a bedroom."

"I'll take her, babe." Rene edged past me, leaned over, and

picked up Eugenie as if she weighed no more than one of the bags of clothes. "There are three bedrooms in the back and more upstairs. I'm gonna put her on the second floor. You and Jean are our best defenses so you're down here. Jake and Collette can go on the third floor."

"What about the other first-floor room?" I asked as he headed down the hallway with Eugenie. "Put Eugenie in there."

Rene laughed. "No can do; it's reserved. Get as much of the stuff out of that transport as you can. I'll get the rest out in a sec."

"Why? Reserved for who?" Jean could ride back with his trunks o' guns. It wouldn't hurt them to make an extra trip.

My only response was his footsteps on the stairway.

"Fine. Whatever." I sloshed my way in and out of the transport with bags, redrawing and repowering the transport every time I accidentally dripped on or skidded across the interlocking marks.

I couldn't budge the trunks, but by the time I hauled out the last suitcase—which had to be either Jake's or Collette's, Rene was back and lifting them out. To be fair, even he huffed and grunted.

"Who's the room reserved for?" I squeezed the bottom of my pink sweater and wrung out a cup of water onto the floor, then began digging in my bags for dry clothes.

"Christof and his stuff." Rene found a bag of Oreos in somebody's bag and tossed one in his mouth, talking around it. "He took The Arch to Barataria and now he's bringing it here. Gotta find a place for it that won't put a target on the rest of us, though."

I stared at Rene. He held out the bag of cookies and I took three. It was that kind of day. "I thought The Arch was a building."

He shook his head. "No, it's a bunch of machines and computers. Hell if I know how that works except Florian moved The

Academy so Christof moved The Arch. As a result, Faery's lost most of its magic except what them Hybrids have and those two crazy bastards've got their crazy magic flying everywhere."

"What else has happened?"

Rene flopped in an oversize ivory leather recliner that had been jammed into a corner next to a delicate-legged round mahogany table—I hadn't noticed it before. Apparently, the king of Barataria had become a big fan of man-cave décor. "I dunno. I heard something about a big snowstorm in Vampyre that has the fangs spitting mad, and I assume that was Christof's doing."

Great, because we wanted to piss off the vampires even more.

I was just about to say so when a shiver of magic tickled its way across my shoulders and I focused my wrath on the transport instead. Sure enough, along with a grim-faced Jean stood a bedraggled Christof and a mountain of equipment the size of three or four industrial refrigerators.

The Arch, I presumed.

CHAPTER 28

What the hell do you think you're doing?" I marched up to Christof and propped my hands on my hips. He looked tired, with smudges of what looked like ash on his maroon sweater and navy pants. I had no idea what the others saw, but mentally thanked Alex for being so damned smart.

"You're bringing all this stuff here where Eugenie is, putting her—putting all of us—in the crosshairs of your crazy brother? Are you insane or just totally self-absorbed?"

Christof crossed his arms, narrowed his eyes, and glared at me. The temperature of the room dropped at least thirty degrees, and I began shivering in my soaked clothing.

"*Jolie,* perhaps you should don something that is not so wet, and then we must talk." Jean wrapped an arm around my shoulders and propelled me down the hallway and into the bedroom on the left.

If he thought he was going to talk me out of being pissed off at crazy fae princes, he was sadly mistaken.

He followed me into the bedroom. "Do you wish me to tarry in the hall while you tend to your toilette?"

"Please."

As soon as the door closed, I collapsed onto the floor and lay on my back. Breathe in. Breathe out. I willed my temper to calm. Failing that, I convinced my muscles to relax, drawing on years of meditation I'd used to control my empathy and strengthen my own mental wards.

When I'd finally gotten a handle on my fury at Christof, I put on my proverbial suit of pink armor and prepared for fury of a different nature. *Rand! Where are you?*

No answer, so I tried again with the same results.

The pink watch, which was still ticking despite the deluge, told me it was a quarter till four. Chances were good that, unless he were in Elfheim, Rand would see what was going on in New Orleans and try transporting to Barataria early. I still felt a strong will to live, so I assumed he hadn't drowned in the waves. Therefore, there was a strong possibility he'd show up any minute.

My anger at seeing Christof and his Mount Everest of Magic would pale beside Rand's response. It would take all of us to keep him from dragging Eugenie straight to Elfheim, and I didn't know but that it might be the safest place for her right now. Christof and Florian and their traveling magic show changed everything. I said a prayer for Alex's safety, then took a deep breath and opened the door to the hallway.

Jean lounged against the wall and looked at me with raised brows, probably waiting to see if I was still angry.

"Come on in. You're right—we need to talk."

"Is your temperament more sanguine, Drusilla?"

"Not on your life, but we still need to talk."

He came in and sat beside me on the bed. "First, I must ask

one thing. How went your conversation with Monsieur Zrakovi?"

That debacle had occurred only a few hours ago, but it felt like a month. In telling Jean about it, the rest of my anger drained. The people in this apartment, and the loups-garou still at Maison Rouge, were my only true allies. By association, that included Christof, whether I liked it or not.

"I don't see any way of changing Zrakovi's opinion of me," I said after telling an abbreviated version of the story. I didn't have the strength or time to explain second-line parades to a 230-year-old undead pirate.

Besides, losing my connection to the wizarding world had torn another jagged chunk out of my damaged heart. Until today, I'd thought I could salvage something, even if I couldn't practice magic openly. The realization that I'd failed surprised me in its hurt.

"Eventually, your wizards will come to you for help, Drusilla, and things might look differently. Our world stands on the brink of great change. Good or bad, I do not know."

My pirate, the philosopher.

For the first time, it occurred to me that Jean Lafitte, who'd always proven very well informed in the affairs of the preternatural world, might know what Rand was up to. I should have asked him earlier. My elf's deadline for making promises approached, so maybe it was time to confide in my unlikely confidant.

"Rand is up to something with regard to Zrakovi." I told him of the demands Rand had made, and the threats. "Obviously, he'd have a cow if he knew I was telling you this, so don't share."

Jean's brows drew together, and I added, "I mean, he would be most upset if he knew I was telling you this, so please don't let him know about it." I also didn't think we had time for a bovine discussion; the cat conversation hadn't gone very well.

"*Oui,* you speak truly. Let us talk of Mademoiselle Eugenie first. Please consider what I ask before you react in anger."

Who, me? "Okay."

"Given the matters I will reveal to you in a moment, consider whether your friend and her *enfant à naître* might not be safer in Elfheim until we understand how things will proceed."

I'd thought the same thing, after seeing Christof's arrival and learning the princes had left Faery toting their peoples' magic with them like so much oversize baggage. "I know Rand will protect his child, but I need reassurance from him that he'll protect Eugenie as well—from himself." He could destroy her mind faster than I could transport to Maison Rouge and back.

Jean nodded. "And Mademoiselle Eugenie might need to be convinced of this thing, but Christof would be able to help in this, I think. He does not wish to endanger her."

True, Eugenie and "Chris" had formed some unholy alliance and he might be able to influence her—but only if Rand behaved. I'd need some way of making regular checks on her, even if it meant making daily jaunts to Elfheim. I *so* didn't want to do that.

"Do you think she would be safe with Rand in New Orleans?" I might be able to sell her on the idea more easily if she could go to her own house occasionally.

Jean pondered the question for a moment, then shook his head. "I do not think it would be as secure as Elfheim, my apologies. In his homeland, Monsieur Randolph would have staff at his disposal to help her and fighters who would protect her if needed."

He was probably right, but I wasn't sure how Eugenie would take it. Then again, between Violette being killed and the vampire attack and now the hurricane, she might have had enough of life on Gilligan's Island in the Beyond. I was getting pretty sick of it myself.

"What's this other thing you have to tell me? I assume it has to do with why Christof is here, along with The Arch."

Jean leaned back on an elbow, forcing me to do the same so that we faced each other as equals.

Equals lying on a bed in the Beyond during a fae hurricane. No amount of talk could make my life normal.

"As you have realized, Christof and his brother are now openly at war."

I arched a brow at him. "Yeah, I kind of picked up on that."

"The rumors that Christof has shared with me, whose truth I have not been able to confirm, are that your elf has proposed to your First Elder a change to the Interspecies Council."

I sat up, looking down at Jean. "Do you know what the proposal is? That has to be the subject of Rand's second promise."

"Oui. Christof says he learned this information through the boasting of his brother, so he believes it to be true."

The fae couldn't lie outright, so that meant it likely was true. "What are the changes?"

"He has proposed that the wizards should no longer lead the council, and that only the wizards, elves, vampires, and fae be represented by one person each, with an equal vote in all matters. A fifth member of the council with voting ability would be chosen from among all the other species."

Oh, boy. The Elders would fight that loss of power with everything they had, and it would render the council hierarchy meaningless. Currently, the wizards, fae, and elves all had three representatives each, the vampires had two, and smaller groups such as the historical undead and the water species had one each. The First Elder held the position of the ranking member of the council by virtue of the fact that the wizards were the largest group, population-wise. But not by much.

"So if you were chosen to fill the fifth seat, your vote would be equal to that of Elder Zrakovi?" I couldn't help but smile, thinking I might have seen a hint of the pirate's endgame.

"*Oui,* in theory." Jean grinned. "But the value of the fifth vote to break a tie would depend on who had formed alliances on behalf of their people, yes?"

Yes, indeed. Rand would only propose such a change if he thought he already had majority votes in his pocket.

"Has he proposed this to anyone other than Zrakovi?" No wonder Z was in such a pissy mood earlier today. He had big problems on his shoulders and I was like an annoying gnat he wanted to squash.

"To my knowledge, no, he is waiting to hear Monsieur Zrakovi's decision before he decides on his next maneuver." Jean sat up. "Is this an arrangement to which your Elders would agree?"

I thought about Zrakovi, who as First Elder would hold all the power for our people. No way in hell my uncle Lennox would go along with that. He didn't trust Z. I didn't know the other Elders but I doubted they'd want Zrakovi holding all the power either. If it were to happen, my guess would be that either Zrakovi would be forced out, beaten down to be a mere spokesman for the larger Elder group, or be killed so someone more politically savvy could take his place. I almost felt sorry for the guy, who was probably a decent person and a strong wizard who'd been thrust by ambition and circumstance into a role to which he was thoroughly unsuited.

Almost sorry for him, but not quite.

"I don't think the Elders would agree to it, no. What do you think of it?"

"It is an interesting proposition, but there is more we do not yet know." Jean paused. "Before he fled the capital of Faery, Christof saw your elf entering the Royal Tower. He assumes it was to speak with Florian."

Rand was meeting with Florian? "If he got Florian to throw his portion of Faery behind the elves, the vampires would happily join them. Rand would rule the council." And by extension, the entire preternatural world. "Holy shit."

Jean didn't even chastise me for my language. "*Mais oui,* and that is what Christof suspects."

I got up and paced the length of the room a couple of times, thinking. "Why would Rand approach Florian and not Christof? I mean, Florian is crazy; Christof would be a much more dependable ally; plus if I'm Rand's 'bond-mate,' why not ally himself with my ally?"

"This is something Christof and I have discussed much. You make me dizzy, *Jolie.*" Jean reached out and grabbed my hand as I paced past him, and pulled me back to sit beside him on the bed. "We have no answers, but perhaps you might get information from Monsieur Randolph that we have otherwise been unable to learn. If the wizards do not agree to his terms, war is inevitable, Drusilla. It will be costly in lives and could expose our kind to the human world. We need to know what your elf is planning so that you and I and our allies may prepare."

Right, because I'd be on Rand's favorite person list once he discovered I had Eugenie stuck in Old Orleans in the middle of a hurricane, riding it out with Christof and his magic.

Unless. . . .

I got up, took a deep breath, and walked toward the door. Rand might talk to me if I gave him one of the things he most wanted. "I need to talk to Eugenie."

CHAPTER 29

Twenty minutes later, I sat downstairs with Eugenie, watching her reapply her makeup after she'd cried away the previous application. Christof and his machines were stashed in his mad scientist laboratory-slash-bedroom, probably seeing how quickly he could form ice crystals in test tubes. He'd promised not to make an appearance until Jean gave him the go-ahead. Rand did not need to see the faery prince and his mechanical minions.

Eugenie's makeup job was so professional that no one would be able to tell she'd been crying. I rarely wore makeup, and wondered if a nice bottle of ivory foundation with a good SPF would help me attract more normal people to my life. Then again, it hadn't helped my poor normal friend who'd found herself pregnant by an elf.

She'd made our discussion incredibly easy. All I'd had to say was something to the effect of, "Eugenie, we need to talk," and she'd said something to the effect of, "Yeah, I've been thinking I should go to Rand's house in New Orleans, or to Elfheim.

Maybe he'd let me visit Matt and the girls for a few hours. He's been acting better lately, and, sorry, but things are getting too weird around you and your friends."

Talk about an understatement. Thank God she didn't realize her favorite faery Christof was in the back of the apartment, playing mad scientist.

Now we were waiting for Rand. He'd show up eventually. If he hadn't made it by four thirty, I'd transport to Maison Rouge and make sure Jake and Collette hadn't blown away. I wouldn't worry about Rand himself until my own will to live waned.

I'd warned Eugenie that I was going to use her as a bargaining chip and made sure she was okay with it. I needed to know what was going on politically and I needed a promise that Rand would let me see her alone whenever I wanted—or, the way things were going, whenever I could escape the latest train wreck. And it had to be a promise I'd believe.

DRU!

I *eeped* and almost fell off Jean's stiff, formal settee. If we ever got out of this mess, I was going to suggest he let Rene update his furnishings.

Rand, where are you? I purposely didn't screech. I didn't raise my voice. I even sucked up. *Are you okay? I was worried.*

Yeah, worried the imperious I-am-Elf version of Rand would show up and ruin my schemes.

He didn't answer. I waited a moment, then was getting ready for some low-key mental screeching when the familiar tingle of transport magic crossed my skin. A second later, a very wet elf arrived in the transport with a half-dried loup-garou.

I tossed Rand a towel I had brought with me for this very purpose. His shoulder-length hair was plastered to his skull. Thanks to Rene staying here when he was in Old Orleans (who knew?), the apartment had a lot more modern conveniences than Maison Rouge. Towels, for instance, and running water.

He caught the towel and glowered at me on his way to Eugenie. Great. He was already developing his inner glow and we hadn't spoken a word. On the plus side, his internal body heat should dry his hair faster.

He knelt in front of her, and I said a silent prayer of thanks that Eugenie didn't tell Rand she'd been cramping earlier. Once she had gotten something to eat and laid down awhile, she seemed okay. Rand would have the official word, though, and he placed his hands on her belly and closed his eyes.

"He's been afraid but is okay now." Rand shot an accusatory glance my way. "We need to talk about your living accommodations, Eugie."

Eugenie had been well coached. "Yes, we do—after you talk to DJ. I'm going upstairs for a little while to lie down." She placed her hand on top of his, which was still resting on her abdomen and communing with his elfling. "We're going to do what's best for him, Rand. DJ's going to have the final say."

Rand watched her leave with a placid look on his face that was as fake as the straggly wet "fur" on the top of his mud-soaked boots. When he stood up and looked at me, nothing on his face said *placid*. More like *dead meat*.

"Where's Jake? Why did only Collette come with you?"

Good, judging by the blank look that crossed his face, the unexpected question had thrown him off-balance and disrupted his planned rant. Plus, I wanted to know.

"Jake wanted to secure a few more things in the house before he came—it's getting torn up pretty badly. He's fine, though. Not hurt."

I nodded. "Good. Would you sit down? We need to talk." I seemed to be hearing and saying that a lot lately.

"Have you thought about the promises I asked you to make?" He spread the towel out on Jean's recliner and sat on it.

"Yes, and here's my counterproposal. If you tell me what your plans are concerning the Interspecies Council, and if you guarantee Eugenie's safety as well as your child's—and I mean her mental health and not just her physical health—then I will convince Eugenie to go with you to Elfheim to live until the political climate has settled down or the baby comes, whichever she wants."

Rand sat forward in Jean's recliner and stared at me as if I'd grown antlers. Really big antlers. "Agreed."

"Not so fast. I want to make sure you understand exactly what I'm asking, because if any part of it isn't upheld, I will tell her not to go with you. If you break the terms once she's with you, I will come down on you with every bit of firepower my elven staff can muster."

He quirked one side of his pretty mouth. "Even if it kills you as well?"

I quirked right back at him. "Absolutely. Even if it kills me. Without hesitating."

He fidgeted a moment, then gave me a brusque nod.

"You will not do anything to change Eugenie's moods, alter her mind, or shuffle through her memories or past. You won't force her to do anything she doesn't want to do. You'll make sure she gets medical care and understands what that care means. I don't want her scared. I don't want her brainwashed. I don't want her hurt in any way. Do you agree to these things?"

Rand didn't hesitate. "Yes."

"Do you swear on the life of your son?"

He winced. Good. Now he knew how I felt when he wanted promises made on Alex's life. "I swear on the life of my son."

"Okay." I had no choice but to trust him, because it really had become unsafe for Eugenie to stay with the Lafitians. If a preternatural world war broke out, she would make an easy pawn. She needed a kind of protection I couldn't provide any longer, and as much as it galled me to admit it, Rand could.

"Okay, then. We agreed, but will Eugenie?" Rand glanced down the hallway where she'd disappeared.

"Yes, she's getting her things ready. Most of her stuff is still in Old Barataria but who knows if it will survive this storm. It would be nice if she could go to her house in New Orleans and get what she needs."

Rand nodded. "I will take her. The weather isn't so bad there—just a lot of rain."

"Speaking of rain, I guess you know this storm was caused by Florian."

Rand got up and came to sit on the floor in front of me, using the towel to dry his hair. I handed him another to wrap around his shoulders. We didn't have time for him to hibernate on Jean's floor and he'd already started shivering. Thank God I only had enough elven genes to worry about hibernation in extreme conditions.

"I've made a proposal to Zrakovi regarding the makeup of the council."

"Wait." I wanted him to make sure I hadn't promised to keep this to myself. "I'm not promising anything on Alex's life. I just want you to understand that."

"We've gone past that stage. You can tell your allies here. Even Christof."

I pasted on my best clueless look. "What do you mean?"

Rand grinned. He was such a pretty man; what a waste of beauty. "You're a bad actress, Dru. Besides, I can sense his aura here. You got that skill from your elven genes, remember?"

Right. I laughed. "Yeah, okay. He's here, although I think he's getting ready to go on the move again." Rand sat up straighter, so I added, "And no, I don't know where he's planning to go." Far, far away, I hoped.

"Anyway, I made this proposal to Zrakovi and gave him twenty-four hours to respond." Rand laid out the plan exactly as Jean had explained it, minus the extrapolation of how it could make him king of the universe.

"And how did Zrakovi respond?"

"He's avoiding me, the coward." The low regard with which Rand held the First Elder dripped from every syllable. "He claims there are wizarding concerns in New Orleans related to this hurricane, which is patently ridiculous. It came in as a category one storm, for God's sake. There's some minor street flooding and a few trees down. Even the local weather guys aren't excited by anything other than the fact that it came out of nowhere."

"It didn't, though. The storm hitting Old Barataria is no cat one—it's easily a four or five. Florian needs to understand that the things he does in the name of war with his brother have implications to the human world and to preternaturals in Old Orleans who have nothing to do with their family feud."

Rand pulled the towel from around his shoulders and refolded it. "I have given my word that I will not interfere in affairs between Florian and Christof, and I won't."

"But which one are you supporting?" This was a test. Unlike faeries, elves could lie all they wanted.

"For now, Florian. He's more willing to take on the power structure of the Interspecies Council. Christof is cautious, which in the long run is good."

So Jean's suspicions were probably right. Rand would get

what he needed from Florian and then the crazy faery better watch his back.

"What happens if Zrakovi comes back and rejects your proposal?" We'd see how far Rand's willingness to be truthful extended.

"I fully expect him to reject it, so I am considering other options."

I just bet he was. "Like war?"

Rand did his best Mona Lisa impersonation. I hated that little smile. "It is one option, but not the only one. That's all I'm at liberty to say."

It was more than I'd expected. I leaned back on the lumpy sofa and wondered why we hadn't transported Jean's La-Z-Boy throne from Maison Rouge. I was so damned tired.

"You need some sleep." I opened one eye to see if Rand was being a smartass, but he looked concerned.

"Too many crises, not enough time. Guess I'll sleep when I'm dead."

"Things are going to get better for you, Dru." Rand's voice softened. "I know it looks bad right now, but Lafitte, as badly as I hate the son of a bitch, has put himself and his allies in a powerful position."

My eyelids popped open; I wondered if the pirate were eavesdropping. My guess would be yes. If so, that statement should please him.

I was prevented from any follow-ups by Eugenie's reappearance, Rene in tow, carrying her bags. Rand got up to help.

They set them in the transport and Rand held out his hand to Eugenie, trotting out the sweet smile.

Standing side by side in the transport, getting ready to travel to Elfheim, I had to wonder how things might have turned out if we'd reached this agreement three weeks ago. I might be at home in New Orleans, snuggling with Alex while the rain beat down. But it probably wouldn't have stopped Zrakovi from wanting the baby issue to go away. It wouldn't have stopped Mace Banyan from his blackmail. Violette still might be alive, though, and Rand might not have lost respect for Zrakovi as quickly.

Things might be just as screwed up, only screwed up in a different way.

Rene stepped into the transport with them, chest to chest with Rand . . . well, more like nose to Adam's apple. He spoke so softly I couldn't understand him, but Rand began glowing. I grabbed Rene's arm and pulled him away before the elf could do some painful mind-meddling.

I waved to Eugenie as they disappeared, and prayed we'd made the right decision. I'd been praying a lot lately, and felt a lot more coming on.

I hoped someone was listening.

Rene and I stood looking at the empty transport, and I fought off a sudden urge to cry. Without Alex and now without Eugenie, the Good Ship DJ was rudderless. I'd been cast adrift in a world I didn't want to be part of. Except for one person.

"If you leave me, I'll kill you," I told Rene.

"Aw, babe, you like me." He pulled me into a hug, patting my back as if I were a toddler in need of consolation. Which is sort of how I felt. "I ain't going nowhere. When we go back to Barataria, some of my family's talkin' 'bout comin' there, too, at least till things settle down."

"You think they will? Settle down, I mean?" I had a feeling things would get worse before they got better. Maybe a lot worse.

"Ah . . . things ain't settling down quite yet, babe." Rene let me go and spun me around to face the transport. I hadn't felt the magic of anyone coming in, but Jake stood there, dripping wet, holding a very tall, very thin body.

"Holy crap," I whispered, moving closer. "It's Audrey."

CHAPTER 30

"S he came in not long after Randolph." Jake placed Audrey on the floor with slow, gentle movements. She was pale, her skin almost translucent. She wasn't breathing.

"Move away from her." Rene pushed up his sleeves and knelt next to my cousin, feeling for a pulse on her neck. "How long was she under, and how long's she been out?"

"I just happened to be looking out when she transported in—the water's way, way up, though, and rough as hell." Jake took the towel Collette offered him and talked while he dried off. "It probably took me ten minutes to get her out because of the surf, but I brought her straight here, so fifteen minutes max."

Rene put a hand under Audrey's neck and tipped her chin back. "Anybody else know CPR?"

"I do." Jake dropped to his knees on the other side of Audrey. "Want me to compress?"

"Yeah, five breaths, thirty compressions, two breaths, then repeat thirty-and-two. Let's do it."

They worked on her forever, it seemed, although I knew it

was less than a minute before she finally made a choking sound. I closed my eyes, relief washing through me so strong I thought I might have to sit down. An arm snaked around my shoulders, and I looked up at Jean.

"What are they doing, *Jolie*?" he whispered.

"Trying to keep her heart beating until they can push the water out of her lungs."

"*C'est un miracle.*"

He was right; it was pretty miraculous. I guess a man of the sea such as Jean would have found CPR a useful skill back in his day.

"We got her." Jake rolled Audrey on her side and held her while she coughed out a gallon of water. Rene and Jake had saved me, and now my cousin, more times than I could count. I owed them so much I'd never be able to repay it. But I would try.

Audrey was trying to talk between coughs, and I took Rene's position next to her. "You're okay, Audrey. You're safe. Don't try to talk."

"Have to tell . . ." She groaned in pain after a round of coughing.

"Keep coughing," Jake told her. His hands remained on her shoulders, holding her down and on her side. "DJ's right. Don't talk."

If this were normal times and we were in New Orleans, I could call a wizard physician or take her to a regular ER and have a Blue Congress team clean up any strangeness with the hospital later. But we were in the Beyond in the middle of a hurricane. Dr. Rene and Dr. Jake were all she had.

Except for Dr. Lafitte. Now that I thought of it, the pirate probably had a lot of experience tending to those who'd survived a close encounter with the sea. He spread a blanket out on the settee. "Bring her here and ensure she does not lie on her back," he told Jake, then turned to Adrian. "Go to the galley and find something warm for her to drink."

I half expected Adrian to remind Jean that he was a wizard-turned-vampire and therefore did not take orders, but he nodded and walked toward the back of the apartment. I assumed the galley was, in modern terms, a kitchen.

Rene picked up Audrey and transferred her to the settee, which I hated to tell Jean was more comfortable than the floor by only the barest margin. Once she was settled and seemed to be breathing more easily, I sat on the floor in front of her, stroking her shoulder. "You have another blanket? She's shivering."

Jean nodded toward Collette, who headed off for more blankets—and probably to check on Jake, who was changing clothes.

By the time Adrian arrived with a steaming cup of tea, Audrey was struggling to sit up. I moved to sit next to her so I could help, holding the cup while she tried to drink.

The first sip set off another coughing fit, which Rene said was good. "She's gotta get rid of any water left in her lungs. Once she can keep the tea down, she's okay."

Eventually, she was able to drink. The whole time, she'd been looking at me and trying to talk. Her aura had radiated fear from the moment she started breathing again, and I'd attributed it to drowning. But now it was rising even more—fear, agitation, more fear.

"Can you talk?"

She nodded just as Rene said, "No."

She coughed again, and through a wave of fear that came off her so strongly it made my skin crawl with imaginary ants, she choked out one word: "Alex."

Oh God. Something had happened to Alex. I looked at Rene and he nodded. "Take it slow."

"What about Alex? Tell me, but take your time." I rubbed Audrey's shoulders and resisted the urge to shake the information out of her. She'd almost died trying to get this news to me so I had to be patient.

"Arrested." Another round of coughing. "Treason."

"*Mon Dieu.*" Jean stood behind the sofa and I looked up at him. "I feared this."

"Feared what? What do you know?"

Jean walked around the sofa and sat on the floor in front of Audrey and me. "I know nothing, Drusilla, but I feared if your First Elder became desperate enough, he would strike at you the most effective way—through the person about whom you care the most."

I'd feared it, too, all along. But why now, and how of all people could they accuse Alex Warin of treason?

Audrey took two long sips of the tea and kept them down without coughing. Her voice, when she spoke, reminded me of a three-pack-a-day smoker. "Zrakovi came to see my dad today. He said he'd just met with you, DJ."

I closed my eyes. God, he'd gone after Alex because of our meeting. Because I'd pissed him off again and then managed to escape. I'd shown him up again.

Audrey closed her eyes and breathed a few moments before continuing. "He didn't know I was there, and my dad didn't know I was listening. Zrakovi said he'd slipped a tracking tattoo on Alex's jacket just after everyone went to Captain Lafitte's house. He knows Alex was in the Beyond most of the night on Christmas Eve, and had someone in place, watching. They have photos of you two leaving that hotel on Dauphine, and Alex getting in a transport that Zrakovi said he had no knowledge of."

Alex's special Christmas surprise. No way Zrakovi could get a tracking tattoo—a wizard's charm—on Alex without him knowing it. It surprised me that the First Elder had been imaginative enough to put it on a piece of clothing.

"So he arrested Alex." Damn it. "Where is he? What have they done to him?"

Adrian had taken Audrey's cup while she talked, and now returned with a refill. I mouthed a thank-you to him.

"He's being held in some kind of cell they've set up at . . ." She shook her head. "I couldn't understand the name and I'm not familiar enough with the city yet. But it had something to do with Mardi Gras and a warehouse across the river. I'm sorry I didn't catch the name."

I knew of only one place that fit the description. "It's okay; I know where it is. Blaine Kern's Mardi Gras World. They design and build the big Mardi Gras floats, and store them during the off-season."

What a bizarre place to stash a prisoner . . . or a brilliant one. It was a monstrous maze of riverside warehouses where the largest Mardi Gras floats were designed, born, built, and then stored, their cast-off decorations from past years lying around until they could be repurposed. It took two hours to even walk around the whole place.

Last time I'd been there, I'd taken a selfie with a twelve-foot statue of Jean Lafitte that looked nothing like him. After the new year began, the place would be abuzz with preparations for Mardi Gras, but between Christmas and New Year's it was probably deserted. The perfect place for a wizarding prison and maybe a farce of a trial.

"Okay, then. We have to get him out."

In a hurricane. When I'd be detected as soon as I crossed the border. And knowing Alex, he'd want to stay and try to clear his name and save his job, something I could identify with.

Damn it.

"Is there more, Mademoiselle Audrey?" Jean had taken up my job of pacing. "Do you know their plans for Monsieur Warin?"

Audrey nodded while she sipped. "Zrakovi said he was calling an emergency meeting of the council tomorrow, that he wanted to make an example of Alex. He said . . . let me remember the words . . . 'With any luck, I can get both of these traitors out of our hair permanently.' I think the trial is going to be in the same place they're keeping him."

Get both of the traitors—that would be me and now Alex. Which was so wrong. Yes, there was a good argument to place the *traitor* stigma on me, but not Alex. He'd been loyal to Zrakovi even when he disagreed with him, even when that loyalty tore him apart. Zrakovi was insane; there was no political gain for him to do anything to Alex, or to me, for that matter, not if Jean's interpretation of the Quince Randolph proposal was true.

"My father tried to talk him out of it, DJ. He really did. He insisted that Alex had always been loyal, and that Zrakovi was making a mistake to treat him like this. He wouldn't listen."

Yeah, I just bet he wouldn't. I didn't realize how angry I was growing until, in the corner of the room, sparks flew off the tip of the elven staff tucked in my bag. I'd never made Charlie spark from across the room, but I was too pissed off to be pleased about it.

I stood up. "If Zrakovi wants me, then fine. He can have me. But I'm getting Alex out of there." Even if I had to hog-tie him and drag him out on the Bacchasaurus float.

Jean stopped in front of me and put his hands on my shoulders. "You must move with caution, *Jolie*. Perhaps you might use your magic stick to watch the proceedings tomorrow as you did before. That will allow us time to make preparations."

"Us?" I looked up at him and the doubt must have been

written in my eyes. Jean did not like Alex; Alex did not like Jean. It was a perfectly workable arrangement.

"We will save your *petit chien,* Drusilla. You are among friends."

I took a deep breath, swallowing down the doubt and fear and a whole lot of unshed tears that would probably make their way out later. For now, I nodded and gave Jean a hug. I did have allies. Jean and Adrian would help because I needed them; the others would help because they genuinely cared about Alex. Jake would be distraught. Despite their differences in the past few months, they were more like brothers than cousins.

"Make a list of what you need for your scrying shit." Rene handed me a pen and a Popeye's Fried Chicken receipt he'd dug out of his wallet. "I'll transport to St. Bernard Parish, to my papa's. They're less likely to be watching up there and the Prompt Lady has probably got some new holy water since I cleaned her out last time."

I smiled for the first time since before Rand arrived. "You're going to be on the Catholic Church's most wanted list."

"Hell, the Holy Water Bandit's probably the most exciting thing that's happened to them since Katrina, babe. I'm enriching their lives."

"I'm sure they'll be grateful."

Audrey still coughed occasionally but she seemed to be rebounding quickly. I sat next to her again and hugged her. "Thank you."

She smiled. "You'd have found out without me. One of the things Zrakovi wanted to talk to Dad about was how to make sure you knew about it."

Zrakovi didn't know about my meeting with Lennox unless my uncle had told him. "Do you think he expected your dad to be seeing me, to tell me in person?" For all I knew, Zrakovi was paranoid enough to have put tracking tattoos on the whole Interspecies Council.

"Oh no, he knows you and my dad haven't spoken more than once or twice. It's just that, well, my dad is right brilliant, if I do say so. He's brighter than Zrakovi, I think, although I haven't been around the First Elder, but the man seems nervous and mean."

He hadn't always been that way, but my capacity for sympathy was exhausted where Zrakovi was concerned.

"What did your dad suggest?"

She grinned. "We were way ahead of both of them. He suggested Zrakovi find a bloody envelope and send it to Jean Lafitte's house in a transport. And he wasn't that nice about it."

I hugged her again. I liked having family. I mean, my maternal grandmother was family but the woman was so very difficult and disapproving that it wasn't a warm fuzzy kind of relationship.

"Sounds like you and your dad are getting closer."

"I think so." She sighed, leaned back, and closed her eyes. "Don't worry, though, I won't ever tell him I've been a runner for you and Alex."

Yeah, talk about treason. Zrakovi would have Audrey in a cell, too.

"How are you feeling?" She looked exhausted, still pale and wet, but we might need her.

"I'm okay. What do you want me to do?"

I tugged on the soggy sleeve of her sweater that poked out from under the blanket. "First, get some dry clothes. I bet you can wear Collette's stuff.

"Then, if you're up to it, we're going to have a crash course in magic 101."

CHAPTER 31

While Rene was off stealing holy water from Our Lady of Prompt Succor, I schooled Audrey in the basics of drawing and powering a transport.

"Try to use your magic on something." I looked around and set a throw pillow on the floor in front of her. "Try to move that pillow, or blow it up or something."

"Oh, seriously? I'm not five years old." She flung her hand at the pillow, and nothing happened. The second time, with some extra exertion on her part, it moved a quarter inch. "I don't understand."

I hadn't expected her physical magic to work. "It's because we're in the Beyond; physical magic doesn't work here. Green Congress magic seems to be okay, but not Red. Mostly, I wanted to see how you tried to throw a spell."

Throw being the operative word. Gerry had been able to do that, but he'd been a lot better trained and his magic was very strong. Because my physical magic was so pathetic, Gerry had found some tricks to help me. I could pass those on to my cousin.

I glanced at her hands, which were free of jewelry. "Did you ever buy a ring to wear?"

"Oh! Hang on." She ran back upstairs to the bedroom, then back down. The girl bubbled with energy and made me feel like an ancient, wizened little person.

She held out a silver ring with an emerald-cut purple stone. "Amethyst?"

"Yes, it's my favorite. I wasn't wearing it because I wasn't sure what you wanted me to do with it."

I explained Gerry's method of teaching me. "Instead of focusing on the pillow, channel all your power into the ring, then from the ring to the pillow." She practiced a few times and, to my surprise, the pillow danced three or four inches.

"Wow. That's so simple." She looked at the ring as if it were magical in itself, then looked at me with adoration. Well, I'd enjoy it while I could. Nobody could destroy a good case of adoration like me. "Why didn't my dad do this? I might have been able to pass Red Congress."

I had a theory, after seeing that pillow move. Audrey's magic had to be strong, and Lennox might fear what she could do with it. Not because he was jealous. I didn't think that for a second. But a young wizard whose power outstripped her experience, maybe even the common sense that grew with age . . . he could be afraid she'd get herself in trouble and discouraged her in order to protect her.

Then again, I didn't know him that well. So I went with a more logical, less psychological, explanation. "I can't do much physical magic. I'm hellacious with a spell or potion, but don't ask me to do much more than power a transport with my physical magic. It was Gerry's way of helping me maximize what I did have."

She smiled with Gerry's eyes. "You really loved him, didn't you?"

I looked away, not wanting to see the resemblance or the pity. "I did love him. And I am still angry at him for not telling me he was my father." It was hard to both mourn someone and be angry at him, but that was the truth.

I took a deep breath. "Time to move on. What is your experience with transports? Not open transports, but powering one with your magic?"

"None." Her pale cheeks flushed a rosy pink. "I know the shape is the interlocking circle and triangle, but that's about it."

"Okay, there's only so much you can do here, but let's see what I have." Dragging over my messenger bag, I pulled out my portable magic kit, which had started life as a small first aid kit.

"You can use ash, unrefined salt, lead, or a precious metal to create a transport. Ash is short-lasting; it won't hold power more than a half hour or so. It's good for making an exit when you don't want to be followed. Salt is most common; it's strong enough to hold a transport open for a few weeks before it has to be infused with magic again. Lead—I usually use filings because they're cheap—lasts even longer and is good for a permanent transport. Rich wizards sometimes use precious metals to have permanent transports inlaid in their floors." I paused. "I don't know any of those personally, so that gets filed under R for rumor."

I handed her a vial of salt and cleared off a spot on the floor a couple of feet from my big transport. "The transport size doesn't really matter—it just needs to be big enough for whatever you want to transport. Yourself, for example. If you can stand inside it, you can use it."

She had a few questions, but seemed to grasp the concept of powering a transport. I wondered . . .

I went and retrieved Charlie and turned my back to Audrey, not because I didn't want her to see what I was doing but because I felt foolish. "Charlie, I want you to work for Audrey for the next five minutes, okay?"

If staffs could whine, Charlie would be doing it. I could just tell.

Turning back, I handed the staff to her. "This might or might not work, but try it. Instead of your ring, channel your magic into the staff and touch the tip of it to the transport." I set the pillow inside her transport. "When you power it, say 'Pontalba Two.'" Pontalba was the name I'd given Jean's transport. I'd been too wet to be creative.

"Okay." She took a deep breath, whispered, "Pontalba Two," and focused on Charlie. The pillow disappeared from her transport and reappeared in the big transport. "That was bloody brilliant." Her eyes widened. "Is it supposed to be on fire?"

Oh, holy crap. She was going to burn down our only safe haven. We stomped on the pillow until the last of the flames disappeared.

"What are you doing?"

I turned to find Christof, looking every bit the mad scientist, his hair askew, crazed look in his green eyes. "We're having a transport lesson."

My audacious Audrey marched over to the Faery Prince of Winter and held out her right hand. "Hullo, I'm Audrey, DJ's cousin."

Christof turned on the charm as he took her hand. "I'm so pleased to meet you, Audrey. I am Christof, prince of Faery and the future king."

Audrey almost fainted, and I didn't think it was fake. She

also needed a big lesson on the Who's Who of the Prete World, including to whom one should suck up and to whom one should not.

Speaking of sucking up. "Christof, I want to apologize for the things I said to you earlier. It took me by surprise, to see The Arch here, but I had no cause to speak to you the way I did." I felt my nose turning brown.

I got a dose of charm this time. He'd be horrified to know I could see his real disheveled self. "I understand, and I know how protective you are of Miss Eugenie. I would never knowingly place her in jeopardy."

Speaking of which. "I probably should tell you that Eugenie has decided to spend the forseeable future in Elfheim." At Christof's outraged look, I talked faster. "We felt it was safer given the instability of the Interspecies Council right now, particularly the wizards."

Liar, liar, pillow on fire. It was because we didn't know what Christof and his whackalicious brother Florian might do next. "I plan to check on her as often as possible to make sure she is safe."

"Perhaps you should check on her now. Might I accompany you?"

Oh hell no. "I'm sorry, but I just learned that my boyfriend has been arrested by the council for seeing me on Christmas Eve. I have to try and help him first, but then I will definitely check on Eugenie." And you, Mr. Frosty, aren't going with me.

"Ah, very well. I'm so sorry for your bad news." Christof bowed to a swooning Audrey and headed back down the hall. "Thank you for letting me know of Eugenie's whereabouts. I was getting ready to send an ice floe into Elfheim but now I shall send it to Vampyre instead."

"Good move," I shouted to his retreating back. I had several vampires I'd like to see buried under a slab of ice. Although I better make sure Terri got out, or Adrian would be in a lather.

"I want to try the transport again," Audrey said, setting a glass bowl in her transport.

Good, that shouldn't burn. Although I wasn't sure how much of the pillow burning was Audrey's power and how much was Charlie having a tantrum because I'd passed him off on someone else.

She tried several times but nothing happened. "What am I doing wrong?"

I reached out and took Charlie, who vibrated in my hand, chastising me. "My staff usually only works for me; I think that was a fluke before." Or a favor. "You get the idea, though. Outside the Beyond, it should work fine using your ring as a focus."

"Cool." She stifled a yawn. "I'm rather tired. Would you mind if I had a nap before we make plans to spring Alex?"

"Sure." Because I needed to talk to Jake. Whatever we decided to do, he had a big say in it.

CHAPTER 32

By the time I huffed and puffed my way to the third floor, where Jake and Collette had claimed a room, I was vowing that I'd stop eating too much mystery meat and start running again as soon as we got out of hurricane mode. I'd have to illuminate a makeshift running path along the strip of beach using the pink flashlight, but at least I wouldn't get so out of shape.

I paused at the door, not wanting to interrupt anything where three would be a crowd, but heard soft voices from inside. I knocked, and turned the knob when Collette invited me in.

They were the picture of what I wanted my relationship with Alex to look like. Collette sat propped against the headboard of the bed, playing with Jake's hair as he rested his head in her lap. They were comfortable with each other, and I'd never seen a harsh word between them. How did they do that?

"What's up, sunshine? You look upset—is Audrey okay?"

I sat on the bed at Collette's feet, trying to figure out how to break this news. "Audrey's fine. The reason she was trying to get to me in that weather was, well, about Alex."

Jake sat up. "What about Alex?"

I swallowed hard. All the way up the stairs, I'd told myself I was not going to cry in front of Jake. I was going to be calm. The last thing we needed was a pissed-off loup-garou—one who already had a warrant out for his arrest by the Elders—charging into Mardi Gras World.

"He's okay. He's not hurt or anything." Not physically, anyway. That reassurance was enough to make Jake relax a little, or maybe it was Collette's touch. She was rubbing his back.

"Tell me what's up, then. Has he done something where I need to go and kick his ass?"

I smiled. "Not this time. Let me back up to my meeting yesterday with Willem Zrakovi."

Jake shook his head. "I knew that was a bad idea. What happened?"

I could tell from his expression that he thought it went a lot better than I did, but then he had no use for the wizards as an organization and no respect for Zrakovi whatsoever. He thought Alex was misguided.

"Anyway, what Audrey came to tell me is that Zrakovi had put a tracking charm on Alex's jacket, so he knows we met in Old Orleans on Christmas Eve."

"Uh-huh." Jake wanted to say something about the red bow, but refrained.

"Zrakovi was so mad when I got away from him again—thank God he doesn't know it was Rene who helped me—that . . ." I took a deep breath. "He arrested Alex and charged him with treason."

Jake laughed. "Right, because treason is Alex's middle name and . . ." He trailed off. "Damn it, you're not joking, are you?"

I shook my head. "They have him locked up, and Zrakovi's holding a special trial tomorrow."

"Son of a bitch." Jake moved to the edge of the bed, and I froze when I saw the amber color bleeding out of his eyes, replaced by a flat yellow. He was going to lose control.

I looked at Collette to enlist her help, but she was way ahead of me. She reached out and pulled him back toward her. He moved reluctantly, but she wrapped her arms around him and his gradual calm was so pronounced I could almost feel it physically. She soothed him until his eyes regained their normal amber color. But they were not happy eyes.

"What's the plan?" Jake asked. "And will Alex be so stupid that he refuses to let us rescue him?"

I shrugged. "We have to try, and I'm about to the point where I'm ready to beat him unconscious and drag him out of there before he gets himself killed. I think that's Zrakovi's plan, by the way. He wants to make sure I'm aware of Alex's situation, because he knows I'll come into New Orleans to try and save him. Then he'll kill both of us."

"Is he that unbalanced?" Collette's eyes held disbelief. "Surely it's a ruse."

Jake flexed his shoulders, and Collette tightened her grip on him. "It's no ruse. I saw a few so-called leaders like him in Afghanistan." Jake had been a Marine who came home badly wounded; being turned loup-garou had done what the human doctors couldn't in terms of healing his damaged right leg, but it had also taken away the life he'd planned for himself.

"In what way?" Collette asked. She was so perfect for him. She knew how to touch him and talk to him to keep him level.

"Most of the guys were great, but every once in a while you'd run across an officer who was a total nutbag. And what it boiled down to was insecurity and fear. They do bad things to a man who's too proud to admit he's in over his head."

I nodded. "That's exactly where I think Zrakovi is. It's made him desperate. But Alex isn't going to pay for it."

"So is there a plan yet?"

"I'm waiting for Rene to get back with scrying supplies—he thought it would be easier to get in and out of St. Bernard, near his dad's place. That way I can scry Alex and see if I can tell where he is. I think he's at Mardi Gras World, in one of the warehouses, but that place is huge."

"Huge, with lots of places to hide." Jake rolled his head from side to side, popping out the tension. It was something Alex did a lot, and sent a wave a panic through me. What if we couldn't save him?

"Hey." Jake's voice was soft. "We're gonna get him out, whether he wants out or not."

I nodded. "We can watch the so-called trial tomorrow and see what happens. From that, we can decide the best way to get him."

"I've planned a few extractions in my Marine days," Jake said. "I want in on it."

"So do I," Collette said.

"And me," said Rene. I didn't know how long he'd been standing in the doorway.

"Did you get everything?" I turned to look at him. He was back in drowned-rat mode.

"Yeah, and this time I got chased across the Prompt Succor cemetery by a priest while I was trying to haul a gallon of stolen holy water," he said, not smiling. "You owe me, babe."

It took almost an hour to find a suitable spot and set up the scrying materials. Rene hadn't been able to find the right kind of bowl, so we had to scour Jean's apartment for something that would work. I finally settled on a chamber pot with roses painted on the side and tried not to think about it too much.

I'd asked everyone but Jake to not participate in this particular scrying. I'd want them all to watch the trial tomorrow, but for my first look at Alex as a prisoner, I didn't want a crowd. I almost asked Jake not to watch because it felt like an invasion of Alex's privacy, but that was selfish of me. Jake loved Alex as much as I did.

"There he is. Damn sons of bitches have beaten him."

"Had to have been recently or he would already be healed," I murmured, shifting Charlie in the water so I could get closer. Alex sat on the concrete floor cross-legged and I saw no bars around him, but I also saw no wall behind him and he was definitely leaning against something.

"They have him in a containment circle." I used my free hand to point to the circle drawn on the concrete. "Damn it, it's so small he can't even stretch his legs out and lie down."

As if to illustrate what he could do, Alex curled up in a fetal position, crooking one arm beneath his head for a pillow. I didn't realize I was crying until Jake reached out and wiped a tear away.

"Look, he's already healing." Jake wrapped an arm around me and we watched as the bloody cut under Alex's left eye reknit itself. His bloody lip took a little longer but soon it, too, had healed.

I chuckled. "Look at that face."

Jake grinned. "Yep, I've seen that whoop-ass look a few times. That is one pissed-off boy from Picayune."

Alex's eyebrows had gathered in a straight line, and I could tell from the way the muscles in his jaw shifted that he was engaged in some serious teeth-grinding. The reason his wounds were fresh was because he was angry and fought back. That was a good sign. I wanted him mad as hell, not reasonable, or understanding, or thoughtful, or rational. Mad.

"Can you tell where he is?" Jake leaned closer to the scrying chamber pot. I hoped it hadn't been used recently . . . or ever.

Shifting Charlie to different angles, we were able to see the things around him, and there were a lot of things to see. Big jester heads, half of an Elvis torso, clowns, dwarves, dragon heads, all about the same size. "This stuff's too generic and there's a ton of it. We need to find something bigger and more iconic."

"What about that giant bull?" Jake pointed to a spot about ten feet behind Alex, and I shifted to get a better look.

That was no ordinary bull. "That's Boeuf Gras—he's perfect."

"You know that bull?"

"He's my favorite bull in the world. It'll make Alex easy to find—at least if they don't move him. But we can check again before we try to get Alex out." The big white bull, about the size of a tractor-trailer rig, belonged to the Krewe of Rex, Mardi Gras' oldest society. He was unique among the recurring Mardi Gras floats as he rolled atop his flatbed tractor-trailer truck, steam snorting out his nostrils. If Alex stayed close to the "fatted oxen," we'd find him.

CHAPTER 33

I slept little that night, and finally wandered into the front parlor about four a.m. to find Jean and Christof deep into a game of poker. Jean looked as he always did—sexy and piratical. Christof was spiffy in a blue sweater and jeans, his hair perfectly styled and a deep reddish brown.

I'd left my paw locket in the bedroom, so I doubted the real Christof looked quite so fresh. As for Jean, I'd never actually seen the man sleep and wasn't sure the historical undead needed it.

"You do not sleep enough, *Jolie*." Jean barely looked up at me, so focused was he on his hand of cards.

"You think?"

"*Oui*. Or else I would not have said thus."

I walked to the front window and opened the shutter enough to peer outside. The wind no longer howled in that scary wail, and the rain had slowed to a sprinkle. The three-inch layer of water topping the ground outside the apartment had drained or soaked in.

The gas lights that usually illuminated the Place d'Armes,

the precursor to Jackson Square, remained dark, however, so there was no way to gauge if the storm had damaged anything.

"I wonder if the hurricane has ended at Maison Rouge." It was more a statement than a question, but Christof answered. "Yes, it's over. Florian is attempting to melt the ice floe in Vampyre, so he was forced to abandon his hurricane."

"What about Vampyre?" Adrian wandered into the room. I had no idea whether or not vampires slept either.

"Have you heard from Terri?" I asked. "There's been an ice floe disaster in Vampyre."

"Bloody hell. You faeries need to get your affairs in order." Adrian stomped over to the transport and stepped inside, giving Christof the stink-eye, which resulted in at least a ten-degree drop of temperature in the room. "Now I must try to slip into Vampyre and find her. I hate that place."

"Wait. Don't you need a weapon?" I wasn't giving him my silver dagger but Jean likely had pistols and knives stashed everywhere.

"I have what I need." Adrian flashed his fangs at me as he disappeared into the ether. Despite flashes of pleasantness, Adrian Hoffman had been a pissy wizard and, overall, he was a pissy vampire. I was stuck with him, however.

Much like the faery and the pirate. "Do either of you know what time the trial is going to be today?"

"My brothers have been gathering information." Jean played his hand and must have won, gauging by the pile of gold coins he raked toward his already-towering stash. "Pierre learned that the trial will be at noon. Dominique has gone to Maison Rouge to assess the damage and should soon return."

I had wondered if the house in Barataria, which existed due to the magic of Jean's memory, would regenerate itself like he did when he "died." If maybe the house was immortal as well.

Guess I'd find out soon because the shiver of transport magic hit me, and I stepped out of the way as Dominique appeared. He really hadn't had time to recover from his vampire death of a week ago, as evidenced by his furrowed brow and quick collapse onto the sofa. The scowl, I assumed, was for my benefit.

Jean left the card game and stood over his brother. *"Donnezmoi un rapport de dommages sur la maison, s'il vous plaît."*

Dominique rattled his response in rapid French. I understood "doors," "windows," and not much more. Whatever damage had been done, I'd have to hear secondhand. He also handed Jean some papers.

Christof joined them. *"Pourriez-vous ajouter de l'électricité à la maison quand vous le réparer?"*

Great, even the faery spoke French.

They all turned to look at me.

I did my impersonation of Dominique's scowl. "I have no idea what you're saying."

"Language lessons would be most helpful to you, *Jolie.*"

"Probably. For now, a translation would help." Like I had time for French 101.

"Christof asks if we might add electrificitationality to Maison Rouge as we make repairs."

Huh. Electrificitationality. "You mean electricity?"

Jean shrugged and looked at Christof, who nodded.

"No." A few places in Old Orleans had electricity, although they were powered by some kind of magic, or they had . . . "Well, make that a yes."

Jean threw up his hands. "Is it yes or is it no, Drusilla?"

"Maybe. Talk to Rene when he wakes up and see if he can figure out a way to use a generator. I'm not sure. Your house isn't wired for electricity, but wiring might be something

Adrian could create with magic and then use a generator to
power it."

The slack jaws and narrowed eyes on the faces of both Jean
and Christof told me they didn't have a clue what I was talking
about. "Rene can explain it, or Adrian." I was too damned tired,
plus I had no idea if it would work or if Adrian could use enough
of his Blue Congress magic in the Beyond to do it.

Actually, now that I thought about it, Charlie would likely
be able to power electrical machines and appliances, but I had
no intention of offering that as an alternative barring an emergency. I had no intention of standing inside Maison Rouge
twenty-four/seven holding my elven staff to a power cord.

"What was the damage to the house?" I hoped it had been
minor.

While Christof accompanied Dominique to a room upstairs,
perhaps to discuss electrificitationality, Jean settled into his recliner. "Windows and doors have been damaged, and there is
a tear in the roof, but the house stands and has already been re-
fortified. It will not be difficult to repair it and we will be able to
return as soon as we wish."

"Where did your men go during the storm?" I'd half expected
several dozen undead pirates to join us, but none had shown up.

"To the north shore of Barataria Bay, where there is greater
shelter," Jean said. "They already have returned to repair the
house and their village."

I looked at my watch. "It's still seven hours until this farce
of a trial. I think I'll try to sleep."

"Before you do, *Jolie,* you might want to read these. I saw
they were written to you, so did not continue to read." Jean
handed me the papers Dominique had brought.

The first one I opened was short, and typed:

Ms. Jaco:

My disappointment in you continues unabated, as I have been made aware that, no doubt at your selfish insistence and the use of your feminine wiles, Alexander Warin has betrayed the trust of myself and the Interspecies Council. He will be tried for treason at noon on December 27 and, if found guilty by majority vote, will face the death penalty. I hope your Christmas Eve liaison was worth it.

—Wm Zrakovi, First Elder

My guilt swelled on instinct, but anger rapidly replaced it as I handed the note to Jean. Feminine wiles, my ass.

I unfolded the second sheet of paper, this one handwritten and scribbled hastily, judging by the uneven lines and messy scrawl:

DJ:

I'm trying to clear Alex, but Zrakovi has constructed an airtight case. He will try to use the death penalty to trap you, but I don't believe it is a bluff, nor does Alex. I talked to Alex this morning and we both agree—both you and Jake Warin must stay away from New Orleans. Alex might be beyond your ability to help, and neither of us wants to see the two of you killed as well. I know Alex has been dating my daughter, and am not sure what to make of those Christmas Eve photos, but that is unimportant now. I will continue to work on Alex's behalf, as long as I am able.

Yours,

Lennox

I handed this one to Jean as well, turned, and walked back to my bedroom, where I closed the door and collapsed on the bed. I should be crying, wailing like a hurricane wind, flailing arms and legs, praying with fervor. I could do nothing but lie on my back, stare at the ceiling, and hate.

❧

I stuck Charlie in the scrying chamber pot, which had been filled with fresh holy water, and was glad to see Alex looking no worse than the night before. The big white forelegs of Boeuf Gras stood in the distance behind him. So far, Alex hadn't been moved, which was a relief. He sat propped against the invisible wall of the cylinder, his arms resting calmly across his bent knees.

To a casual observer, he probably looked relaxed. I knew better. That was his tense, ready-to-attack stillness. He was looking for a chance to make his move. If they were stupid enough to lift the cylinder, he'd shift into Gandalf, his pony-size dog form, and make a run for it.

In front of his containment circle sat a row of six chairs. Lennox sat in one, deep in conversation with Elder Sato. Rand sat next to Sato and, next to him, drawing a curse from my peanut gallery, sat Florian. Fred Flintstone was conspicuously absent, as was Toussaint Delachaise. The were-and-shifter representative was on trial.

Zrakovi walked into our view and took a seat at the end, next to Lennox. I thought I'd felt hatred before in my life, but I hadn't. Not compared to this.

We had our crowd of onlookers in Old Orleans. I'd been joined by Audrey, Jake, Collette, Rene, Jean, and Christof. Adrian was still off in Vampyre and Dominique had returned to Maison Rouge to oversee the repair work.

Without the full moon to help, the sound from the scrying pot came through like a bad radio signal. I pushed more of my will into Charlie, and it cleared up enough to hear.

"... to view the evidence against Alexander Basile Warin on the charges of treason against the wizarding leadership and against this council," Zrakovi was saying.

Rene leaned closer and whispered, "*Basile? Seriously?*"

I nodded. His middle name was a sore point with Alex so we rarely mentioned it.

What followed was the biggest pile of horse manure I'd ever seen or heard. Morning in the mule pen for the French Quarter carriage tours wouldn't be this deep in shit.

Alex Warin had conspired to help me escape the week before Christmas, which Zrakovi, in his forgiving nature, had chosen to let pass.

Alex Warin had hidden the fact that his cousin Jacob had infected the New Orleans sentinel with the loup-garou virus and, again, Zrakovi had overlooked it.

Alex Warin had known that the sentinel, his lover, bonded with Elven Synod representative Quince Randolph to avoid turning loup-garou, and had hidden that from his superiors. Yet again, in an attempt to be as fair as possible and out of respect for Mr. Randolph, Zrakovi had elected to settle for a reprimand.

Once the sentinel had been charged with treason herself and had escaped, Alex Warin had continued to visit with her in the Beyond, quite possibly revealing council secrets.

"With photographic evidence of this betrayal, it is with profound sadness that I must admit to this august group of my peers that I allowed someone into our ranks who was undeserving of our trust. In an attempt to right that mistake, I have, as you see, taken Mr. Warin into custody. That he is guilty of treason, I feel certain. But I wish to put it to a vote of this council in order to be fair."

My heart pounded in erratic, staccato bursts as Zrakovi gave a dramatic pause and looked down the row at his fellow council members. Alex hadn't moved a muscle, including the blank expression on his face.

"I will begin the voting, and I vote that Mr. Warin is guilty as charged. Elder Sato?"

I prayed that Sato would recognize this madness for what it was, but he and Zrakovi had been colleagues a long time. "Guilty."

Zrakovi jotted on a pad. "That is two votes guilty, zero votes innocent. Elder St. Simon?"

Lennox stood up. "This is a complete farce, and we all know it. Alexander Warin is innocent."

Zrakovi stared him down. "Understandable, given your blood relation with your niece. That is two votes guilty, one vote innocent. Mr. Randolph?"

Rand also stood. "Drusilla Jaco is my mate, and therefore Mr. Warin and I have had our share of difficulties. Nevertheless, I agree with Elder St. Simon. Of these charges, Alexander Warin is innocent."

Zrakovi's eyes widened. He might not have expected it, but I wasn't surprised. Without the other members there, Rand's vote didn't matter. Zrakovi didn't need it.

"Very well. That is two votes guilty, two votes innocent. Prince Florian, that places the deciding vote on your shoulders."

Christof began softly cursing in some language I didn't think any of our roomful of multilingual people had ever heard.

Florian stood and stepped forward. "Given that Mr. Warin's paramour is a proven ally of my brother, who is no friend to this council, I must regretfully vote guilty."

This paramour would like to regretfully fry his ass with her elven staff.

"Very well. Alexander Warin, will you please stand?"

Alex stared at him without speaking, and didn't move a muscle.

"Defiant to the end, then. So be it. On behalf of the Inter-species Council, I declare you guilty of treason. The punishment is death. You are allowed to choose whether you prefer to die by a lethal shot of physical magic or a gunshot to the head. Which do you choose?"

Alex smiled, or at least his mouth did. His eyes were dark brown pools of fury.

"Very well, I choose death by firearm." Zrakovi took two steps toward Alex. "It's more painful, and it can be slower. It will take place at six p.m. tonight, in approximately six hours."

Behind me, both Audrey and Collette gasped, and I heard whispers. Zrakovi was so damned predictable. He could pull out a gun and shoot Alex now, but he wanted to make sure I had plenty of time to get there and attempt a rescue. Alex wasn't his target; he was the means to an end.

There was no response from Alex. I'd never loved him more, or been more exasperated with him. Although he would accomplish nothing by pleading for mercy or for another chance; Zrakovi had this outcome in the bank. And six hours? What could we get planned in six freaking hours? Just enough to form a half-assed plan with a high risk of failure, which is what Zrakovi was relying on.

One by one, the council members wandered away, leaving only Lennox behind. He walked over to the containment circle and knelt next to it, talking so low that even with Charlie at full strength, I couldn't hear what he was saying.

Alex shook his head and responded, also too low to hear, until he finally raised his voice.

"DJ, I know you're probably watching this—Lennox said Zrakovi made sure you knew. *Do not come here.* I know you want to grab that staff of yours and come charging in here to save me, but all you'll do is get yourself killed and I can't deal with that."

He dropped his chin to his chest for a moment, and when he spoke again, his voice was rough. "My beautiful DJ. I can handle this, but only if I know you're okay. Please do this for me. Rene, Jake, you stay away, too, and keep her safe." He raised his head, defiance in the set of his chin but I saw the tears in his eyes. His voice gave away nothing. "On our friendship, I ask this of you."

Lennox spoke a few more words to him and Alex nodded. Then my uncle walked away, Alex curled back into a fetal position, and I could no longer see his face.

Wiping away the tears I couldn't help spilling down my cheeks, I pulled Charlie from the water, stood up, and faced the others.

"I don't care what he wants. Who's going with me?"

CHAPTER 34

We gave ourselves an hour to plan, which included Rene and Collette going out for supplies. We would spring Alex as soon as we could get there. Obviously, it was a trap, and there would be guards. The earlier we arrived, the more time we had to create chaos if we couldn't get him out quickly.

First, I needed materials to make more of the aura-camouflaging swill. We all needed to drink some—they could easily be on the lookout for Rene or Jake, who'd accompany me in.

Although he wasn't happy about it, Jean finally agreed to help us plan but not to participate in the "extraction," as Jake called it. He'd snapped into U.S. Marine mode.

"I need you to be at Maison Rouge and have your men ready to fight, should it be necessary." I grasped Jean's hand. "We need a safe place to go."

He nodded, but his compressed lips told me he didn't like it. "Monsieur Warin may come to Maison Rouge today, but unless he is willing to pledge fealty to Jean Lafitte, I'm afraid he will not be allowed to remain after the morrow. My apologies, *Jolie,* but this is as it must be."

I closed my eyes, trying to decide whether to laugh, cry, or beat Jean over the head with my staff. He and Alex hated each other. It went way beyond any feelings they had toward me. And there was a lot at stake. As much as I wanted him to throw aside his feelings, and his common sense, to accommodate me, I respected his decision.

I squeezed his hand. He was giving me what he could. "Thank you."

"I shall be happy to assist you as well," Christof said. "I have not met Mr. Warin, but I liked the way he handled himself at the last council meeting I attended." Yeah, because Alex had helped Eugenie and me escape after Christof had put so much snow on the roof of the museum that it caved in.

"Thank you, Christof, but if you don't mind, would you also wait at Maison Rouge? We might need you there if your brother follows us." In truth, I didn't want to officially be seen as an open ally of either faery prince, not yet anyway. The less I was seen with him, the better.

"Certainly, whatever you wish." He gave me a formal nod. "Jean, with your assistance, perhaps I should transport The Arch back to the island."

I'd hoped the traveling magic show might stay here in Old Orleans so we'd have less of a target aimed at Old Barataria, but I had more important plans to make than the location of Tinkerbell's laboratory.

While Jean and Christof clomped in and out with Jean's trunks and Christof's mountain of magic, Jake, Collette, Audrey, and I talked out our options. They were pretty simple. Find out which among the long row of warehouses Alex was in. Get rid of his guards. Break the containment circle. Drag Alex out of there, even if it required knocking him unconscious. Get him to Maison Rouge. Then worry about the rest.

I hesitated about including Audrey, partly because of her inexperience and partly because I didn't want to see her hurt, which would also hurt Lennox. I'd come to respect my uncle. She saw the reluctance in my face.

"I'm in on this, DJ." She held up her right hand and wiggled her index finger to show off the amethyst ring. "You need access to physical magic, even if it's mine, plus no one will be expecting me. Rene, Jake, and Collette have plenty of muscle, but you need magic, too."

Damn it, she was right. I needed her. With a limited time to premake potions, she would be valuable backup. Even if her physical magic was unfocused and scattershot, it would cause chaos. This time, as much as he loved order, chaos could be Alex Warin's friend.

"Okay, but stick with the plans. Don't freelance." And after this was over, if we were still alive, my cousin and I were letting Lennox in on our growing friendship.

After Rene and Collette returned, I made up a couple of confusion charms and freezing potions with my limited supplies, double-checked that the dagger and Charlie were ready to go, and mixed the noxious aura-masking potion.

"Audrey, you and Collette probably don't need this—no one's on the lookout for you, so it's optional. I recommend you take a pass." I handed generous cups to Rene and Jake. Jake made a face; Rene gagged but kept it down. The girls said if I could do it they could do it, so we all drank.

After we'd chased it with enough of Jean's brandy to get rid of the taste, we got in the transport, and I checked Jean's list of secret faery transports. There were several along the Mississippi

River riverfront, one just east of the convention center at Race and Henderson. That was our way in.

I prayed again, even though my response so far had felt far from divine, and said, "Port of New Orleans."

We landed at the transport at a quarter until four; thanks to lingering clouds from the storm, dark had already begun to settle over the city. We had a two-block, slightly uphill walk to reach the end of the row of warehouses that made up the working part of Mardi Gras World.

It might be two days after Christmas and technically a workday, but the place was deserted—except for the guard I spotted walking near the end of the nearest warehouse. I opened my senses and got nothing but shapeshifter, loup-garou, and wizard, all of which seemed to be coming from us. Human security guard, then.

We had all dressed in black, which meant I'd borrowed a sweater from Rene to avoid being the pink member of the crew. In some macho ritual, Jake had found black markers and made straight dark lines beneath our eyes, and since Jake and I had blond hair, Rene had brought us both black Saints caps. We looked like the world's worst football team, back from the days when locals rightly called the Saints by another name: the "Ain'ts." The shifters all had guns; Audrey and I were our own weapons, plus I had Charlie.

Jake motioned us to gather behind a semi parked near the warehouse entrance. "Let's give him time to get out of sight." He gestured toward the guard. "No point in hurting anyone until we have to."

Sounded good to me. I checked my pockets for the charms and potions—freezing on the left, confusion on the right. The dagger remained clipped to my forearm. I couldn't spring it out one-handed like in a movie, but I could get at it quickly. Charlie was clutched firmly in my right hand. The wood was warmer than usual; he was ready to rumble.

Once the guard was out of sight, Jake went first, running in a slumped position to make himself look as small as possible. In the darkening dusk, he was almost impossible to see. We followed one by one, with Rene bringing up the rear.

Once we reached the big warehouse door, I used Charlie to magically pop the lock and we slipped inside. Security lights gave us enough visibility to see where we were going and yet not so much light that we couldn't hide in shadows. So far, so good.

I'd never given much thought to what hell might look like if it were a physical place, but this might come close. When a dragon head was on one of the big Mardi Gras floats, it looked reasonably small. Standing beside it, detached and lying on the ground, it was the size of a VW Beetle. And that was the small pieces.

This was obviously the Land of Mardi Gras Detritus, cast off and set in the back room until someone else had a need of a troll, a giant plaster Chucky doll head, or a chicken foot.

Walking in single file through the first long warehouse, we passed Elvis, a herd of three-dimensional representations of artist George Rodrigue's Blue Dogs, Queen Elizabeth, several kings I didn't recognize, and four different Marilyn Monroes.

What I didn't see was Boeuf Gras. Not yet.

I took the lead, kept my empathic senses open, and scanned around us, learning the auras of my companions so I could discern when any new prete came nearby, hopefully not savvy enough to be wearing peridot to keep me from reading their auras. Of course, I couldn't read elves or fae anyway, but I wasn't worried about elves for a change. I thought Rand wanted to stay far, far away from tonight's nasty business, although he had to be worried that I'd screw up and get myself killed.

He should be worried.

"Wait." I sensed the buzzy energy of a werewolf ahead of us. Two of them. I held up two fingers and pointed at Jake and Collette, then pointed ahead—our agreed-upon shorthand for two werewolves in front of us.

These could be general guards, or they could be Alex's guards.

It seemed as if we'd walked a quarter mile of warehouse already. A wide path ran down the middle, with Mardi Gras heads and tails and animals and vehicles jammed into both sides.

I stopped and held up a hand. I'd heard something, and turned to look at my shapeshifting companions. They had a lot better hearing than Audrey or I. Jake pointed ahead, repeated the two werewolves sign, mimicked talking, and mouthed "next section."

Okay, almost showtime. The long warehouses were open to each other, so entering the next one wasn't such an obvious transition. We slowed down, moving in silence, looking everywhere. The werewolf auras weren't too far ahead now, so I skirted behind a big statue—as in maybe fifteen or twenty feet tall—to take a look around.

Rene poked me in the arm and, when I turned, pointed up. I craned my neck only to see a bad representation of Jean Lafitte. I gave Rene a grimace and moved out.

Another ten yards or so and I caught a flash of white ahead and to my right. Again, I stopped, this time behind a giant gator head. Through his open mouth, I pointed out the massive white bull, Boeuf Gras. By shifting a little farther toward the center aisle, I was able to spot Alex. He was sitting up again, facing the bull, so we'd be coming in on his right side.

Jake pointed just past the bull, and there were our two werewolves. He gestured to himself and Collette, then across the aisle to a big plaster version of St. Louis Cathedral, then criss-crossed his downturned fingers to symbolize walking. Rene pulled out his pistol to provide cover and I held Charlie at the ready as first Jake, then Collette, sneaked across the aisle. They'd be able to slip up on the guards from behind now. Of course, chances were good that Alex would spot them as well.

That, I didn't worry about. Alex was a damned good enforcer. He could keep a blank face better than anyone I knew, as evidenced by his response to his travesty of a trial.

I knew the moment he'd spotted Jake and Collette, or at least when he spotted movement. He didn't change position or expression, but there was a minute tensing of his shoulders.

From our position behind the faux cathedral, I couldn't tell Jake from Collette, only discerned movement behind the two weres, who were chatting, none the wiser. Until suddenly, both of their heads were facing the wrong way on their bodies. Audrey let out a high-pitched noise, then stopped abruptly when Rene clamped a hand over her mouth.

I closed my eyes, queasy. Like two well-oiled machines, Jake and Collette had clamped hands on either side of the werewolves' heads, twisted, and snapped their necks like gruesome synchronized athletes. Then the guards were gone, dragged back into the shadows, where their bones would eventually repair themselves but not anytime soon and not without a lot of pain.

I reminded myself why we were here, and that this had never promised to be a pretty business. I turned around to Audrey and put a finger over my lips, warning her. No more noise. She nodded.

Slowly, Alex stood, hands propped on his hips, staring into the shadows where the guards had disappeared. I spotted Jake nearer us again, across the aisle. He pointed to his head and his nose; he wanted me to check for auras again.

I closed my eyes and opened my senses, weeding out my companions and Alex, dismissing the smells of motor oil and paint and adhesive and plaster, reaching for anything that felt out of place. There was at least one more werewolf here besides the dead ones.

I held up two fingers, pointed at Jake, and held up my hand, palm outward: *wait.* Closing my eyes again, I focused on the new werewolf auras; they seemed to come from overhead. I looked up, squinting into the rafters. Sure enough, two guards were standing directly over Alex's circle, and they were looking hard back at the corner where Collette remained with the first two guards.

Two fingers, pointing at Jake, then pointing at Alex, then upward. Jake followed the track of my fingers and gave a short nod. He disappeared for a moment, then reappeared.

A clang from Collette's direction distracted the guards, not to mention almost giving me a heart attack. It gave Jake enough time to get back to our side of the aisle, exchange some motions with Rene, and wait to see what our guards would do.

If they came down to our side, Rene and Jake would take them. If they went to the sound of the noise—Collette's distraction—Jake would go back and we'd have two more broken werewolf necks. At least in theory.

The guards were smarter than they looked; they split up. The taller of the two, pistol drawn, jumped down with an enviable nimbleness and edged into the shadows toward Collette. I'd have broken an ankle on this concrete—or my skull.

Rene eased his way toward Alex, so he was waiting when the second guard jumped from the rafters. Never mind that the guy had at least fifty pounds and four or five inches on him. Rene grabbed him and snapped his neck before he had a chance to react.

I didn't see the other guard, but Jake and Collette appeared across from me again, asking me to again sniff out any pretes. I went through the routine, but this time the place was clean. At least for now.

I nodded, and stepped out from behind the cathedral. Alex sensed movement and turned, and the look on his face dug another crack into my fractured heart. Such love and joy and misery and, yeah, grim frustration. "You aren't martyring yourself for me," I said softly, approaching the containment circle. I reached out with Charlie and broke the plane, freeing Alex. "And I'm not leaving you here."

He pulled me to him with such fierceness that my breath was cut short. I didn't care.

"What the hell are you doing in here?"

We both whirled to the source of the voice and saw the same human security guard as before. Behind my back, I gestured with my palm down: *I've got this.*

I gave my best girlish laugh. "I'm sorry. We just thought it would be cool to come in here and, I don't know, take some pictures or something. We didn't hurt anything."

"Ma'am, this is private property." He was an NOPD officer working security off-duty; his badge identified him as Mc-Garrity. "I'll have to escort you out now. . . . Alex, is that you? Man, you know better than this."

Oh shit. It would have to be somebody Alex knew. Then again, he knew a lot of NOPD cops from having worked in the local FBI office.

"Ah yeah, sorry, Jack." He wrapped an arm around my waist. "But hey, could you resist this face?"

Please. This face had barely been washed in the past two days and had black football player grease on its cheeks.

We didn't have time for this. I walked over with my hand out, as if to introduce myself. "Hi, Jack. Sorry about this."

Then I pulled a vial from my left pocket, flipped off the top, and slung the contents in his face, turning Jack McGarrity into a big old NOPD statue.

"Jake, can you and Collette haul him somewhere out of hearing range?"

They finally emerged from the shadows, and Jake grinned. "Hey, cuz. I'd like you to meet my fiancée. Collette, Alex. Alex, Collette."

Alex was going to strangle him, judging by the look on his face. "Do none of you follow directions?"

"Hell no, shifter." Rene joined us and Alex clapped his hands over his eyes. "Who else is here?"

"This is it," I said. "Now, let's get the hell out of here."

A crackling noise sounded from the floor. "Hey, Jack, check in. Everything okay?"

The police radio. We all stared at it for a few seconds, but finally Alex picked it up, clicked on the talk button, and drawled, in a pretty good local accent, "All good here. Gonna finish my round, over."

"Roger that."

Alex turned off the radio. "You guys need to leave."

I stared at him, not believing what I'd heard. "We are not leaving you here." I spoke in an exaggerated whisper. "I don't know if you missed the memo, but you're going to get shot in the head in about"—I looked at my pink watch—"an hour."

He shook his head. "I can't live on the run, DJ. I thought about it, and I don't know how to live that way. I'm . . ." He paused and lowered his voice. "Damn it, I'm not strong enough to live that way. It scares the hell out of me."

Oh good grief. Now was not the time for an existential crisis of self-confidence. "You'll figure it out. Now get your ass out of the middle of this aisle and let's go."

"DJ!" Jake hissed from behind me. "I hear somebody coming. More than one. Lots more."

Crap. "Let's go." I grabbed Alex's wrist and pulled him exactly nowhere. He wasn't budging. I tried to beat him over the head with Charlie and he took the staff away from me. Damn it.

"Charlie. Come to me."

The staff shot sparks, making Alex hiss and open his grip. The staff flew into my hand.

I sensed wizards, plural. And werewolves. Also plural. "Stay in the circle and pretend you can't get out," I whispered, backing into the shadows and finding Rene and Audrey. Across the aisle, Jake and Collette also backed up.

Alex sat down in the middle of the containment circle with his legs crossed, and turned to watch the newcomers.

Damn it to hell and back. Zrakovi led his little procession of death, accompanied by another man—a wizard, I assumed from the aura—and two werewolf guards.

Time for Plan B. If we had one.

CHAPTER 35

I held my breath as Zrakovi approached Alex. He stopped several feet away. "Where are your guards? Didn't you send guards, you fools?" The last was directed at the burlier of the two werewolves. I wonder how they felt about the execution of one of their own?

"There were four here; I talked to 'em less than an hour ago."

He sniffed the air and pointed toward the corner where the four broken-necked werewolves had been laid out like chickens in a meat case. The other guard followed his nose and in a few seconds, he said, "Dack, you better come back here."

Dack, the burly guy, disappeared and I could tell when he saw his buddies by the loud round of colorful cursing in a heavy local accent.

"They're not dead but they won't be doing any work for a while," Dack said, walking back to Zrakovi with his proverbial tail between his legs. Guess we knew who was alpha wolf in this pack. "Necks have been broken. All four of 'em."

"Damn." Zrakovi looked around him, squinting into the

shadows, suddenly aware that—duh—someone might be watching. "The next question is why you are still here, Mr. Warin." Zrakovi reached out and waved his hand where the containment circle's cylinder was supposed to be. "Especially since you have been freed."

Alex stood up, holding his hands up in a gesture of no-trouble-here. He towered over Zrakovi but he didn't have a weapon and he didn't have magic. "I'm still here because, as I explained to the people who came to free me, I am innocent of the things you've charged me with. I have done nothing wrong. I've done nothing to betray you. Ever. I hoped you'd realize that."

Zrakovi managed to look up at Alex and look down his considerable nose at the same time. "And the people who came to free you. I assume that's our former sentinel and her band of misfits? Perhaps your out-of-control cousin?"

"I never said that. Maybe it was who you say, maybe it was a vampire, maybe it was faeries. Maybe it was goddamned Peter Pan."

Good. Alex was getting mad, and it was about damned time.

Zrakovi didn't seem to appreciate Alex's humor. "Let me introduce you to my associate, Mitchell. He is a Blue Congress wizard, and quite good at the art of re-creation. Mitchell, why don't you re-create the events of the past hour here in this spot."

"Sure thing." Mitchell was about five two, maybe weighed a hundred and thirty pounds, and was dressed in green from head to toe. He was a freaking leprechaun.

A leprechaun about to set up a show. He did some pretty magic with his fingers, creating a holographic image of a trapped Alex next to the live Alex. He spread his fingers to expand the image, which included more of the aisle and side areas. Damn it. If he went all the way through this he'd see Jake and Collette and Rene as well as me. At least Audrey had remained hidden.

I turned back and put a warning finger over my lips to Audrey and Rene, then stepped out into the aisle. "You can stop your freak show, Zrakovi. Here I am."

"And me." Jake stepped out from the other side. He was going to save Collette and, if I could, I was going to save Audrey and Rene. Although if I knew Rene, he'd be in the middle of whatever was going to happen. The merman liked a fight, he liked Alex, and he hated every wizard except me and, maybe, Audrey. It would be more than he could resist. But Audrey and Collette could walk out of here, if we were lucky.

Zrakovi couldn't keep the broad smile off his face. "Finally. Do you know how much trouble you've caused?"

I took a move out of the Alex Warin playbook and just smiled.

"I've tried really hard," Jake said in his best Mississippi drawl, earning a sharp look from Alex. I hated to tell the love of my life, but since turning loup-garou, his cousin had become a smartass with very little filter between his brain and his mouth. Jake was gonna say whatever Jake was gonna say.

I've never been a patient person, but I had no choice. The next move had to be Zrakovi's.

Fortunately, I didn't have to wait long. "Dack, please disarm Mr. Jacob Warin; Carl, please handcuff Ms. Jaco—as I recall, she is afraid of guns." Just to prove he wasn't, Zrakovi pulled out a pistol. I wondered, not for the first time, how much physical magic Zrakovi had at his disposal; like me, he'd been a Green Congress wizard. I'd never known if he had magical talent or was just a good politician.

Carl, who'd drawn the DJ card, was a muscular black guy with a killer body and a killer's eyes. It would be a pity to set him on fire, but before he could get within two feet of me, I'd pulled out Charlie and pointed the staff at him. "Just try it, Carl. I can't miss from this range."

My move distracted Dack enough that Jake had time to pull out his own pistol and point it at the werewolf.

"I should warn you that my enforcers are shooting with silver bullets," Zrakovi said.

"Ain't that a laugh. So am I, wizard."

Damn it, Rene. I closed my eyes, cursing inwardly as Rene stepped from behind Alex, his own gun trained on Zrakovi and the leprechaun. Mitchell looked like he was close to having an unfortunate gastric accident.

Zrakovi stared at Rene a few moments before putting an identity with the face. "Mr. Delachaise, correct?"

"Dat's right." Rene affected his heaviest parish accent. "Your mismanagement caused the death of my brother a few months ago, in case you done forgot."

Zrakovi managed to look startled, offended, and arrogant all at the same time. The man had a talent. "I believe it was Ms. Jaco who killed your brother, if you'll recall. I'd suggest you walk out of here now and, out of respect for your father, I'll forget you were here."

Rene spit on the concrete near Zrakovi's feet. The First Elder took a step back, alarm and fury fighting for space on his face. "There's your respect for my father, wizard. Noticed he wasn't at your little trial today. Forgot the invitation to the representative from the water species?"

"How do you know who was at the trial? Your father wasn't told of . . ." Zrakovi seemed to realize he'd just stepped in his own shit.

"That explains a lot," I said, waving Charlie around so that Carl tried to move away from Zrakovi in case I tried to shoot him. "No representatives there from the water species. Only one of the two elven members. No at-large member. No leader of the weres and shifters . . . oh, wait . . . that would be the coun-

cil member you were railroading for your own petty, vindictive
satisfaction. I can't believe you got Elder Sato to vote with you.
What do you have on him?"

Zrakovi's eyes widened with every sentence I'd spoken. He
looked like a bug-eyed cartoon wizard. "You were here," he
hissed.

"I scryed the trial," I said, giving him my sweetest smile.
He'd always underestimated my elven magic. "It's an elven skill.
You really think I haven't been watching your every move?"

Okay, maybe I exaggerated a little. Or a lot.

A hacking cough from the corner drew our attention, and I
watched in horror as one of the first werewolves staggered into
the aisle, his head pointing straight to his right side. He used a
giant purple fleur-de-lis as a crutch.

Zrakovi ignored him, but I couldn't. He wasn't armed but
even with a half-broken neck he was more muscle on the other
side. A wizard, a leprechaun, and two and a half werewolves
against one wizard, two shifters, and two loups-garou, assuming
Alex would fight and Collette was still here. I hoped Audrey
had run for the hills.

I liked our odds . . . until Mitchell began his blue magic
again, and the giant Mardi Gras heads and torsos came to life.

Holy crap. The twenty-foot Jean Lafitte was walking. If he
stepped on one of us we'd be pancakes.

"Kill them all," Zrakovi said, flinging a burst of physical
magic at me. It was nothing like what Gerry had been able to
do, but it was enough to kill anyone it hit.

I threw myself to the ground, aiming Charlie at Zrakovi's
right hand and knocking his gun halfway across the warehouse.
He clutched his left hand around his right, looking down as if,
perhaps, I'd burned him. Tough.

Zrakovi flung another round at me, and I set his jacket on

fire with Charlie's next shot. He danced around like a go-go dancer and flung his jacket to the ground, stomping out the fire. Damn it, what was wrong with me? If I couldn't bring myself to make a killing shot at Zrakovi when he was trying to kill me, what use was I?

Around me, I was aware of fighting, growling, movement. But I stayed focused on Zrakovi and my own weakness of character. This was the man who was prepared to execute Alex. He'd taken my life from me figuratively, and wanted to take it literally. Why couldn't I just kill the man?

As the Mardi Gras madness continued around us, two shots rang out and both Zrakovi and I turned.

Next to me, Rene wiped his mouth with the back of his forearm. The werewolf whose head had halfway straightened itself wasn't coming back this time. His head lay three feet from the rest of his body.

Alex and Jake stood side by side, the bodies of Dack and Carl at their feet.

"Damn you all." Zrakovi looked at me. "Can't kill me, eh, little girl? You aren't your father's daughter after all. At least Gerry St. Simon could kill his enemies."

My voice was soft. "I've never considered you my enemy, Elder Zrakovi."

He looked surprised for about half a second. "We'll see how you feel about me after this. Obviously, you care nothing for your own life, but there is one you care about."

"No!!" I screamed a second too late, as he flung a strong burst of physical magic, so strong that it was white, straight at Alex.

I didn't remember raising my arm. I didn't remember aiming the elven staff at Zrakovi. I didn't remember sending magic shooting at the man I'd once admired and respected.

I only became aware of the dark, of lying on the ground, still holding the staff, of something holding my legs down.

Above me, I heard crying. "Audrey?" God, please let her be okay.

I shoved against whatever was plastered to my legs. "Stop that, babe. You're gonna break a rib. I was just gettin' you out of the way in case they tried to shoot you."

"I wish they had." I shoved him again, and he finally rolled off me. As I got to my feet, the emergency lights came on. I saw Alex moving in my peripheral vision, so I focused on the scene directly in front of me.

The first thing I saw was Zrakovi and Mitchell, both lying on the floor. Dead or unconscious, I wasn't sure which. Smoke rose from Zrakovi's clothing; his face was red in some spots, charred black in others. If he was alive, the pain he felt would be no more than he deserved.

I turned to look at Audrey, who was sobbing. Tears coursed down her cheeks and around the fingers of both hands, which she had clamped over her mouth. Frail tendrils of smoke drifted from her amethyst ring. Mitchell looked as dead as Zrakovi but he hadn't been burned; had she killed him?

"No no no, please no." A woman's voice morphed into the howl of a wolf, and I twisted to see Alex sitting in the floor, holding Jake in his arms. His lips quivered, his jaw muscles clenched, but it wasn't enough to stop his tears.

Jake was dead, a scorched strip of shirt marking the spot where Zrakovi's magic, meant for Alex, had hit Jake instead. Even a loup-garou couldn't come back from a magical shot to the heart.

"He jumped in front of me." Alex held Jake's body against his and rocked back and forth. "It should be me." He looked at me, tears flowing freely. "Why did you bring him here? Why couldn't you listen to me, just once?"

I was frozen in place. I wanted to run to him, whether he wanted me to or not. And I wanted to run away.

A red wolf nosed against Alex's arm, and he lowered Jake's body to the floor. Collette lay on the concrete with her head on Jake's chest and howled again.

Footsteps rang from farther down the warehouse, coming closer. I spun toward the noise, holding my staff at the ready. *If you had just shot Zrakovi when you first got the chance, this wouldn't have happened.* I readied myself for a makeup shot. I wouldn't hesitate this time.

Unless, of course, it was my uncle, which it was.

"What the bloody hell happened?" He stopped a few feet from Zrakovi, knelt, and felt for a pulse, then did the same with Mitchell. "This man is dead, from an attack of physical magic. Zrakovi is still alive, but badly burned." Lennox looked up at me. "You did this?"

"Yes, sir." If I could do one thing here, it would be to keep Audrey out of it. "Zrakovi was trying to kill Alex and I used the staff on him, and the other guy—"

"I killed him with my magic." Audrey stepped from behind me, then burst into tears again.

Lennox walked to his daughter and pulled her into a hug. They talked, but I couldn't listen to them. I couldn't take my eyes off Jake, remembering every time he'd called me his "sunshine," of the man he'd been when I first met him, his amber eyes filled with laughter and the light glinting off his sun-streaked hair. He was a good man, and he was my friend.

Rene slid an arm around my shoulders and pulled me against him. He and Jake had been friends, too, but for the moment his aura held pure fury.

"How is Alex going to live with this?" I asked him, not expecting an answer because there wasn't one. I'd imagined myself being killed. I'd even imagined the possibility of losing Alex. But not Jake. After all he'd been through, he'd finally found a way to be happy.

"Why are you here?" Audrey asked her father.

"DJ." Lennox stepped between me and my view of Alex. When I tried to move around him, he put his hands on my shoulders and forced me to look at him. Beside me, I felt Rene's fury ratchet up another notch. "I have news. You need to listen."

I tried to pretend I didn't see Alex still sitting with his head bent, or Collette's wolf, licking Jake's lifeless face. "What news?"

Lennox looked around at werewolf bodies, wizard bodies, and Jake. "The rest of the Elders are on their way to New Orleans. The elves have taken their stand against the wizards, claiming Florian and his followers as allies. All negotiations have ended."

He gave me a hard look, then looked back at his daughter. "The preternatural world is officially at war. God help us all."

CHAPTER 36

A full moon shone over Maison Rouge, Old Barataria. I sat on the verandah with my legs dangling off the edge, looking into its milky brightness and thinking about character. Strength of character. Weakness of character. Failure. I'd been stuck in this mode for the three days we'd been back to Lafitian headquarters.

A quarter-mile down the beach, a wolf sat on the sand, emitting an occasional howl of pain that raced across my skin like knife cuts. Collette had disappeared for two days after Jake's death, but had returned this morning in her wolf form. So far, she hadn't shifted back.

"Can I sit with you?" Audrey stood next to me, waiting for me to turn her down again, as I had since we returned. This time, I nodded and patted the wooden verandah next to me. It smelled of fresh cypress, as did much of the front part of the house that had been either rebuilt or reinforced after the hurricane.

"How can it look the same when everything has changed?" The same beautiful full moon shone over the same black waves. The flambeaux had been lit, casting shadows over the banquette stretching to the same narrow sandy beach.

"I don't know." She sat next to me without talking for a while, then finally said, "Have you heard from Alex?"

"No." He had refused to come back to Barataria with us, and I didn't blame him. It wasn't because of Jean, but because of Jake.

We'd held each other in the middle of that warehouse while Lennox paced around us, frantic for us to leave in the new transport he'd drawn before the rest of the Elders arrived. Elders who didn't know me, or Alex, or Audrey, or Jake. Elders who'd known Willem Zrakovi for years, like Elder Sato. Elders who might well believe whatever he said.

His anger at me had been short-lived, and we held each other until Lennox tried to physically pull us apart. "I have to take Jake home, to his parents, to our family." Alex's eyes were rimmed in red, and still the tears fell. "What am I going to tell them?"

I brushed off his tears with my fingers, something he'd done for me a hundred times. "You will tell them he died bravely. That he died protecting the people he loved." Those things were true.

"Will you come to me after you've taken him home? We'll go wherever you want. We'll figure out how to make a life for ourselves." I was so afraid once the shock wore off, he'd blame me as much as I blamed myself. That he'd never be able to look at me again without seeing Jake lying in his arms with the life burned out of him by wizards' magic.

"I don't know yet. I can't think that far ahead. I can't . . ."

He'd looked away, unable to finish, and that's how I had left him, without a kiss or a protestation of love. Just that I'd respect whatever he decided.

Audrey hadn't heard it all, but she'd seen and heard enough. "He'll contact you. One of these days, soon, you'll look out there and see a plastic bin with a note in it, asking you to meet him somewhere."

I gave her the best smile I had left in me. "I hope so." It's why I stayed out here, watching, waiting for something that might not happen. "Have you heard from Lennox?"

"Dad, on the other hand, sends notes every day. Twice a day, actually." She smiled, which made me smile. I was happy that my uncle had turned out to be a good guy. He wasn't going to throw himself on his sword and give up his position to clear us, but I thought he had the guts to stand up for his principles. We'd see where that got him.

"Any movement in the war-that-isn't-yet?"

"No," she said, picking a splinter out of her finger. The new verandah hadn't yet been sanded and painted. "He says there are reports of a lot of activity in Elfheim and in Faery, and that the vampires are courting all sides, looking for the best offer. You haven't seen anything in Elfheim?"

"Nothing, but my access to Castle Rand is pretty limited." As in, I transported to Eugenie's wing of the manor house, visited, and then transported back. The one time I'd tried to slip into the main house, an imperious elven housekeeper had shooed me away. "Eugenie's doing great, though. She doesn't see Rand that much, but she likes the midwife and the crabby housekeeper, and she has run of the house except when I'm there. He's behaving himself so far."

Although I trusted Rand about half the distance to the frog that was hopping along the banquette a few feet away.

Adrian was on transport duty, and until he stood up, I didn't notice that someone was wading in. I scrambled to my feet; I knew those broad shoulders and slim hips anywhere.

My throat closed up so tightly I could barely breathe.

Alex stopped for a few moments, talking to Adrian, who pointed toward the house. Did I need to warn Jean? Walk in with Alex to remind Jean that he'd promised him twenty-four hours' asylum—never mind that his offer had been issued three days ago?

Alex strode up the banquette, and I saw with alarm that he was heavily armed. He carried his big .45 semiautomatic in his shoulder holster, a rifle in his left hand, and had a knife sheath clipped to his belt loop.

"Alex?" I had to stop him. He was just asking Jean to shoot him. Thank God it had been Adrian on guard duty instead of Dominique, but even Adrian shouldn't have let him pass carrying this much gear.

"I need to talk to Lafitte." He stopped and gave me a quick kiss. An almost brotherly kiss, void of emotion. "It can't wait. Will you tell him I'm here?"

This was not any version of Alex I'd seen before. He was somber, his voice steady but soft. He spoke without a trace of warmth.

"I'll tell him," Audrey said, and disappeared through the study window.

"Are you okay?" Dumb question, DJ, of course he wasn't okay. "Are *we* okay?"

A faint trace of a smile finally showed up. "We'll talk. There's something I have to do first."

I nodded and looked around when Jean appeared in the main doorway into the house. I'd lay odds there were pirates with guns trained on that entry parlor from a half-dozen directions. As for

Jean, he had pulled on his formal jacket, the one I called his "captain coat," a deep indigo blue with gold epaulets and buttons.

"Monsieur Warin, you wish to see me?"

"Please."

"Come inside, then."

Jean turned and disappeared. I followed Alex inside and stood next to him.

"*Jolie,* would you please allow Monsieur Warin and me to speak privately?"

Oh hell no.

"DJ, do as he asks." Alex's voice had that somber, even tone again. Damn it, they were throwing me out.

"Fine. I'll be in the study with Audrey and Rene." Eavesdropping.

I went in the room and closed the door behind me. "What's going on between Jean and Alex?" Audrey whispered. Rene put down the book he was reading.

"I don't know—they tossed me out. But I'm gonna find out."

I knelt in front of the door and quietly pulled the large key from the keyhole. I loved these old antique doors. They were perfect for spying, and the subjects of my snooping stood only a couple of feet from the door.

"What may I do for you, Monsieur Warin?" Jean was neither angry nor friendly. Like Alex, he was extremely formal.

Alex laid the rifle on the floor in front of Jean, unclipped the knife sheath and lay it next to the rifle. He reached in one boot, then the other, pulling a dagger out of each. They joined the pile.

Finally, he took off the shoulder holster, threw the holster on the floor, and handed the gun to Jean, butt first.

"Captain Lafitte, we've had our differences but I've learned something that DJ has been trying to teach me for a long time."

Jean looked down at the gun but didn't take it. "And what is that, monsieur?"

"That loyalty and truth are more important than blind duty. That one must think for himself and follow his heart. It was a hard lesson to learn."

Jean nodded, and for a moment he allowed sorrow to show on his face. He had truly liked Jake, had considered him more a friend than an employee. "The price for that lesson was very, very high, Monsieur Warin."

Alex nodded and swallowed hard.

"Now, I must repeat my question of you, monsieur. What is it you request of me?"

"Captain Lafitte, I have laid down my weapons for you and am willing to take them up again in your service, if you see fit to grant me asylum and accept my pledge of loyalty."

The tears built behind my eyes again. Only I knew how much that speech had cost Alex Warin. He had been taken under the Elders' wings when he was sixteen, trained in the ways of the enforcer, taught how to survive as a shapeshifter in a human family and in a human world, and promised to always protect his mentors.

It had taken losing Jake to open his eyes. It had taken incredible inner strength for him to come here and humble himself before a man he'd fought against for so long.

But he had done it.

Jean hadn't answered, and I wanted nothing more than to rush in there and shake him. Alex would be an asset for us when this war finally started. The sides wouldn't sit around plotting and planning forever, and we as a group would have to decide who we'd support.

Jean took Alex's pistol and held it up to the light. "This is a finely made weapon, Monsieur Warin. I quite admire it." Then he turned it around and handed it back to Alex, butt first.

"I accept your oath of fealty. It took a man of much courage and strength of character to come here as you have."

Alex's face relaxed a smidgeon. "Thank you."

Jean smiled. Not the friendly smile he reserved for strangers, or the sexy smile he reserved for me, but the devilish smile he saved for those he planned to torment. "You will be willing to begin . . . how do you modern folk say it . . . at the bottom, of course?"

Oh God, he was going to make Alex cook and clean and empty chamber pots.

The muscle under Alex's eye twitched a couple of times, and he began thrumming his fingers against his thigh. "Of course."

Jean raised an eyebrow in an unspoken question.

Alex swallowed hard and choked out, "Of course, *sir.*"

I collapsed in a heap, leaning against the door, not sure whether I should laugh or cry, or both.

"What's wrong?" Audrey, who'd been looking out the front window, rushed toward me. Rene leaned down and offered a hand to pull me to my feet.

"Alex is joining the cause, and Jean's going to make his life miserable for a while," Rene told Audrey, earning a look of shock from me. "I knew he would. Only question was how long it would take Alex to suck it up and ask."

"How did you know?" I stared at him. I'd envisioned any future with Alex not here fighting alongside the Lafitians but on the run in some semi-romantic comedy of escapades which, quite frankly, I would enjoy and Alex would hate. "Oh, right. Because you could hear them without listening through the keyhole."

"I didn't hear a word they said."

"Then how did you know this was going to happen?"

Rene leaned over to whisper in my ear, and I waited for some pearl of Cajun wisdom that would make sense of Alex Warin and his new boss, Jean Lafitte. " 'Cause I'm just that good, babe."